"For a good-looking woman, you sure are hard to get along with."

Her green eyes bolted wider in the shade of the tree they now stood beneath, gangly branches sprawling overhead and all around them. "Is that a compliment or an insult?"

He shifted his weight from one dusty work boot to the other. "A little of both, I guess."

She still stood very close to him—he could feel the closeness, especially when she let out an irritated breath and said, "Then I'm not sure whether to slap you or kiss you."

And at this, he couldn't keep himself from flashing a cocky grin. "You'd never get away with the first one, honey."

"And the second?" she challenged, planting her fists on her hips.

His eyes flitted down her body, then rose back to her face just before he said, "That you'd have a shot at."

Their gazes stayed locked now and he'd have given anything to know what thoughts flashed through her pretty head. An invisible heat moved between them that had nothing to do with the late-day Florida sun.

By Toni Blake

TONI BLAKE

TAKE ME ALL THE WAY

A CORAL COVE NOVEL

AVONBOOKS

An Imprint of HarperCollinsPublishers

This is a work of fiction. Names, characters, places, and incidents are products of the author's imagination or are used fictitiously and are not to be construed as real. Any resemblance to actual events, locales, organizations, or persons, living or dead, is entirely coincidental.

AVON BOOKS
An Imprint of HarperCollins*Publishers*
195 Broadway
New York, New York 10007

Copyright © 2015 by Toni Herzog
ISBN 978-0-06-239258-9
www.avonromance.com

First Avon Books mass market printing: December 2015

Avon Trademark Reg. U.S. Pat. Off. and in Other Countries, Marca Registrada, Hecho en U.S.A.
HarperCollins® is a registered trademark of HarperCollins Publishers.

Printed in the U.S.A.

10 9 8 7 6 5 4 3 2 1

To my amazing agents,
Meg Ruley and Christina Hogrebe,
and everyone at the Jane Rotrosen Agency.
Thank you for ten wonderful years of support, guidance,
faith in what I do, and for being funtabulous cheerleaders!
You rock the casbah!

Acknowledgments

My sincere appreciation goes to:

Renee Norris, for reading this book ever-so-swiftly and providing your always insightful feedback, allowing me to work out the kinks before deadline. And during the revision stage, you came to my rescue yet again! I so appreciate the time and effort you put in on every single book I write and your consistent enthusiasm about the process.

Lindsey Faber, for brainstorming help on this and most of my stories. In particular on this one, thank you for your assistance in finding the right classic to tie in, your endless encouragement when I'm saying things like, "I don't think this is going well," and that brilliant moment when you suggested, "Maybe in this one the cat is his." Purrrrrfect!

Lindsey Faber (again!) and Alisa Adams for running "Team Toni" on the home front—keeping the website informing, the newsletter delivering, the mail arriving, and the social media fires burning.

Lisa Koester, talented pottery and stained glass artist, for completely inspiring Tamra's art, and also for kindly helping me with the details.

Sarah Jane Stone, talented Avon author, for the wonderful discussion we had in San Antonio about your PTSD research, which gave me a jumping off point as I shaped Jeremy's past and present. Thank you for sharing so generously.

Meg Ruley and Christina Hogrebe, my fab agents, whose praises I sing on the dedication page of this book.

And May Chen, editor extraordinaire, for being so fun and supportive and enthusiastic to work with, as well as Shawn Nicholls, Pam Spenger-Jaffee, Dianna Garcia, the Avon Books art department, and everyone else at HarperCollins who has embraced me and my books and make it such a wonderful place to publish.

"Do you want to live?"

Frances Hodgson Burnett, *The Secret Garden*

Prologue

JEREMY SHERIDAN crushed his empty beer can in his fist. Nothing felt right. Staying or going. But he disliked the idea that he might be a burden.

He sat on the deck of the little shop where his brother-in-law, Lucky Romo, painted motorcycles for a living. The same little shop where Jeremy had been living for a while, next door to his sister, Tessa, and Lucky, thanks to their kindness.

He'd spent a lot of time with Lucky since his return from Afghanistan. He'd never have expected the guy to become his new best friend, but he found Lucky easy to be with. Maybe it helped that Lucky didn't talk a lot. Funny, most people looked at Lucky and saw nothing but a big burly biker with long hair and tattoos. But the guy was an artist, the real thing, a freaking Picasso with a paint gun.

And people who looked at Jeremy saw a war hero. *The* war hero. Destiny's official Boy Wonder.

It was a role he'd thought he wanted. One he'd

pretty much played all his life. Star athlete in high school, homecoming king, all around good guy. And he'd thought coming back to his hometown and being that same guy again would be easy, the natural thing to do. But turned out he'd brought some heavy baggage home with him. The kind you couldn't unpack.

He walked into the house, to the fridge. Opening the door, he rummaged around and at the same time heard Lucky come in from working in the garage.

"Any more beer?" Jeremy asked.

"Had the better part of a six-pack in there last night," Lucky replied. "You drink it all?"

"Guess that's possible." Jeremy cursed under his breath. "Sorry, man," he murmured.

"Don't need to apologize," Lucky said, "but . . . you don't seem like you're doing too good."

"I'm okay," he claimed. But he still stared into the fridge, because it was easier than meeting Lucky's gaze.

"Listen, you sure you don't want me to paint that old truck? I've got some down time right now."

Jeremy glanced up to see Lucky hiking a thumb over his shoulder to the driveway. Lucky had probably offered to paint Jeremy's old Ford pickup half a dozen times since he'd come home. Jeremy knew it looked like crap—a mottled, sun-beaten red. But it had *always* looked that way, from the very day he'd bought it used right after high school with the money he'd saved from working at Edna Farris's apple orchard. It felt like one little piece of his old life he hadn't lost. "Nah, man. But thanks."

Though now it hit him for the first time that maybe it was an eyesore in the driveway of a guy who painted vehicles for a living.

Now he met Lucky's gaze. "If you want me to move on, just say the word."

"No, it's not that. There's plenty of room, and you're family. And hell, you spent most of your adult life in war—that's bound to mess you up. But . . ." Lucky stepped closer, spoke lower, even though they were the only two people anywhere nearby. "People are beginning to talk. To worry."

Jeremy finally shut the fridge door, stood up straight. "People?"

"Tessa. Your parents." He stopped, sighed. "Everybody really. Tessa and your folks are pretty sure some stuff happened in Afghanistan they don't know about."

"You say anything?" Jeremy asked. He had confided in Lucky. Lucky had come through some bad shit himself and landed on his feet. *Better* than on his feet—he had a great life. Maybe Jeremy had hoped Lucky's change of fortune would rub off on him somehow.

"No," Lucky assured him. "You asked me to keep it just between us and I have. But . . . guess I worry a little, too, dude. Thing is . . . I've been wondering if maybe you should think about talking to somebody."

Jeremy's gut tightened. "I talk to you. That's enough."

"I'm not sure it is," Lucky told him.

"I already did that kind of talking," Jeremy pointed out. "Before I was discharged. I passed with flying colors."

"You mean you lied."

He crossed his arms. "I just wanted to come home, man. Put it all behind me."

"A shame that last part didn't work."

Jeremy didn't answer. But he knew it was true. And he knew Lucky was right. Last summer he'd worked some construction in Crestview, the next town over—but it had been a temporary position and when it had ended, he'd let it. He'd let himself go right back into the solitude up here at Whisper Falls.

Over time he'd discovered that he liked just keeping to himself, here at Lucky's. He liked looking off the deck out into the thick woods that surrounded the place. He liked thinking about walking into those woods and just getting lost there. Sometimes he took those walks, into the trees and up to the falls. Sometimes he napped because it turned off his thoughts for a while.

He kind of wanted to walk into the woods and get lost right now. *But war heroes don't spend their days holed up in the woods drinking beer.* He'd hidden from that reality almost as well as he'd hidden from everything else. Until now.

"Maybe I should go somewhere new," he said, voicing the thought he'd been turning over in his head for days now.

"No, man," Lucky told him, shifting his weight from one workboot to the other. "Like I said, this isn't about that. You're always welcome here."

And Jeremy let out a breath. "I know, and I appreciate that. But . . . maybe a change of scenery would do me good."

"Where would you go?" Lucky asked.

Jeremy considered options. On one hand, there weren't many—he didn't have a lot of ties outside Destiny. But on the other, there were millions—it was a big world.

"Maybe I'll go to the beach," he offered up. No particular reason, but the beach was a peaceful place. "Maybe I'll head to that that little town where your parents live." Lucky's mom and dad had moved to Florida years earlier, and Jeremy had even gone with his own parents on vacation to visit them right after his return from overseas, back when he was wearing the war hero persona better. "It's nice there."

"Yeah, it is," Lucky agreed.

Although Jeremy wasn't really sure what a change of scenery would do for him. Other than stop him from hiding himself away in those woods forever. At the beach there was only the ocean and horizon. A lot harder place to hide.

Maybe a move would help him make a new start.

"What's the town called again?" he asked.

And Lucky replied, "Coral Cove."

"It's time to open your eyes!"

Frances Hodgson Burnett, *The Secret Garden*

Chapter 1

"PACK UP your stuff, go home, and get dressed—we're going out!"

Sitting behind her sales table at the community's nightly Sunset Celebration, Tamra Day looked up to see her neighbor friend, Christy Knight, who'd just barged onto the Coral Cove pier like she owned it.

Well, *this* was sudden. She and Christy didn't usually "go out."

Then she glanced down at the shorts and T-shirt she wore before raising her gaze back to her friend, a little dumbfounded. "I *am* dressed. And out where? This is Coral Cove, remember?" She loved the little beach town where she'd made her home for the last eight years, but there was no place in Coral Cove that required "getting dressed" in anything fancy to "go out." In fact, the Sunset Celebration, where she sold the pottery and stained glass pieces from which she made her living, was about as "out" as it got around here.

Even now, as dusk descended, she was surrounded by other artists and shopping tourists, and music played over loudspeakers to vie with the occasional call of seabirds passing overhead. Being at the Sunset Celebration always made her feel good, talented, valued. It was the most festive place to be in Coral Cove. And she'd been having a perfectly good evening—up to now.

Which was when Christy pursed her lips, looking only slightly as if she'd been caught at something. "Well, I'm not sure where we're going, but we're meeting Cami for a girls' night." Then she raised her eyebrows hopefully. "Fun, right?"

Okay, what was going on here? Something was definitely up.

It wasn't that Tamra didn't enjoy a night out with girlfriends, but she didn't trust this situation. She tilted her head, squinting lightly into the vibrant colors left from the recent setting of the sun. "Did Fletcher put you up to this?"

Their friend, Fletcher McCloud, had long been on a mission to find Tamra a man. And lately, she'd had the feeling everyone else was in on it, too—except for her.

And she wasn't opposed to dating but she simply hadn't met a lot of eligible, handsome guys in Coral Cove, not in the entire time she'd been here. So she doubted her Prince Charming was suddenly going to show up tonight just because she "got dressed" and "went out."

Christy gave her pretty blond head a light, cheerful shake in reply. "No, Fletcher has nothing to do with it. We just want to have some fun."

She kept using that word—*fun*. But fun, Tamra thought, were the lives Christy and their friend, Cami, were already living. They were both in relationships with great—not to mention *hot*—guys. They were both blond and svelte and gorgeous and rocked a bikini like nobody's business. And she loved them to death and was grateful for the joy they brought into her life, and she was glad they were happy. But the upshot was, she didn't need anyone feeling sorry for her or trying to make something happen that . . . well, frankly, just didn't seem to be in the cards for her.

"Chop-chop," Christy said, clapping her hands so suddenly that Tamra flinched in her folding chair, hit her knee against a table leg, and shook her entire collection of pottery and stained glass. "Let's go get you dolled up."

Tamra grabbed on to the table to steady it—then drew back, frowned. "Dolled up? Really?"

Christy sighed, planting her hands on her hips. "Look, I'm not asking for diamonds and an evening gown here—just a skirt or something would do."

And okay, the truth was that Tamra used to wear skirts a lot more than she had lately. And maybe she used to pay more attention to her appearance in general. As a local artist, long, flowy skirts had always been her usual style for the nightly event at the pier. Again, until lately, since she'd become more of a khaki shorts and T-shirt sort of gal.

So yeah, maybe she'd let herself go a little. But she'd been doing so much work helping to beautify the town, it was the only practical way to dress. It so happened that Cami was the head of the new Coral Cove planning commission, and Tamra was taking part in lots of projects that called for dirty hands, not skirts.

Or . . . maybe she'd also let herself go since . . . well,

since Cami had gotten together with Reece Donovan, a longtime friend Tamra had once carried a torch for. She didn't like admitting that to herself, but it had been a blow. Not Cami's fault, and she was truly over it now, but it had stung at the time. And maybe even left Tamra feeling discouraged about something she hadn't quite realized she cared about: romance.

"Okay, fine," she finally told Christy. "I'll put on a skirt. But I'm pretty sure we're just going to end up sitting at the Hungry Fisherman drinking beer."

"No," Christy said adamantly, shaking her head. "We'll find something better, something new and exciting! It'll be fun."

Now it was Tamra who raised her eyebrows, albeit in a manner more doubting than hopeful, as she replied, "I can't wait to see what it is."

JEREMY sat on a picnic table behind the Happy Crab Motel in Coral Cove, Florida. He'd been here a couple of weeks.

He was living at the kitschy little row motel built in the fifties for free, just because the owner, Reece, was a hell of a nice guy. *That's what you get when you show up someplace without a plan—you're suddenly homeless.* He hadn't exactly thought of that when he'd gotten in his pickup and headed south down I-75.

Most people would have made a move like this with more of a strategy in mind, he supposed. And maybe a little more money in their pocket, too. But after he'd come home from Afghanistan, he'd given most of the military pay he'd accumulated over the years to the widow of his friend Chuck and their four kids, who lived in Texas. Chuck hadn't made it back and Jeremy had—so helping out his buddy's family had seemed like a no-brainer.

A cold, dark fist closed tight around Jeremy's heart, even in the Florida heat, at the very thought of Chuck. The moment he'd seen Chuck fall flashed in his mind.

Push it away. Get back on track.

What track?

You need a plan, man—a fucking plan.

And that's what he told himself every single day as he dragged himself out of his room. That's what he told himself every night while he sat around watching the palm trees sway. Sometimes he walked the beach, but that took about all the energy he could muster. And so far, no fucking plan.

When he'd first arrived, Reece had asked him if he could swim. "Yeah," he'd said. "Why?"

"Town's looking to hire a new lifeguard," Reece had told him. "You should apply."

And Jeremy had said, "Uh . . . maybe, sure. Thanks for the info, man." But inside he'd been thinking: *Hell no.* The beach on a busy day? No way—too many people, too much uncertainty. And being in charge of protecting people was the last thing he wanted. The military had deemed him a hero; so had his hometown. Because he'd once made a move that had kept his whole platoon from being decimated by an ambush. But funny thing about being that kind of savior—sometimes what people saw, knew, was only one side of the coin.

You need to find a job, man. Not as a lifeguard, but some other job.

The sun had just set, but the air remained warm.

September in Florida. A long planked sun-washed dock stretched along the bay behind the motel, providing more than half a dozen boat slips. Two of the boats tied there—a catamaran and a sleek white sloop—belonged to Reece, but the other spots Reece rented out.

Now Jeremy watched two college-age boys in the distance, clearly rich and entitled as hell, downing shots of something dark on the lower deck of a big, ritzy cabin cruiser. Daddy's boat. Part of him resented them and their youthful good looks, their loud voices that carried too far. And another part of him just wanted to go drink with them and forget things.

Next door to the Happy Crab stood a run-down seafood joint called the Hungry Fisherman. Movement from near the back of the restaurant drew Jeremy's eye to a big but equally run-down gray tomcat sniffing around the trash bin, on the hunt for scraps. The cat appeared about as down on his luck as Jeremy.

Try though he might, he couldn't block out the frat boys' raucous laughter and snide comments—they were talking about sex now, about what one of them wanted to do to a particular girl—but he kept watching the cat, and stroking the beard he'd let grow over the last few months.

He wasn't much of a beard guy usually, and he wasn't much of a cat guy either—more of a dog man—but he found himself vaguely wondering what particular wars this cat had fought. He kept trying not to hear the loudmouth frat boys.

The big cat padded slowly away from the restaurant's back door, apparently striking out. Jeremy suspected the scent of fish from inside was probably torture, that the cat was like a thirsty man staring at an ocean—water, water, everywhere, but not a drop to drink. The lanky cat—too skinny for his size—took long strides across the parking lot and past the motel's pool, approaching Jeremy.

Stopping at Jeremy's tennis shoes, he looked up and let out a plaintive meow. That was when Jeremy realized the cat was missing an eye, one permanently closed.

"Sorry, got nothin' for ya." Truth was, he'd eaten a lot of seafood himself lately, because Reece wasn't the only generous person in Coral Cove—Polly and Abner, owners of the Hungry Fisherman, had been more generous with him than they or anyone else had reason to be. *Gotta get a plan, man.*

An image flashed in his head—him at a younger age, in his parents' yard with his dog, Dakota. He'd gotten the German shepherd as a puppy when he was fifteen. Loved to play fetch, that dog. And acted like a big tough guy to outsiders, but he was more bark than bite—a big lovable hulk of an animal.

Whenever Jeremy had come home on furlough or between tours of duty, Dakota had been one of those things that stayed the same for him, just like that old truck. Pulling into his parents' driveway to see Dakota run out and greet him had always taken him back to simpler times.

Dogs can only live so long, though, and Dakota hadn't outlasted Jeremy's dedication to serve his country. He'd gone in to the Marines at twenty-one and come out eleven years later. His dad's email about Dakota's death, only a few months before his discharge, had hit Jeremy harder than it should have. He still missed that dog.

Since Jeremy had nothing to offer, the one-eyed tomcat moved on in more long, lanky steps, heading out onto the dock, still clearly seeking dinner. The cat must have been drawn by the voices, since he padded toward the cabin cruiser, and right up a small plank walkway onto it.

And it was only a short moment later when the more obnoxious of the two boys barked, "What the hell? Get off my goddamn boat, cat!" with far more passion than the situation called for. Then he shot to his feet and kicked the cat, hard, catapulting it off the vessel.

For Jeremy, the cat's airborne body moved in slow motion. His chest tightened as he watched it strike the trunk of a palm tree just off the edge of the dock with a *thud*, then land at its base.

The cat lay there, stunned and unsteady, disoriented.

And Jeremy's gut clenched as the frat boys both laughed, and the other one said, "Shoulda thrown the dumb thing in the water to see if it could swim."

More cruel laughter. "Maybe I will," the first replied.

Jeremy saw from the corner of his eye when the cat got its wits about it and finally darted away into the night. But it was too late. Something inside him broke loose, taking him back, to the darkness that hid inside people, to pointless cruelty, to other falling bodies— soldiers, friends. He never made the conscious decision to act—he only felt the ground beneath his feet and the fury filling his lungs and heart and head as he bolted from the picnic table into a full-on sprint toward that boat.

All thoughts left him—it was only action now.

And he never said a word—simply punched the quieter of the two in the mouth, knocking him from a chair onto the deck, just before he picked up the louder one by the throat, slamming him against the wall of the cabin with the words, "You messed with the wrong cat on the wrong night, pal."

THEY were drinking at the Hungry Fisherman.

"I know what you're thinking," Christy said to Tamra across the table. "We're drinking at the Hungry Fisherman."

"You're a mind reader," Tamra said. "Thank God I got dressed up for this."

"I need to add 'create nighttime hotspots' to my to-do list," Cami said, holding up one finger as she shifted into town planner mode. She tilted her head, clearly pondering it. "Though it would have to be a place with just the right blend of elements."

"A beach bar," Christy suggested, wide-eyed and happy as always. "A fun, casual, open-air place."

Cami's gaze brightened at the inspiration. "In the empty lot across from the Happy Crab, at the end of the beach," she added with a smile, pointing vaguely in that direction. She'd already talked Christy's handsome fiancé, Jack DuVall, into buying a long-closed used car lot and opening a miniature golf business there, on which construction was just starting. Jack wanted to mostly just be the money behind the project, so he'd hired Cami to organize it all, and she in turn had hired Tamra to design the course and oversee the building of it.

"That would be perfect," Tamra agreed, liking the idea.

But then Cami's smile began to fade. "Now all I need is someone to finance and run it."

Perennially cheerful soul that she was, Christy said, "Well, the more the town gets refurbished, the more new businesses it will draw. And look!" She held out both her hands to motion around them. "Outdoor seating at the Hungry Fisherman! If you can make Polly and Abner change, you can do anything."

True enough, only a month ago, the patio they sat on just across from Coral Cove Beach had been pockmarked asphalt, part of the parking lot. But Cami had succeeded in getting the owners of the seafood restaurant to put in a small patio enclosed with a wooden fence draped with fishing net and a few white, round life preservers, and also to add a festive new drink menu, designed with Cami's help. Music, another new feature, played over newly installed speakers—at the moment Bastille sang about flaws. And since then, business had picked up and they'd even started staying open later.

"And at least we're not drinking beer!" Christy announced triumphantly with a short nod in Tamra's direction. In fact, Tamra was drinking her second Ahoy Mateys, a rather tasty tropical rum concoction, while her friends both sipped on a couple of All Hands on Decks, the Hungry Fisherman's version of a Long Island iced tea.

"You know what else?" Christy said in her merry way. "The more good changes that keep taking place around here, the more new people there will be to meet."

Tamra glanced absently across the table at Christy—just in time to realize the statement had been targeted directly toward her.

So she arched one eyebrow in reply. And decided it was time to address the elephant on the patio. "Christy, I know you mean well—but why do you think I want to meet new people?"

"Well, I just thought—"

"And given the resorts up the road"—which kept Coral Cove's beach and Sunset Celebration thriving despite the businesses in this older part of town needing a boost—"there are already plenty of new people coming and going all the time. So as much as I'm on board with sprucing up the area, I don't think it's going to have any impact on my social life. Which is fine just the way it is—promise."

The women across the table from her went quiet. And Tamra realized she'd probably sounded annoyed. Crap. "I'm sorry," she said immediately. "Maybe rum makes me defensive or something. And I don't mean to sound unappreciative. It's just that . . ." She let out a sigh. And, for lack of any better options, blurted out the ugly truth. "Okay, I know everyone feels sorry for me because I have no love life. And that's nice of you all, but it's really all right."

"It's not that we feel sorry for you," Cami rushed to say.

"It's just that . . . well, wouldn't you like to find someone?" Christy asked. "I mean, deep down, isn't that what everyone really wants if they're honest with themselves?"

Whoa. This had suddenly turned into a deep conversation. Or deep by Tamra's standards anyway.

Being an artist, she certainly had the capacity to be deep, but . . . she didn't always let it show. It was easier that way.

Both Christy and Cami really did have great lives. And she didn't begrudge them that—but she often wondered if they really understood how different their existences were from hers. They were both so outgoing, whereas she tended to be a little more reserved, even guarded. They were pretty and perky and vibrant, while she was just more . . . well, average in all those ways.

She'd never been the life of a party, or "the hot girl," or even "the pretty girl." And she was fine with that really, because the one time in her life when she'd truly felt pretty and special had ultimately ended up making her feel ugly inside, and she'd begun to suspect that being pretty was sometimes actually more of a detriment to a woman than a help. So she was good with who she was.

"The fact is," she began slowly, thoughtfully, "some people just aren't meant to have the whole big dating-and-relationship thing. And I'm not interested in chasing after it. And I really *do* think you guys feel sorry for me—but stop, okay?" She tried to laugh, like it was all fun and games. "It's really fine."

The other two women stayed quiet for a moment, until Cami asked gently, "Then why don't you *look* like it's fine?"

Oh hell. It was the rum. She'd forgotten to *keep* laughing, keep her smile in place. And maybe the rum was bringing out something else, too, something she'd just been trying to ignore. And she'd been doing a pretty good job of it . . . until this very moment.

Trying to concoct a reply, she peered out over the beach as a sea breeze lifted her long, wavy, auburn hair, which she'd pulled back in a low ponytail lately to keep it at bay. And she wasn't sure how to account for her expression other than with . . . stark honesty. An honesty and awareness suddenly bubbling inside her, almost actually *wanting* to come out. Damn rum.

So she took a fortifying sip of her Ahoy Mateys and said, "You want to know the truth?"

"Of course," Christy said.

And Tamra dropped her gaze to her colorful drink, another wistful sigh escaping her. "I really am okay with the situation, except for . . . the sex part." She'd muttered the last few words. More to herself than to her companions. Then realized she'd really, truly said that out loud, and added, "Oh crap. Apparently rum makes me spill my guts, too."

"Wow," Christy said, looking as stunned as Tamra felt.

But . . . didn't women talk about sex all the time? Not *her*, *ever*, until now—but wasn't this normal? "Wow?" she asked, a little embarrassed, worried. Had she breached some social protocol she didn't know about?

"It's just that . . . you're usually so reserved and— and straitlaced, I guess," Christy mused, flashing a little grin. "I mean, don't take this the wrong way, but you just don't seem like someone who thinks about sex. Or at least you never talk about it."

Tamra sheepishly lifted her glass. "It's the rum talking."

Christy's smile broadened. "Then I think maybe I *like* you drinking rum."

All three of them laughed, but Tamra was quick

to move forward with more of an answer. Even if she didn't know exactly what she wanted to say now that she'd opened this personal can of worms. "Well, normally I'm *not* someone who thinks much about sex."

Only then she decided that was enough, right there. Because sure, there was more she could say on the topic—much more—yet why put herself through that? The rum, apparently, had decided to shut up now.

"But . . . enough about that. Let's talk about your wedding," she said to Christy with an enthusiastic tone she hoped would catch on. "Are all the plans set? What's left to be done?"

"W-h-h-hait a minute," Cami said, sounding a little intoxicated. "Not so fast."

Tamra just blinked.

And Cami went on. "You can't say what you just said and not tell us the rest."

"Well, sure I can," Tamra insisted. "And there *is* no rest. Not really."

"No," Christy argued. "Cami's right. I like this side of you."

Tamra's back went a little more rigid, though she worked to keep sounding casual. "What side of me? I've really said very little if you think about it."

"But just enough," Christy pointed out, "to make me feel like we're . . . getting to know you more. I mean, I know we know you, but . . . you don't open up a lot. This is probably the most personal conversation we've ever had about you. And I already feel like I know you way better than I did just five minutes ago."

Tamra could have responded to that in many ways. There were plenty of reasons she wasn't as open and trusting as a lot of other people. She almost envied the quick way Christy and Cami bonded with people—whereas Tamra's bonds formed much more slowly.

And she supposed it was that which made her choose the simplest reply, the one she thought she could just spit out and get over with the quickest—which was, yet again, frank honesty. And yeah, it felt *super* personal to tell them this, but maybe the rum's gut-spilling effects were on the upswing again.

"Okay . . . here goes." Though she paused, nibbled her lower lip a second, and then made the mental push forward to share the things she was just now admitting to herself. And it all came out in a rush, like a big bucket of words being dumped out of her mouth. "Like I said, usually I don't sit around thinking about sex, but lately I'm just feeling . . . those urges. A lot. As in it's driving me crazy. Yesterday I saw a hot construction worker out on Route Nineteen and practically drooled.

"But I'm not the sort of person who just wants to hook up with someone, and even if I was I have no idea where I'd find a suitable guy, so no matter how you slice it, it's . . . frustrating." She stopped, giving her head a nervous little shake, predictably uncomfortable with the topic. Time to shut up again. "And that's really it—all there is to it."

Though she was quick to lift a finger high into the air then, because she needed to make something perfectly clear. "But that doesn't mean I'm desperate to meet men, okay?" After which she lowered her voice, since a woman at another table glanced over. "Which is good, since there are so few around here who aren't taken."

The truth was, even most of the vacationing men were usually married. Coral Cove drew families and couples. Occasional groups of young women or college boys, but mostly it was a crowd of matched pairs.

"Happy now?" she asked.

And she was just gearing up for the next assault, preparing to defend her position—since well-meaning people who were parts of happy couples always seemed committed to convincing everyone else they *also* belonged in a happy couple—when the blare of a siren cut through the Coral Cove night.

A siren in Coral Cove was as rare as . . . well, as rare as sex for Tamra—she was pretty sure she hadn't heard one in all the years she'd lived here. So it halted the conversation instantly, and they all looked up to see the glow of bright blue lights atop one of Coral Cove's three police cruisers as it came screeching into the Hungry Fisherman's freshly paved parking lot.

Two of the town's half dozen cops rushed from the car, running into the space that separated the restaurant from the Happy Crab, toward the dock that lined the bay a short distance behind the buildings.

Polly hurried out the front door in the same rust-colored waitress uniform she always wore, the outdated beehive hairdo atop her head slanting this way and that as she struggled to see what was happening. "What in the Sam Hill?" she asked, looking after the cops.

She turned to the girls and other patrons on the patio, as if *they* knew what in the Sam Hill, but of course they didn't. Christy held her hands up in silent reply to Polly, as if to say, *Who knows?*

A few minutes later, both cops reappeared, coming

from the direction of the dock, but now they escorted between them a scruffy, bearded guy in handcuffs. Leading him to the cruiser, they pushed him into the backseat as everyone on the patio gaped.

"Lord, who on earth is that?" Tamra asked.

And Cami said, "Uh oh. That's the guy Reece has been letting stay at the motel for free. I'd better call him."

And as the police car's blue lights faded into the night, leaving the Hungry Fisherman quiet and peaceful once again, Tamra said, "Well, there you go—case in point. If that's the best this town has to offer me in the way of new men, I think I'll just stay celibate."

What could you do for a boy like that?

Frances Hodgson Burnett, *The Secret Garden*

Chapter 2

"THE THROAT? You picked a guy up by the throat?"

Jeremy sat on a hard cot in a small holding cell in the Coral Cove Police Station, looking through the thin bars at Reece Donovan, who'd pulled a folding chair up close on the other side.

"Yep," Jeremy replied. He wasn't exactly proud of what he'd done, but on the other hand, he still thought the punk had earned it.

Reece, however—sitting there in his usual flip-flops and cargo shorts— just shook his head, looking perplexed. "Why?"

Jeremy kept it simple. "He kicked a cat."

"A cat?" Reece blinked.

And Jeremy nodded.

Reece squinted, clearly trying to make sense of this. "You a big cat lover or something?"

"Nope. But the guy had no cause. Kicked it so hard it went flying into a tree trunk." Just then he noticed the two cops who'd arrested him standing on the other side of the room gawking at him like he had horns sprouting from his head. He knew he didn't look good lately, but damn. He switched his glance from them back to Reece. "What the hell are those two staring at?"

Reece looked over, too, then back through the bars. "I'm guessing it's the first time in a while they've had a prisoner in here. They probably don't quite know how to handle it."

"My first time being one, too," Jeremy informed him. Then muttered, "And I'm starting to feel like an animal in the zoo."

"The cops were asking me if you had an anger problem," Reece informed him.

But Jeremy shook his head. "It wasn't an anger problem—it was an asshole problem."

Outside the cell, Reece leaned back in his chair and ran a hand through his hair. Finally he said, "Shit, dude—I like you. And I wanna help you out. But . . ."

Jeremy let out a breath he hadn't known he was holding. Or maybe he'd been holding his breath for weeks, months, possibly even years.

Something colored Reece's voice, and it was . . . burden. Most people in Jeremy's life never quite let that out, let it show. They cared about him and knew he'd been through bad things. But Reece . . . Reece didn't know him or his past.

"This isn't me." The words left him in a murmur, unplanned.

"What?" Reece asked.

Jeremy looked up, met Reece's gaze for the first real time since he'd walked in here. "This isn't me," he said again. "But after I got back from Afghanistan, things changed." Then he let his eyes drop to the floor between them. He didn't like letting weaknesses show.

"Damn, man," Reece said. "I saw your tattoo, so I knew you were military." Jeremy had gotten a U.S. Marines emblem, along with the words *Semper Fi*, tattooed on his right biceps only after returning home. Something about trying to hold on to that hero persona. But stamping it on his arm hadn't made him any more of a hero than he'd been in the first place. "I didn't know you'd been in Afghanistan, though."

Jeremy didn't reply to that because he had nothing else to say. He'd already said too much. He didn't regret defending a helpless animal. But he regretted garnering anyone's sympathy. Silence stretched between them, expanding to fill the room like something heavy and smothering.

"Can we make a deal?" Reece said a long moment later.

Jeremy flicked his gaze tentatively upward to the guy outside the bars. "What's the deal?"

"I'm gonna bail you out," Reece said. "And I'm gonna talk to the guy who owns the boat and whose son you attacked and try like hell to get him to drop the charges because you're a military veteran and my friend. And you can keep staying at the Happy Crab. But in return, I'm putting you to work. On some projects around town. My girlfriend is the town planner and she's looking to hire someone for some heavy lifting, landscaping, and light construction. You be able to handle that?"

A job. Someone was offering him a job.

One that had nothing to do with protecting people, thank God.

And hell, that felt unexpectedly good. "Yeah," he said simply.

"All right," Reece told him. "Your first few paychecks can go toward paying off your bail and back rent on the room. Can you handle that, too?"

"Sure," he said again.

Reece just looked at him for a long, sizing-up kind of minute—probably trying to decide if he'd made the right call here. Jeremy didn't know the answer any more than Reece did. Finally Reece commented, "You don't say much."

"Nope."

At this, Reece just laughed, then pushed to his feet. "Hang tight, I'm gonna go bail you out."

But as he started to walk away, Jeremy decided there was one more thing he *should* say, even if he kept it quiet, short. "Reece," he said.

Reece stopped and looked back.

And Jeremy added, "Thanks."

TAMRA wrapped a sweater around her and warmed her hands on the big mug of hot tea she'd just made for herself. It wasn't that cold out, but fall had brought cooler nights to Coral Cove, the temperatures dropping after dark, and she found herself wanting to bask in the softer air.

It was late—nearly one A.M.—and she sat in the garden she'd created behind her small beach cottage on Sea Shell Lane. She'd had the yard enclosed with a tall privacy fence almost as soon as she'd moved in—common in Florida because so many people had swimming pools. Yet no one had known her well enough at the time to ask why, and even though she'd made friends since then, no one had particularly inquired about the choice.

She'd wanted to create a sort of private paradise, a serene place for her and her alone, and since that time, her garden had been an elaborate work in progress. Always in progress—she was always adding things, changing things. Just last week she'd added snapdragons in a sunny spot, which she knew would grow taller and more robust than they ever had the chance to do in northern climes, and several pottery birdbaths she'd crafted hung from the branches of various trees. She sat surrounded by orange marmalade and white plumeria and giant elephant ear plants as a soft sea breeze riffled through a set of windchimes she'd made as well, and the sweet scent of the bougainvillea draping the west wall wafted past her.

It had indeed become her secret haven, the place she went to just be with her own thoughts, find peace when she needed it, feel *more* peace when she already had it.

Sometimes she napped in the hammock strung between two tall palm trees, but tonight she sat curled up in one of the white Adirondack chairs she'd placed in a semi-circle around the fire pit she'd installed. She used the fire pit often when the weather was cool enough, but not the other chairs.

She looked at them now, wondering for the first time why she'd even bought more than one when she never invited anyone into her garden, never let it be enjoyed by anyone but herself.

Of course, her friends had *seen* the garden—they'd either peered out at it through the French doors at the rear of the cottage, or they'd helped her carry things in and out through the side gate. Fletcher, who lived right across Sea Shell Lane from her, was always quick to notice out the window if she was toting in new shrubbery or big bags of potting soil and coming over to help. And her friends always seemed complimentary and even in awe of the space she'd tucked away back here when they had occasion to view it—but they never invited themselves over. Even Christy, who was so perky and sociable and lived right next door. Tamra couldn't help thinking that, while it had never been said, on some level they knew it was a place she'd created only for herself.

Wouldn't you like to have them over? Wouldn't it be nice to have drinks around the fire with Christy and Cami? Wouldn't it be pleasant to roast marshmallows and make s'mores with Fletcher? Or maybe invite John and Nancy Romo, the nice older couple a few streets away, over for a glass of wine?

Yet something in her core tensed slightly at the idea. She didn't know why. And yet it remained there, floating heavy inside her.

Her discussion tonight with Christy and Cami had been oddly warming. She usually just found it annoying when her friends pushed romance on her, suggesting she should be out chasing men and making her feel almost abnormal not to be doing that. But tonight, even as uncomfortable as she'd been blurting out frank truths about herself, it had touched her when they'd openly wanted to be closer to her, know her better. And it had made her realize how many walls she'd put up—not just around this garden, but inside herself, too.

Yet . . . when all was said and done, she was still happier here alone. Happier to just be completely at ease, completely comfortable, by herself.

There's nothing wrong with it. Enjoying your own company is healthy. You can't love anyone else until you love yourself. And though it had taken a little time after her unconventional upbringing on a commune in Arizona, she really did love herself now. But she still didn't trust easily. And she wasn't sure there was an upside to changing that. It was better to take care of yourself, and easier to stay happy and productive if you didn't put yourself at risk with people.

How on earth would inviting Cami and Christy back here for a drink put you at risk, for heaven's sake? It wouldn't, that simple. So maybe this wasn't even *about* risk. Maybe it was just about personal comfort and ease. Everyone needed a place that was strictly their own and this was hers.

Now if only your stupid body would quit aching with lust. She prayed this was only a phase, one that would end quickly. And good Lord, she still couldn't believe she'd told Christy and Cami about that tonight. Word vomit. Even if it had it resulted in making her friends feel more connected to her, it had still been word vomit.

She'd been trying to deny it even to herself for a while now. But the truth was that she suffered the warm spread of sexual desire flowing through her like hot lava almost all the time lately.

She'd suffered it this morning during a walk on the beach, where she'd seen all the things she normally saw there—but now she suddenly saw them differently. Felt them differently. She'd witnessed a couple kissing on a blanket and envied what they shared, hungered for what they experienced. The feel of wet sand on her toes, the cool ocean water lapping up onto them, had affected her in different ways than ever before, affected other parts of her body.

And she'd thought about it this afternoon when she'd worked in the art studio in her cottage. Digging her hands into the same clay she always worked with had held a fresh . . . awareness. Touching it had made her want to touch other, far different things. A man's body.

And she'd felt it still more while weeding beneath her banyan tree just before the Sunset Celebration. Rich soil on her fingers, even the trowel in her hand, had held a newness for her, a strange yearning she couldn't seem to shake free of. Being in her garden usually brought her an enormous sense of peace—she'd filled it with things she loved, after all—but today the overriding emotion had been frustration.

At thirty-five, she hadn't thought much about sex in a long while. She knew most women were more into sex, but she'd just never suffered that compelling need for it that so many seemed to.

In her teens and early twenties, there'd been guys, experiences—but since then, not so much. And mostly, she'd been okay with that. Until now. The spot between her thighs ached even as she sat clutching the mug between her hands. People acted like sex was so fun, but when your body wanted it and couldn't have it, well . . . she didn't see anything fun about *that* at all.

Maybe it's the birth control pills. She'd started taking them just recently—her doctor's remedy for an irregular cycle that often came with bad cramping. And it had worked—thank God. But she knew the pill affected various hormones and wondered if this new rush of sexual need had perhaps been instigated by the change.

And while a part of her suffered the urge to pull up her skirt, bare herself to the bright moon peering down from a clear, dark sky, and just take care of her own needs, the thought made her feel . . . more needy than sensuous. She knew plenty of people took care of the issue that way, but the very idea made her feel lonely. And she didn't *want* to feel lonely. She'd felt lonely in Arizona. She'd felt lonely all through her growing up years, even with people all around her. She'd finally *quit* feeling lonely when she'd left—because being alone wasn't what made you lonely; it was about something else. And why do something that would make her feel lonely in any way whatsoever? She'd rather lose a little sleep over the physical frustration and just pray, again, that it would subside.

Was it possible, though, to be content in her private world here and . . . still feel a little empty inside? That didn't quite add up, did it? *It's the sex issue making you feel empty, that's all. Your life is great otherwise.*

And even if there *was* something missing . . . well, maybe it was just easier not acknowledging that. She'd built a wonderful little life for herself here—so she was going to keep right on telling herself that it was enough, all she needed to be happy.

CAMI had arranged for an empty lot along Coral Street, which ran down the strip of land that stretched between the beach and the bay, to be paved and made into a municipal parking lot. It would serve the "Coral Street Business District," as she'd recently dubbed the area she was busy bringing back to life. Three days after Tamra had "gotten dressed" to "go out" with the girls, she was joining up with Cami, Reece, Fletcher, Christy, Jack, and anyone else who was willing to pitch in, for the task of planting shrubbery and perennials around the small lot's perimeter to make it visually appealing.

With Fletcher's help, Tamra unloaded the signs she'd hand-painted for the lot from the back of her small SUV.

"Ready for a day of work in the sun?" Fletcher asked cheerfully.

Her friend was an unusual man. His small brown beard and ponytail made him look like a time traveler from 1969, he made his living by walking on a tightrope every night at the Sunset Celebration, and he stayed unusually positive no matter what. Case in point: His wife had left him nearly four years ago, turning his world upside down, and he had no idea where she was—and yet for some insane reason he remained happily convinced she'd come back any day now.

Tamra worried about Fletcher because he was a good friend and she cared about him. She feared his pie-in-the-sky attitude about his marriage would leave him with a seriously broken heart one day and that his denial was only delaying the inevitable.

"Definitely," she answered him. In fact, she hoped some hard physical labor might be just the thing to take the edge off her sexual frustration. It was like a monster inside her, clawing at her constantly.

"You know," he said, "if you don't mind my saying, you don't seem yourself lately."

Oh crap. Her sexual deprivation showed? "Of course I'm myself," she assured him, trying for a light laugh. "Who else would I be?"

He shook his head, not buying it. "I don't know—you just seem . . . on edge."

Yep, her sexual deprivation showed. Great. And it occurred to her that she could explain it to Fletcher—he was an evolved enough man that he wouldn't be creepy or perverse about it. In fact, the idea made her wonder for the first time if he didn't suffer similar issues himself given how long his wife, Kim, had been MIA.

But she thought better of it. Especially here, now, with people all around. Bad enough she'd spilled something that personal to Cami and Christy—but at least they were women.

So finally she just said, "Nope, fine," and hoped it didn't come out sounding too stiff. Besides, the one thing about Fletcher that bugged her was his tendency to push her toward finding someone to date. Of course, *everyone* seemed to do that lately, but Fletcher had been at it longer than most. And she knew they all meant well, but why couldn't they understand that it just wasn't that easy?

If she ever met someone, she wanted it to happen naturally. And she didn't want to settle. So many women settled, just because they were desperate to be validated by having a man in their lives. She wasn't that desperate and never would be, her recently activated sex drive be damned.

Within a few minutes, work had begun—an ample crowd of Coral Cove residents had shown up to help with the project, so Tamra suspected it would be a short day. Cami commandeered the whole operation—

clipboard in hand, she went from person to person, giving out instructions. And soon enough, wheelbarrows were being pushed this way and that, shrubs and decorative grasses were being unloaded from truck beds, and dirt was being shoveled.

Normally, Tamra would be among those digging in the dirt, avid gardener that she was, but since so many others were on hand, Cami asked her to take charge of getting the signs she'd created in the ground. A main sign was to be placed at the lot's entrance, and two more, indicating the lot was for patrons of Coral Street businesses only—as opposed to beachgoers—were to be erected at each side, facing the parking spots.

Tamra knelt, working with a large trowel, enjoying the feel of the sun on her face and shoulders, glad she'd pulled her hair back into a ponytail as usual—when a deep, shockingly rude voice sounded in her ear. "Can you get outta my way?"

Caught off guard, she looked up. She couldn't see the face of the man standing next to her—it was blocked by a large juniper bush. She saw only dirty brown workboots and two burly hands wrapped around a large burlap-covered ball of roots towering above her. "What?" she asked.

"I said, 'Can you get outta my way?' This thing's freaking heavy."

She just blinked, her back going ramrod straight where she squatted in front of him. "Can *you* not be so rude?"

"Jesus Christ, woman. Just move before I drop the damn thing on you."

Tamra tried to hold in her gasp. But given this Neanderthal's manners, she feared he might make good on the threat, so as much as she didn't like obeying orders from rude strangers, she grudgingly stood up and got out of his path. Then watched as he plunked the bush on the ground next to her feet.

She looked from the bush to the Neanderthal, now that she could actually see him, and—oh Lord, was she mistaken or was this the same Neanderthal who'd been hauled away from the Hungry Fisherman in handcuffs the other night? Same scruffy beard, same longish, messy hair.

"That bush had to go right there, huh?" she asked. "Right at this exact moment?"

His expression didn't change—he wasn't the least bit cowed by her scolding. "That's where it goes," he said. "It's heavy, so why should I move it twice?"

"Well, maybe because I was already working there," she pointed out, raising one critical eyebrow in his direction.

"Was it that hard for you to move?" he asked in the same tone, as if she were being unreasonable.

"Well, I—"

"Wait, don't answer that," he said, holding up one hand. "Didn't know I'd be dealing with the princess of Coral Cove over here. But now that I know, I'll steer clear of you."

And with that, he turned and sauntered away.

And Tamra stood looking after him, bewildered. Where had this guy come from and what was his problem? And why did she actually feel a little like she was in the wrong here when she knew good and well that she was in the right?

No one had ever in her life accused her of acting like a princess. She just wasn't that girl—not by a long shot. And she sure as hell didn't like it. Who on earth did Mr. Scruffy Beard think he was, anyway?

Normally, she would turn around and go back to what she'd been doing. But she was so taken aback that she suffered the unusual urge to seek out some friendly faces rather than stand there alone stewing over some asshole she didn't even know. Spotting Cami and Reece talking with Fletcher and Christy, she crossed the parking lot toward them.

"Who *is* that guy?" She rolled her eyes and motioned toward the rude stranger, who now unloaded another sizable bush from the tailgate of a faded red pickup truck.

"His name is Jeremy Sheridan," Reece said.

And Christy added, "He's from Destiny, Ohio—my hometown. I just didn't recognize him the other night when we saw him getting arrested. I still can't believe that's him." She shook her head, then appeared a bit wistful. "You should have seen him when he was younger. He was so handsome—big town heartthrob, football hero, the works."

They all glanced over to where the Neanderthal now lugged another bush toward some unsuspecting helpers who Tamra figured were probably about to get yelled at for being in his way.

"Him?" she asked, not bothering to hide her skepticism. Okay, he had nice arms—muscular, tan—but otherwise . . . "That's hard to imagine."

Then Christy lowered her voice to inform Tamra, "He's been in war. In Afghanistan."

And Tamra tipped her head back slightly. "Ah—so *that's* what's wrong with him."

When everyone just stared at her, clearly aghast, she

said, "I don't mean to be cold, but I'm not sure going to war gives someone a license to be rude to every person they meet. And I don't want anything to do with him."

Which was when Cami made a slightly troubled face and said, "Well, that could be a problem."

And Tamra blinked. "Why's that?"

"Because I just hired him to build the golf course you're designing."

She began to feel hot and as contrary
as she had ever felt in her life.

Frances Hodgson Burnett, *The Secret Garden*

Chapter 3

*T*AMRA FELT her eyebrows shoot up. "Him?"

Again, everyone just stared at her.

"What?" she said, defending herself.

"He's a veteran," Christy said, almost as reverently as if they were in a church. Tamra supported veterans and appreciated their sacrifice, but that didn't mean she was going to let one treat her like crap.

"And he gave me a reference," Cami added, "which I called and who spoke highly of him. Apparently he's a great worker and knows what he's doing. Once we get the concrete poured, he should be able to do everything else we need. With your help." She added that last part with hopefully raised eyebrows.

And Tamra just stood there. The fact was, whoever did this job was someone she'd be working with closely. From erecting a small hut for money collection and equipment storage to laying the Astroturf for the holes to constructing the miniature features for each—which Tamra had designed to look like Coral Cove landmarks, she would work hand in hand with this guy.

No matter what he'd been through, he seemed like a jerk. A jerk with nice arms maybe, but still a jerk. She didn't particularly want to spend the entire autumn butting heads with some ass who thought she was a princess just because she didn't like rudeness. And though she was being paid for her work on the golf course, most of what she'd done this summer for the town had been on a volunteer basis, and she'd been generous with her time and skills. So she knew she'd be within her rights to tell Cami she just couldn't work with him and that she'd have to find someone else.

She flicked another glance his way in time to see that he'd dropped the next sizable bush pretty much right in the middle of where other people had been working and that they all stood there looking after him with the same stunned expression she probably had. Because he was a Neanderthal.

But when she glanced back to Cami, her friend's eyes still glimmered with hope. And a look that said, *You'd really be helping me out if you can do this.* She even added, through slightly clenched teeth, "He's within the budget I promised Jack. Most guys with any experience aren't."

Tamra loved Coral Cove. It was the best home she'd ever had—the *only* home that felt *real* to her. The few people in the world who she cared about, and who cared about her in return, lived here. And the reason she'd been happy to give of her time to the town was because she valued her warm, safe seaside haven so much.

And this golf course was about bringing new business to the town.

And she was a team player.

And not a princess.

So finally she said, "Okay."

The group of friends standing around her broke out into big smiles, and Cami's face lit with relief. "You'll work with him?"

"Sure," Tamra said. Even if a bit stiffly.

Freeing one hand from her clipboard, Cami reached out to warmly squeeze Tamra's arm. "Thank you! And I'm sure he won't be so bad. Just a little rough around the edges, that's all."

"Hey, heads up—can you all move it? Heavy bush coming through."

Everyone standing with her raised their eyes in time to indeed find another big bush headed their way, and as the Neanderthal dropped it heavily to the ground between them, they all took a quick step back.

Tamra looked up to see his broad shoulders and cargo shorts already walking away—then flicked her gaze to Cami, who smiled nervously.

FLETCHER McCloud knew he made it look easy. He made it look easy to be happy and mild-mannered all the time. He made it look easy to have faith—constant faith—that his wife was coming back. And he believed that with his whole heart.

But the truth was . . . there were moments when he began to doubt.

Only moments, though, and that was the important thing. As long as he came back to believing, as long as his crises of faith were short-lived, infinitesimal blips in his brain, it would all be okay. Kim's note had promised him that very thing, in fact.

Standing in the living room of his beach cottage, he found himself studying the gifts he'd bought for her since she'd been gone. Pieces of jewelry he'd known she'd like, small and sometimes silly keepsakes he'd picked up on a lark—like the little stuffed parrot that had reminded him of the real one that had once sat on her shoulder during a stint in Key West and how she'd suddenly loved parrots after that.

Now he reached in the back pocket of his shorts and drew out his wallet, and from it the note Kim had left for him upon her departure.

I'm sorry, Fletch. I love you, but I just have to go. Don't let this hurt too much. Everything will be okay.

Kim

It would only be okay again—fully okay—when Kim came back. And that was how he knew deep in his soul that she would.

Some days it was still hard to believe she'd left him. They'd been happy. Or at least he'd thought so. They'd spent the previous ten glorious years traveling all over the country, living simply but comfortably from the money his tightrope act drew in.

Kim had been his assistant. He still missed that, even now. He missed looking down at her from atop the rope, feeling that perfect connection, looking into the eyes of the one woman who got him, who understood him, who loved him.

For the first month after she'd gone, he hadn't been able to walk the tightrope. He'd simply been unable to regain his balance, mentally or physically. Everything in our heads, and in our hearts, was linked to how our bodies operated.

He'd only started to perform again by tricking himself, telling himself Kim was in the crowd watching him, cheering for him. When he remembered she wasn't really there, it all felt emptier, hollow, and he came to understand that what he'd taught himself to do as a boy, through painstaking practice and faith and repetition, he'd eventually begun doing . . . for her. He'd realized that when he climbed up onto the tightrope every day or night, in every city or town, at every street fair or carnival, it had been to impress his wife, to show her the magic she inspired in him.

Even now, each night when he ascended to the rope, he scanned the crowd looking for her, and each and every night, he believed he would find her there. And when he didn't, he simply pretended that he did, that she had come back and was watching him, and that was what enabled him to keep his balance.

He flinched when a loud *knock knock knock* sounded on the side door. No one used Fletcher's front door—everyone entered through the one on the porch that overlooked the ocean, the porch that had become a place to pass lazy afternoons with friends, commiserating their losses or celebrating their successes. He liked having that kind of a door, that kind of a house. It had been here, in Coral Cove, that Kim had so suddenly left him, and he'd sold their well-used motorhome to get the down payment for the cottage—so that he could wait for her here.

As much as he missed his old life with Kim, there were certain aspects of living in Coral Cove he valued greatly now and would never have known otherwise. Life on the road had taught him to make fast friends with people but also not to get attached—and it was nice that now he *could* get attached, nice that everything wasn't temporary. Everything happened for a reason, and the worth he'd found in building a new life here provided for him some of those reasons. And when Kim came home he'd understand the rest of it, why it had to happen this way.

When the knock came again, he realized how lost in thought he'd gotten. "Fletch, you home?"

It was his neighbor and good friend, Jack. "Yep," he called. "Come on in."

As Jack stepped inside, his gaze dropped to the note Fletcher still held in his hand. "You, uh, reminiscing?"

He'd shared the note with Jack early in their friendship, but it wasn't like he sat around holding it in his hand all the time, and he felt as if he'd been caught at something.

So he let out a chuckle, laughing it off. "Only for a minute." Then he refolded the note on its well-worn creases and put it back in his wallet as he smiled into Jack's eyes. "What's up, my friend? Can I get you a beer?"

"Actually, I need your help with something. Christy has me building this elaborate arbor for the wedding. I just picked up the wood and was hoping you'd help me unload it and get started."

"Happy to," Fletcher said. He was always pleased to help his friends. "Though"—he stopped, tilted his head—"I think most people just rent that kind of thing. You could probably save yourself a lot of trouble."

"I know," Jack said, "but Christy wants to put it in the yard afterward, like a keepsake."

Ah, keepsakes again. Fletcher understood about those. So he began to nod. "That's a nice idea." He'd learned the value of putting down roots somewhere, of making a house a home. He only hoped Kim would like the home he'd made for them when she finally got here.

Midday Florida sun beat down on the two men as they crossed Sea Shell Lane toward Jack and Christy's bungalow. He supposed Jack might prefer to wait until a cooler hour to unload and start constructing his wedding arbor, but Fletcher's friends had learned to work around his schedule, knowing he made his living performing at the Sunset Celebration every night.

"You okay?" Jack asked, slanting an inquisitive glance Fletcher's way as they began carrying the thin strips of wood, tied in bundles, from the bed of Jack's pickup to his backyard.

"Fine, as always," Fletcher replied. And he meant it. Yeah, he had his moments when he wasn't as fine as he generally portrayed himself to be, but they were few and far between. Jack had just happened to catch him in one, but it was past now.

"Because . . . the way you were holding that note before—"

"Every now and then I look at it. To remind myself everything will be okay. That's all. And it will, so no worries."

They both lowered their armfuls of wood to the grass behind Jack's house. Jack looked from the wood up to Fletcher and the hot air felt weighted with tension until he finally said, "Four years is a long time, buddy."

"I know," Fletcher answered quietly, calmly.

"And sometimes I just worry . . ."

"Don't," Fletcher assured him quickly. Assuring himself at the same time. "All is well."

Just then a burst of female laughter cut through their somber tones, breaking the mood, making them both look up. Christy rounded the corner of the house with a young woman Fletcher didn't know. Dark hair hung nearly to her trim waist, and she wore a short tie-dyed dress belted at the hips. She had a unique look that he instantly dug and related to, and she appeared wholly out of place on quaint, idyllic Sea Shell Lane.

"Oh hey, Fletch," Christy said in greeting. "This is my friend from Cincinnati, Bethany. She's here early for the wedding—I'm so excited that she's staying for so long!"

"Ah yes," Fletcher said, remembering the stories Christy had relayed about her old roommate. She was an artist, a painter—and if his perceptions from Christy's tales were apt, maybe a slightly lost soul searching for something she hadn't yet found. Though his first impression was that she didn't *feel* lost—and something in her eyes instantly told him that she saw the world through a slightly different lens than most people. Like him. "I've heard a lot about you," he greeted Bethany. "Fletcher McCloud, your friendly neighborhood funambulist. Welcome to Coral Cove." He held out his hand and she took it.

"Funambulist?" the dark-haired woman said with an easy confidence that nearly dripped from her. Not arrogance, but an obvious comfort in her own skin—she clearly knew who she was and embraced her individuality. No, not lost at all.

"Technical term for a tightrope walker," he explained. "I like to think I put the *fun* in funambulist."

She laughed, the sound a pretty trill that seemed to fall all around him like happy raindrops. "And I," she said, "am Bethany Willis, officially Christy's dark side."

And Fletcher laughed. He recalled from Christy that indeed her friend walked more on the wild side than her. "You don't seem so dark to me," he said anyway. There was a big difference between darkness and wildness. "More of a free spirit, I think," Fletcher said. "More light than dark."

The slight, saucy tilt of her head and the quirk of her bright red lips made him think she liked that. Even when she laughed and said, "I don't know about that. Just ask Christy—hang around with me long enough and I'm bound to get you in trouble."

That made Fletcher let out another laugh, Jack and Christy joining in. "I love her, but she's telling the truth," Christy added with a grin.

"Ah, I'm not afraid," Fletcher replied.

And Bethany smiled at him. She had a lovely, honest smile. He knew already that she didn't give it away easily, automatically, like most people—but that when you got it from her, it was the real deal.

"Well, we'll let you two get back to work," Christy said, an excited-about-my-wedding gleam in her eye. "We're going inside to make some plans for the shower."

And as the two disappeared into the side porch door of the small house, Fletcher couldn't help feeling uplifted, and as if he'd just stumbled upon a kindred soul.

"Cute girl," he told Jack, thinking out loud.

Causing Jack to glance up from where he'd just begun to focus on the instructions for his arbor, a speculative look in his eye.

And Fletcher read his mind. "Don't get ahead of yourself, my friend. I simply made an honest observation. You know I'm unfailingly honest."

Jack gave a short, accepting nod. "That I do."

And then they got down to the task at hand, Jack studying the arbor plans, Fletcher helping him sort the wood into various piles.

It was a few minutes later when Jack's cell phone buzzed in his pocket, and he pulled it out to take a look. After which he raised his gaze to Fletcher and said, "I don't want to blow your mind—or risk getting ahead of myself—but . . ."

"But?"

"But according to Christy, she thinks you're cute, too."

JEREMY used a spade he found on the jobsite at the miniature golf course to begin moving a thick layer of dirt and sand that an overnight rainfall had washed onto the concrete for what he assumed would soon be Hole 1. He'd arrived early and this seemed like as good a thing to do as any. He liked how quiet and empty the area was this early in the day—less to keep an eye on, less uncertainty around him. He listened to Pearl Jam sing about sirens through a pair of earbuds.

It occurred to him that for a guy who had nightmares about gunfire and sirens and bombs, maybe lighter music would be wise—but he didn't like lighter music. Despite himself, he still felt drawn to a certain darkness.

That's what you came here to get away from, get rid of.

Well, regardless, at least he was doing something useful for a change. It felt good to use the muscles in his arms, shoulders, back—good to feel them stretch taut. One of the ways he'd spent his time at Lucky's was lifting the weights Lucky kept in his shop. Using his muscles, experiencing that pull, had been one of the few things that had helped him keep feeling alive—and it still proved true now, but it was better to be doing something productive with them.

As the song faded to its end, a voice, at once brash and feminine, cut into his solitude. "Hey!" it was saying. "*Hey!*" And it sounded damn impatient.

He stopped shoveling and turned to see—oh, the princess. Figured. She seemed like a damn testy woman. And she looked downright put out—already, this early in the morning.

Most people had no idea how good they had it, how tiny their problems were. The things they bitched and complained about were so small in the big picture. And whatever this chick's problem was—it was small, too. So he simply leaned on the handle of his spade, reached up to remove his earbuds, and said, "Good morning."

And at this, she appeared even more annoyed. "*Good morning?*"

He stood before her bewildered, but still unruffled. "Is that not a greeting you're familiar with?"

If it was possible, her green eyes sparkled with a bit more irritation. "Is answering someone when they address you repeatedly something *you're* not familiar with?"

At this, Jeremy let his eyes widen slightly. Then he reached down and picked up an earbud that dangled from his jeans pocket now. "I was listening to music."

She blinked and looked a little embarrassed. But then she went right back to sounding snippy. "Well, I'm not a psychic—and I couldn't see through all that hair that you had anything in your ears."

"Well, now that you know, maybe you can cut me a little slack, huh?"

Uh oh—wrong thing to say. Now that sparkle in her eyes shifted toward being irate.

And even though at 6'1" he was considerably taller than her, she took a step closer and stared pointedly up into his eyes. "Look, I just expect you to be on time, do what I say, and be respectful. We don't have to like each other—but we have a job to do, so if you can follow those few simple rules, this will be much easier."

He just looked at her. This from the woman who had shown up fifteen minutes late—which was why he'd started shoveling the overflow of dirt and sand in the first place.

"Are you hearing me?" she asked.

Wow, she could be brusque for a little slip of a thing. Not that she was tiny actually. He supposed, now that he was really looking at her, her build was . . . average. But in a nice, curvy way. Though that might have been easier to see if she weren't so irate.

"Yep, princess, I sure am."

This time he could almost feel her bristling before he saw it in her big round eyes and stiffened posture. "And that's another thing. Don't call me princess."

At this, Jeremy just shrugged. "You got something against princesses? Most women dig that sort of thing." Then he winked. Because at this point, she was egging him on, kind of asking for it.

"Well, I'm not most women. And I'm not a princess, by any stretch of the imagination. Understood?" Still asking for it.

So he delivered. "You got it, babe."

She kept on looking put out. "I'm not your babe— I'm your supervisor."

"And you might just need to relax a little," he muttered under his breath. But apparently loud enough to be heard, given the look she flashed him. Oops.

She crossed her arms beneath ample breasts. "Who do you think you are anyway?"

"Just a guy trying to do a job," he said. "Didn't know I'd get told off before I even started." Jeremy had thought he was going to like doing this work, but now he suspected his non-babe boss might make that difficult.

"Listen, I just want to work peacefully here."

"I could go for some peace, too, believe me," he informed her.

"Good," she replied with a terse nod, sounding a little too satisfied for his taste. Like she'd conquered him or something.

And he knew he should shut up, just ask her what she wanted him to do to get started here, yet instead he heard himself beginning to talk. "But for the record, all this started when you snapped at me because you didn't know I had earbuds in. So a little respect goes both ways, ya know."

She pursed her lips and sized him up beneath half lowered lids. "No," she said, sounding a little more calm, but also a little more calculating. "This started when you rudely told me to get out of the way and nearly dropped a big root ball on my toes."

Something about that made Jeremy laugh, though he wasn't sure why. Maybe because he thought she was taking that a little too seriously. He'd known in retrospect he probably could have been more polite, but he'd just been trying to get the damn bushes in place, and they'd weighed a ton. "They were heavy," he said.

"I know. You told me."

"So I didn't have time to be nice."

Her tone got a little more indulgent then; she sounded slightly more appeased. "Well, maybe *I* didn't take the time to be nice just *now*. But we'll get along a lot better if we can both take the time going forward. It's not that hard."

Jeremy turned that over in his head. There had been a time when he was the nicest guy in the world—when that had come naturally. He supposed spending so much time alone had screwed with his people skills. "Okay," he said. "I'll try."

"Thank you," she answered quietly. "Me, too."

And he realized her face had changed. Calming down had taken away the sharp edges, the harsh lines, and left behind a much softer, prettier woman.

Huh. He hadn't seen that coming, thinking she was pretty. But she was. Not Barbie doll pretty, not supermodel pretty, not schoolgirl pretty—but pretty in a more . . . solid sort of way with her large green eyes, wide mouth, and the long, auburn hair that hung down behind her in messy spiral waves, pulled back in an elastic band. He wondered vaguely what it looked like loose, falling around her face.

"Why don't we get started?" he suggested.

She gave a short nod. And even though she still regarded him warily, at least she'd quit raking him over the coals.

She opened the large three-ring binder she held and said, "Why don't we take a look at the project plans and discuss the best route to move forward. As you can see, the course has already been designed and the concrete forms are in place." She motioned at the flat lot they stood in, surrounded by slabs of concrete that had been poured in what was otherwise a sea of the same dirt/sand mix he'd been shoveling. "Our job is . . . to do everything else."

As she began to unfold a large map of the course, Jeremy said, "Why don't we take this to my truck—I can open the tailgate to use like a table."

The surprised light in her eye told him she hadn't expected him to be smart, even in such a small way. "Sure," she agreed, and they walked together toward the old red Ford.

Once he lowered the tailgate, she showed him the course and began outlining the various aspects of construction. "I'm not an architect or anything," she said, "so you'll need to be able to take my drawings and build from them without plans. Can you do that?"

He looked down at her sketches of the obstacles that would sit on the course—miniature versions of the Happy Crab, the Hungry Fisherman, the pier, the lifeguard stand on the beach, and other Coral Cove landmarks. "Not exactly the Taj Mahal—think I can handle it."

When she reached the part about the small building where the cashier would take money and hand out equipment, he said, "Would make sense to get that erected first thing—be a good place to keep tools where they can be locked up at night and under roof when it rains. And a good home base for paperwork and other things. Don't ya think?"

Again, she looked slightly surprised he'd come up with an intelligent idea. "Um, yeah."

And he let out a small laugh.

"What?" She was instantly back to looking wary again.

"You don't have to act so shocked I have a brain," he told her. "Just 'cause I don't bend over backwards to kiss anybody's ass, that doesn't make me an idiot."

Her face colored slightly with a pretty pink blush. "I didn't think it did."

He flashed an I-know-better expression and tapped his head with one finger as he said, "Don't underestimate what I got goin' on up here, pri—" He stopped himself and let out a small chuckle.

"If you're so smart," she pointed out, "I'm sure you can stop yourself from calling me princess."

He arched one eyebrow in her direction and said, "I just did."

The woman next to him pulled in her breath, but he couldn't read her thoughts. The only thing he knew for sure was that she didn't want him to get the best of her—which meant that even if they'd technically made peace, they were still secretly at odds. And which, of course, made him want to get the best of her—just because she still seemed to be asking for it a little.

After briefly meeting his gaze, she quickly pulled her eyes away, down to the open binder. "Let's . . . look at the supplies you'll need to get started."

"Sure," he said easily, dropping his gaze there as well. He found himself watching her hands, turning pages, using her fingertips to point at particular pieces of information. Her nails were longish but not well manicured. And there was something in that he liked. Natural. It seemed . . . feminine but natural. There was no trying, no affectation—it was just real.

They went over what he'd need and decided he'd head to the Home Depot out on Route 19 to get it.

After which she closed her notebook, picking it up to walk away, and Jeremy followed. Only to hear an *oomph* as she fell, sprawling in the dirt before him, the binder flying out of her grasp to land nearby.

"Damn. You okay?"

She sat up, gave her head a quick shake to clear it, and said, "Yeah." Then, "I tripped over something."

Jeremy bent to find a large root jutting from the ground. "This."

She drew in her breath. "We paid to have this lot completely cleared and graded before the concrete was poured."

"Eh, sometimes something gets missed," Jeremy said reasonably. If war had done anything positive for him at all, it had made it so he didn't sweat the small stuff.

"I didn't pay for things to be missed," the woman on the ground informed him. Man, she was tightly wound.

He reached a hand down to her, helping Tamra to her feet. Then murmured under his breath, "You really could stand to lighten up a little." After which he glanced up in time to see his new boss flashing him a death glare.

"What did you just say?"

She was right—she wasn't anybody's princess. "I said . . . why don't I go get a shovel and see if I can dig this thing out?" Then he dared cast her a small grin, since they both knew that wasn't even remotely close to what he'd said.

To her credit, she simply brushed the dirt off her shorts and quietly answered, "Okay.

Not to Jeremy's credit, as he began digging up the wayward root, he found himself watching her ass when she bent over to pick up her binder. Her shorts were loose, but he still thought she might have something nice underneath them. Pretty legs anyway, even if a little paler than he might expect from a woman who lived at the beach. And he considered asking about that, but thought better of it, pretty sure it would only get him snipped at some more.

As she turned to face him, he darted his gaze away from her shorts and pretended to be engrossed by his work. Turned out the root ran deep. The earth around it was fairly loose, consisting largely of sand, so the digging was easy—but no matter how deep he went, he couldn't find the base.

"Maybe if you just pulled on it, it would come out," she suggested.

Jeremy doubted it. But he wasn't inclined to argue with her, so he dropped his shovel, bent down, and used both hands to grab hold of the root.

As he'd suspected, it remained firmly attached to the ground, but he continued to pull, putting to work all those muscles he'd built on Lucky's weight bench. "Damn," he muttered—but then something loosened beneath his grasp and he knew part of the root had broken free. Grabbing onto it a little farther down, he gave it every ounce of strength he had, yanking hard. So hard that the root came loose from the earth's grip and sent him flailing backwards.

Instinct made him shift his body forward, midair, not wanting to land on his ass—just as he felt himself connect with the softer female flesh of his boss and he knew he was taking her down with him.

They hit the soft dirt with a gentle *plmmmp*, and his fall was made even softer by having her body beneath him. They ended up face to face.

When Jeremy met her gaze—filled with a little bit of shock and little bit of something else he couldn't quite read—a small, unplanned grin left him just before he said, "We gotta stop meeting like this."

The woman beneath him didn't smile back. "You can get off me now."

Yeah, he knew that. But for some reason, he didn't really want to. It wasn't a bad place to be. "Before I do," he said, "I just realized we were never officially introduced. I'm Jeremy."

Mary's heart began to thump and her hands to shake a little in her delight and excitement.

Frances Hodgson Burnett, *The Secret Garden*

Chapter 4

"Yes, I know," Tamra said. She couldn't believe the Neanderthal was lying on top of her. How on earth had she gotten herself in this situation? "Get off me."

"And you are?" he asked.

"Getting angry," she said through slightly clenched teeth.

Which made him let out another of those deep laughs of his. Which might have charmed her on some human level if he weren't a belligerent wiseass and if she didn't have to deal with him. "You're Tamra," he said, since she'd refused to play along.

"Very good," she said dryly, rolling her eyes. "Now get up."

And when he didn't immediately make a move to do so, she pressed her palms to his chest. It felt warm, solid. In a way that somehow seemed to echo through her fingertips and up her arms.

Oh. Ugh. She didn't know what was happening

here, especially as their eyes met. His . . . weren't bad. They were maybe even kind of nice. Blue. Flecked with gray. And something hard, masculine—not the kind of thing you could really see, but more sense, feel. Yet the rest of him was unkempt and hairy and rude and cocky and a host of other things that held no appeal for her. He was so not her type. So she was back to ugh.

And why was he still lying on her? And dear God, right in view of Coral Street. "Get up! Now!" She pushed on his chest again, harder this time. And ignored any other feeling besides the intense desire to bring this awkward connection to a quick end.

Finally, her rude worker pushed upward to his knees, separating their bodies, and she suffered a startling awareness of the way he hovered above her, their legs still mingled.

When he got to his feet, relief rushed through her veins—along with a more subtle underlying current she couldn't put her finger on. The heat of the tropical autumn sun beat down on her, making her hotter than usual.

As he reached to help her up for the second time in just a few minutes, he said, "You're no fun."

And the accusation put her on the defensive. "Not wanting to lie around in the dirt with a stranger on top of me has nothing to do with whether or not I'm fun."

The last time he'd pulled her to her feet, she'd become more aware of the touch than she should have. The same thing happened this time, too—only more so now. Just as when she'd touched his chest, a zing of unwanted electricity rippled up her arm, then spread all through her.

"So are you?" he asked.

"Am I what?" She tugged at the hem of her shorts, then smoothed the tank top she wore as she scanned the area, looking around to see if anyone had witnessed Jeremy Sheridan, war veteran and jailbird, lying on top of her at the jobsite.

"Fun," he said easily.

Okay, why did that question catch her off guard?

Because . . . it's flirtatious. No matter how she sliced it, Mr. Scruffy Beard was flirting with her. And she supposed he'd been doing so for the last few minutes, but the reality was only fully hitting her now. "None of your business." She had no idea where the reply came from.

Yes you do. You don't want to say yes and have him think you're flirting back. But you don't want to say no and have him think you're not fun. Ugh again. Why on earth did she care what he thought of her?

When he flashed a speculative grin through that messy beard of his, it moved all through her—and made her nervous as hell even as it irritated her.

"And quit smiling at me like that. I'm not *that* fun."

"I'd be surprised if you were," he said, stooping to pick up the shovel he'd abandoned.

And she was on the verge of feeling insulted—when he winked at her. Oh Lord. She wasn't sure what was worse—that it was officially overt flirtation or that her body responded with a thin burst of desire flowing through her lower regions when she'd least expected it.

"Was it so horrible to have me on top of you?" he asked. Lord, he was direct. She wondered if her eyes betrayed her and wished desperately for sunglasses to hide them, but she'd left them all the way over on his tailgate.

"*I* didn't mind it so much," he added when she didn't reply.

"That was clear," she quipped, not wanting to let him think he was getting the upper hand. "And yes, it was extremely unpleasant."

As usual, though, he just laughed. "Why's that, prin– . . . Tamra?"

She raised her eyebrows. Was he seriously asking her? She'd met his gaze, but now looked away. "Well, I don't even know you, and I don't lie around with men I don't know."

"But if you knew me you would?" Another grin through that beard.

She prayed he couldn't see the heat rising to her cheeks, or that he would mistake it for a touch of color from the sun. "No! You're not . . . not . . ."

"Not what?"

Did the man never stop? Well, fine, she'd just be direct, too. He was asking for it anyway. "My type," she said. "You're not my type."

He appeared completely undaunted as he asked, "What's your type?"

So she tried to keep being honest. "Well—not so much of this," she said, motioning around her head with her hands, meaning he had too much hair for her taste. "Or this." She motioned to her chin, meaning his beard. "And I like men who are nicer, and more polite—two things you seriously have working against you." She ended with a brisk nod, just to drive the point home and make sure he knew exactly how much she was *not* into him.

And she supposed it shouldn't have surprised her when he simply laughed in reply, but it still did.

So she heard herself ask, "What's so funny?"

"Methinks the lady doth protest too much," he said, still looking amused.

And her jaw dropped. "You're quoting Shakespeare now?"

He lifted one hand, used his index finger to point at his head, and let his eyes grow big. "Like I said," he told her, "lot going on up here, sister."

Tamra rolled her eyes once more. "That's another thing I am not. Your sister."

"Don't worry," Jeremy said, one more small, bold grin unfurling across his hairy face, "I could never confuse you with my sister. Because I would never like lying on top of my sister so much."

TAMRA couldn't deny feeling a little emotionally disheveled by the time she sent Mr. Scruffy Beard off to Home Depot to buy the supplies needed to start the golf hut. She almost wondered if she should think twice about handing him the credit card Cami had issued her for such things—he was such an unknown quantity in ways, and so far he didn't exactly come across as a fine, upstanding citizen. But the whole encounter with him had her so flustered that she'd have probably handed him her *own* credit card just to get rid of him for a while.

As she watched him drive off in the old red pickup in need of a muffler, her heartbeat slowed. And life began to seem normal again. The beach lay serene in the distance as families and couples began to dot the sand now that the sun had risen higher in the sky. A seabird cawed as it flew by overhead. Coral Cove was at peace, and so was she. But that was a far cry from how she'd felt while caught in a verbal sparring match with Jeremy Sheridan. Not to mention when he'd been lying on top of her.

Ready to push the whole incident from her mind, she crossed the street and walked toward the Hungry Fisherman, visible in the distance. *Yes, talk to other people, clear your head. That's a good idea.* Any distraction at all from what had just transpired seemed wise.

As she approached, she found Polly sitting at a table on the patio with Cami and Reece. All of them smiled at her—too boldly.

"Um, hi," she said, wondering why they all wore goofy grins.

"That was a nice show there," Polly said.

Oh crap.

"Maybe a little early in the day for something like that, though," Reece added. "Might want to keep it a little more G-rated for the little kids headed to the beach." He finished with a good-natured wink, but Tamra could scarcely recall a time when she'd been more embarrassed in front of her friends.

"That was no show," Tamra assured them. "That was the Neanderthal Cami hired being a clumsy lout and using the opportunity to be totally inappropriate."

At this, Reece's eyes narrowed. "Inappropriate how? Did we make a mistake here? Do I need to have a talk with him? Or get rid of him altogether?"

Tamra hadn't expected Reece to come flying to protect her honor, and now she almost felt bad about the accusation. Mr. Scruffy Beard had been inappropriate—but . . . did it still count as inappropriate if it had made her heart beat faster with excitement? She didn't like admitting that to herself, but she couldn't deny the truth—the hard, cold reality that it hadn't been completely one-sided. "Well . . . he was just very flirty when he fell on me, that's all. But I handled it and I'm sure it won't happen again."

In response, Cami still sat there smiling, looking almost as if she had a secret.

Tamra lowered her chin and squarely met her gaze. "What?"

"You just look . . . flushed or something. Maybe a little flirting isn't a bad thing." Cami finished with a wink, as if to emphasize the point. Ugh, why had Tamra spilled her guts about her sexual needs? It was so much easier to just keep private things private.

She tilted her head and said, "Really, Cami? Have you seen him?"

Cami just shrugged. "Under all the hairiness, he might be cute. Christy says so anyway."

"And he's got some nice muscles on him, that's for sure," Polly said. "Hubba-hubba."

Reece spun to look at Polly. "Don't take this the wrong way, Polly, but I don't think people say 'hubba-hubba' anymore."

She planted her hands on the hips of her rust-colored uniform. "Well, they might if they saw *him*."

"But back to Tamra and Jeremy," Cami said, switching her attention from Polly to Tamra.

Rats, Tamra had thought maybe she was off the hook. And she was extremely uncomfortable with this whole conversation. "Let's get something straight. There *is* no me and Jeremy. The guy works for me. Which I didn't even want, if you'll recall. And he's a handful, but I can manage it. And that's all there is to it."

"Handfuls of *some* things can be fun," Polly mused.

But Tamra didn't return her playful expression, even as Cami laughed out loud. Instead she just said, "Can I please have a Coke? I need to restore my energy before the handful gets back from Home Depot."

As Polly stood up to get Tamra's soda, Reece rose from the table, too. "I'm gonna go check on Fifi, work on getting her habitat winterized today." Fifi was Reece's six-foot-long giant iguana who lived in a room behind the Happy Crab's check-in desk.

And as soon as he was gone and the two of them were alone, Cami said, "Don't get mad at me, but you really do look a little flushed, and I really do think he's cute underneath the hair. And given that you're—you know—feeling certain urges, maybe you should just be . . . more open-minded."

"Let me get this straight," Tamra said. "You think it's a good idea for me to hook up with an unkempt, impolite, homeless guy who was arrested for attacking a stranger."

Cami pursed her lips. "Well, when you put it that way . . ."

"Thank you," Tamra said with a terse nod of victory.

"But he's a war veteran. So he has reasons for . . . not being at his best," Cami argued. "It really doesn't mean he's a rotten guy."

"It doesn't mean he's a good one, either. But no matter what he is, he's made a terrible impression on me and I'm not attracted to him one iota, and that's the end of the story."

It was a relief when the restaurant's patio door opened and Polly reappeared with her drink. And thankfully, conversation shifted to preparations for Christy and Jack's wedding. Tamra, Cami, and the maid of honor, Bethany, were throwing an engagement party and there were lots of plans to be made.

"I met Bethany," Cami told Tamra. "I think you'll like her. She's an artist, like you."

Tamra smiled. She always appreciated that, being called an artist—recognizing her creations as art was the highest compliment someone could give her. Her mission in life was to leave the world a little richer in that way than she'd found it.

But as the discussion went on, Tamra's thoughts drifted unwittingly back to what she'd said about Jeremy. The last part might have been a lie. She might have been a little bit attracted. Maybe more than even an iota.

But she didn't like that—not at all. Because it wasn't logical; it didn't make sense. He was unkempt and hairy. They'd been at odds since the moment they'd met. At best, he was cocky and presumptuous; at worst, downright rude. So why on earth had she suffered any twinges of desire for him?

Was she *that* desperate? Was her body *that* hungry for sex? Would *any* able-bodied man who'd fallen on her and refused to get up have elicited the same reaction?

Ugh. Don't even think like that! You are not desperate. You are not needy. This, too, shall pass.

After all, it was her first morning working with Jeremy, so this was . . . growing pains in their work relationship. It was new and awkward. *He* was awkward . . . as in too forward and having too much attitude. But soon enough, what had just happened would be further in the past and their time together would start seeming more normal, less fraught with tension. Working with him would become just "another day at the office."

But maybe for right now, while things *were* awkward, she'd just arrange it so they didn't spend a ton of time working directly together. She'd provided him with architectural plans for the hut, so assuming he was as capable a builder as she'd been promised, she wouldn't really need to be on hand for that. While he worked, she could do other things: tend to the landscaping, design the remaining course obstacles. There were a million things to be done, after all. He'd do his part, she'd do hers, and they didn't have to be Siamese twins about it.

Meanwhile, Cami was busy scribbling names into a notebook—a result of Polly asking how big this wedding shower party thing was going to be, since she and Abner were providing the food. "It's nice for Christy," Cami added, "that there are a few people from her hometown who live here. More will come down for the wedding itself, but for the party, we'll definitely want to invite John and Nancy Romo. And Jeremy, too."

At this, Tamra's eyebrows shot up. "Jeremy? Are you serious?" She made a face. "He's becoming part of our social circle now?"

Cami shrugged and opened her eyes wider, as if to say: *Deal with it.* "He's one of Christy's few links to her hometown here. And besides, everyone else we know will be coming—it would seem weirder *not* to invite him. And it might be nice to make him feel included."

Tamra just sighed. "If he doesn't get included in things, maybe it's because he's . . . say, homeless. Or rude. Or gets arrested because he attacks people."

Now *her* eyes went wide, silently expressing that she was making excellent points.

But Cami seemed unmoved. "Riley was homeless once, too, you know." Riley was the manager of the Happy Crab. Reece had taken in the old man out of the goodness of his heart—and now Riley was a beloved member of the community. "Sometimes people just need a little help, someone to believe in them."

Tamra took that in. She knew it was true. She hadn't believed much in *herself* when she'd arrived in Coral Cove with nothing but a car full of pottery and stained glass to show for her first twenty-seven years of life. The kindness of the people here had changed that. And yet she still felt the need to argue, grousing, "Reece needs to be more careful about taking in homeless people—one of these days he could end up with a real nut on his hands."

But at that, Polly just laughed and Cami said, "Well, we're still inviting Jeremy Sheridan to the party."

As Jeremy walked in the door at Home Depot, he scanned the area, high and low, as he automatically did when entering any new environment. As he turned each blind corner, he kept on the alert, ready for anything. He knew there weren't snipers at Home Depot, but his body didn't seem to know—his body stayed tense in any unfamiliar surroundings.

He walked down the tool aisle, then flinched at the sight of a man holding a drill, testing the feel of it in his hand. *It's a drill, not a weapon. Breathe. Slowly. Inhale through the nose. Count four. Exhale through the mouth. Count four.* It always helped.

The truth was, he fucking hated being here. He hated being anyplace with a crowd, with strangers milling around. That was a lot of the appeal of Whisper Falls. No crowds. No unpredictability. It had taken some of the tension out of his day. Most people could walk around a store or a town and feel normal, but for Jeremy it wasn't that easy.

And even at the beach, there were vast open spaces—it was easy to stay aware of what went on around him. In a store, though, he was confronted by aisles, and tall shelves, things you couldn't see around.

But it'll get easier. It'll get a little easier every time.

As he found a large cart and began collecting what he needed, his mind drifted back to the jobsite, to his interactions with the princess who refused to be anybody's princess. He didn't know what he thought of her. Shades of light and dark there. Shades of challenge. And he wasn't up for mysteries these days, so it was probably best to just do his work and let it alone. *It* being her. *It* being whatever weird pull he'd felt moving between them.

It hit him, as he located the size 10p nails he needed for framing, that she'd actually made him laugh. Unwittingly maybe, but still—he couldn't remember the last time he'd laughed and really meant it. Maybe that was why he'd kept egging her on.

She stayed on his mind as he gathered the rest of the building supplies, and it was only as he headed to the checkout that he realized he'd spent the last few minutes *not* looking around waiting for something bad to happen.

And by the time Jeremy left the store with his purchases loaded into the bed of his truck, he felt a little stronger than he had going in.

As the sun sank over the ocean in the distance a few days later, Jeremy sat eating takeout from Gino's Pizzeria up the street at one of the picnic tables behind the Happy Crab. It had become a favorite spot for him since arriving here, a peaceful spot. He supposed in summer, when the place was more crowded, the motel's pool might be busy with laughing, splashing kids, or the dock area more bustling with boaters, but for now it was a relatively tranquil place where he could quietly take in this little corner of the world.

The thing that made it even better tonight was that he'd bought his dinner. No one had given it to him out of generosity. He *appreciated* generosity—he'd elicited more than his fair share since returning home from Afghanistan—but it was nice not to *need* it for a change. Although he'd only worked a partial week so far, today he'd gotten his first paycheck signed by Jack DuVall, proprietor of the Coral Cove Mini-Golf Paradise.

After cashing it, he'd promptly headed to the motel's office and paid Riley for at least a little of his bill—it had felt good to start chipping away at that. Then he'd bought a couple slices of pepperoni pizza and a large soda, bringing it back here to the peace and quiet he found peering out over the masts and sails of the boats lining the dock area and the bay beyond.

He'd spent these last days erecting the small building Tamra had put him in charge of. He'd forgotten how much he enjoyed working with his hands. Or . . . maybe he hadn't ever really liked it as much as he suddenly did now. Seeing something begin to grow that hadn't been there before made him feel worthwhile. Even if it was only a mini-golf course. He supposed it just felt good to be doing something right for a change.

He hadn't seen much of Tamra—she'd informed him she'd be working on other things. And he was pretty sure he'd just scared her off that first morning. But still she stayed on his mind. Maybe he'd liked the idea of having company as he worked. A surprising thought for a man who'd chosen to isolate himself for so long. Or maybe he'd just *expected* company—normally you get a job, you deal with people on that job.

Once upon a time, he'd been smooth with women, good with girls. What had happened with her that first morning on the job didn't make him feel smooth, but flirting had come shockingly easy—even if it might not have been appropriate.

These days he didn't examine stuff like that. Unlike the Jeremy Sheridan of old, he didn't have much of a filter these days, and he kind of liked it that way. It made life a little more interesting anyway.

And maybe he'd liked pushing her buttons. He wasn't sure why—except maybe because they were just so easy to push.

Oh well, probably didn't matter much if she was going to keep her distance. He supposed that was a hint and that he should probably take it.

Even if there was something about her . . . under the surface. Something he could sense more than see. She was so prickly on the outside—yet he suspected there was something softer, gentler, underneath. It made him want to uncover it . . .

But take the hint, like you just told yourself.

Even if she's the first woman to spark any interest in you, of any kind, for a very long time.

Just then a certain gray tomcat came trotting up the dock, almost blending into the weathered wood. Camouflage, Jeremy thought. Looked like the cat had recovered from what had happened the last time they'd crossed paths.

The big, lean cat paused at the end of a ramp that led to—oh hell—the same boat the frat boys had occupied that fateful night. Jeremy hadn't seen any movement on the boat—tonight or since he'd been arrested—but still he silently willed the cat: *Don't go there, bud. I can't save you this time.*

His throat seized slightly then, and his chest tightened, realizing the words that had just passed through his brain.

You can't save anyone. Not even a damn cat.

When the cat finally moved on, Jeremy whispered, "Good."

And the small sound made the cat look over at him with his remaining eye.

And he realized that this time he could give the cat something to eat.

Pinching a bit of thick pizza crust off in his fingertips, he held it down where he hoped the cat would see it. It was dark out, but the area was lit.

The cat didn't hesitate—he walked right up to Jeremy and took the offered bite of food, and then another, gobbling them down.

"There you go, buddy," he whispered. "Eat up." He found himself scratching the cat's head for a second, then reached up to tear off more crust for him, along with a little cheese this time, too.

"What's your story?" he murmured toward the cat. "You got a death wish or something, hanging out around that boat again?" He chuckled. "Or you want to be the captain, head out on a big fishing trip."

Just then, the motel office's back door opened and Jeremy looked up to see Reece walk out. "This the guy whose honor you were defending last week?" he asked, peering down at the cat.

"Guilty as charged," Jeremy replied.

"Speaking of that," Reece said, reaching the picnic table, "got some good news for ya."

"That's something I could use," Jeremy said. Though, in fact, he already felt more at ease inside than he had in a long time. Maybe good news was just the icing on an already pretty decent week or so. Relatively speaking anyway.

"The assault charges were dropped," Reece told him.

And though Jeremy hadn't let himself think much about that, it had placed a weight on his chest that he'd been ignoring because it was easier than facing it. He'd gotten too damn good at that. But things were changing now, thank God.

He didn't hide his relief. "That's more than good news—it's the best damn news I've heard in ages." He released some of that pent-up tension with a sigh, then asked, "How'd you make that happen?"

Reece shrugged. "The kid's been in some trouble—didn't need any more. And I think his dad realizes he's an ass and probably had it coming."

Jeremy met Reece's gaze again. "I owe ya, man. Big time."

Reece let out a good-natured laugh. "You're right,

you do. But lucky for you, I don't keep score. Just glad things are going better for you."

Yet Jeremy still needed to say more. "You've really . . . kept me on my feet here. I won't forget it."

Reece took the gratitude as easily as he did everything else. He just nodded comfortably and said, "So the work's going good then? You and Tamra aren't gonna kill each other?"

Jeremy let out a quick, unplanned laugh. Clearly word had made it around that the two of them had butted heads a little. Even though, technically, it had been more like butting bodies. Which was a lot more fun, and a memory that still made him feel . . . alive, in a man/woman kind of way, more than he had in ages.

"I won't kill *her* as long as she doesn't kill *me*. She's keeping her distance, though, so guess we're both safe for now." He tossed a sideways glance in Reece's direction to add, "Don't think she likes me much."

When Reece didn't reply to that, only keeping an amused expression in place, Jeremy added, "What's her deal, anyway? Seems uptight."

Reece shifted his weight from one flip-flop to the other. "She is, a little. But . . . she had a rough time earlier in life."

Jeremy let that statement hang in the evening air for a minute. It was easy to forget that most everyone had demons of some kind, especially when you were battling your own. "Don't suppose you're gonna tell me in what way?" It was none of his business, especially since he barely knew Tamra, but he couldn't help being curious.

"Nope," his landlord said. "That'd have to come from her."

Now it was Jeremy who nodded, letting it drop, but still wondering what made Tamra . . . Tamra.

"She's one of my closest friends," Reece said then. "Just so you know." A gentle warning came through in his tone.

And Jeremy replied, "Understood and respected." He got the point.

After which Reece's gaze took on a speculative look as he tilted his head and observed, "You seem . . . cooler than you have up to now."

Jeremy couldn't argue with that. "Guess getting out, working, is good. A step in the right direction."

"That's good to hear. Keep it up." And with that, Reece pointed over his shoulder in the general direction of the shore to say, "Well, I've got a date with a hot blonde for a late walk on the beach, so I'm gonna take off."

"Okay, man. Enjoy," Jeremy said, watching him go.

That was when a meow drew his attention back to the big gray tomcat at his feet. He'd continued dropping bite-size bits of pizza down to him, but had run out as he and Reece had talked. "Sorry, pal," he said now, peering down at the cat, "but you cleaned me out."

Though he instinctually reached down to scratch the cat behind the ear anyway, watching his one pensive green eye fall contentedly shut. There was something satisfying in bringing the cat a little peace that way. Maybe it brought him a little peace, too.

But that kind of peace, he knew, was only temporary—you could only pet a cat so long.

So after a while he stopped, sat back upright on the picnic table's bench.

When the cat opened his good eye again, their gazes locked. Until, after a few seconds, the cat suddenly turned and trotted away, over toward the Hungry Fisherman's back door, clearly in search of a bigger dinner.

"Don't get yourself in any trouble, bud," he murmured as the cat disappeared into the darkness.

Yeah, that kind of peace was only temporary.

*. . . it was curious how much nicer
a person looked when he smiled.*

Frances Hodgson Burnett, *The Secret Garden*

Chapter 5

THE NEXT day Jeremy sat at the Hungry Fisherman
in an old orange booth with cracked vinyl seats which
he suspected had seen decades of use. He'd spent the
morning working in the hot sun on the golf course
hut—again without Tamra's company or supervision—
and was getting a fish sandwich for lunch. The place
was completely empty at noon on a Wednesday, so he
was glad he could actually pay for his meal this time
around.

After he gave Polly his order and tucked the plastic
menu back behind the napkin holder on his table, his
cell phone notified him of a text message. He looked
down to see it was from Marco, an old Marine Corp
buddy. WHAT'S UP, MAN?

He typed in an answer. NOT MUCH, BUD. YOU?

He and Marco had been close in Afghanistan and
it was good to hear from him. If he hadn't fallen into
such a funk, he'd have probably done more to keep in

touch. As it was, Marco reached out to him every few months and they texted a little until it died down and they went quiet again for a while.

SAME HERE. JUST SORRY TO SEE SUMMER GO—HAD A GOOD ONE WITH THE KIDS. Marco lived with his wife and two little girls in St. Louis.

Before Jeremy could fashion a response, another text from Marco arrived. YOU GETTING OUT AND ABOUT ANY, BUDDY?

He'd sensed Marco's concern over the hermit tendencies he'd developed, so he was glad to tell him he'd made a change. YOU COULD SAY THAT. I HEADED SOUTH LITTLE PLACE IN FLORIDA CALLED CORAL COVE. DOING SOME LIGHT CONSTRUCTION.

YOU SHITTIN' ME, SHERIDAN?

The reply made Jeremy chuckle. NO. WHY?

I KNOW THAT PLACE, MAN. PLANNING TO BRING BRITTANY AND THE KIDS TO A BEACH NOT FAR FROM THERE ON THEIR FALL BREAK FROM SCHOOL. WE SHOULD CONNECT.

Damn. That sounded good. To see an old friend. A friend who really understood.

Well, at least he understood *part* of the stuff that haunted Jeremy—not all of it, because there were some things he'd told only Lucky.

But still, close enough. He typed back: THAT'D BE AWESOME, DUDE.

SOUNDS LIKE YOU'RE GETTING BACK ON YOUR FEET. THAT'S DAMN GOOD TO HEAR.

He probably wasn't quite as on his feet as his friend thought—yet things were sure as hell looking up. YEAH, THINGS ARE A LITTLE BETTER.

GOOD DEAL.

Then it occurred to Jeremy to ask: YOU DOING OKAY,

MAN? He wasn't the only one who'd been through heavy shit, after all.

OKAY ENOUGH.

Hmm. Usually Marco was the one who sounded like he had his life together, like he'd left the past in the past. But now Jeremy wondered if he'd missed stuff—hints—in their brief bits of correspondence because he'd been too mired in his own issues.

He wasn't sure what to say, though, because he wasn't used to being on the other side of this equation. Finally, he settled on: IT'LL BE GOOD FOR BOTH OF US TO CATCH UP.

I'LL BE IN TOUCH, JER.

SOUNDS GOOD, MAN.

When Polly brought his lunch a few minutes later, movement near her feet drew Jeremy's eyes downward—to see a lanky gray cat trotting along with her. He let out a surprised laugh. "Well, if it's not the captain."

After which Polly followed his eyes to the floor, let out a screech, and nearly threw his fish sandwich up in the air.

Jeremy just chuckled and said, "It's okay, Polly—it's a cat. Not a bat. Or a rat."

"I know good and well what it is—and these cats are gonna be the death of me, I tell ya." She lowered his plate to the table, sandwich intact, though a few fries had hit the floor in the upheaval.

Jeremy let his eyes widen as he looked up at her and her very tall, hair-sprayed hair. "Cats? There are more than one?"

The older waitress released a tired-sounding sigh. "Well, I've only had to deal with one at a time so far.

But seems like one gets a home and another stray shows up to take its place." Then she darted her glance around the room. "And thank God you're the only person in here right now and you're not raisin' Cain about it, because believe you me, the health department don't cotton to cats in restaurants." Then it was *her* eyes that grew wide as she focused her gaze tight on Jeremy. "Would *you* like a cat?'

The answer was easy. "I don't have a home to *give* a cat, Polly—remember?"

At this, Polly took on a sneaky look and cast a sideways glance in the general direction of the motel. "Wouldn't be the first time somebody secretly kept a cat at the Happy Crab."

Jeremy raised his eyebrows. "Is that so?"

She gave a succinct nod. "Cami had pretty much adopted her kitty, Tiger Lily, when she was staying there. And it all turned out fine. Reece was real understandin' when he found out." She finished with a triumphant nod.

"Well, I don't care to impose on his kindness any more than I already have. And I think Reece has a soft spot for Cami that he might not quite have for me." Jeremy added a wink. "And besides, you just said yourself, when one cat gets a home, a new one comes along—so since you seem destined to have a cat issue here, I'll just let you keep the one you've already got."

Polly put her hands on her hips. "Just so you know, Reece told me defendin' this fella's furry little honor is how you got yourself in trouble with the law. So I know you like him."

He smiled up at her. She was something else. "The fact is, Miss Coral Cove Sleuth, just because I got pissed off when somebody was mistreating him doesn't mean I'm—like—a cat guy. If I was gonna have a pet, it'd be a dog. Man's best friend and all that. And like I said, I live in a motel room. I'm not in the market for a pet. I'm more in the market for . . . a life." A short laugh left him. "First things first, ya know?"

Now she smiled back, but remained undaunted in her quest. "Sometimes a pet is *part* of havin' a life. A good ingredient, anyway. So you just think on that, why don't ya?" Then she motioned to his plate. "And eat your fish before it gets cold, while I put this guy out the back door before anybody else sees him trespassin' around here." She rolled her eyes toward Abner, who sat on a booth on the far side of the restaurant, going over paperwork and wearing a straw hat reminiscent of one you might find on a scarecrow in the fields surrounding Jeremy's hometown of Destiny. "If there's cat hair in the buffet, somebody'll have a cow."

"I'd think *anybody* would have a cow if there's cat hair in the buffet," Jeremy pointed out with a grin. Then picked up his sandwich as Polly hefted the cat into her arms and headed to the kitchen.

After Jeremy finished his sandwich and fries, he paid his bill, pleased to leave Polly a healthy tip as she made him a to-go cup to take back to the jobsite. But as he turned to leave, his eyes landed again on Abner.

Since his arrival in town, he'd seen Abner wear many hats—literally, not figuratively. A fire chief's hat, a motorcycle helmet, an airline pilot's hat, a felt fedora, and more. Reece had explained that the man was just a little eccentric, that no one knew why he wore the hats, no one asked, and no one cared.

Even so, it made him sort of hard to approach—

made him seem like a guy who was probably a little weird.

And still . . . Jeremy thought he himself probably seemed pretty weird to a lot of people here, so he followed his gut, and instead of heading out the door, he instead crossed the restaurant, past the buffet counter, to the darkish corner where Abner sat wearing his straw hat with an otherwise entirely normal outfit of a golf shirt and khaki shorts.

When Abner raised his eyes to Jeremy, his expression stayed stern, which Jeremy had noticed was the usual. But he didn't let that deter him, either—since he hadn't exactly been a barrel of laughs himself the last couple of years.

"Help ya?" Abner asked.

"Just wanted to thank you," Jeremy said. "For your generosity since I got here." The two men had never actually spoken before, but he knew from Polly and Reece that Abner had been fine with Polly giving him meals on the house. "I'm making some money now, so I intend to pay my debts."

Abner's face never changed or softened the tiniest bit as he said, "Everybody needs a little help sometimes." And then he looked back down.

The briskness of the conversation, the way the harsh planes of Abner's face conflicted with his kinder words, was a little jarring. "Well . . . you have a good day, Abner. And thanks again," Jeremy said. Then he started toward the door.

"Wait."

The command drew Jeremy up short, made him turn back around. He met Abner's eyes beneath the brim of the straw hat.

"Most people steer pretty clear of me. I don't blame 'em. I understand why that is. So I respect you for comin' over. Most people wouldn't. They'd just pass it through Polly. And that woulda been fine. But I appreciate the gesture. You're a good man."

Jeremy barely knew how to respond. He was taken aback. By the whole thing. Abner's acknowledgment that, basically, he *was* kind of a weird dude. And the last part. It'd been a damn long time since Jeremy had felt like a good man.

Finally he said, "You are, too." Since that much seemed clear. Might be weird. Might be gruff. But again, Jeremy could relate. *We all have our secrets, our reasons.*

He finished with a nod, then headed back out into the hot Coral Cove sun to get back to work.

TAMRA held a cool glass of iced tea in her hand as she sat on Fletcher's porch with him on a sunny afternoon. It was one of her favorite places to be, and Fletcher was one of her favorite people to be with. Their friendship was a nice, easy one—comfortable enough that they could discuss almost anything, or nothing at all. Well, except maybe sex. Just because she wasn't particularly comfortable discussing that with *anyone*.

"If Kim ever comes back, I hope she'll understand about our friendship," she mused out loud.

With her eyes still on the shore in the distance, she felt Fletcher's piercing gaze. "First of all, it's when, not if." Then a warm smile unfurled beneath his dark mustache. "And second, of course she will. She'll love you the same way I do."

And Tamra knew this wouldn't make him happy, but she spoke her mind anyway. "Well, I won't love *her*."

Nothing more needed to be said on that topic—Fletcher knew Tamra held a grudge against his wife. She'd met Kim only in passing during the brief time she'd been in Coral Cove before Kim'd disappeared. She had no idea what she would think of Kim's personality—their meetings had been too brief—but she knew what she thought of a woman who would leave her loving husband so mysteriously and hurtfully. No rationale Kim could invent would ever be enough.

"When she comes back," he said calmly, evenly, "everything will change. You'll see. Things will suddenly all make sense. And even if you never find it in your heart to forgive her, I know you'll be nice to her, for my sake." He added a wink, driving his point home. "And over time, all this will be forgotten—it'll blend into the past because we'll all be focused on the present." He was peering out over the sea then, an idyllic, faraway look in his eyes, and Tamra thought, as she had so many times before, what a remarkable person he was. To forgive even before Kim returned. To forgive a crime he didn't know the true extent of—why she'd left, what she'd done since she'd been gone, when she would come back. *If* she would come back. *Like it or not, Fletcher, none of us still has any actual reason to believe she will.*

Not sure how to respond—because Fletcher had a way of making you not want to dash his hopes, even if you thought they were farfetched—Tamra opted to say nothing and took a sip of her tea instead.

"How's work on the golf course coming?" he asked. They both watched a large white sail cross the horizon in the distance.

"Early days yet, but fine," she said. In fact, she was enthusiastic about the project—besides being pleased with the creative aspects, she liked adding something lasting to Coral Cove's future.

"I heard you were lying around in the dirt with that guy." Only the tiniest hint of smugness colored his voice—he clearly enjoyed knowing something she didn't know he knew.

"Um, you heard wrong then," she corrected him. "He fell on top of me, that's all. A far cry from lying around. Trust me."

"Well, I'm sorry to hear that." He slanted a sly grin in her direction. "Because I thought it was an interesting development. Like maybe you'd decided he wasn't so bad after all."

"No, he is," she assured him. And even if she had seen signs of the guy being a little more human—and maybe even a little more interesting—than she'd initially thought, Fletcher didn't need to know that. It would only encourage his pushiness. She even added, "I've been working with him as little as possible, in fact," just to drive the point home. Sheesh, why was everyone so desperate to make something happen between her and Mr. Scruffy Beard?

"You know," Fletcher observed, "you practically bristle when I even suggest anything between the two of you."

"Maybe it irritates me that everyone *keeps* suggesting it—when I've expressed no interest in the man whatsoever."

"You have a habit of doing the same thing to me," he pointed out.

"True," she admitted. "Because I think it's for your own good."

"Likewise," he countered simply.

"But then you also know how annoying it can be," she pointed out reasonably.

"True," he replied. "But . . ."

She turned toward him, her look filled with warning. "But?"

He met her gaze. "But if there's anything there at all, any slight hint of attraction, what would be wrong with exploring that? What would be wrong with having some fun with him? It wouldn't have to be some big, serious thing if you don't want it to. It could just be a little fun. A fling."

Tamra thought back to earlier times in her life, times when she'd surrendered to a man, trusted a man, and how horrible the results had been. Years had passed since then—she was older and wiser. And she tried not to be a slave to her past—she lived for now and was happy to leave bad things behind her, where they belonged. She was open to the idea of love, or any other kind of relationship. But . . . only with someone who had all the right ingredients. She had no intention of giving in to any sort of pursuit from a man who seemed all wrong for her.

"Why are you all so eager to fix me up with someone who, frankly, seems like trouble?" she asked Fletcher, truly wanting to know.

He didn't answer for a minute, clearly weighing his reply. Until he said, "Honestly?"

She nodded. "Of course."

"I've known you for four years. Reece and Polly and other people around here have known you since you got here, eight years ago. And as far as anyone knows, you haven't dated anyone since then. And it's a long time, Tamra. Especially for someone who has as much to offer as you. So maybe we just think you should . . ."

"Date any loser who comes down the pike?"

Fletcher finished his thought in a different way. "Not be so picky."

And Tamra's back went rigid. "Okay, now I'm bristling. Because you're saying it's wrong to have standards. Or that I can't get a guy who doesn't have major stuff wrong with him. Which is insulting. If you think I'm going to be into just any yahoo who happens to have a penis, you're sadly mistaken."

At this, Fletcher let out a laugh. "That's not exactly what I was suggesting."

"Well, it feels that way." She raised her eyebrows. Then calmed down a little to add, "I have an idea."

Fletcher appeared relieved, probably at her less abrasive tone. "What's that?"

"From almost the beginning of our friendship, you and I have been pushing each other in romantic directions neither one of us seems to want to go in. So . . . maybe we should just stop. It's never led anywhere anyway, except to getting on each other's nerves. Agreed?"

In the wicker chair next to hers, Fletcher pursed his lips, obviously thinking this over. "I guess you make a decent point," he finally said. Then added a short nod. "Okay—agreed. No more unsolicited advice or suggestions between us in the romance department."

* * *

OVER the last year or so, much of Tamra's pottery work had focused on fish. Fun, colorful, silly, happy fish. Some of them were plates, others bowls. Still others hung on walls. Smaller, more three-dimensional fish became knickknacks for tables or shelves, or were incorporated into windchimes.

Before fish had taken over her art, she'd gotten into crabs—making red crab-shaped dishes Reese had commissioned for each room at the Happy Crab, and making more crab plates and bowls to sell. And before that, she'd been drawn largely to creating more abstract pieces that were reminiscent of the sun or waves, and her stained glass suncatchers had often followed that same general design dynamic, as well.

But fun fish, it turned out, sold enormously well to the vacationing masses who patronized the Sunset Celebration at the pier each night, and she'd discovered they also made her happy. Something about just working on a silly smiling fish with big eyes or brightly colored fins made her feel uplifted. Sun and sea pieces had made her feel relaxed, calm, peaceful—and that was what she'd needed for a long while after coming to Coral Cove. Yet somewhere along the way, she supposed, she'd started needing less peace and more happy.

She generally kept the cottage quiet when she worked. Sometimes, though, in the mild weather of spring or fall, she could open the windows and let the sound of the surf echo in, as it was doing on this September morning the day after making her new agreement with Fletcher. An added benefit of the art studio in her cottage was the large window above her worktable that allowed her to look out on her garden as she created new pieces.

After using her string cutter to cut a fresh slab of clay for a new fish plate, she used a rolling pin, same as you would on cookie dough, rolling the clay out to about a quarter inch thickness. Then came the fun—the freehand design of a brand new happy fish.

Mostly it was shaping it with her fingers, but once she accomplished that, she would smooth down the edges with a wet sponge, then use a knife or the tip of a small paint brush to carve in indentions and detail. And later, she would add in additional pieces of clay—a fin, a tail, a mouth—to make the plate three-dimensional.

As the piece of simple clay became a fish in Tamra's hands, she wondered how Jeremy was doing on the golf hut. As far as she could tell, the work had been looking good, but since that first morning, she'd only stopped by in her SUV a few times to check in with him, then driven away.

It's stupid to let that one uncomfortable-yet-heart-rippling event keep you from spending time on the jobsite. After all, since when do you let anything or anyone intimidate you?

And yet, as she crimped one edge of clay with her fingertips to create a scalloped tail, she couldn't *not* be honest with herself. The thought of going back to the jobsite brought about other feelings, as well.

It's stupid that you want to see him. You don't even like him. And yet, the truth was, every time she thought about him, even when Fletcher had brought him up yesterday and she'd so vehemently stuck to her story of having no interest in him, she'd continued suffering a reaction. A tingling sensation that ran the length of her body yet was undeniably centered at the crux of her thighs, emanating outward in waves, like radio signals coming from a tower.

Eventually pleased with the new fish she'd created, she placed it in a plastic container, where it would dry for a week or so before the first firing. Otherwise, it would crack or explode in the kiln.

Three fish later, she decided to go up to the golf course and start behaving like an adult here. She had a job to oversee, after all.

But this wasn't because she wanted to see him. It was . . . to stop avoiding him.

Part of Tamra was tempted to put on one of her long, flowy skirts. Because so far she didn't think Jeremy had seen her looking her best. *But that's ridiculous. Especially since you're not interested in him. Or so you keep claiming.*

Instead, she opted to just change the simple tee she'd been working in to a nicer top—perfectly casual but more fitted. There was no crime in showing off her shape a little, after all. Not particularly to him, but to just . . . anyone.

As she parked her car in the mini-golf course's recently paved parking lot, she spotted Jeremy in the distance. Working in the hot sun, he'd tied a dark bandana around his head as a sweatband and wore a snug white T-shirt, dingy and soiled from work, but which still managed to outline the muscles in his chest and upper arms. His khaki shorts were loose, and a low-slung tool belt draped his hips above dirty workboots. He appeared to be hammering nails into a large window frame. His skin, more tan than the last time she'd seen him, glistened with sweat. And the spot between her legs tingled hotly. Oh hell.

Turning off the engine, she drew in a deep breath, let it back out. Looking again, this time she tried to focus on less pleasing aspects of his appearance—his longish, messy hair hung in unkempt waves and tendrils about his head. His pale beard remained gangly and ungroomed.

Unfortunately, she still suffered an almost giddy sense of nervousness to know she'd be approaching him. It made no sense.

Unless . . . this is what chemistry is.

If so, it was . . . well, either something she'd never truly experienced before or she'd entirely forgotten what it felt like. Like yesterday, her mind flashed on past men in her life, from when she was younger. Maybe she'd felt this then—a certain need, a fathomless magnetism that defied logic—but had chosen to forget, given how those relationships had ended. Maybe she'd *wanted* to forget—maybe she'd decided nothing good could come from a feeling that stole so much of her control, in such a non-sensical way.

Because, good Lord, if anything was non-sensical, it was that the man in the distance made her feel that. She barely knew him, she didn't much like him, she found his unkempt hairiness unattractive, and she truly questioned whether he was a good guy or a bad one. And yet, under the surface remained a tingling that had intensified to a ridiculous degree since parking the car. Craziness.

Okay, pull yourself together here and just go talk to him. Like a normal human being. And his boss, for that matter. And . . . see how things go. More of her conversation with Fletcher came back to her now—the part about being open, and about fun. Maybe . . . she would be open to letting Jeremy change her opinion of him. Maybe.

One more deep breath and she exited the car and crossed the jobsite to where he still hammered nails into the little building, which appeared to be mostly done. He concentrated on his work as she grew nearer and made no indication that he knew she was there until he looked up and asked, "What do you think? Looking pretty good?"

He didn't smile, but sounded proud. Almost like a guy who cared about his work.

Upon closer inspection she had to agree. "Yes, looks great. Good job," she added. Trying to be nice. Even though it made her feel a little vulnerable with him. Maybe because they'd gotten off on the wrong foot. Inside, she supposed she feared seeming even the least bit weak to him—and sometimes in life, nice equaled weak. Sometimes, nice *made* you weak.

"Be ready to start painting it soon. And gotta build the doors that'll close over the windows when the course isn't open. We'll need to paint those and the trim boards before I put them on."

She nodded.

"You have the colors picked out, right? Should I buy the paint or is that something you want to do?"

The truth was, for someone who was usually on top of a project, Tamra hadn't thought through any of the next steps—too waylaid by Jeremy Sheridan's insertion into the situation. A realization that was all the more reason to get her head back in the game and just get used to having him around. Especially now that it actually appeared he was going to be a good, dependable worker, despite his other faults.

"I can pick up the paint. I can start painting, in fact, while you work on making the doors and cutting the trim."

He returned his eyes to his work. "Never thought I'd say this, but might be nice to have some company."

And the comment begged the question, even if she asked it cautiously. "Um, why did you think you'd never say that?"

He shrugged, looked solemn. "Been more of a keep-to-myself guy the last couple years."

Now she returned the nod. And wondered out loud, feeling a little braver, "What's changed that?"

For the first real time since she'd arrived, he fully met her gaze. Reminding her how piercing it was. She felt as pinned in place by it as a butterfly in someone's collection case. "Maybe I like the idea of this particular company."

Her heart fluttered nervously. Lord, it had been so long since anyone had flirted with her—and here he was, at it again, this fast. She'd totally forgotten how to respond to flirtation. Perhaps she'd never really known in the first place. Her chest tightened as she drew in a tense breath.

"Oh."

That's what she said, what left her. She felt frozen in place. Socially inept. What on earth was wrong with her?

His eyes. It was his eyes. The way they held on her, so intently. It was nearly unbearable.

"Maybe," he went on, "even though we didn't exactly hit it off, I'm cool with giving somebody a second chance."

Okay, that was easier to deal with. And it was fair—

they'd both been at fault in ways so far. So she managed to say, "Me, too."

"Second chances have been good to me lately," he added, ending with a soft, deep laugh that seemed to vibrate gently all through her. And she could scarcely understand how she'd felt his laugh that way, as if it had somehow entered her, become part of her. And she was all into this second chances thing, but even this small exchange of flirtation had been enough to make her want to get away from him, just a little, so she could mentally regroup.

"Um, it's hot out here," she said.

A hint of amusement reshaped his eyes. *He knows I'm nervous.* "Yeah," he said.

She pointed vaguely over her shoulder toward the strip of businesses including the Hungry Fisherman and Gino's. "I think I'll walk over and get us both something to drink."

For the first time since her approach, he actually grinned. And just like his laugh, it moved all through her. "That'd be great—thanks."

And with that, she turned and made a beeline for Gino's Pizzeria.

Her heart beat too fast as she walked away.

She still didn't get it, this effect he had on her.

He had a nice smile, when he chose to use it. And his blue eyes held a certain sparkle, along with those little crinkles around the edges that were always so much more attractive on a man who was beginning to age a bit than they ever seemed on a woman.

So . . . you're going to work a little more closely with him. And that meant one of two things would probably happen.

Either you'll start getting to know him and ultimately decide you really don't like him in that *way and all the weird, tingly feelings will disperse.*

Or . . . the weird, tingly feelings will stay and you'll want to act on them. A thought that didn't do anything to calm the frantic beating of her heart.

But you're getting ahead of yourself. What you need to focus on right now is just . . . acting normal with him. Pleasant when warranted. And not nervous. After all, you can't go dashing away for a Coke every time he smiles at you.

By the time she had two cups of Coke in her hands and began making her way back up the street, she felt more like her usual self. In control. Normal. Ready to communicate with him like a regular human being, even when he flirted. It was something of an art, flirting. And it had caught her off guard. *But I can learn to flirt back. Or at least be pleasant about it while I'm trying to learn.*

And . . . maybe Fletcher and her friends were right. Maybe she needed to loosen up and be more open-minded. Maybe after the bad experiences of her youth, she'd put up some sort of invisible wall—not only about not getting too close to people, but one that didn't let men in. And maybe it was time to slowly, carefully begin taking that wall back down.

But when she crossed the street toward the jobsite and Jeremy came back into view, he wasn't alone anymore. Two younger women stood talking to him, wearing sexy little shorts and bikini tops. And every cell in Tamra's body went on red alert.

The three of them were laughing. Clearly flirting. So flirting with *her* was nothing special. He was one of *those* men. He flirted with *every* woman.

Though . . . as Tamra grew closer, she realized that one of the girls was actually Christy. And she remembered that Christy had known Jeremy growing up. And of course she was getting married soon, too. But still . . . who was the other one? She was tall, thin, a pretty brunette with bright eyes and a confidence Tamra could never hope to muster. And not a day over twenty-five.

Tamra never considered her actions—simply followed her instincts.

Marching right up, she shoved one of the drinks into Jeremy's fist and said, "Here's your Coke. Now I'll thank you to get back to work. We're paying you by the hour, and not to stand around flirting with pretty girls."

"You are a selfish thing!"

Frances Hodgson Burnett, *The Secret Garden*

Chapter 6

As soon as she said it, Tamra realized her mistake. She was mainly tipped off by the three people standing in a semi-circle, looking utterly dumbstruck, as if they didn't know what had just hit them.

And she knew she should say something—something nicer, something to smooth things over—but she couldn't think of what. She couldn't believe she'd fallen victim to sudden jealousy. Over a man she kept telling herself she wanted nothing to do with. And that she'd attacked him for it.

It was finally Jeremy who spoke, directing his words to the dark-haired girl. "Well," he said pointedly, "it was nice to meet you, Bethany, but looks like I'm a slacker who needs to get back to work before the boss fires me." And the roll of his eyes indicated his sarcasm, just in case Tamra could have possibly missed it.

And so this was Bethany. Christy had never mentioned her being so striking. And despite herself,

Tamra still remained a little jealous, even if this was Christy's friend.

Then Jeremy switched his gaze to Tamra and said, "Thanks for the Coke," so harshly that it managed to embarrass her yet a little further.

After which he was gone, heading back toward the little building he'd constructed across the lot from them.

Okayyyyy, time for some damage control.

"I'm sorry," she said quickly to the other two women, flicking her gaze from Christy to Bethany. "It's just that . . . he's been in some trouble since he got here, so I'm just trying to keep him focused on his work, walking the straight and narrow."

Bethany looked uncomfortable, understandably, as Christy spoke softly, clearly not wanting Jeremy to hear. "He's really not a bad guy, Tamra." She looked put out, and Tamra felt like an ogre.

"I know," she said, letting out a breath. "And I don't mean to seem so rude. It's just . . ." Just what? What on earth could justify her bad behavior? The fact that he'd nearly dropped a root ball on her foot a couple of weeks ago was water under the bridge. Even his arrest before that was old news now. "There's just been a lot of weird tension between us." That was true. And the best explanation she could come up with at the moment without revealing things that felt too personal.

"Well, you might have just made it worse for no reason," Christy told her.

And . . . wow. This was Christy. Sweet, cheerful Christy. If *she* was scolding Tamra, that meant her actions had been pretty inexcusable.

"You're right, I know." She shook her head, ashamed, and getting more honest. She supposed what it boiled down to was just . . . fear. It was scary for her to be attracted to a guy who seemed like trouble. It was scary to let down her guard, even just a little.

Then, awkwardly, she remembered that she and Bethany still hadn't been introduced. "Hi Bethany, it's nice to meet you," she said. "I'm Tamra and I'm really not as bad as I seem right now."

She was relieved when Bethany actually laughed. "We all have our moments. I can go from relatively nice to bitchy in a heartbeat."

Okay, even if she was striking in that tall, confident way, Tamra had to like her. If for no other reason, because she was kind enough to try to put Tamra at ease right now.

"But if you don't mind some advice about dudes," Bethany went on, "don't let 'em stress you out. Because most of them have weird issues you'll never really get to the bottom of, and they aren't worth it. Men are best used as playthings."

Of course, next to her, Christy was rolling her eyes. "Um, hello? Jack is a prince."

"You're right," Bethany said. "Jack *is* a prince. I'm convinced you got the last good man on earth. The rest . . ." She swiped fingertips manicured in bright red down through the air. "Meh. When it comes to guys, I go into it with an attitude of having some fun and knowing everything is temporary—it takes all the drama out of it, trust me."

"Don't listen to her," Christy told Tamra. "There are still good guys out there. You'll find one."

And now it was Tamra joining in on the eye rolling. "Again," she directed forcefully to her well-meaning girlfriend, "who said I even want one?"

"Well . . ." Christy said, and Tamra read her thoughts. She was remembering the night Tamra had shared with her and Cami that she was dying for sex.

Now she warned Christy with her eyes that this was not a topic up for public consumption, not even with Bethany, not even if Tamra liked her. "Well, nothing. I'm fine," she said emphatically. "With or without a man."

"Preach it, girlfriend," Bethany said, holding up her hand, and Tamra realized she wanted to high five her—Bethany thought they were totally on the same page about guys. And actually, she realized as she indulged in one of the only high fives of her entire life, she was probably closer to being on Bethany's page about these things than on Christy's.

"What about Fletcher then?" Christy asked, and Tamra wondered what she was talking about—until she realized the question was directed to Bethany. "I thought you liked him."

The news made Tamra draw back slightly, stunned. "Really?" she asked. "Fletcher?"

Bethany let out a self-assured laugh. "I said he was cute. And he seems interesting. But it's no big thing, Christy. Especially considering what you told me about this wife of his who he's so sure is coming back. I thought he just might be . . . fun to hang out with while I'm here."

As Christy and Bethany went on talking, wheels in Tamra's head began to turn. Bethany wanted to have fun with Fletcher of all people? And she thought men weren't worth getting emotional over and had learned whatever magic trick it took to keep that from happening? And she somehow used guys for fun the same way so many *guys* used *girls* for fun?

On one hand, she knew she and Bethany were very different from each other. Bethany clearly had her act together, on the inside, way more than Tamra did. Tamra instantly envied her confidence, something she could sense was very real, not faked. But that aside, they had certain things in common. Christy had long pointed out to Tamra that they were both artists, which made her feel an instant connection. But more than that, she just liked Bethany's attitude. Not taking things so seriously. Not taking *men* so seriously. She might be on to something. *And I could probably stand to learn from her.* And maybe Fletcher could, too—in a far different way—if he'd only let himself.

By the time Bethany and Christy walked away, Tamra felt almost transformed inside. Strange how quickly and easily something like that could happen, and brought on in a way she never could have predicted—through meeting Christy's friend. Her head swam with new ideas that fit nicely together.

Maybe Fletcher could let himself have fun with Bethany while she was here. And maybe it would change everything for him.

And maybe, just maybe, Tamra could learn to let loose a little, have fun herself, without getting all caught up in all the stuff that usually held her back with men: expectations, worry, doubt, fears. Maybe she could learn to be just a little bit more like Bethany. And maybe it would change everything for her, too.

And with that brave new thought in mind, she crossed the sandy work lot toward where Jeremy took some measurements. Like earlier, he never looked up or indicated he even knew she was there until he said, "Need to run to Home Depot to get the wood and hinges for the doors. You got any problem with that?"

She sucked in her breath at his harsh tone. Then fell on her metaphorical sword. "I'm sorry," she said. "About before. I was out of line."

As his gaze met hers, she could see his surprise. She could also see him weighing his response.

Before he made one, she added, "I'd like it if we can put everything that's happened up to now behind us and start fresh. Is that possible?" She spoke kindly and hoped he could feel her sincerity. Talk about making herself vulnerable in front of him.

And she didn't even know if it was a good idea, but she was going for it—truly trying to do what she'd just suggested, start fresh. She wanted a do-over. She wanted to be different with him. She wanted to take Bethany's advice, and Fletcher's advice, and not take everything so seriously and see if . . . if there was perhaps some fun to be had with Jeremy Sheridan. Even if he did desperately need a shave and a haircut.

Finally, Jeremy said, "Sure."

But he'd still sounded stiff.

So she decided to be brave, to put herself out there still a little more. "Maybe . . . we could get together, later, tonight, have dinner or something. To work on that fresh start."

And his hesitation made her feel it before he said it—he was going to turn her down. Her stomach sank like a stone.

"Thanks for the offer. A little while ago, I'd have taken you up on it, but . . . now I'm thinking it's probably better we keep this all business. Okay?"

Wow. "Okay." There was nothing else to say. And even that came out more softly than intended.

"I'll, uh, head to Home Depot now if that's all right with you."

"Of course," she said quickly, still embarrassed.

And as she watched him get in that beat-up red truck that went rumbling away, she wanted to just sit down on the ground and cry. Seemed like no matter what she did when it came to men, it was wrong. Trust them and you get hurt. Don't trust them and you put up a wall that keeps them away. With Jeremy, she'd followed the instinct to protect herself and been too gruff, and now that she was trying to let go of that, it was too late—she'd driven him away. Her timing seemed backwards.

It always had.

Maybe that's why I never try. I know I'll just screw it up.

Deep in her heart, she knew she was destined to be alone and might as well just accept that and move on with her life.

VAGUE shouting, darkness, gunfire.

Hot—it was so fucking hot. Thirst clawed at his throat like dry, scaly fingers.

Running, running. Through a labyrinth of small stone structures, bleak and dank and humid.

More gunfire. Waiting to be hit, waiting to experience that, to find out how it felt.

But the gunfire never hit him.

Other people, yes. Whoever he was running with. Cries of pain came, but he kept running, running, away from it all—only to eventually realize he was alone, the lone survivor. But was being the lone survivor really . . . surviving?

Jeremy jolted awake with a gasp. He lay in bed in his room at the Happy Crab, drenched in sweat. Jesus God, it wasn't real. He let himself begin to breathe again.

Except . . . it *was* real, in a way. The part about surviving that had hit him in the nightmare. He wasn't the lone survivor, of course. But when you saw so many good men go down, when you lost so many good friends . . . well, surviving it didn't feel exactly like some grand victory. It felt . . . at best, random, and at worst, like a mistake.

He'd *made* mistakes. Mistakes no one knew about.

Reaching up, he ran a hand back through his bushy hair, his scalp wet with perspiration. Sometimes it surprised him to realize just how much hair he had now, too lazy to get it cut.

Not lazy lately, though. He tried to let the thought make him grateful for changes inside him. But at the moment it was a little difficult to get to grateful. *I'll work on that tomorrow.* Right now, he needed to get out of his head. If he let himself fall back asleep right now, it would only happen again. Or so the pattern usually went.

He hadn't had any nightmares in a couple of weeks. Again, he tried to be thankful for that, but it was hard so fresh on the heels of one, and he suffered a fear that they'd never go completely away, that a part of him would always be stuck there, in war, in darkness, in gunfire. Though maybe he deserved to be.

He forced himself to sit up in bed.

Then he got up, walked to the mini-fridge across the

room, and grabbed a bottle of water. Unscrewed the cap, took a drink.

Setting it down, he found a pair of loose gym shorts and pulled them on over his underwear, then walked to the door and opened it up. Cool air and the salty scent of the ocean rushed over him, reviving him a little. And reminding him he was in a very different place now. Very different from Afghanistan. Even very different from his hometown in Ohio, where it had gotten so easy to hide, and so easy to . . . atrophy.

The thought made him step outside. It was the middle of the night in Coral Cove and the only sign of life was the all-night neon of "The Happy Crab Motel" sign, that bright red crab smiling in the dark. Beyond that, across Coral Street, the beach lay in blackness—he couldn't see it, but he could smell it and hear the soothing sound of the surf rushing in, then flowing back out, rushing in, flowing back out.

Pulling the door shut behind him, he started away from his room in bare feet. He wasn't going far—just wanted to walk around a minute, soak up the breeze, keep clearing his head.

The parking lot asphalt beneath his feet was neither cold nor hot—just solid, hard. But enough of a connection to the earth to give him a still stronger sense of being alive, and being someplace far different than his nightmares took him.

He strode across the empty street to the beach, its perimeter dotted with tall palm trees, fronds swaying in the wind. He stood at the base of one, looking up, drinking in the calming rhythm of the tree's movements—it seemed to mimic the ocean waves.

A glance up the street brought the golf course

vaguely into view and took his thoughts back to what had happened with Tamra yesterday. Yep, if anything drew him fully out of the past and into the present, it was her. Here he was, doing his damnedest to pick himself up, change his life—and this woman just seemed determined to knock him back down. And every time he thought she was softening to him, she swayed back the other way—her moves as unpredictable as a palm frond in the breeze.

For the first time in two long years, he was out among people, learning how to be human again—but damn, she made it difficult. If she'd had any idea how challenging it had been just to have a conversation with Christy Knight and her friend—especially given that Christy had known him as a far different guy—would she still have come down on him like that?

Of course, it wasn't her job or anyone else's to give a shit about his issues.

And maybe he hadn't been so nice to her in the beginning, either. But back then, he'd just been starting to function around other people again. And he'd felt less at ease about his life even just a couple of weeks ago than he did now.

So it wasn't her fault he'd acted like an ass when they'd first met.

And it wasn't his fault she'd been a jerk to him yesterday.

But when it came to his boss, he was done trying. Done being drawn to her. Because that had clearly been a bad idea.

And the way he'd so brazenly flirted with her that first day on the jobsite when he'd fallen on her—*really* bad idea. He'd been following old instincts that had actually felt familiar, surprisingly easy. Something about her had brought out the bad boy in him, made him want to rub and polish away her rough edges and get to what was underneath. But it wasn't happening, wasn't *gonna* happen.

He'd been wide awake after that bad dream, but now he was tired and ready to give sleep another whirl. And a brisk wind was suddenly beginning to kick up anyway, rustling the palms overhead harder now.

A few steps through cool sand led him back to the sidewalk, then the street. As he crossed, he caught a bit of movement from the corner of his eye and glanced toward the now-dark Hungry Fisherman to see his buddy, the big gray cat, lurking in the shadows. It surprised him when the cat began padding toward him, taking long steps with that big, gangly body.

"Got nothin' for ya tonight, pal," he said, knowing the cat sought food.

Despite that, the big tom fell into step with him as he headed back to his room. And when Jeremy opened the door and went inside, the cat did, too—before he could stop it.

Jeremy looked down. "Nope, bud—good try, but that's not gonna work." And with that, he picked the cat up, opened the door, and put him outside.

Then he got back in bed, pulling the covers over himself without bothering to take his shorts off. Tamra stayed on his mind a little, but sleep came quickly anyway.

When he awoke some time later, it was to the sound of rain. A windy, blowing rain that pattered against his window, making its way up under the awning that ran the length of the building.

And then he heard a meow.

Oh hell.

Go back to sleep. He shut his eyes again.

And heard another meow.

Ignore it. He focused on the sound of the wind and rain, tried to let it lull him back into slumber.

But the big cat kept right on meowing.

With a tired sigh, Jeremy sat up and swung his legs over the side of the bed. *Damn cat.*

Walking to the door, he unlatched the chain and pulled it open. The damp, gray, one-eyed cat came trotting in like he belonged there.

Jeremy looked down at him, the room dimly lit by the neon crab sign in the distance. "Don't get too comfy, dude. You'll get me thrown out of here."

Then he lay back down. And a moment later felt the soft *plllmp* as the cat silently bounded up onto the bed. Damn, did he think he owned the place?

When a slight, warm pressure came alongside Jeremy's thigh through the covers, he realized the cat had now gone so far as to curl up beside him. *Oh brother.*

"This is only for one night."

In response, the cat began to purr.

"I'm a dog guy, got it?" he said.

Of course, Captain didn't answer. So Jeremy just rolled over, intent on going to sleep—and the cat resituated behind his bent knees, filling the space with a solid warmth that hadn't been there before.

Mistress Mary, quite contrary,
How does your garden grow?

Frances Hodgson Burnett, *The Secret Garden*

Chapter 7

THE NEXT morning, Jeremy waited until he was dressed and heading out for work to put the cat out. "Stay outta trouble," he said in parting as he headed toward his truck.

He could have walked to work easily, but he chose to drive, not only because he often ended up needing the truck to run an errand or haul something, but because it seemed like a good routine to get into, an official way of "going to work"—driving there, like the majority of Americans did every day.

Slamming the slightly rickety pickup door, he walked up to the hut to find that Tamra had begun painting it a retro beachy coral color. Other accents, like the borders on each green, would be done in the same shade, reflecting the town's name and echoing a vintage Florida feel.

She greeted him with a smile. "I'm excited to start the painting—makes it seem like real progress, like it's really coming together."

So she was bending over backwards to be nice, huh? Well, fine, but he wasn't biting. Because sooner or later, she'd pull back the bait. So he'd just save them both the trouble and not take it in the first place. "Great," he said, but didn't bother meeting her eyes. Or taking in the rest of her, either. Even if he'd already noticed that she looked cute today in slightly shorter-than-usual shorts and a fitted yellow tee that hugged her curves and showed just a hint of cleavage.

But quit noticing her cleavage. She's your boss, not a woman to be trifled with—she'd made that abundantly clear.

He knew his short response had injected a little tension into the air, but he didn't care. Even when she tried again. "I think this will be a good system—you build and I paint."

"Sounds good." He added a brief nod this time, but that was it.

And he sensed her disappointment, but he didn't care about that, either. Especially when it made her start getting less friendly again. It was what he'd expected, in fact. She'd proved his predictions true.

And that was how their days began to go. All work, no play.

Even as the tension continued to rise between them, daily, sometimes hourly.

Of course, it wasn't easy to act distant all the time. And they were completing a big project together. So as it progressed—as the hut was completed, as other pieces took shape—there were moments of shared . . . something.

It should have been shared joy, or a shared feeling of accomplishment. But instead it was as if they were each forced to celebrate silently, refusing to acknowledge the teamwork involved.

When they completed the final touches on the hut together and stood back to look, Jeremy felt a pride that wasn't quite complete if you didn't share it with someone. He glanced over at her and almost smiled. But he couldn't quite go there.

And he sensed *her* wanting to smile, too, but instead, as their gazes met and then dropped quickly away from each other, she said, "It looks great."

He still didn't smile, either, as he said, "Yeah, it does. We did good work."

She nodded stiffly. "You did a good job. I . . ."

"What?" he asked when she stopped.

She sighed, shifted her weight from one tennis shoe to the other. "I . . . know we've had our differences, but I would be remiss if I didn't give credit where it's due. You're a good carpenter."

Huh. Jeremy hadn't expected that. It was gratifying to know that someone—okay, maybe not just someone, but her in particular—saw that he was good at something. So for the first time in days, he let himself relax, let an honest, easy smile spread across his face. "Thank you," he said. "I appreciate that."

And he thought she'd smile back.

But instead she just said, "Sure," and looked away.

And . . . shit. That easily, she'd let him know they weren't friends or anything else. Again. What on earth made this woman so icy? He knew what *he'd* been through—what on earth could have turned her into an even colder version of him?

Well, it didn't matter. Back to business. It *was* what it *was*, and that was fine.

Of course, it would be finer if he could quit noticing her—her hair, the curve of her breasts beneath the more fitted clothes she'd begun wearing lately, the smooth, pale legs that had started to darken just a bit beneath the sun. It would be finer if he still didn't wish he could make her smile, put her at ease with him, make her want to put him at ease, too. It would be finer if he didn't wish for something more with her.

But he moved forward by just trying to focus on the work they did. He focused on getting another check at the end of the week and repaying more of his debts. He focused on things that made him feel good—like sitting out behind the Happy Crab in the evening. Like buying an extra piece of fish if he picked up dinner at the Hungry Fisherman, and crumbling it into bits for Captain when he came around.

One night he even called his mom on the phone. His sister or Lucky called him every few days to check on him, and when Tessa told him their parents were asking after him but had gotten reluctant to call ever since he'd become so reclusive, he decided to ease his mother's worries. "I'm doing better, Mom," he'd told her, sitting at the picnic table one night.

He could hear her joy through the phone. "That's so good to hear, Jeremy."

He still didn't want to socialize a lot, though. Even when Reece invited him to a bonfire on the beach one night, he declined, claiming to be too tired from work. And when he saw Christy Knight at Gino's one evening and she suggested he venture over to the Sunset Celebration, he'd told her maybe—knowing good and well he wouldn't go. He'd come a long way, but he still didn't like crowds and probably never would.

It was that very night, sitting at the picnic table, when he looked up to see Polly crossing the Hungry Fisherman parking lot toward him in her usual rust-colored waitress dress.

Jeremy tossed her a grin. "How many of those dresses you own, Polly?" He'd gotten comfortable with Polly fast.

"Fourteen," she said without missing a beat.

He couldn't stop his eyes from widening.

"Got a nice two-week rotation goin'." Stopping in front of him, she peered down at her dress, pulling out the wide, pointed collar a bit, studying it. "Just between us, though, they're gettin' a little worn. I try to take care of 'em, but I've had 'em a long time."

Jeremy only nodded.

"Cami keeps tellin' me I should update my style, get more current. She thinks I should wear khaki pants and a shirt of some sort. But I don't know." She shook her head doubtfully. "I been wearin' these dresses 'bout as long as I can remember—I'm real used to 'em. I go straight from my nightgown into this dress and back—don't own much else, because I'm here all the time. What do *you* think?"

Jeremy pondered it a minute. "I think you should do whatever makes you feel best," he told her honestly. "But . . . change can be good."

Polly seemed to take that in, think it over. Then she glanced down at Captain, who'd been at Jeremy's feet under the table the whole time, unnoticed by her until now. "Looks like you got yourself a friend there."

"Seems that way," he agreed grudgingly. "He, uh, shows up a lot."

She drew back slightly, studying the cat more closely.

"Seems to be puttin' on a little weight, not lookin' as scrawny as before." Then she gave Jeremy a thorough once-over as well. "And you don't look like you're puttin' on *any* weight for a fella who eats as much as you seem to lately." She ended with a wink, making it clear she knew he was feeding the cat.

"Fish isn't very fattening," he joked. "And I do hard, physical labor every day."

In response, she stooped down, scooped Captain up in her arms and held him high, until she was face to face—almost nose to nose—with him. "Just as I suspected."

"What's that?" Jeremy asked.

"This cat has fish breath." She set the big gray tomcat back down. "And I didn't give him anything tonight, and we been lockin' our garbage cans up. Not because I don't like feedin' him, but that whole health department thing, ya know. I hate to do it, but . . ."

Seeing her remorseful look, Jeremy set her at ease. "I get it, and yeah, you caught me. I've been making sure he gets at least one meal a day."

She smiled, then cast a conspiratorial look. "Tell ya what. Now that I know you're lookin' out for him, when you come in, I'll just toss an extra piece of fish or whatever we got left over in a separate bag and slide it across the counter to ya, sneaky-like, free of charge. Abner never needs to know. And together, we'll get this fella fattened up some more."

"Sounds good," Jeremy said.

"Well, I'd better get back over there." She hiked a thumb toward the restaurant behind her. "Now that we're pickin' up more night business, I might have to hire some other waitresses soon."

Jeremy voiced his thought out loud. "Wonder how they'll like wearing dresses like yours." Though he finished with a wink.

And Polly's brow knit with worry. "They might not, now that you mention it. And I like things to match." She sighed. "Guess I oughta give that some thought."

As she turned to go, she motioned down at the cat one last time to add, "You two make a pretty good team."

Jeremy just laughed. "Guess us homeless guys get each other."

Polly stopped walking, looked back, and said, "You're not homeless, Jeremy. You mighta been when you got here, but you're not anymore." Then went on her way.

THE following morning, Tamra looked in the mirror.

The truth was, Christy had been right hinting that she'd let herself go. And ever since she'd started putting just a little bit of thought and care into her appearance, she'd felt better. Inside. Not like it changed her whole world or anything, but she'd just felt a little more confident.

Of course, the further truth was that, if she got really, really honest with herself, part of the impetus was about . . . Jeremy. Even if that made no sense. *You don't want him, but you want him to think you look good. You don't want him, but you want* him *to want* you. The man was a walking contradiction—who created more and more contradictions inside *her*.

She still thought his beard and unkempt hair were awful. And yet his eyes, his smile—underneath all the hairiness, something continued to beckon her.

Maybe it's still just your unfulfilled sexual desires. Because they continued to torture her, making her wonder how someone so focused on higher creative endeavors could at the same time be drawn in to also focusing on something ultimately as meaningless as sex. And sure, she knew sex had meaning when you cared for someone, but when you just wanted it, independent of love or affection . . . well, to Tamra, that felt meaningless with a capital M.

Truthfully, though, she feared her strange attraction to Jeremy Sheridan had come to be about more than just overactive hormones. She'd come to like certain things about him. She respected his work ethic, and his carpentry skills. She'd seen him, in small ways, begin to be nice to people. Not her, but other people.

He can't be nice to you because you won't let him.

And why was that? Why, every time the man attempted any cordiality with her, did she shut him down?

Walking to the kitchen, she poured herself a cup of hot tea from the bright yellow kettle on the stove on which she'd hand-painted flowers. Then she walked out her French doors onto the back porch and down into her garden. The morning sun had just begun to burn off the misty chill of an autumn Florida dawn and the vines and trees and flowers glistened with dew.

She sat down in an Adirondack chair, and as she gazed into the palm trees and bougainvillea and other thick foliage and blooms that seemed to cocoon her in safety there, she finally understood. Why she couldn't be nice to Jeremy. It was about exactly that—safety. It was . . . one more cocoon. Only not a physical one.

Something about him scares you. Something about want-ing him scares you.

It's high time you got over that, you know—being afraid of a man, assuming he's going to hurt you.

But Jeremy was such an unknown quantity. Even the beard and messy hair made him seem . . . hidden. She wished she could really see his face.

And his past was a mystery, as well. She didn't know what he'd suffered, but clearly his experiences in Afghanistan had him pretty screwed up if he'd shown up in Coral Cove with no money and no plan.

Though she didn't even know if she was afraid of having sex with him—because it had been so long for her—or afraid she might start to care for a man who was broken in ways she could never fix. Or maybe it was both of those things—and more.

She took a sip of tea and let the hot liquid trickle down her throat, warm her up inside, remembering that sometimes fear was healthy. Early life in a com-mune had taught Tamra to respect her fears and trust her instincts.

She supposed she just liked things safe. Coming from a place where she'd had no control, she'd made a life where she had *total* control. For a while, money had been tight—it wasn't easy making a living as a craft artist—but over time she'd built a healthy business. And now she was getting extra income from Jack and even managing to save some for a rainy day. So she felt more in control of her life than ever.

If you didn't count sex or lack of it.

And if you didn't count Jeremy Sheridan.

But you don't have to count Jeremy Sheridan. You've pretty much counted him out already, in fact. You've decided you're not brave enough to explore your attraction to him. You're too afraid to go there. And maybe that was best. After all, lately he hadn't exactly seemed interested anymore anyway.

When tears welled behind her eyes, she pushed them back. Lord, she hadn't cried in ages. And if she wanted to cry a little now . . . well, it wasn't about Jeremy! It was about . . . accepting that, as wonderful a life as she'd built for herself, there were some things she just probably wouldn't ever let herself have. Romance. Love.

You told Christy and Cami you didn't need those things. And you don't. Really, you don't. You've gotten by fine without them all this time. And you'll keep right on getting by.

It was mid-morning that day when, at the jobsite, a local nursery delivered an entire truckload of shrubbery, ornamental grasses, and other plants—several days early.

"Looks like we'll have to change gears and get these in the ground," she told Jeremy.

As they both stood watching the guys from the nursery unload the bushes, Jeremy said, "I'm glad you got big ones. They're extra heavy to move around."

Tamra replied in the same dry tone. "I'll be sure to stay out of your way when you're carrying them."

"Good idea."

Of course, that was easier said than done, especially since the nursery had delivered different amounts of different things than she'd thought she ordered. Since the invoice amount was what she'd expected anyway, she decided to just make it work rather than sort out the mess. But that meant having Jeremy move shrubs around as she pointed and told him where to put things, only to sometimes change her mind.

It happened enough that she began to cringe each time she asked him. "Um, can you move that hibiscus over about five feet?" Unfortunately, it was probably the fifth time she'd requested he move that particular one.

"Sure," he said, clenching his teeth slightly as he hefted it back into his arms. "It's not like it's breaking my back or anything."

"I'm sorry." She meant it. "But once it's in the ground, it's in the ground. We need to make it look right."

After two more hibiscus moves, he appeared exasperated, finally saying, "You really think it makes a difference? Whether this bush is here or five feet from here?"

She took a deep breath. "Yes, actually. If you were a landscape designer, you'd understand."

"Are *you* a landscape designer?" he asked skeptically.

She gave him a pointed look. "For your information, I could be if I wanted to. I garden a lot."

"Oh. Well. Then you're definitely the expert here. So go ahead, tell me the ten new places you want me to move this bush before you make up your mind."

It took the rest of the day before Tamra was satisfied with the layout. "It's too late to plant now, but we'll get them all into the ground and watered tomorrow," she told him.

"Good—I can get a little rest before you start cracking the whip again," Jeremy grumbled. Then he looked to where a large bush still rested in the parking lot. "Uh, what about that one?"

Tamra looked, too. Crap. She'd known it was sitting there, but had totally forgotten about it at some point. Where could she incorporate it in the design?

And then Jeremy seemed to tune in to her thoughts— and said, "Oh-ho-ho no. No more rearranging. I mean it. I'm done."

So she thought a minute and said, "I suppose I could use it at my house and just reimburse Jack."

He seemed appeased. "Good idea. And I bet Jack would even let you have it for free."

But then she pursed her lips. It was a big bush. Too big for her lift. "Of course," she began cautiously, "I, uh, can't really get it where I need it to go by myself."

And he let out a tired sigh. "Let me guess. You want me to take it there for you."

She tried for a softer expression—though he made that difficult. Or maybe it was her fault—she wasn't sure anymore. "Could you?"

"Do I have a choice?"

She shrugged, relented, tired of feeling at odds with him. "You don't have to do it," she said. "I'll just call Jack or Fletcher or Reece and ask one of them."

But at this, he only sighed. "No, you won't. Of course I'll take the damn bush to your damn house. Let's go."

It was the sweetest, most mysterious-looking
place anyone could imagine.

Frances Hodgson Burnett, *The Secret Garden*

Chapter 8

"THANK YOU," she said softly.

Her sudden gentleness made it hard for Jeremy to
keep feeling put out. "You're welcome," he replied, his
tone quiet.

He moved his truck closer to the bush in question,
then got out, lowered the tailgate, and heaved the heavy
shrub up into the bed. As he slammed the old tailgate
shut, he said, "Where to? I don't know where you live."

"Sea Shell Lane."

"Which way?"

From the look on her face, that was a surprising
question.

"Am I supposed to know already?"

She tilted her head, the red spirals of her ponytail
falling to one side. "Well, Reece and Cami live there.
And so do Christy and Jack. So I just assumed . . ."

He felt the need to remind her, "I don't know any of
them very well. Even Reece."

She leaned her head back the other way. "You don't get out much, do you?"

"No," he answered simply.

After which she motioned to her SUV in a nearby parking space and said, "Follow me."

When Jeremy saw how brief the drive to Sea Shell Lane was, he almost understood why Tamra had expected him to know where it was. After turning left behind her, in the direction of the ocean, he found himself on a short street of pristinely kept pastel cottages that harkened back to a simpler time. Not much put Jeremy at ease, but there was something instantly inviting about the little street that came to a dead end just above the beach, the asphalt meeting up with a little set of wooden stairs that led to the sand.

Turning into her driveway behind her, he noticed that Tamra's little yellow house was as perfectly well kept as the rest—maybe even more so. Her small lawn was thick and well-trimmed, with a healthy flower garden and a couple of small trees. More flowers spilled from hanging baskets on her wide front porch, trimmed in white. It looked like something out of a storybook, and was, in his mind, a much softer looking place than he'd have expected her to live.

And something in that one tiny idea forced him to begin . . . rethinking her a little. Maybe he'd been right about her in the beginning—maybe there was more to her than met the eye.

They exited their vehicles at the same time, and she called to him, "Bring it around back," pointing to a narrow stone walkway that led around the left side of the cottage. "I'll go open the back gate."

A moment later, Jeremy hefted the bush from the

truck, unable to see around it where he was going. As he proceeded toward the rear of the house, he watched his workboots, glad when he hit the stone walkway to let it guide him.

He was only vaguely aware of nearing a tall privacy fence, painted a weathered sort of white, before passing through the open gate. He caught sight of Tamra's legs and tennis shoes, too, and said, "Am I about to walk into anything?"

"No, you're good," she said.

"Where am I going with this thing? I want to put it down once."

"Well, I haven't had a chance to plan for this, so it might have to be twice—unless you want to stand there holding it while I think."

"Nope," he said, and let it drop right in front of him on the stone.

And then he took in everything around him. It was as if he'd entered a whole new world. One of lush greenery and bright blooms. Her entire backyard was a beautiful garden. "Shit, you weren't lying," he said without thinking.

"About what?" she asked.

"You *could* be a landscaper if you wanted."

"Thanks." She sounded shockingly bashful. It threw him, drew his gaze to her face.

She was actually blushing a little. He wondered why, but didn't spend much time trying to figure it out as his attention was drawn back to the garden.

From the trees hung delicate windchimes and other pieces, all made of colored glass. He caught sight of a blue glass bird that seemed to be flying past, and numerous butterflies in yellow, purple, pink. From the ground sprung the occasional birdbath, and more pieces of glass mounted on wrought iron sticks—a green glass dragonfly, a row of glass daisies. In between it all ran the stone path—it seemed to make a circle around the yard, and near the house, where they stood, it widened to encircle a large fire pit. Wooden chairs rimmed the pit, and farther back in the garden he caught sight of a hammock that looked like the perfect resting spot.

"This is . . . freaking amazing," he told her.

"Yeah?" she asked. Again, she sounded so much more delicate than usual.

"Yeah." He nodded, still taking it in.

The truth was, he kind of never wanted to leave. It was . . . the perfect place to be alone, the perfect place to hide.

And then . . . he understood. The same way he liked to hide—so did she.

When his gaze returned to her, he saw her differently. He understood her better now—not completely, not by a long shot, but better. He'd sensed a certain beauty in her before— he'd witnessed hints of it wanting to creep out from around her more rigid persona— but now he really saw it. Looking down at her, here, she was . . . prettier. Her eyes more innocent. Her lips fuller, softer. Maybe he was crazy, or maybe the late day shadows were playing tricks on him, but she was truly beautiful here in a way he'd never seen her look before.

"What are you staring at?" she asked. Like an accusation. Softness vanishing before his eyes.

"Nothing." No way would he tell her the thoughts in his head—she'd just reminded him that she liked to keep that wall up between them, that employer/employee thing. "Where do you want the bush?"

She looked around the garden and he realized that, even as dense as it was, she knew it like the back of her hand.

"That back corner," she said, pointing.

"Okay." He hefted the massive bush's rootball up into his arms.

When he reached the spot where it was necessary to leave the stone path, he again couldn't see where he was going. Which earned him a "Don't crush my ivy!"

"How am I supposed to get it in the corner then?"

"Just watch where you're stepping. This garden is a lot of work."

"Well, I can't see where the hell I'm walking."

That's when her fingertips touched his arm.

And he felt it—damn—in a lot of other places.

"This way," she said, now guiding him, leading him with the gentle pull of her hand.

And hell, it felt good. To be touched. At all.

When was the last time he *had* been? By anyone? Other than having handcuffs put on him. Or a cat rubbing up against his leg.

It almost made him forget how heavy the bush was, focusing on that touch, the ripples it sent up his arm, the slight reaction that tingled through his thighs, groin. Shit. From a touch so simple, so practical.

"Here," she finally said, pulling her hand away. And the bush suddenly weighed a ton again, so he let it drop directly in front of him on the ground.

Though next to him, she gasped. "Not there!"

"What?"

She pointed slightly to the left of where he'd dropped it. "There."

Another sigh. Stooping to lift the bush from hell once more, he found himself murmuring through slightly clenched teeth, "Mary Mary, quite contrary, how does your garden grow?" Then he plopped it back down about two feet from where it had just been. "Is that right?" he asked as he stood to face her again.

Though he hadn't realized the move would put them in much closer proximity—suddenly only a few inches lay between them.

"Yes," she said, except now she looked annoyed. "But what's that supposed to mean? What you just said."

Jeremy wasn't in the mood this late in the day to pull any punches, even if she *was* his boss, even if he'd learned to mostly try to keep the peace with her. So he replied, "Guess I was just thinking that for a good-looking woman, you sure are hard to get along with."

Her green eyes bolted wider in the shade of the tree they now stood beneath, gangly branches sprawling overhead and all around them. "Is that a compliment or an insult?"

He shifted his weight from one dusty workboot to the other. "A little of both, I guess."

She still stood very close to him—he could feel the closeness. Especially when she let out an irritated breath and said, "Then I'm not sure whether to slap you or kiss you."

And at this, he couldn't keep himself from flashing a cocky grin. "You'd never get away with the first one, honey."

"And the second?" she challenged, now planting her fists on her hips.

His eyes flitted down her body, then rose back to her face just before he said, "That you'd have a shot at."

Their gazes stayed locked now and he'd have given anything to know what thoughts flashed through her pretty head. An invisible heat moved between them that had nothing to do with the late-day Florida sun.

But then, in the very split second Jeremy thought something amazing was about to happen—Tamra let out a *harrumph*, rolled her eyes at him dramatically, and turned to walk away.

Only he wasn't going to let her. No way. They both might like to run from things, but he wasn't letting her run from *this*. As she took the first brisk step away from him, his hand closed warm and firm over her wrist.

She gasped, her gaze rising back to his. He still couldn't read her eyes—he had no idea if he was seeing fear or wonder or hope or—hell, maybe it was a little of everything. His heart beat like a hammer and every instinct he possessed told him to go for it. Still gripping her wrist with one hand, he lifted the other to her face and brought his mouth down on hers.

Tamra had a split second amidst her shock to decide: Push him away the same as she did everything else . . . or be in it, all the way. And while her initial instinct was to do the first, some tiny ounce of courage and desperation rose up inside her and made her choose the second.

She didn't know the last time she'd been kissed. She barely remembered how, and she felt a little foolish as she tried to kiss him back—but she stayed with it, moving her mouth against his, and soon reveling in what it felt like simply to be kissed, to know he'd wanted to, that something in her had drawn this from him.

Soon she even quit thinking—and progressed only to feeling. His hand cupping her face, the warmth of his mouth. She drank in the scent of him—they'd been working all day, but a little sweat and dirt had never smelled so very masculine and powerful to her. His mouth moved over hers in a slow, firm rhythm she felt in her gut, and she matched it.

At some point, the hand that held her wrist let go—and moved to the curve of her hip. Her own hands rose to his chest, her fingertips pressing lightly through his T-shirt.

As he eased her back, back, she soon realized he was leaning her gently against a thick tree trunk—and then bringing his body closer, until it connected with hers, their legs intertwining. His thigh lodged between hers and she let out a gasp as pleasure spread outward from the spot between her legs.

Oh God—this was too much.

What was she thinking, doing?

This wasn't her—it was reckless, crazy!

And she had to stop—*now*. If she didn't . . . it would get out of control. And her whole *life* would feel out of control. And she couldn't have that.

At the same moment she turned her face, ending the kiss, she pushed him away to bring an end to this madness.

They were both panting. God. How had things turned so downright feverish so quickly? Who *was* she? And who was he? That, she realized, was the bigger question. She really didn't know him at all, so what on earth was she doing making out with him as if she did? As if, as if . . . they shared some connection.

"We have to stop."

"Why?" he asked on labored breath.

She looked into his eyes—or tried to. But she still found it so hard to see past the beard, and all that hair. *I can't see you. I don't know you. I don't have sex with strangers.* None of those things were answers she could really give him, though, so she blurted out, "We're so different."

"Are we?" he asked without missing a beat.

"Yes. Of course." She spoke emphatically. Because wasn't that obvious?

"How?"

Sheesh. Really? He was going to argue this with her? She let her eyes go wide. "In . . . every way." But she didn't elaborate, because all the ways she could think of seemed . . . cold. *You have no home or direction. You've been screwed up by war. You've been arrested.*

"Tell me how," he insisted.

She let out a sigh. Lord, why was he making this so difficult? *When a woman pushes you away, does it really matter why?* But Tamra closed her eyes and tried to summon an answer that would make him understand . . . without hurting his feelings. A few days ago, she wouldn't have cared about that, but now she did. She supposed that if he'd been worthy of kissing, even just once, that he was worthy of her kindness.

"I . . . don't really know anything about you," she said. "And I . . . I can't even really see your face." She finally drew one hand from his chest and motioned vaguely to his beard. "And I guess that all just makes me . . . nervous. Working with you is one thing, but this . . ." Lord, simply looking down, seeing their bodies still so close together, remembering how much closer they'd just been, nearly stole her breath. "This is another." And she concluded by finally drawing her other hand away from his chest, as well.

As she stood there awaiting his reply, she grew more aware of his body again, aware of the sinews in his arms, the tattoo on his right biceps, the muscles in his chest she'd unwittingly felt beneath her palms. In that way, she knew him far better now. It was one thing to see a man's body, but another to feel it, experience it, press into it. Yet it was the rest of him she still didn't have a handle on.

"The truth is, Mary Mary Quite Contrary, that we have a lot more in common than you think—you just don't want to see it."

Her eyes flitted from his chest to his gaze, unplanned. "What are you talking about?"

"The very fact that you're pushing me away," he said. "That's what *I* do to people. Neither one of us wants to let anybody get too close. Or I haven't until now. But I'm trying to change. Trying to start being more like . . . like the guy I used to be."

"Well, I don't know *him* any more than I know *you*." Which kind of sidestepped the whole point of what he'd just said. Because she didn't like it—it felt too personal.

"He was . . . a nicer guy than me. I think you'd have liked him." His voice held a certain wistfulness, a vulnerability she'd never heard from Jeremy before. And looking into his eyes now made her see something more. Regret. Lost youth. A strange innocence. A man who . . . needed to be loved.

She sucked in her breath at that last thought, though. Was she losing her mind? Nothing about this had anything to do with love—it was two lonely people succumbing to physical urges in her backyard. And that . . . just wasn't enough for her.

Fletcher and Christy and Cami—they all wanted her to have fun, loosen up, be more casual about romance and sex . . . but she didn't know how. She didn't know how to join her body to someone she was completely uncertain of in every way.

She finally pulled her gaze from his, even turned her body away. Her eyes fell on a patch of fiery red snapdragons as she said, "I'm just not in the habit of making out with men I don't really know. And given that we're working together, it seems like it could only complicate things. So no matter how you slice it, it's a bad idea. Okay?" She went so far now as to step out onto the stone path, put more distance between them, move this encounter toward a conclusion.

Still, it almost surprised her when, a few seconds later, he quietly said, "Okay."

When she sensed him following her out from under the tree, she kept walking, back toward the garden gate. Silently saying it was time for him to go.

She almost stopped when she reached it, but decided no—to stop and turn toward him now would still be . . . awkward and tempting at the same time. Behind the garden wall, there was just too much privacy. So she walked through the open gate, following the path around the house and back to the driveway.

Suddenly they were back out in the bright sunlight, the sound of the surf in the distance more audible now, signs of vibrant life all around them—from seabirds cawing overhead to Jack backing out of his driveway next door and tossing up a wave as he drove by.

Upon reaching Jeremy's truck, she really had no choice then but face him. And nothing had changed. He was still unkempt and not her type and still somehow sexy as hell. She dropped her gaze from his immediately. "I suppose things will be weird between us now," she mused.

He just shrugged, the corners of his mouth turning up. "Things have *always* been weird between us."

And she couldn't help it—it made her laugh. But then she added, "Well, weirder probably."

Jeremy tilted his head. "Doesn't have to be that way. I'll do my best to be normal. Well, as normal as possible. For me." He ended on a small wink that, for some reason, she felt at the crux of her thighs.

She pushed down the response as best she could. "Me, too."

Then she stepped back, away from the faded red door of his truck—and he took the hint, opening it and getting inside. Through the lowered window, though, he said, "I'm sorry if I made you uncomfortable."

"It's fine," she said quickly, shaking her head as if it were no big thing. "Forgotten." Ha. As if. Where was she getting this stuff?

He gave a short nod. And something in it almost made her sorry she'd said that last word—she didn't want him to feel forgettable.

But she stayed quiet as he put the truck in reverse and began to back out. "See you tomorrow," he said.

"Yeah," she replied. "See you then."

Her heart beat fast as he drove away, and she realized that maybe it had been beating fast for a while now. When he was gone, she walked the short distance to the sun-bleached steps that led to the beach. She kicked off her shoes at the bottom and let her toes sink into the warm, soft sand. She stood facing the ocean, drinking in the wind it sent blasting over her. She wanted to . . . feel. Normal things. Anything that wasn't as surreal to her as what had just happened in her backyard.

Only then she lifted her hand to her cheek. The cheek he had cupped. She cupped it again, the same way, remembering how that had felt. Such a simple touch, and yet . . . even now, reliving it made her close her eyes. Remember the kissing. And the other touches, too.

She'd raced out here onto the beach to run away from those things. But the unavoidable truth was . . . it had turned her inside out. It had been amazing. Almost transforming.

Only the further truth was . . . deep down inside, she still didn't think she'd ever really be brave enough to truly open herself up to a man again.

> . . . she did not intend to look
> as if she were interested.
>
> Frances Hodgson Burnett, *The Secret Garden*

Chapter 9

*T*HE NEXT morning, Tamra followed her instincts and did what she felt was best. Rather than put on a pair of work shorts, she dressed in one of her long, flowing skirts, a coordinating top, and sandals. Then she got in her SUV and drove to the jobsite, where Jeremy was already at work, digging the first hole for the plants and bushes they'd laid out yesterday. He wore a T-shirt with the sleeves cut out and sweat glistened on the muscles in his arms beneath the sun, even though it wasn't yet nine A.M.

Instead of parking, she pulled to the curb along Coral Street beside where he worked. As she put down her window, he stopped, perching his hands atop his shovel's handle.

"Morning," he said. Just that. But she almost thought she heard something sexual in the word. *Or maybe it's just your crazy body, responding to anything.* And after yesterday, it was impossible not to see him in a sexual light, even more than she had before.

"Um, hey," she began. "Would you mind doing the planting alone? I know it's a lot, but there's no rush as long as you keep the roots watered. I need to work on some other things."

"That's the reason you're giving me?" he asked evenly.

She kept it simple. "Yes."

"Seriously?" Now his eyebrows rose just slightly beneath the bandanna stretched across his forehead.

And she let out a sigh. *Why was he always so difficult?* "Okay, no," she admitted. "I just think it would be a good idea to put a little distance between us, okay?"

He tilted his head, clearly weighing her words. "Well, at least that's being honest."

She decided to change the subject, get back to a more practical matter. "The company installing the artificial turf on the greens is due to arrive this morning to start laying the material. They have my number if any questions come up, but you can monitor the situation." She motioned vaguely around the work site. "Just plant all this stuff and . . . supervise."

"All right, Mary," he replied. "Whatever you say."

This time it was she who raised her eyebrows. "I'm Mary now?"

He shrugged. "I can call you princess if you'd prefer."

"Um, no." Then she let out a sigh, informing him, "And just so you know, I'm really not that contrary."

A slow smile transformed his face. "That might an eye-of-the-beholder kinda thing." Then he winked, before letting the grin fade. "It's okay, though—I get it more now."

"You get what?"

"It's just . . . what you do to keep people at arm's length. It's your way of protecting yourself. I'll try not to take it personally anymore."

She had no idea what to say to that—she was too stunned. Until something hit her, something that would perhaps make him see that her whole life wasn't about keeping people away. "I don't know if you know this," she said, "but I'm an artist. I make pottery and stained glass."

"I might've heard that somewhere," he said.

"I sell my work at the Sunset Celebration. If you wanted to come over some night. It's a nice way to pass an evening. And there are people there you already know, like . . . me."

And, all things considered, it surprised the hell out of her when he said, "Thanks for the invitation, but . . . probably not my thing."

"Oh." Great. Embarrassment. Not what she'd been looking for here—not at all. She'd been trying to be nice, trying to show him she wasn't a total shut-in and that he shouldn't be, either. So much for that.

"Have a nice day, Mary," he said.

"You, too," she answered quickly, and then she drove away. Though this shored up for her that she was right to be wary of him. It reminded her that her reasons for stopping last night were good ones. When all was said and done, she still had no idea who he really was inside, what he was about, or what he really wanted—other than maybe sex. Being kissed by him might have been the most exciting thing to happen to her in a very long time—but not exciting enough to make her lose her head. She'd already spent too much time getting it screwed on straight in the first place.

FLETCHER stood atop his tightrope on Coral Cove Beach, taking careful steps across. It was second nature to him now—funny how you could get so good at something that once seemed so impossible. Concentration, balance—they were still required, but those were the parts that came effortlessly now.

It was never lost on him that the tightrope provided a unique vantage point. A golden orange sunset tinged with thin slashes of vibrant purple burned on the horizon in the distance, and he counted it as a perk of the job that he'd gotten to take in hundreds of sunsets, night after night, and that such beauty never got old.

And below him stood the patrons, the people who kept him up here, walking, juggling, smiling, joking—the people who made this life possible for him. And now that he'd built a real home for himself in Coral Cove, the crowd—albeit a slightly thinning one this time of year—held the added gift of often being dotted with friends, people he'd come to know.

It was habit, though, to also look for Kim—as second nature to him now, sadly, as the rest of it. No, not sadly; sadness got you nowhere in life. And as he scanned the gathering below, their faces all turned upward like flowers toward the sun, he remembered to do it with joy. Because one day she'd be there, too. Smiling up at him. Making everything in his world right again.

He envisioned her in the crowd now; he felt the vision in his soul so deep that it sent a pure joy bursting forth in him—it was that real. And as he let a smile unfurl upon his face, he moved on with the next part of the show, saying to the crowd at large, "Could someone be so kind as to toss those three pins to me please," pointing to where he knew his juggling pins lay without even looking.

He did look, however, when a young woman stepped forward, gathering the pins, then peering up to toss him the first—and he found himself gazing down into the dark, arresting eyes of Bethany Willis, Christy's friend from Cincinnati.

The smile he wore instantly widened on her as their eyes met, and he kept his gaze on hers as he softly said, "Thank you."

"My pleasure," she returned just as warmly, pitching the pins up into his waiting hands.

He found it strangely unpleasant to draw his focus away from her and onto the act of juggling. She was easy to look at. Although not in a way everyone might see. She wasn't classically pretty and didn't try to be. She was her own animal; she embraced her differences and understood her strengths and played to them. He knew all that instinctively.

And his heart welled with an unexpected pride as he continued the show. Because he knew it was impressive to someone who'd never seen it before, and it felt good to know he was impressing *her*.

He mostly didn't look directly at her again—because after he juggled the pins he moved on to juggling lit torches and, second nature or not, he had to pay attention to what he was doing. Yet he still stayed aware of her—he almost felt her presence, some invisible energy emanating from her direction in the crowd. And he thought he probably performed better because of it.

Toward the end of the act, he asked again for someone in the crowd to pass him an item from the sand, this time an old top hat. And once more Bethany was quick to step forth, stoop down to retrieve the hat, and toss it up. They exchanged another smile he felt in his solar plexus.

Though necessity required him to turn his attention back to the entire crowd once more, putting on a little showmanship. Placing the hat on his shoulder, he rolled it artfully end over end into his hand, then twirled it on his fingertip a moment before ceremoniously placing it on his head. "And this, kind spectators," he announced, "concludes my little balancing act for your amusement."

And even as the crowd began to applaud, he quickly whipped he hat back off and, speaking more loudly added, "This hat is not only for wearing, but for sharing! I'll be passing it amongst you now, and if you enjoyed my show, I'll appreciate any kind thanks you care to drop in." Then he winked. "Make my living doing this, folks, so thanks for helping me keep a roof over my head and a tightrope under my feet."

And then he did a well-practiced forward flip off the rope to land upright in the sand, as he did each and every night—one last little feat of daring for the vacationers. After which he spied dads reaching for their wallets or the occasional mom digging in a purse and passing a bill to a small child to bring his way. He mingled among them, accepting their tips graciously and gratefully, thanking them each, chatting and patting awed little boys on their heads.

And then, at last came Bethany and Christy—and Bethany's beguiling eyes as she prepared to drop a ten-dollar bill in his hat. Only he grabbed her wrist and said, "As I always tell my friends, your money's no good here."

A pretty laugh trilled from her throat. "That's no way to make a living at this, you know."

He smiled at her. "But for my friends—and that extends to *their* friends—coming to my shows is uplifting enough to me." Then he glanced toward Christy, who had already faded out of the conversation to talk to John and Nancy Romo, who appeared to be out for an evening stroll. "After all, if I accepted Christy and Jack's tips every time they were kind enough to come to a show, they'd be going to a Justice of the Peace instead of having a nice wedding."

Yet Bethany insisted. "Well, this is the first of your shows I've seen, so just let me be another tourist for tonight." She winked at him. And his chest went a little warm. "Besides, from one artist to another, I know how important it is to have your work supported. Who knows," she added on a shrug, "perhaps you'll buy a painting from me someday. Or even a painting by someone else—doesn't matter, because it all pays forward."

He still held her thin, delicate wrist—but now he let it go with a simple, "Thank you." And a small bow. "From one artist to another." Because he understood what she was saying—artists of all kinds supported each other, knowing that it could be a challenging career path.

"That hat is fantastic, by the way." She pointed at the old top hat, now filled with a mix of green bills and coins.

She was the first person in a decade to ever really

notice or compliment the hat, and the mere gesture reached down inside him and grabbed hold of his soul. She was a kindred spirit. "I bought it from a re-tired ringmaster who sold and traded circus antiqui-ties at an odd little shop in upstate New York."

Her big eyes, boldly outlined, widened further. "That sounds incredible! I want to go there!"

"If it even still exists—the hat's been with me for over ten years. But it was a wonderful and wacky place."

They traded another smile, this one easier, one of mutual understanding. Not everyone in the world would get how magical a circus antique store is, but *they* both did.

"Your show was amazing," she told him. "And what a unique art form!"

"I've been called unique a time or two," he admitted on a light laugh.

Which she returned. "We have that in common then." After which she added, "I'd love to get to know you better. We should hang out some while I'm here." And reached out to gently touch his arm.

His eyes dropped there, to the touch. Tamra had oc-casion to touch him every now and then, in a friendly way. As did Christy, and even Polly. But this felt . . . different. *Where* he felt it was different. His gut. His groin.

"I'd . . . like that," he said.

And when he lifted his gaze back to hers, something there looked . . . electric. Magical. Invigorating. "Good. See you soon," she concluded, then squeezed his arm lightly before letting go and walking away.

He stood there for a minute, rooted in place like

a palm tree in the sandy earth. Then he got hold of himself—because he didn't want anyone to see him looking dumbstruck by the interaction. So he took a deep breath and allowed himself one last glance at her walking away, hips swaying, her long legs dropping from a flirty, flouncy short dress and ending in cowboy boots of all things. And then he forced himself to turn away, toward the business of packing up his props and taking down his tightrope.

What the hell had just happened here?

A vibrant woman had flirted with him. And he'd experienced a connection with her. And she'd suggested sharing more of that connection. And he wanted to see her again.

And she wasn't Kim.

Not much caught Fletcher off guard. Even less usually scared him. But this did both of those things.

Two days after Tamra bailed on him at the jobsite, Jeremy finished planting all the shrubbery and grasses. The digging had been backbreaking work—he returned to the Happy Crab dirty, sweaty, and tired. And with a cat attempting to trip him up at every step.

As soon as he slammed the door of his truck, the gray cat was at his feet. "Hey buddy," he'd said. "Let me get cleaned up and then I'll go get us some dinner."

"Meow," the cat replied, as if he understood.

Jeremy just rolled his eyes—maybe at the cat, maybe at himself; he wasn't sure. Somehow he'd become responsible for this cat's supper every night?

Pulling a crab-shaped keychain from his pocket, he shoved the key in the door of his room and pushed it open—to look down and see an envelope near the toe of his workboot that someone had shoved beneath. It was pale yellow.

Huh. What the hell could this be?

As he bent down to pick it up, Captain went trotting past him right into the room.

He'd worry about his trespasser in a minute, but for now was busy checking out the envelope, where he saw his name written in a nice script. He still had no idea what this was, but seeing something addressed to him so officially made him feel . . . human, maybe. And it made him open it more gently than he probably would have any other piece of mail. He guessed he didn't want to tear up being human.

With dirty fingers, he drew out a matching yellow card that said:

You are invited to a wedding party and shower for
Christy Knight
and
Jack DuVall

"He was never as puzzled in his life."

Frances Hodgson Burnett, *The Secret Garden*

Chapter 10

THE DATE on the invitation was this coming Saturday night. And the card indicated that the party was being thrown by Tamra, Cami, and Bethany—the girl he'd met with Christy last week.

He just stared at it. Good thing it had had his name on it or he'd think it had been shoved under the wrong door.

As he stripped off his clothes and got in the shower, he wondered what on earth had prompted the invitation. Mainly he was curious if Tamra had been involved in this decision.

She was such a wild card. One minute kissing him, the next telling him all the reasons she didn't want to be kissing him. One day telling him off and the next inviting him to come see her art. He shook his head as he ran a bar of little motel soap over his arms, torso.

He didn't know if he'd go. Just like the Sunset Celebration, it probably wasn't his thing. Once upon a time, back in Destiny when he was younger, sure. But he wasn't that same guy. And there was the whole crowd thing—he would never like crowds. He remained glad he'd come here, glad he'd started slowly inching forward into having some kind of life—but damn, keeping to himself up at Whisper Falls sure had been easier.

Upon exiting the shower, he was surprised to nearly trip over a cat, naked. "Damn, I forgot you were here." He shook his wet head, then moved past the cat and dressed in a clean pair of faded blue jeans and a red T-shirt.

Stepping up to the sink outside the bathroom, he looked into the wide mirror above it. Truth was, it had been easy to let his hair grow and not give a damn when all he did was sit around at Lucky's, but now that he was working, it was irritating and hot. Today, he'd gone so far as to pull it back in a rubber band. At the moment, it hung in twists and waves around his head and shoulders like tentacles. He considered trying to comb it, but the sad-bordering-on-ridiculous fact was that he didn't have a comb.

So he just ran his fingers through his sandy-colored beard, then grabbed up his wallet and room key and headed for the door. "Come on, Captain, out we go," he said. He made his usual short walk across the parking lot to the Hungry Fisherman, the cat still faithfully on his heels, and managed to get inside without Captain following.

He passed by a life-size statue of a fisherman that looked suspiciously like Abner, and which he'd learned in passing that Polly had actually carved herself many years ago. She was a simple woman in most ways—but a woman who would carve the man she loved from a giant block of wood, especially a man like Abner . . . well, that was pretty special. Weird maybe, but special.

It caught him a little off guard to see that what had become his usual booth was filled with women—in particular, Tamra, Cami, and Christy. They all looked up and waved as Christy called, "Hey, Jeremy!"

"Hey," he said, trying for a smile. But he was tired. He found himself wanting to make eye contact with Tamra but at the very same time wanting to avoid her since he never knew what to expect from her.

So he leaned toward the avoiding by making a bee-line toward the opposite side of the restaurant beyond the seafood buffet. The only table in that area occupied was the one where Abner frequently sat. Tonight he wore a bright yellow hard hat with a red golf shirt and khaki pants. He didn't look up, so Jeremy left him alone and slid into a nearby booth. Most nights he ate out behind the Crab, but wind had started kicking up a couple of hours ago, so eating inside sounded better tonight. He'd feed the cat after he left.

Polly brought over his usual soft drink and told him to help himself to the buffet with a wink that he figured had something to do with Captain. And as Jeremy dug into a big plate of food, he occasionally heard the girls on the other side of the restaurant laughing. Though . . . never Tamra, he realized. *Even with her girlfriends, she never laughs. She should laugh more.*

Then he shook his head. *Who the hell am I to give advice?*

He'd just finished his plate and was ready to go back for a light helping of seconds—including something for a certain one-eyed cat—when Abner and his hard hat slid into the orange vinyl seat across from him.

Abner greeted him by throwing a familiar-looking yellow envelope down on the table between them, clearly grouchy as hell. "You going to this damn wedding shower?"

Jeremy wiped his napkin across his mouth before answering. "Don't know," he said. "Don't really want to, so probably not."

"I don't want to, either," Abner groused, "but I have to."

Jeremy raised his eyebrows. Abner didn't strike him as a man who did much against his will.

"We're providin' the food," Abner explained. "Plus Polly says it's only decent. Suppose she's right. But I don't like parties."

"Me neither," Jeremy agreed.

They sat in silence a moment and Jeremy took a sip of his soda.

He'd sort of thought they were done talking, so it surprised him when Abner spoke back up, motioning vaguely across the room. "Why aren't you sittin' with them gals?"

Jeremy thought the bigger question was why Abner would assume he *would* sit with "them gals." But he just said, "Uh . . . guess I prefer keeping to myself."

Across from him, Abner gave a solemn nod. "Me, too. Maybe that's why I like you." They sat in silence another moment until Abner mused aloud, "Not always good, though, keepin' to yourself. Maybe you oughta go. To the party."

Jeremy wasn't sure if it was actual advice or if Abner just wanted his company there. Safety in numbers and all that. All the quiet outcasts sitting at the same table looking miserable together rather than separately.

Finally he replied. "It's nice to be invited, but . . . not sure I fit in around here very well. At least not yet."

Abner gave another small nod. "Me neither."

"How long have you been in Coral Cove?" Jeremy asked.

"Since 1972."

Now it was Jeremy who nodded. That was a hell of a long time not to fit in.

"If you want to fit in," Abner said, "you need to show 'em you're not so different from them."

Again, it was difficult to summon an answer because A) Jeremy hadn't indicated that he *cared* about fitting in, and he wasn't sure he did, and B) Abner didn't exactly seem like the guy to be doling out guidance on the subject. The good thing about talking with Abner, though, was that you didn't have to answer if you didn't feel like it and it still felt totally comfortable. So Jeremy just gave the man another nod and left it at that.

Then he went to refill his plate, and Abner departed the booth as well.

After eating a little more, Jeremy wrapped a few strips of breaded cod in a couple of napkins, then slid them into the front pocket of his jeans, left Polly a good tip, and walked to the counter to pay his bill.

"Be right with ya, hon!" she yelled from a table where she was refilling drinks, and as he stood waiting, he could hear the conversation from Tamra's booth.

"She likes Fletcher!" Christy was saying.

And Tamra and Cami both said, "Really?" almost in unison.

As they chattered on, he realized they were talking about Bethany.

"Only," Christy went on, "she's not really into his look. You know, the whole long hair and beard thing. She thinks he looks . . ."

"Like 1970 exploded all over him?" Tamra asked.

"Exactly," Christy said. "But she's all into his personality and she thinks he might be cute under the beard."

"Hmm," Tamra offered, "I never thought about that before—or what he would even look like without it."

"Do you think he'd ever change things up?" Cami asked.

"Unlikely," Tamra answered. "I mean, he's so . . . Fletcher. He's not a guy who changes to suit other people, you know?"

"And he'd probably be all like, 'How will Kim recognize me when she comes home?'" Cami said, imitating Fletcher. Jeremy had only met the guy once, the day the whole town had worked on the municipal parking lot, but he thought Cami did a pretty fair take on him.

"Well, if you ask me," Christy said, "a change would do him good. In more ways than one. And being open to getting to know Bethany would do him good, too."

"Amen to that," Tamra said.

Then Christy added, "And just between us, I wouldn't mind if Fletcher tidied up his look, too. Like, for the wedding. He's the best man, after all. And I love Fletcher, but . . ."

"1970." Tamra and Cami again spoke in unison.

And Jeremy thought Tamra sounded more hopeful as she said, "It really is past time for him to join us in the twenty-first century. I have no idea if he'd even consider it, but sometimes he listens to me, so . . . I'll see what I can do."

Oh boy. Jeremy already sympathized with poor Fletcher. He didn't think he had much in common with the dude, but what guy wanted to have to change to suit a woman? Or maybe *more* than one woman in this case.

Just then, Polly came dashing up behind the cash register, and as Jeremy paid, she said in a low, secretive voice, "Do you have you-know-what for you-know-who?" Then she gave him the biggest "secret wink" he'd ever seen in his life.

He patted his front pocket easily and said, "We're good."

When he walked out the door a minute later, he immediately found a gray cat at his feet and, again, nearly tripped over him. He stopped, looked down. "Not cool, dude," he said. "Not cool."

"Meow," the cat said.

And then it started to rain a little. And Jeremy said, "Shit. I suppose now you're gonna wanna eat your dinner in my room. Like you're freaking royalty or something."

"Meow," the cat replied as they made their way across the lot.

He'd already nearly forgotten the conversation he'd just overheard, and the one he'd had with Abner, as well. But as he glanced up and caught sight of his own reflection again—this time in the plate glass window that fronted his room—he kept thinking about changes.

He'd already made a lot of them.

But maybe there were still more to make.

"The boy is a new creature."

Frances Hodgson Burnett, *The Secret Garden*

Chapter 11

THE NEXT day Tamra sat with Fletcher on his porch facing the ocean. They discussed some of the pottery Tamra was ready to put in the kiln later tonight, as well as how nightly attendance at the Sunset Celebration was waning with fall. For both of them, the change of seasons meant using much of what they'd earned during summer to pay the bills during winter.

It was a quiet afternoon like most on Sea Shell Lane, and their conversation a typical one. Tamra was trying to ease into some of the things she *really* wanted to discuss with Fletcher today, near to bursting inside.

So finally she blurted out, "Bethany likes you. As in . . . *like* like. Like she's attracted to you."

At this, Fletcher lowered his glass of iced tea to the table between them and just looked at her. She couldn't read his silence, so she went on.

"I know we agreed not to push each other, but I think you should be open to this, Fletch. She seems nice and she seems . . . like you, in ways. Like she . . . appreciates the same sort of weird stuff you do."

"My hat," he murmured.

"Huh?"

"She liked my top hat. The one I collect tips in. In ten years, no one has ever complimented that hat before her."

Tamra smiled because she could see how much meaning that one little thing had held for him, and that he knew she was right. "See?"

"Still, there's a lot to consider."

"Not really," she argued.

He just gave her a look. It clearly screamed, *Kim!*

And the look she gave him in return said, *Forget Kim. Finally. Now.*

Fletcher let out a sigh and asked her, "You want to know the truth?"

"Sure."

"I'm thinking about it. Considering it. I'm . . . drawn to this girl. She seems . . . potentially amazing. And . . ."

Tamra leaned toward him across the table when he trailed off. "And?"

An even bigger sigh left him. "I never thought I'd say this, Tam, but . . ." He stopped, swallowed visibly. "What if everyone is right? What if you're all right, all this time, and Kim isn't ever coming back? I hate thinking that—it feels like a huge betrayal to everything I've held faith in these past four years. But . . . what if I'm wrong about it and I let an opportunity to know someone incredible pass me by?"

For Tamra, it was as if a huge light had just clicked magically on in Fletcher's brain. And it shone directly on her heart. "Yes!" she said. "What you just said! It's so, so true, Fletch! It's one thing to have faith, but another to let opportunities pass you by. You have to be open to this! And I'm so happy to hear you say you are!"

But Fletcher held up both his hands. "Hold on just a minute, Speedy Gonzales. I said I was considering it, that's all. So don't go putting any carts before any horses. Just . . . give me some space on this and I'll see where my heart leads me, okay?"

Knowing Fletcher well, Tamra understood it was time to just be agreeable. "Okay," she said. "Okay." But inside, her soul filled with more excitement and hope for Fletcher than ever before.

"So what's new in *your* life?" he asked, eyebrows lifting.

And Tamra panicked as visions of making out with Jeremy in her backyard flashed through her head. "Nothing," she replied too harshly. "What do you think you know?"

Fletcher's eyes went wide. "What are you talking about? It was just an honest question, to change the subject. But what aren't you telling me?"

Oh shit. Now she was pretty sure *her* eyes were wide, too. They were in a Mexican standoff of wide eyes.

Until Fletcher said, "Tam, don't bother lying. What's happened that I don't know about? Spill." And when she just sat there, he threatened her. "If you don't, I won't consider getting to know Bethany better. I'll just keep right on sitting around waiting for Kim. How's that?"

"*That* is a threat I'm not going to take any chances

on you carrying out." She hadn't planned to share this with him, but she wasn't a good liar. And he was her best friend, so . . . "Okay," she began. "It's possible that . . . I kissed Jeremy."

"What?" Talk about wide eyes—Fletcher's now looked on the verge of popping out of his head.

"Or, well, actually, *he* kissed *me*. In my backyard." She rushed ahead, just ready to put this out on the table now that she'd started. "He was helping me get a big bush into the garden. And he just kissed me. And I guess I kissed him back. And . . ."

"How was it?" Fletcher asked. "The kiss?"

She was tempted to lie. Because the truth—*this* truth—made her feel so vulnerable somehow. But again, this was Fletcher, so she was honest. "It practically curled my toes."

Now a big smile unfurled beneath his mustache. "And then what happened?"

"Well, I eventually pushed him away, made him leave, and have been avoiding him ever since."

She could feel her friend's disappointment. "Because?" he asked pointedly.

She met his gaze again. "Same reason as before. He's such an unknown quantity. Everyone here might be embracing him, but that doesn't mean he's a good guy or a bad one—it just means people here are nice. And most of what I know about him is bad. He returned home from war mentally messed up. He got arrested a few weeks ago for attacking some guy. He doesn't take an interest in personal grooming. The list goes on."

It surprised her when Fletcher didn't immediately argue with her, but stayed quiet a long while. And it surprised her even more when he eventually said, "You know, you make some decent points. We *don't* know much about him. But we do know some good things, too. We know Christy vouches for him. And we know he seems to be pulling himself together. And we know he shows up for work each day and does a good job. So . . . I think you should be brave. Give him a shot. Be open to exploring this."

But already Tamra was shaking her head. "I keep trying. But I also keep coming back to the reasons not to. And that's where I am right now. And I have to follow my heart, right?"

At this, however, Fletcher just shrugged. "Your heart doesn't always know what's good for it, Tamra."

"Neither does yours," she countered reflexively.

And they seemed to find themselves in another staring contest—until Fletcher said, "It seems we are destined to advise each other on romance, my friend."

"That it does," she agreed.

"And so . . . I have a proposition for you."

Hmm. She hadn't seen that coming. "What is it?" she asked cautiously.

Even as he spoke, he looked as nervous as she felt. "I'll make you a deal. I'll be open to the Bethany thing if you'll be open to the Jeremy thing."

Huh. That was a hell of a proposition. The thing she most wanted *him* to do required *her* doing something scary as hell. And she supposed the thing he most wanted *her* to do in turn required something scary for him, too. It was perfect. Perfectly horrible. Horrible because Tamra couldn't bear for Fletcher not to take this chance, and if she could do anything at all to help him to move on from Kim . . . she had to.

"Okay," she whispered.

Fletcher blinked. "Really?"

"Really," she said. "That's how much I want this for you."

He nodded. "And that's how much *I* want this for *you*."

He held out his hand and she took it, held it.

"And we both really, seriously do this," he said. "We're both honestly in it."

She nodded. Even if the very notion terrified her.

But now she changed the subject. "And another thing. You need a haircut."

His jaw dropped. "A what?"

And she sighed. "Spoken like a man who needs a haircut." She rolled her eyes. "I was sort of elected to tell you. Or I volunteered. But either way, you need one."

He continued sitting there looking at her as if he didn't speak English and had no idea what she was saying.

So she went on. "For Christy and Jack's wedding. And really for the party, too."

He was back to blinking now. And he sounded completely perplexed as he said, "Wh-why? I mean, this is who I am." He motioned toward his head.

"And we love you for who you are," Tamra explained as sweetly as she could, wincing slightly as she added, "but . . . you're a little out of style, Fletcher. Even more than I am. And since you're in the wedding . . ."

Fletcher let out one more big sigh, taking in the request.

So Tamra rushed to reassure him. "Change can be good, right? And that's what we're really talking about here, isn't it? Being brave enough to make healthy changes."

He sounded a little defeated when he replied. "I'm not sure what my hair has to do with being healthy, but . . . tell you what." Another blink. Another sigh. "I'll make you one more deal."

Oh boy. She braced herself. "Let's hear it."

"You wear something to the shower besides a long skirt."

Tamra gasped. "What's wrong my skirts?"

"You're hiding in them," he said without missing a beat.

Which made her gasp again. "Then—then . . . you're hiding, too! Under your beard."

Fletcher tilted his head. "Maybe we all hide a little, have our little bits of protection. But . . . do they really protect us from anything?"

Ah—typical, philosophical Fletcher, back on the scene. But it was a good question, and they both stayed quiet for a minute, pondering it. Until Tamra finally said, "Okay, deal. I'll shop for a cuter, more stylish dress like the other girls are wearing to the party and you get a haircut and a shave."

His back went rigid. "I have to shave, too?"

"Yes."

"But . . ."

She didn't let him get any further with an argument. "You want me in some sleek, short dress, you shave. That's my final offer—take it or leave it."

He looked a little frustrated. And staring contest number three commenced for a long minute until he replied, "For you—and for Christy—I'll take it." He held up one finger. "But you'd better appreciate this!"

"It's for your own good," she insisted. And then admitted something she wouldn't have even five minutes ago. "Maybe . . . maybe we're both in ruts. Maybe we both need to be a little more . . . daring, willing to take chances."

"You're making me take a bigger chance," Fletcher said. "Just so you know."

She tilted her head, made a doubtful face. "If I were to . . . let something happen with Jeremy, that would be the most daring thing I could do."

"Same with me if I were to get involved with Bethany. Just in a different way."

"Fair enough," she had to agree.

At this, Fletcher wordlessly got up and walked in the house, returning a moment later with two cans of beer. He lowered them to the same table where their iced teas sat, abandoned, clearly having decided they needed something with a little more *oomph* right now. He popped the top on both, then picked them up and passed one to her.

He held his up in a toast. "Here's to taking chances."

She took a deep breath and tapped her can to his.

"PERFECT day for a party," Reece said to Tamra when she got out of her car at the Happy Crab on Saturday morning, ready to help set up for the shower. Indeed the sun was shining bright, and though it would be dark by party time this evening, pleasant temps and light breezes were predicted.

"How are things looking?" she asked as they walked together through the breezeway that led to the back.

"Wait 'til you see. The tables were delivered a little while ago."

Just then, they exited into the open area behind the Crab—and wow! Round tables covered in white linen dotted the space, and strings of white lights draped from lamppost to lamppost and palm tree to palm tree. With the boats and dock nearby, it suddenly felt almost like a miniature yacht club.

Tamra hadn't been sure this was the best setting for a party—despite the Happy Crab's retro charm, she hadn't thought it romantic enough. But it had been Bethany's brainchild—because Christy and Jack had fallen in love while staying at the Happy Crab. Now the open area edged by the dock and bay had become more romantic than Tamra could have imagined.

"This looks amazing!" she said, stunned.

Cami and Bethany exited the motel office then carrying centerpieces—jars filled with flowers, each decorated with a piece of the repurposed jewelry Christy made her living creating.

Near the pool, Polly stood setting up long tables where the seafood buffet would be. "I can't believe you people want to eat fish at this shower," she called to them all. "Don't you ever get tired of fish? Lord knows I do."

"Quit complaining, Polly," Reece called back to her with his usual good-natured smile. "You need the business."

"Maybe so, but I'd still think you people coulda found a more romantic food than fish."

"From what I hear," Bethany said, "they fell in love at the Hungry Fisherman just as much as they did here." She pointed to the motel. "So that makes it perfect."

Just then, Fletcher arrived, and Tamra made note of two things: He still had the same ponytail and beard he had the last time she'd seen him, and his eyes fell instantly on Bethany. Well, the second one was good anyway.

When Fletcher spotted Tamra, she reached up and gave her own hair a little tug, as a reminder. He replied by reaching down to give one leg of his shorts a small pull. As if he expected her to wear something new now, while setting up. So she made a face at him

Reece turned on some music to echo through outdoor speakers near the pool as they all dove in on the party preparations. Fletcher and Reece set up white rented chairs around the tables as Cami, Bethany, and Tamra worked on decorations.

And the whole time, Tamra kept her eyes peeled for any sign of Jeremy.

He lived here, after all, so he could appear at any moment.

She'd spent the last few days continuing to work apart from him, on other projects, for practical reasons, both work-related and personal. She'd made progress on her own art, creating some seahorse-shaped plates and firing some already dried dishes in the kiln she'd invested in a few years ago. She'd also worked on some stained glass pieces already in progress, wrapping the edges of colorful butterfly-shaped suncatchers in copper foil, then attaching the copper with the burnishing tool before soldering them together. She'd also made more progress on the designs for the kitschy theme pieces for the golf course, adding plans for a hole that would require balls to zigzag past tiny pastel cottages built to resemble those on Sea Shell Lane and the surrounding neighborhood.

All of which had indeed kept her out of Jeremy's path other than the night she'd seen him briefly at the Hungry Fisherman. And given her some time to think, mentally prepare.

She couldn't believe the agreement she'd made with Fletcher. After all, instinct had told her to push Jeremy away in her garden. And she still believed she'd responded smartly, for all the reasons she'd given Fletcher on his porch.

And yet . . . she'd kissed Jeremy for quite a while before that instinct had kicked in. And those kisses had stayed with her. And when she'd seen him walk into the Hungry Fisherman, her heart had begun pounding against her rib cage so hard that it hurt. Just from the memory.

Thank God no one but Fletcher knew about that. If the girls knew, no telling what lengths they'd go to in shoving her toward him. And if she was going to truly open herself to this, she had to do it her own way, in her own time.

Though she knew tonight would be a darn *good* time. She knew Fletcher was expecting that, same as she was expecting him to get closer to Bethany tonight, too. The only problem being: When it came right down to it, could either one of them really go through with it?

By early afternoon, everything for the party was in place. And everyone was gone—except Fletcher and

Bethany. When she'd offered to take care of a few last things, he'd volunteered to help.

But being alone with her, even just doing a few party tasks together, was different than seeing her in a crowd. Her gaze was so direct, and so filled with . . . expectation. An expectation he still wasn't sure he could meet. No matter how drawn to her he was.

Music still played through the speakers, currently the Sick Puppies reminding him that it was time to change. But he still wasn't sure. About any of it.

When they finished tying fabric ribbons around the backs of the wedding party's chairs, Bethany plopped down into one, the move suggesting she was tired, but her eyes, on Fletcher, shone as bright and bold as ever.

"Guess that's it," he said.

"Except for one last thing," Bethany said as he pulled out another chair and took a seat next to her.

"What's that?"

"Me asking you a question, something I've been trying to figure out."

Fletcher pulled in his breath, tried not to feel guarded. Normally, he was just as direct as she was—it was a trait they shared. But right now, he felt uncharacteristically shy. "Let's hear it."

The hint of a coy smile reshaped her lips as she said, "I want to know what your deal is."

Hmm. That was to the point, all right. And it was a fair question. So he began to tell her. "Well, I have a wife. But I don't know where she is right now."

It surprised him when the dark-haired girl beside him shook her head. "No, I know that part from Christy. But what's your *real* deal, inside? What's it about? What's so special about this woman?"

And that was even much *more* to the point. The calm, sure, inquisitive way she posed the question nearly stole his breath. Even though it shouldn't. *You're just two people. Two honest, open people. Just tell her the truth, what's in your heart.*

And really, the answer, when he broke it down, was simple. "She's . . . my wife," he said. "Isn't that enough?"

Bethany tilted her head, appeared knowing, and maybe a little cynical. "Millions of men have wives, even wives they love, but they wouldn't wait patiently for four years, ready to forgive them for total abandonment." And when he met her gaze, she added, "I've heard you're shockingly honest. So am I."

"I can see that," he said, trying for a small smile.

And when he said nothing more, she went on. "How is it that you go on believing? Because I have trouble having faith in things I can't see—like love, and loyalty, and dreams coming true—on a daily basis. But you . . . you seem at the opposite end of the spectrum—believing in something you have zero evidence for, never stopping. What is that about? Why is it so important?"

Fletcher contemplated the question. He talked a lot about his endless faith that Kim would return, but Bethany was asking him something deeper, asking him to dredge up a more private part of himself. So private that he wasn't sure he knew the answer, and so he sat there digging through all the feelings in his heart—until it struck him.

And it was . . . a *hard* answer. An almost *frightening* answer. An answer so enormous and personal that he almost didn't want to tell her.

And he knew he didn't have to—he barely knew her. And yet, he still felt that connection happening, that kindred soul thing. And there had been moments with her today when he'd almost wished . . . that he wasn't waiting for Kim at all so that he could feel truly *free* to explore everything about Bethany that called to him, everything about her that woke something up inside him.

And he felt the burning urge to keep right on being who he was—the guy who had no secrets, the guy who spilled his soul. Even if this had been a secret to *him* until just now and didn't feel like . . . a good or flattering one.

"If . . if Kim is really gone . . . I don't know what my life is about anymore, what my purpose is. She's my cornerstone, my foundation—I built my whole life on her. When I was young, I wanted to perform, to make magic, to do something impossible that would make people feel amazed and in awe, and would maybe make them think *they* could make magic, too, in whatever way they wanted. But somewhere along the way, I started making that magic for *her*. I wanted to see the world with her. I bought my house on Sea Shell Lane for her. If she's not there anymore, in my life, in my future, what's it all about? What's it all for?"

Bethany let her gaze drop from his for a moment, clearly considering her reply—until she looked back up at him and said, "I understand how big a thing marriage is. And I've never been married so I won't pretend to have shared that kind of intimate, long-lasting connection with someone." She stopped, pursed her lips. Then stood up from her chair and looked down at him. "But there's such a thing as holding on too tight to something that doesn't really exist anymore. And sometimes it's best to let go of the past and look to the future.

"There's more than one kind of magic in the world. I feel like she stole yours—ran off with it and hasn't brought it back. How long are you going to let her keep it when you could be . . . sharing it with someone else?"

She spoke the last word with invitation in her eyes.

And then she walked away, leaving Fletcher to sit there alone and to feel that, the aloneness of it, and to decide . . . that maybe he didn't want to be alone anymore.

TAMRA looked in the floor-length mirror on her bedroom door. She barely recognized the woman looking back.

The woman before her wore a fitted, above-the-knee dress of pale yellow. She'd bought it yesterday at Beachtique, a shop in the same stretch of retail as the Happy Crab and Hungry Fisherman—which she'd always thought a little too classy and upscale for its surroundings. But when she'd needed a dress for tonight's party, she'd been glad it was there.

She continued taking in her reflection, trying to get used to what she saw—what other people would see. There was cleavage. And leg. Basically more skin than most people probably even knew she had. She wasn't sure she was comfortable with it. But she'd promised Fletcher, and unlike the promise about Jeremy, this was the part she felt she had more control over—so she had to follow through.

And she'd even gone him one better. This afternoon, totally unplanned, she'd walked into the hair salon on Route 19 where she got her hair trimmed every few months—and made what was, for her, a radical shift. This morning, her long auburn spirally locks had hung to her waist, a big curtain of hair. Now, it was four inches shorter and laden with layers that made it lighter, bouncier, fuller around her face. And she had bangs!

She could scarcely believe she'd done it—she hadn't changed her hair in years. But maybe the talk she'd had with Fletcher had suddenly made her realize she was judging him, and Jeremy, for not caring how they looked, when she was just as guilty. So she'd just gone for it, walked the talk.

The truth was, she thought she looked prettier now. Something in her face was softer. The hair framed her features more. Maybe she was crazy, but she could have sworn her eyes looked larger, her lips fuller.

Even so, she was nervous—her stomach swam with anxious butterflies. *She* thought she looked prettier—but what would everyone else think? It was scary to show people you were trying to make yourself into something a little bit new and to not know how they would react.

And there was more to be nervous about tonight than just her new look. The very thought forced her to expel a breath she hadn't even realized she'd been holding. Had she really made this agreement with Fletcher? About Jeremy? Wearing a shorter dress to a party was one thing, but pursuing romance—or good Lord, sex!—with Jeremy was another.

Jeremy had told both Reece and Polly he would

be at the party tonight. And she supposed she could just avoid him the same way she had all week, but regardless, she would see him. And probably—no, definitely—be swept back to the memory of those unbelievably tantalizing kisses they'd shared in her garden.

She decided to text Fletcher. To distract herself from her nervousness. She was ready early and had a little time to kill. She scooped her cell phone up from her dresser and typed in a message. WHAT ARE YOU DOING?

It took a few minutes for him to answer. SHAVING.

She gasped. She knew he'd agreed to, but it still caught her off guard. The truth was, she couldn't quite envision Fletcher without his beard. Wow. CAN I SEE A PICTURE?

He answered more quickly this time. No. THIS IS HARD FOR ME. CAN'T TALK RIGHT NOW, OKAY?

It made her feel bad. Fletcher didn't complain about much and she'd seldom heard him admit anything was difficult. Cutting off some of her hair today had felt a bit like . . . cutting away a little of her own identity. And in the end, it had felt refreshing, like it had lightened something inside her, cleared away something old to make room for something new. But maybe Fletcher hadn't quite gotten to that part yet.

She kept her reply simple. OKAY. GOOD LUCK. IT'LL BE GREAT, FLETCH.

It surprised her when her phone buzzed again with another message from him. ARE YOU WEARING SOMETHING NEW?

YES.

GOOD. WE CAN DO THIS.

She smiled. It was strange to see Fletcher vulnerable—he always acted so in control. But she admired him for showing her that part of him right now, and it heartened her that they were doing this—all of this—together.

You're right, we can! See you at the party.

. . . and the whole world looked as if
something Magic had happened to it.

Frances Hodgson Burnett, *The Secret Garden*

Chapter 12

*T*AMRA'S HEART beat too hard as she exited the car
after parking in front of the Happy Crab. *What have
I done? I made these changes now? On the one night I'm
going to see every person in town?*

She steeled herself, though, as she took careful
steps—on heels she seldom wore—toward Christy and
Jack's pre-wedding party. *There's no going back now—it
is what it is. And tonight is about Christy and Jack and their
new life together, not about you.* She carried a wrapped
gift—a stained glass heart-shaped suncatcher with the
date of their wedding soldered at one edge.

When she exited the Happy Crab's breezeway
into the party, music played and the smell of seafood
wafted through the air. The first people to see her were
Cami and Reece—and both their jaws dropped.

"Tamra?" Reece said, eyebrows lifting.

She blinked nervously. "I don't look *that* different. I
got a haircut, for God's sake."

Yet both still appeared completely dumbstruck. "You look that different," Cami said. "As in *amazing*."

Something in Tamra's chest expanded. She didn't want to care that much how she looked. She didn't want to care that much how people saw her—the outside her, the physical her. There was so much more to a woman, after all.

And yet . . . Cami's words lifted her spirits in a way she couldn't have anticipated. "Really?"

Reece and Cami exchanged glances, clearly still trying to absorb the differences that must be bigger than Tamra had realized.

"Um, yeah," Reece said. "You look like a million bucks!"

Again, her heart soared. And as more people began to arrive and mingle and say hello—and to compliment her—something new grew inside her. Or at least something she hadn't felt for a very long time. Feminine confidence. Not just confidence about herself as a person, or an artist, or a friend—but a confidence borne of knowing people saw the woman in her, the feminine side she didn't always display, and that they liked it.

"Good gravy, Tamra," Polly said, stepping up to her, "where you been hidin' all that gorgeous, girl? You're gonna have to beat the fellas off with a stick!"

Polly herself had switched things up tonight, as well, wearing an old-fashioned but brightly flowered dress. "Looks like you broke out of your normal shell tonight, too," Tamra pointed out. "I like seeing you in some color!"

A blush rose to Polly's cheeks as she said, "Well, that's nice to hear, hon."

And though he wore just a simple button-down shirt and pressed khaki pants, even Abner had spiffed up in his own unique way, topping his look off with a shiny silk top hat.

After suffering from self-consciousness less than an hour ago, Tamra now felt prettier than she had since she'd been a much younger woman. The cherry on top of the sundae of compliments was when Bethany—clearly a woman with style—gave her a once-over and said, "This. Yes. So much hotter." And ended with a thumbs up as she walked away.

Tamra stood chatting with Reece and Cami when a lean, handsome dark-haired man walked in, slightly overdressed for the party in a stylish pale gray suit and plum-colored shirt underneath. Tamra only noticed him for two reasons—she was keeping her eyes peeled for Jeremy and Fletcher, and this was the only person there who she didn't know. She was about to ask her companions about the new arrival when he walked up to them and said, "Sorry I'm late."

And they all three blinked. And gaped. Because the voice coming out of the guy's mouth had sounded astonishingly like Fletcher's. But that was the only resemblance to the bearded, pony-tailed tightrope walker they all knew.

"Quit staring," he said. "I know it's weird, but you're making it worse."

After a little more blinking and gaping, Reece finally managed to say, "Fletcher?"

"Yeah?" the guy said.

"Holy crap," Tamra remarked.

Fletcher—or the man purporting to be him—

stepped back and gave her a long look. "I could say the same to you. You look great, by the way."

She drew in her breath, dumbfounded. It was hard to believe the attractive man standing in front of her was her best friend. "Um, um . . . thanks. So do you." She stood there, still taking him in, now shaking her head. "I just didn't know . . ."

He let out a heavy breath, looked uncomfortable. "Didn't know what?"

It was Cami who spoke up—which was good, because Tamra remained stuck for words. "Fletcher, you're . . . handsome!" Though she still appeared as confused as Tamra felt. He looked like a different person.

"Thank you. I think. Although the level of your shock tells me what a surprise that is."

"Well, um . . ." Cami fumbled.

"You've been hiding it," Tamra said. It was easier for her to be honest with him due to their close friendship. "But she's right. You really are a handsome man, Fletch." She gave her head another shake. "That beard and ponytail were doing you a disservice."

He continued to discuss it in his usual matter-of-fact tone. "I always felt they suited my performance persona. Looked circus-y."

"That's fair," Tamra said. "But this . . ."

"Is better," Cami finished for her. "Way better. Even though I sort of feel like I'm talking to the handsome new stranger in town." She leaned a little closer, looked a little harder. "Are you sure this is really you?"

"It's me—I promise," he said. "But I'll be honest. I feel a little naked. Not quite myself."

"Join the club," Tamra said.

Reece started wagging his finger back and forth

between the two of them. "Did you two plan this or something?"

Tamra and Fletcher exchanged glances, and Tamra said, "Sort of. I promised I would if he would."

"Why?" Reece asked. "I mean, you both look great—so great that I'm totally freaked out right now. But what brought this on?"

Tamra and Fletcher stayed quiet. The answer was complicated. And clearly Cami hadn't filled Reece in on their conversation about Fletcher and Bethany. Finally Fletcher gave a simple but true reply. "We both thought it was time the other made some updates. So we agreed to do it together. To make it easier."

Tamra was still caught up in looking at her newly made-over friend. Who knew he had such a strong jawline? Or that short, tidy hair would make him appear so much more . . . commanding or something. He simply looked like a guy who had it going on. He even appeared a little taller somehow. "There's a cleft in your chin," she couldn't help pointing out.

"I know," he said.

"But no one else did. We've never really seen you before. It's . . . nice. To really see you, Fletch."

Just then, Bethany came strolling up carrying a tray of little green mojitos she'd been handing out to party guests. She addressed Tamra, Cami, and Reece as she said, "Christy just texted. She and Jack will be here in five minutes, so we should get ready for their big entrance." Then she turned to Fletcher. "Hi, I'm Bethany Willis, the maid of honor. And you are?"

"Fletcher McCloud," he said slowly. "Best man."

And Tamra watched as Bethany's eyes grew slowly large.

Reece took the tray from her hands. "That's too much alcohol to risk you dropping it all."

Bethany just kept her eyes locked on the cleanly shaven man before her. "You're not the same Fletcher McCloud I spoke to earlier today."

"Afraid I am," he told her.

But she shook her head. "No. No, this is like some weird movie where you've switched places with some other version of yourself from some other dimension."

Tamra realized he looked even more alluring when a slight smile reshaped his face—another thing the beard had hidden. "Is it a *good* movie?" he asked.

"Oh, it's a *really* good movie," Bethany replied. "Blockbuster, in fact. I hear there's Oscar buzz." Then she bit her lip. "We need to get ready to announce Christy and Jack, but . . . I'll tell you more about it later. The leading man is to die for."

And then she took Cami's arm and pulled her away to announce the couple's arrival, leaving Reece to hold the mojitos. He arched one eyebrow in Fletcher's direction. "Did I miss something?"

"Like?" Fletcher asked.

"Like I'm thinking this movie she's talking about has a hell of a lot of sexual tension in it. Going both ways. And that it's suddenly not the Kim story anymore."

Tamra watched Fletcher draw in a deep breath, then let it back out. "I'm . . . trying to be more open-minded."

Reece looked back and forth between the two of them. "Don't get me wrong—I dig everything that's happening here. But I'm starting to feel like I'm in the freaking Twilight Zone."

A few minutes later, Cami stood next to the small

bridal party table—for the couple, maid of honor, and best man. Bethany exited the breezeway, nodding to Cami that Jack and Christy had arrived. The crowd had grown and now most of Coral Cove gathered behind the Happy Crab, mingling and sharing mojitos on a beautiful late September Florida night.

"Ladies and gentleman," Cami said through the microphone, "please join me in welcoming the lovely couple who fell in love right here at the Happy Crab Motel, Jack and Christy."

Hand in hand, the two came whisking into the party looking like a fairy tale come to life. Christy appeared radiant, her long blond hair adorned with a flowered wreath, the colors echoing that of her dress. Tamra felt the happiness just dripping off them, flowing out to everyone around them who applauded their entrance.

It would have been easy to be jealous of such idyllic happiness, but Tamra loved them and enjoyed just soaking up their joy in that moment. More than she ever had before, in fact.

Maybe . . . maybe it has something to do with new hope.

Hope that maybe, someday, I could have that kind of happiness, too.

She hadn't believed that, not really, since she was a young girl. She hadn't believed that even last week. And she wasn't sure she truly believed it now, either— but the difference was . . . all these new things in her life. A week ago she hadn't kissed Jeremy. A week ago she hadn't seen how pretty she could look. A week ago she'd been more afraid of change than she suddenly was right now, tonight. Tonight, it seemed almost like anything was possible.

After Jack took the mike and thanked everyone for

coming, he went on to say a few words about Coral Cove. "As Christy and I fell in love here, we fell in love with Coral Cove at the same time. You've all taken us into your lives, made us part of your community, made this place home for us. Words can't express how blessed we feel and how much we appreciate you all celebrating our upcoming wedding with us." Then he lifted one of the mojitos Reece had just shoved into his hand, adding, "To friends, and to always having a place to call home."

"And to Jack and Christy!" Bethany said, holding up her glass for a second toast.

"And to Coral Cove—indeed a true home for many a wayfaring stranger," Fletcher chimed in, offering up his glass as well.

After which someone asked, "Who's that talking?"

And Fletcher replied, "Mrs. Mendoza, I'm Fletcher. I live around the corner from your shop, on Sea Shell Lane. I buy ice cream from you a couple of times each week."

And a low gasp went through the crowd as Mrs. Mendoza said, "The only Fletcher I know is a tightrope walker and you're not him."

"I am," he assured her. "I shaved, that's all."

And from behind the buffet table Polly piped up. "Hon, if you been hidin' that face under that beard all this time, that's a crime. That's all I'm sayin'. Now can we all eat some seafood before every stray cat in town shows up and turns things ugly here?"

Laughter rippled through the crowd then, even though Tamra could still feel them all collectively trying to grasp that this was the same quirky fellow they'd come to know at the Sunset Celebration these past few years. Reece took the opportunity to turn the music back up and people got in line for the buffet.

A few more acquaintances approached Tamra to tell her how great she looked, and though she normally might not have enjoyed standing alone at a party, once they drifted away, she found she didn't mind a moment to herself at all. To take it all in. To feel her own new sense of confidence and comfort.

Only . . . where was Jeremy?

He lived right here at the motel, after all, so it didn't make sense for him to be late.

It doesn't matter. Maybe he'd just be an awkward addition at the party anyway. And it's not like you really care if he sees you looking pretty.

Of course, she knew those very thoughts meant that she did care.

But it's okay anyway. If he doesn't come, his loss.

She almost considered asking Reece which room was his, then walking around the motel and knocking on his door.

But again, no. You're being open here—but that doesn't mean you have to chase him. Especially since you're still not even sure it's wise to want him.

Across the way, Fletcher and Bethany had their heads together, smiling, even laughing. *Wow, that's really happening.* She was so happy for Fletcher, so happy he'd finally decided to look beyond Kim.

A few minutes later, as she straightened the gift table and gathered up envelopes there to make sure none got lost or blew away, someone touched her elbow—and she looked up to find her newly transformed best friend. He smiled at her. "Come join Bethany and me for dinner?"

"Oh—that's sweet, but no. I can hang with Cami and Reece, and you two are supposed to sit at the bridal party table anyway. And I wouldn't dare interrupt the blossom of new romance, regardless." She winked.

"We do seem to be hitting it off."

"I noticed," she told him with a smile.

He tilted his head. "No Jeremy so far?"

"Nope," she answered, trying to keep a small smile in place.

"Well, he's missing out if he doesn't get to see you in this dress, Tam."

"Thanks," she said, "but . . . whatever. It's all good."

Though she knew Fletcher could tell she felt a little sad. "Worst case scenario, you see him on the job Monday, right?"

She nodded. "Actually, I was nervous about seeing him tonight, so I should be relieved, right?"

"Right," Fletcher agreed.

"But . . . I'm not." The honesty snuck out because with Fletcher, it could. More than with other people anyway. But she put her smile back on to say, "Get back to Bethany—I'm fine."

Fletcher gave her hand a light squeeze and a small, consoling smile from the face it was still hard to reconcile as being his—but his eyes, she noticed, were filled with the same wisdom and kindness as always.

As promised, she sat with Reece and Cami at one of the round tables eating Polly's seafood buffet. Talk continued to revolve around things like Fletcher's big transformation and Polly wearing something other than her waitress uniform. And people kept telling Tamra how great she looked.

She hadn't realized it, but maybe somewhere along

the way she'd stagnated. And she supposed people who stagnated never realized it—that was part of stagnation. But she felt revived, re-energized, and like a long forgotten part of her had been set free: the part of a woman that simply wanted to feel pretty.

At some point she noticed a big gray cat standing at the leg of her chair, staring up at her longingly as she bit into a hush puppy. And oh—the poor thing was blind in one eye! So Polly hadn't been kidding about stray cats coming around. And Tamra didn't really want to encourage that sort of thing, but it was hard not to let a hungry, one-eyed cat tug at her sympathy, so she gave it a chunk of the crabcake she hadn't yet eaten.

"Well, look who just came rolling in," Reece said then—and Tamra looked up quickly, a wisp of hope lifting her heart, but immediately realized Reece had meant the rolling part literally. Christy's grandfather, who lived in a nearby retirement home and was in a wheelchair, had arrived. He was the reason Christy had originally come to Coral Cove.

"Where's Fifi?" good-natured Charlie asked as his lady friend from the home, Susan, pushed him up to greet them. The old man always seemed fond of Reece's giant iguana.

"Thought I'd put her on her leash and bring her out in a little while, after dinner," Reece replied. "It's good to see you out."

Charlie grinned. "Wouldn't miss my grandgirl's party for the world."

"Heard you're giving her away at the wedding," Cami chimed in.

"You better believe it." The older man beamed. "I'll

be there with bells on. Now, mind you," he added, letting only a tiny shred of doubt show in his expression, "not sure how I'm gettin' her down the aisle in this thing. Wheelchairs, and even walkers, don't move too good in the sand. But where there's a will there's a way, so we'll get it figured out, that's for darn sure."

After everyone else had gone through the buffet line, Polly and Abner joined them with plates of their own, sitting down on the other side of Tamra. "See you met Captain," Polly said.

"Huh?" Tamra asked.

Then she followed Polly's gaze to the scavenging feline who still lingered. "He's been . . . what you might call an unwelcome customer at our place lately." Polly's eyes grew bigger as she made a slight motion toward Abner, indicating the cat was more of a problem for him than for her.

"But you gave him a name anyway?" Tamra asked, a little perplexed.

"Oh no, not me," Polly said. "That's what Jeremy took to callin' him. Don't know why, really. But they seem to be buddies."

The mention of Jeremy brought her down a little. Why hadn't he come tonight? She knew it was only a party, but . . . it had also been an invitation to be part of their community. And if he chose not to, the same way he'd chosen to decline Tamra's invitation to the Sunset Celebration . . . well, it made it clear he didn't care much about getting to know any of them.

And if he was just her employee, it didn't matter much. But on a more personal level, it mattered. His not coming tonight meant passing up an opportunity to be around her, that simple.

Of course, that's probably your own fault. She'd pushed him away. And she'd avoided him all week. So maybe she couldn't blame him. But . . . it would have flattered her, moved her, if he'd made just one more effort to give her a chance to change her mind, to try to win her over.

It doesn't matter, though. It's still a great night and a great party.

After dinner, the music was quieted for more toasts, and Tamra shoved thoughts of Jeremy aside in favor of letting herself enjoy everyone else's happiness.

Like Christy and Jack's as they again thanked everyone for coming—their love was evident as they stood hand in hand, addressing the crowd.

And when dancing began, Cami pulled Reece into a slow dance, her arms looped around his neck, and Tamra could see how in love he was and was so glad her longtime friend had found that.

Fletcher and Bethany stood beneath a streetlamp talking, laughing, looking like people who might be on the verge of falling in love. Maybe she was romanticizing that, but no matter *what* it was, it was the happiest she'd ever seen him.

And even Polly and Abner seemed a little bit romantic tonight—Tamra watched Abner take Polly's hand, the older woman's eyes lighting with surprise as he led her to the dance floor. "Didn't break out my fanciest hat for nothin'," he said, and it made Polly laugh.

Tamra sat alone, taking it all in. Sometimes watching someone else's life, someone else's happiness, was enough—if it had to be. The party was in full swing now—most of Coral Cove was mingling and dancing away a beautiful autumn night beneath the stars next to the bay, the tall sails and rigging of the boats along the dock providing the backdrop.

Everyone was having so much fun, in fact, that Tamra realized they'd forgotten to cut the big sheet cake from the Beachside Bakery. They'd already gotten pictures of it, though, so she decided to make herself useful and start slicing and handing out dessert.

She'd gotten through the first row, cutting and placing little slabs of white cake on yellow paper plates—when someone touched her arm. She looked up, slicer in hand, to see a handsome man with short, sandy hair and a small, well-groomed beard. "Hi," she said politely.

But then she stopped, froze. Because . . . his eyes. She knew those eyes.

"Hey," he said deeply, gently.

She sucked in her breath. "Jeremy?"

"Yep, it's me, Mary." Then he let his gaze run the length of her, head to toe and back again. "You look beautiful tonight."

She sucked in her breath harder. "Um, you too." Because he did. He really, really did. But then she shook her head nervously, because that wasn't what she'd meant to say at all. "I mean . . . what happened? What's this all about?" She found herself motioning to his much-shortened beard and tidy hair with the cake slicer as if it were a pointer and he were a chalkboard.

"The night we kissed you said you couldn't see me," he said. "So . . . guess I wanted to let you. See me."

Wow. It was a night for miracles in Coral Cove.

When new beautiful thoughts began to
push out of the old hideous ones,
life began to come back to him . . .

Frances Hodgson Burnett, *The Secret Garden*

Chapter 13

"*You* . . . DID this for me?" She found herself blinking, repeatedly. Nervous and still trying to wrap her
head around this new and improved Jeremy Sheridan.
He *looked* improved anyway. He looked like . . . a hot,
sexy dream come true.

"It was time," he said. "But . . . you gave me a reason."

She sucked in her breath once more, and finally let
it out in a rush. Crap, she kept forgetting to breathe.
But it was hard with him standing in front of her suddenly looking so . . . wow. Drop dead gorgeous. She
could really see him now. And she couldn't get over
how much she liked what she saw.

"Wanting to let me really see you," she clarified,
still taking that in, too.

He nodded. "After you said that, I guess I wanted to
let you see me more the way . . . I used to be. More like
I used to see *myself.*"

She didn't know how to respond. It seemed like a profound gift at a moment when she'd least expected it.

"In case it matters," he went on. "In case it fixes anything. Between us."

When she pulled in her breath this time, she reminded herself to let it back out. And she was honest. "It matters," she said. And it wasn't just that he was suddenly so much more attractive to her—Lord, he even wore a short-sleeved button-down shirt with nicer-than-usual shorts—it was that he'd *done* it. He'd made the effort. For her. A big one.

"There's something about you," he continued. "Something about *us*." He moved his fingers back and forth between them. "War changed me. It made me see things clearer—but not in a good way. It made my life feel . . . small. And pointless. And like I didn't deserve to be happy. But since I came here, I've started . . . feeling a little better. Sometimes. And a little more normal. Sometimes." He let out a small, self-deprecating laugh, then shook his head. "Maybe I should shut up. Maybe I'm saying all the wrong things when I want to say the right ones. But . . . I'm trying. Because you make me want to do that. You make me feel things I haven't for a while. And maybe I just don't want to let that go."

A lump had risen to Tamra's throat. Because he was pouring his heart out to her. He was doing exactly what she'd asked of him and never expected him to do—really let her see him. And not just on the outside, either.

So even as hard as it was—and had always been—to let herself be that open, too, she knew she must. And not only because she'd promised Fletcher. But because

Jeremy made her want to. He made her feel like she could be real with him. Like she *had* to, in fact. Because if someone was real with you and you couldn't give that back to them, at least a little, what was the point in even living? "You . . . make me feel things I haven't felt in a long time, too."

"Why?"

"Huh?" she asked.

"Why haven't you felt them? I know why *I* haven't felt them—but why haven't *you* felt them, Mary?"

Just then, John and Nancy Romo came walking up. "Cake!" John announced happily, like it came as a surprise.

As his wife said, "Why, Jeremy Sheridan as I live and breathe. I heard you were here—why haven't you come and seen us?"

Once again, Tamra let out a breath she hadn't quite realized she was holding.

"John, Nancy—hi." He lifted a small wave, and Tamra could feel him being as nice as he could but also wishing they hadn't been interrupted.

"I owe your mother a phone call," Nancy was saying now. "I'll have to tell her I saw you. You look wonderful, by the way." She was reaching out, grabbing his hand. "You'll have to come over—we'll grill out, make shish kebobs. You know how John loves his shish kebobs. And I want to hear how you're liking our little town—we were thrilled to hear you'd come down to stay for a while. And you know if you need anything, you just give us a call. Or knock on the door, for that matter. You're family, after all."

After a little more small talk, the Romos departed and Tamra asked, "Family?"

"My sister is married to their son. And our parents are close friends. I visited here with my mom and dad once."

She nodded.

And he said, "You didn't answer my question."

"I didn't have a chance before they walked up."

"You have a chance now." His eyes burned with the same intensity as the sun shining down from a bright, clear sky—even though it was long past dark and the lighting behind the motel was dim, so it was something she could feel more than see.

And when it looked like more people might be heading toward the cake table, Jeremy removed the slicer from her grip and set it down, then took her hand and drew her away into the shadow of a palm tree near the dock.

His question, though, was a complicated one, and she didn't know how to make her answer simple. But she bit her lip, thinking it through, and tried her best. "I . . . I was raised in a commune out west," she began.

"Wow," he said.

And she appreciated that he instantly grasped the gravity of what a different sort of life she'd led than most people.

"Yeah—wow," she repeated numbly. "It's . . . not the most normal environment."

"I can imagine."

"Relationships of all kinds there were . . . strange. I trusted the wrong people a couple of times. And I guess I just let it . . . harden me or something."

He stepped closer, their eyes locking. "I felt that. That you were softer underneath. Under whatever made you act so tough on the outside."

"Really? You could?" Tamra didn't know *anyone* could see that part—sometimes she forgot it was there herself.

He nodded, his sexy eyes falling half shut, and she thought maybe he was going to kiss her—until she heard Christy's voice. "Jeremy! Oh my God, is that you! Look at you! You look fabulous!"

One more breath Tamra had to let out—as Jeremy spun to face Christy. "Yeah," he said, "thought I'd try to make myself a little more presentable for your party."

"You look so much more like I remember you now!"

And then Reece approached behind Christy. "Whoa. Is that really you?"

"Guilty as charged, bro."

And Reece just shook his head. "I can't handle much more of having my mind blown tonight."

And when Jeremy looked at Tamra, confused, she explained, "You're the third person, including me, who's shown up here tonight looking different."

"We seriously need to start throwing more parties around this town," Reece said. "Apparently it really makes people clean up."

Everyone laughed, and Tamra stepped up and gave Reece a teasing slug in the arm.

"The good thing for you," Reece told Christy, "is that everyone in your wedding pictures is going to look like they came off the cover of *GQ*."

And Christy playfully lowered her chin to reply, "Um, speaking of that, you could use a trim. It didn't seem important when everyone else around here was looking so shaggy, but you might be the weakest link now."

More laughter erupted, and the next thing Tamra

knew, Grand Funk Railroad's version of "Locomotion" blared from the speakers, and Tamra spotted Polly trying to move Fifi out of the way in the area serving as a dance floor.

"Polly, Polly, Polly," Reece said, leaving them to approach her, "you can't make a conga line with an iguana." And he grabbed her, spun her around, and put his hands on her waist. "You can make one with an iguana *owner*, though."

Tamra laughed, beginning to realize Reece had downed a few mojitos.

"Come on, people," he said, "don't make me and Polly look foolish."

"Um, you might be managing that on your own!" Cami called laughingly, but fell into line behind him. And the rest of the party joined in. Even Riley. Even Charlie in his wheelchair. And even—holy crap—Abner!

Though Jeremy and Tamra still stood on the sidelines. He looked at her said, "I'm not much of a party guy these days, but . . . if Abner's having more fun than we are, something's wrong."

"We should probably join in," Tamra agreed, and they fell in at the back of the line, Jeremy behind her. And she couldn't deny immediately liking how his hands felt on her hips.

As is wont to happen during a conga line, there were occasional stops and starts that caused people to bump into the person in front of them. And when Jeremy bumped into Tamra from behind, it was . . . nice. Warm. It sent ripples all through her. Especially when he refastened his hands to her hips. His thumbs pressed into her flesh, just a little, more than if the person in front of him were a stranger. And then—mmm—his body came flush against hers, resulting in . . . a firmness against her ass.

She looked over her shoulder, found his face right there, an inch or two away. She dropped her gaze from his eyes to his mouth, his jaw, his chin—all visible now, even through his short beard. And she liked them. And she liked that they were so near. To *her* mouth. If she wasn't mistaken, his hold on her hips tightened, his fingers splaying wider, somehow feeling as if he was touching a little more of her.

When the song ended, Meghan Trainor's "All About That Bass" took its place and everyone fell into dancing the normal way—except for Tamra and Jeremy, who stood facing each other uncertainly. "I'm not much of a dance guy, either," he said.

"We have that in common," she informed him. And yet, she sort of wanted to. Maybe it was the mojitos. Or maybe it was just the vibe of the night. If she couldn't release her inhibitions tonight, when miracles were taking place right and left, when could she?

So that was why it made her happy when he said, "But . . . when in Rome, what the hell, right?"

She laughed and said, "Right. Let's dance like fools and not give a damn."

And that's exactly what they did. They danced to fast songs, and they danced to slow ones, too, Tamra melting gingerly into Jeremy's arms, secretly happy when the tempo slowed and Colbie Caillat began singing lyrics that told her she didn't have to try so hard. And it was true—she didn't. It was . . . easier than she could have dreamed even a few hours ago to lean against Jeremy, feel his warmth, welcome his embrace as his muscular arms cocooned her. It was no less new, but it was less . . . scary. Because . . . he'd let her see him now.

They laughed together, talking about nothing and everything. She knew people wondered who she was dancing with—she felt them watching, whispering— but she didn't care. She was simply having fun. A kind of fun she couldn't remember having had . . . ever.

When they took a restroom break, Tamra came out first and spotted Fletcher, also on the dance floor, looking like he was having as much fun with Bethany as she was with Jeremy. On impulse, she grabbed up a black pen to write on one of the little yellow napkins at the cake table:

It's a night for miracles!

And she whisked past the two of them on the dance floor and gently tucked the napkin into Fletcher's pocket. Just because. Whenever he found it, she wanted to remind him. Things were shifting. For both of them. Suddenly nothing seemed impossible. A happiness she'd never quite envisioned—for both her and Fletcher—seemed within reach.

And yes, she barely knew Jeremy. But as Fletcher had said, this was just about being open, having fun, living. She was taking this one moment at a time and enjoying the hell out of it.

When a hand closed over her wrist, she turned to find Jeremy—looking as handsome and strong as he had all night. She still couldn't believe this was the same unkempt man she'd come to know on the jobsite. She still couldn't believe he'd changed that—for her. "Dance with me some more, Mary?"

Another slow song was starting. "Yes," she said.

Her arms circled his neck as his closed around her waist. As they swayed back and forth, it held all the tension and heat and new intimacy of a pair of teenagers dancing at the prom. But Tamra had never been to the prom—this was her first time dancing like that. She never wanted the music to end.

But when it did, Jeremy whispered in her ear, "Take a walk with me."

It never occurred to her to refuse—she wanted to be alone with him, wanted to know him better.

When he took her hand, she didn't balk—she let him hold it, liking the connection. Even that, just holding a man's hand, was something she'd done so little of, and something in the simplicity of it felt special.

They walked in silence for a few moments, up the dock, away from the party, the noise and music fading as they strolled past the line of boats.

"I met your cat friend," she volunteered.

She felt him look at her in the dark, then refocus his attention ahead. "I wouldn't say we're really *friends*. We just . . . hang out some. I'm more of a dog guy."

"Okay," she said, smiling inside as he tried to hide his affection for the cat.

"What made you change your hair?" he asked.

She considered her answer carefully, but it was hard because there was so much else to concentrate on and feel—his hand in hers, the soft breeze, the stars overhead. "I guess I was just trying to . . . embrace change. Be open to new things."

"New things like me?"

"Maybe," she said.

"New things like . . . kissing me?"

She pulled in her breath. Hesitated only a second. Then admitted "Maybe," once more.

"It looks great," he told her.

"You . . . look great, too." It wasn't easy for her to be openly complimentary of a man that way—she simply wasn't accustomed to it and she'd spent so much effort trying to convince *this* one that she wasn't into him.

"Thanks," he said. "For, like I said, giving me a reason." Then he stopped, turned to face her, and took both her hands in his. "I hope you're open to it *now*."

"Open to what?" she asked—right before he kissed her.

Unlike earlier when they'd kept getting interrupted, she wasn't completely ready for it. She'd been totally in the moment with him, enjoying his company, not thinking ahead. And now—she felt awkward. Was she kissing him right? She didn't know. She barely remembered *how* to kiss—just as when it had happened in her garden.

Only then . . . she stopped worrying. She stopped thinking altogether. Because it just felt good. To kiss and be kissed. To have his hands on her—they gripped her waist firmly, warmly. Like when they were dancing, hers circled his neck—and she liked that it was bare now, no longer covered with his hair, because she could feel his skin.

The kiss was slower than when he'd kissed her in her garden—now he came off like a calculated lover, a man who kissed well and often, even if he'd told her that wasn't the case. When his tongue pushed into her mouth, she didn't hesitate—she followed the instinct to touch it with her own. A low groan rose from his throat in response and she felt it between her legs.

He stopped the kisses to speak low and raspy into her ear. "Maybe you're right—maybe you're not so contrary after all."

Her own voice came out breathy, girlish. "See, I told you."

He pulled back slightly, just enough for her to see his small, flirtatious smile. "I just had to get *past* the contrary."

She'd drawn her hands down, pressing her palms against his chest, and she used one of them to playfully swat at him. "You had a pretty good dose of contrary in you, too, mister."

He just shrugged, looking a little smug about it. "Part of my charm."

She laughed, and gazing down into her eyes made Jeremy chuckle, too. He'd never seen Tamra like this, so gentle and sweet, and he'd begun to think he never would. Damn, he was glad he'd been wrong about that.

As he leaned back in for more kissing, she was less tentative than before—he could tell she'd relaxed into it now, could feel it in her touch, in the way her lips melded more sensually to his. Each time he'd started kissing her, it had been as if she was afraid to let herself go, afraid to let him see she wanted it, too. But now she wasn't trying to hide it anymore—she was kissing him more freely, more confidently, and he liked it. A lot.

He still couldn't get over the way she looked tonight. He'd known she had curves, but this was the only time he'd ever seen them shown off to full advantage. And the way she'd changed her hair made her appear somehow both . . . prettier and *wilder* at the same time. It was hair a man's hands could get lost in. But right now he was too busy exploring her *curves* with his hands, so he'd save that for later.

It moved him—and hell, turned him on—to know she'd made those alterations with him in mind. The same way he had for her. And God, it felt amazing to connect with her like this. After having her put the brakes on, it felt like the sweetest of rewards that her tune had changed now.

Jeremy sunk deeper, got lost in their kisses. He'd grown hard behind his zipper and now followed the urge to lean into her, to let her feel what she'd done to him.

She gasped, breaking the kiss, as he pressed his hips more fully against hers. Their eyes met—hers wide and wanting. He wanted to kiss her into oblivion.

As he brought his mouth back down on her soft, pliable lips, her fingers clutched at the front of his shirt. And his hand slid unthinkingly, unplanned, upward from her hip to the side of her full breast.

Another short, heated gasp. More need expanding inside him.

But shit, why did I start this here? *Out on a dock just a stone's throw from a big party.* He wanted to take her right here anyway, though—wanted to just push up her dress and thrust himself into her warmth.

Yet as tempting as it was to proceed where they were, he had a feeling Tamra wouldn't be into that kind of risk—and besides, he wanted to take his time with her, not rush this. And fortunately an easy solution hit him. He stopped kissing her just long enough to rasp in her ear, "Let's go to my room." Because, like the party, the Happy Crab lay only a stone's throw away.

Her eyes changed then, and he couldn't read them— but . . . uh oh. He had a feeling that this change wasn't a good one. "I—I can't," she said on labored breath.

Aw hell. "Why not?" he asked. "No one has to know. They're all busy—they won't even notice us."

Now she shook her head, looked distressed. Her fingers still clawed into his shirt. "It's not that."

"What then?" He pulled back, gazed down into her eyes. She'd wanted to see him and he'd shown her. Now he wanted her to see the rest of him. "Tamra, I want you."

He watched her pull in her breath, saw the fear glistening more clearly now in her green eyes, the air around them lit dimly by lamps that lined the dock. "I'm sorry," she said. And then, fast as that, she was racing away from him in the night, back toward the party, looking unsteady on the low heels she wore.

Well, shit. She was back to being contrary again.

He could have chased her but didn't.

If she wanted to run away, who was he to stop her?

Even if his cock ached at her departure. A low groan left him as he tried to push down his rising frustration.

He didn't know what was wrong with the woman. But he wasn't in the business of fixing people, that was for damn sure. He couldn't even fix himself—or it was still a work in progress anyway.

He stood in the pale lamplight running his hand back through freshly cut hair, surprised for a second to find so little of it—he'd forgotten for a moment that he'd cut it all off. Trying to be better. Trying to be his old self.

His mind flashed on the tiny little nugget of her past she'd given him earlier—that she'd been raised in a commune. What had that been like? How badly was she screwed up inside and why?

But it didn't really matter. Familiar feelings flooded him. *Can't fix anybody, can't save anybody.*

He'd come to the party tonight because Abner—of all unlikely people—had inspired him. But the truth was, he didn't like crowds any more tonight than he had a few days ago and he'd sat in his room for a good long time before making himself come out. And right now, he was just tired of trying.

Trudging toward the party, he decided he'd just head back to his room. If he was lucky, he'd make a clean getaway without having to talk to anyone.

His chest tightened as the music got louder, the lights brighter. Re-entering the party area was a slight assault on his senses, same as when he'd walked in earlier, but just like then, he didn't let it show. Most of the crowd was dancing, though some people sat at tables eating cake or stood talking near the make-shift bar. Abner sat by himself near the buffet tables, and Jeremy accidentally made eye contact with him. He gave a slight nod, hoping that would be enough to allow him to walk away unbothered.

He was about to pass through the breezeway that led to his room—when his eyes fell on a pale yellow sweater draped over the back of a white chair. The chair Tamra had sat in earlier, where her purse had been resting as well. She'd left her sweater behind.

Jeremy knew it would likely make its way back to her—her friends would know it was hers. But he picked it up anyway, then exited through the breeze-way. It would be easier if he just returned it himself—that way he'd be sure.

As he left the party, though, he realized the only question was: Did he go back into his room and go to bed, holding on to the sweater until Monday? Or . . . did he return it now?

FLETCHER and Bethany had just left the dance floor and found drinks to quench their thirst. He held his up, grinning into her eyes, and said, "Here's to new friends."

In response, she lowered her chin slightly and flashed him a coy look. "I hope you don't mean that."

He didn't understand, tilted his head. "What?"

Her smile held confidence. And mystery. "I like you, Fletcher," she said. "And I want to be more than just friends." And with that, she lifted one well-manicured hand to his freshly shaven jaw, her touch as soft as an angel's, then lifted a kiss to his cheek.

"Be right back," she told him then, quick as that walking boldly away toward the bathroom, and he realized he'd felt that kiss as keenly as if it had been on his mouth. It tingled all through him. He'd forgotten that—how good a woman's touch could feel, the sensations it could send echoing through his body.

He wasn't quite sure how this night had come into being. In ways, he felt like someone else—like she'd said earlier, some other version of himself from some other dimension. He looked different than he had just this morning. And he felt different, too. But at the same time, he was still himself. He just hadn't expected to suddenly have shaved off the beard and cut off the ponytail he'd worn his whole adult life. He hadn't expected to be dancing the night away with a beautiful, alluring young woman he'd just met. He hadn't expected her to kiss his cheek, touch his face, tell him she wanted something more. And most of all, he hadn't expected to want it, too.

A glance down drew his eye to something sticking out of his jacket pocket. Reaching down, he drew it out—a yellow napkin with something written on it in ink.

It's a night for miracles!

He just stared at it, took in the words. The last time he'd found a note like this, it had ended life as he knew it. These words were so much better than those others had been. And he wasn't sure where the napkin had come from, so it felt almost as surreal as the rest of this evening. But it also felt true. A night for miracles indeed.

When he saw Bethany returning, walking toward him with that same bold, purposeful stride, he shoved the napkin back in his pocket. And decided to embrace miracles. He smiled boldly, hoping she'd see, understand, that he was ready. For her.

That was when someone tapped on his shoulder from behind—and he turned to find his wife standing there, four long years after he'd last seen her. "Hi, Fletch," she said. "I'm home."

"You are real, aren't you?" he said.
"I have such real dreams very often.
You might be one of them."

Frances Hodgson Burnett, *The Secret Garden*

Chapter 14

FLETCHER FELT like he was seeing a ghost. He blinked, stared, tried to figure out if she was real.

She looked almost the same. Her hair was shorter, curlier than before. And her face perhaps showed a few signs of aging, the kind he'd never have noticed if he'd seen her every day. But her smile remained just as electrical, her eyes as bright.

"Kim," he murmured, trying to wrap his head around this.

He'd spent all this time waiting, wanting, knowing she'd be back one day. But lately, just since meeting Bethany, he'd begun to think less about it, put his focus elsewhere—on what was in the here and now, in front of his eyes. If Kim had tapped him on the shoulder two weeks ago, he wouldn't have been nearly as stunned as he was right now.

"Look at you, Fletch," she said, taking him in, same

as he was doing with her. "I barely recognized you. You shaved and cut your hair! You look great! It's so good to see you, my love." She was shaking her head in a heartfelt way, the way of lovers long parted, the way he'd dreamed she would someday.

He just hadn't expected someday to be *tonight,* right now, when for the first time ever he'd been gathering the strength to finally move on.

Fletcher tried to think of words—but none came. He'd played this moment over in his head a thousand times—but it hadn't happened like this, in the middle of a party, in front of the people who'd become his friends, in front of a woman he'd been ready to kiss. Nothing about this felt the way he'd thought it would.

When finally he found his voice, he said, "Wh-where have you been?" From his peripheral vision he could see eyes upon him. Music still played, but the people who knew him best were watching, understanding that this long awaited place in time had finally come. He could barely hear anything over the pounding of his heart in his ears.

The question made Kim's smile fade. Funny thing was, he'd always planned to make it easy on her. To welcome her back with smiles and hugs and joy—and sort it all out after the fact. But that wasn't turning out like he'd expected either.

His wife swallowed visibly. "I'm so sorry, Fletch. No words can make up for it, I know." She reached out, grabbed his hand. Her touch felt strange—both familiar and foreign. "Let's go somewhere and talk. Is there a place we can be alone?"

"I . . . I have a house. I bought a house."

She looked surprised, understandably. They'd never

wanted to own property, be tied down—they were ad-
venturers together. "A house?"

He just nodded. "It was a long time, Kim. Had to
live somewhere."

She looked appropriately guilty. Which he hadn't
intended exactly—and yet he wasn't sorry to point out
the obvious: Her actions had been monumentally life
changing, and monumentally hurtful.

"Can . . . can we go there? Talk privately?" Clearly,
she'd tuned in to the fact that even while some people
around them still danced, they had an audience.

Fletcher felt . . . assaulted. By what he'd thought he
wanted. *No, I do want it. Of course I do. I love her. I've
always loved her.*

I just can't believe . . . she's really back.

"Yeah," he murmured. "Of course." And then he
remembered Bethany behind him. Lovely, vivacious
Bethany. He turned to her. "I'm sorry," he said.

She appeared nearly as dumbstruck as he felt. But she
said, "It's okay. I understand. Do what you need to do."

He just looked at her, torn inside. Somewhere in the
last few minutes, he'd mentally committed to this, to
letting something amazing happen with her—and he
was sorry he wouldn't see where it led.

But God, Kim was back. Really back.

So of course he needed to take her home, to her *new*
home, to *their* home, the home he'd bought to wait for
her, and share with her.

He'd just never expected to feel so . . . lost.

*But she's home, like you've always wanted. You'll go with
her now, you'll hear what she has to say, you'll forgive her.*

No, you've already *forgiven her. Or at least that's what
you've always told yourself.*

You'll go with her and you'll start over and somehow all this will make sense. He'd always assumed it would. He'd always thought the very moment she walked back into his life that he'd understand and there would be nothing but joy.

Why didn't it feel that way?

TAMRA sat in one of the Adirondack chairs that circled the fire pit. It had started to get chilly now that the hour had grown late, so she'd started a small blaze. It had kept her hands and mind busy after getting home, and now it kept her warm— good because she thought she might stay out here awhile. She needed more peace than usual tonight, the kind of peace her private garden gave her.

Part of her wanted to go inside and change—get rid of the dress that now suddenly made her feel like . . . like she'd been masquerading as someone else. Turned out she was still just her plain old self, afraid of her own feelings, afraid to be with a man. Perhaps it had just been too long. And she still carried too many scars. It was the only explanation she had for running away from him.

She hadn't changed, though, because she hadn't wanted to leave the garden for even that long. She wasn't sure anything could really heal her soul at this point, but the garden at least soothed it.

She wished the night hadn't ended this way. She'd wanted to claim her miracle, same as she wanted Fletcher to claim his. She'd thought she'd abandoned her fear and trepidation. Having Jeremy show up like that, transformed, for her, had truly *felt* like a miracle, one she should honor. He'd seemed so much more . . . like someone she could really be with, in that way. He'd given her a reason to trust, to believe . . . at least a little.

But in the end, it hadn't been enough. A heavy sigh escaped her, seeming to weight the air. But then the light, pretty sound of a breeze tinkling through windchimes caught her ear, and she leaned her head back and took in the stars shining down through the tree branches above, and she was back in her safe place where nothing could hurt her.

The sound of the gate opening caused her to flinch and swing around to look.

Her heart began to pump painfully hard when she saw Jeremy walk in.

Oh God. It hadn't occurred to her that he'd follow her.

And he looked so good. She was still getting used to that—how handsome he suddenly was. Another reason for her heartbeat to hammer out of control.

He walked up next to her by the fire and held out her sweater. Oh—she'd totally forgotten it in her hurry to leave.

"Not exactly a glass slipper," he said, "but I think when a woman rushes out of a heated moment and leaves something behind, the guy's supposed to take it to her and see if it fits, right? And then good stuff happens."

She just looked at him, adjusting to the moment. And said, "I'm no Cinderella."

He gave his head a speculative tilt. "I don't know. You were all dressed up at a party and went running. If the shoe fits . . . or in this case the sweater." And then he drew his gaze from hers and began looking around, as if searching for something.

"What are you looking for?"

"A pumpkin. Maybe some mice. That sort of thing." He flashed a small grin that nearly buried her.

"Afraid they're not here," she said. "You've got the wrong girl."

He raised his eyebrows as he held up the sweater. "No, this is definitely yours, Mary."

She shook her head, uncertain what to say, but a little honesty spilled out. "I meant the wrong girl for . . . other things." She met his gaze only briefly before jerking it away, staring into the fire.

"I don't believe that, either," he told her. "You want other things as much as I do. The only question is why you won't let yourself have them." He sat down on the arm of the chair closest to her. "Is it because we don't know each other well? Because we haven't dated? I could fix that."

She peered up at him. It was nice to see he understood that even in this day and age some women wanted to get to know a guy before hopping into bed with him. It wasn't exactly hearts and flowers romance, but he wasn't a bad guy. He just had some issues—like her. And two people with issues . . . well, that sounded like a recipe for disaster.

She replied as openly as she could. "That might be part of it. But it's more than that."

"Tell me," he said, no longer smiling. "Make me understand."

"No," she said with another shake of her head. "I can't. It's . . . personal."

"My tongue was in your mouth a little while ago. That's personal, too. We're into personal now. Tell me."

Tamra drew in her breath—she didn't like being put

on the spot. She'd run away from him to escape that—and all of this, after all. So she simply shook her head one more time, more emphatically now.

"You really are pretty contrary," he insisted.

"I'm not," she argued.

His brows rose again. "What would *you* call it?"

She could hear her heartbeat in her ears. "Nervousness, I guess," she confessed. "I'd call it nervousness." A blush of humiliation crept over her.

She'd expected him to perhaps laugh at her childishness. But he simply told her, "Nothing to be nervous about here, Mary, I promise. I'm just a person, just like you."

"The thing is," she said, a little short of breath—because of what she was about to say, "it's been a long time since I've . . . had sex. And maybe I'm afraid . . . I won't know what to do."

His eyes sparkled with understanding—because she'd let him in, into her fears, just a little. "Truth is, Mary, it's been a long time for me, too. Longer than I'd like to admit. And maybe you're not the only one a little . . . on edge about it."

"You don't *seem* on edge," she countered quickly.

"That's because . . . I want it more than I fear it. That's all." He pushed back to his feet. "I wish you felt that way, too." And with that, he let her sweater drop over the arm of the chair he'd just vacated and turned to walk back toward the gate, which had fallen shut behind him.

She felt like a loser. She needed to make him better understand.

"I'm really *not* like Cinderella," she said behind him, standing up.

He stopped, looked back.

"I'm not . . . pretty."

"I'd beg to differ," he said, taking a short step back toward her. And her heart warmed. Until tonight, no one had made her feel pretty in a very long time. And even just since coming home, tonight's compliments had begun to wear off. Maybe . . . maybe she hadn't *really* believed them. But when Jeremy said it, it felt a little more real, for reasons she couldn't easily explain.

Yet still she argued. She got even more real with him. "I'm not a size six. Or even eight."

At this he looked perplexed. "Who gives a shit what size you wear?"

"I'm not like Christy or Cami or Bethany. I'm not skinny, or even thin. I'm not a Barbie doll."

"If you haven't noticed, Mary, I like your body just fine." He took another step in her direction. "Maybe I like having a little more to hold on to. And I *like* holding on to it—when I've had the chance to do that anyway."

Huh. He liked her body. Her body, which . . . wasn't horrible, but she couldn't help comparing herself to her thinner, younger, more stylish friends. It took a second to absorb what he'd just said—and that he really meant it.

But maybe it boiled down to one more thing. One more secret envy. "There's another way I'm not like them, too. They go after what they want in life. They're so confident and bold—they never let fear stand in their way. But . . . I do."

"Then that's the one and only thing I want to change about you, Mary."

She stood there, considered that.

And he went on. "A month ago, I was afraid to walk out the fucking door. I was afraid to leave the fucking yard. And then I did. And guess what? It's okay. Nothing terrible happened." He shifted his weight from one foot to the other then, looked a little troubled, like he'd realized how much he'd just admitted to her. But he went on. "I'm the last guy to say I've dealt with my shit well. But I'm doing better. Because you just . . . have to. Otherwise you wake up one day old and alone and wonder if things could have been different. Sometimes you gotta be bigger than your fears."

Tamra stood before him, frozen in place. By all his honesty. And by the challenge he'd issued. God knew she hadn't planned to tell him any of this—and it remained embarrassing, even if he'd admitted big weaknesses of his own. She'd thought the night was over. She'd thought she'd escaped all the challenges. She'd thought she was safe here.

But then he'd come into her garden. He'd entered her safe place and made it not safe anymore. It struck her that he was the only person to ever do that, the only person to ever let himself into her private place without being invited.

When she didn't reply to all he'd just said, he finally gave up, turned to go again.

But there were moments in life when a person was tested. And Tamra knew this was just such a moment—she could feel it in her bones. She'd run from him twice. And now he'd entered her sacred space— he'd made himself . . . a part of it suddenly, in a way. She'd promised Fletcher she'd open herself to Jeremy. And more than that, she'd promised *herself*.

"Jeremy, wait."

Once more, he stopped and looked back. This time the expression on his face was a skeptical one. But she wanted to fix that. She wanted to be brave, too. And she prayed she wouldn't regret it.

"I . . . don't want to be afraid anymore. Of anything."

"You don't have to be, baby," he told her deeply.

"Make me . . . not afraid," she said.

And their gazes locked as he came toward her.

Oh! The things which happened in that garden!

Frances Hodgson Burnett, *The Secret Garden*

Chapter 15

JEREMY SQUEEZED her hand gently, trying to put her at ease. Something about her honesty tugged at his heart, and left him feeling that knowing her fears made this easier. Because there was no reason to be nervous now—for either of them. If anything awkward happened, it wouldn't feel so awkward. He suspected he probably had more sexual experience than Tamra, but it *had* been a while, and now that didn't matter as much.

He met her gaze and hoped she could read his thoughts. *We're in this together.*

"I want you to forget," he said, "anything except how much I want you right now."

"Okay," she whispered, and it came out sounding tentative, but he still felt her trust and that made everything better.

When he ran his thumb over the back of her hand, a ribbon of heat rippled up his arm. Damn, they had some wicked chemistry for sure.

And now . . . now there was no stopping it.

Stepping closer to her, he lifted his free hand to gently push the curls back from her cheek so he could see her face. Moonlight, along with the strings of tiny white bulbs she'd draped through the trees, allowed him to take in the innocence in her eyes, the fullness of her lips, the blush of anticipation coloring her cheeks. Tamra was not a woman he'd ever thought of as innocent before tonight, but that was what he saw in her now. It was an innocent faith that what was about to happen would make her happy and leave no room for regret.

"You really are beautiful," he said. "I need you to know that. I hate that you've ever thought otherwise."

She lowered her chin slightly, peered at him through soft eyes. "When did you become so sweet?"

He just shook his head. "It's not being sweet. It's telling the truth. That's what we're both doing right now, right? Telling the truth. And the truth is—there are a lot of different kinds of beauty in this world besides looking like a Barbie doll. And you have plenty of them."

And he meant every word. It had never crossed his mind that she wasn't tiny and slim. It *had* crossed his mind that he liked the fullness of her curves. It had never crossed his mind that she didn't look like a supermodel. It *had* crossed his mind that her smile—when she let it out—made her whole face shine and that her eyes were the deep, warm green of the woods surrounding Whisper Falls.

"Tell me something true," he said to her. He liked this truth business between them. It made her more open with him, made them go places they wouldn't otherwise.

He watched as she drew in her breath, devising a reply. "I like that you're letting me see you," she said. "Both inside and out. I like that you cut your hair and trimmed your beard. I like the way your eyes sparkle. I like that I can see so much more of your face now. I like seeing . . . who you used to be, because . . . from what I hear, he was pretty great."

Jeremy managed a half smile. But it was bittersweet to be reminded of that other him, and that he'd lost so much of himself somewhere along the way.

And he'd thought she was done, so it surprised him when she went on. "I like . . . that a guy like you . . . wants to be with a woman like me."

He needed more on this one, though. "What do you mean? A guy like me, a woman like you?"

"I've heard what you were like once. Football hero, war hero, general heartthrob. And a guy who can have any girl he wants usually goes after . . . well, the Barbie dolls."

"I'm not really that guy anymore, though. Even if I'm getting my shit together, I'll never really be that guy again. That guy was . . . so fucking obvious. He was . . . predictable." He thought about when he'd come home from war. For a while he'd worked damn hard trying to be that perfect guy, live up to the hype. He'd even briefly pursued Lucky's sister in Destiny, the beautiful Anna Romo. And then the bottom had dropped out. It made him realize, "I never thought I'd say this, but maybe there's actually some good in the ways I've changed. Maybe I . . . look a little deeper now, see a little clearer. I don't want or need a Barbie doll to have a good time."

A rare but lovely flirtatious smile unfurled on Tamra's face before she said, "That's convenient for me tonight."

And he felt more in sync with her than he ever had, enough that he wanted to quit talking now and get to doing.

When Jeremy kissed her this time, Tamra . . . surrendered.

Something had changed here, something big. Maybe it was the things he'd said to her; maybe it was the honesty she'd shared. But she knew already that she wouldn't run away or pull back this time. The ghosts of lovers past that had haunted her ever since he'd entered her world were no longer hovering nearby. As he moved his mouth over hers in her secret garden hideaway, they were the only two people who existed.

When his arms closed warmly around her waist to settle on her hips, she didn't hesitate to embrace him just as fully. And finally, finally, she let herself begin to get lost in it all—in a whole new way. Lost in the kissing, lost in the touching, lost in Jeremy himself. And she'd never have imagined something like this happening here, in her garden—and yet it made all the sense in the world. It was the perfect place to finally let go, finally be as real with someone else as she was inside, by herself.

This time, when Jeremy's palm eased onto her breast she didn't panic—she tensed slightly, but then . . . then . . . she just let it feel good. As he molded her flesh in his hand, she followed the instinct to kiss him harder. And when pleasure flowed south, into the region between her legs, she let herself drown in the sensation.

"I want this so much," she heard herself breathe between kisses, unplanned. And the confession was the ultimate final surrender—because words that bared so much of her soul couldn't have spilled from her an hour earlier.

"Come here—come with me," he rasped, and led her deeper into her own garden as if he belonged there—until they came upon the big netted hammock where she sometimes napped strung between two palm trees. His seductive grin lured her. "I've never made love in a hammock."

"Me neither." And she couldn't deny that it sounded like a nice idea.

"Hop in," he said playfully, and as she lay back in it, he joined her, stretching out alongside, wasting no time leaning in to kiss her again.

As his body connected and intertwined with hers from shoulder to toe, his hands drifted from her face to her waist to her breast—and his kisses drifted as well. Mmm, she found herself stretching like a cat, eyes fallen shut in pleasure, as kisses to her neck vibrated through her whole being.

Soon enough those wonderful kisses migrated down onto her breasts, through her dress. And as her fingers threaded through his freshly trimmed hair, his hands grazed their way up her thighs, and under her dress.

And now that she was in this, fully committed and trusting in the moment, in the night, in Jeremy—it was easy. To part her legs when his fingers dipped skillfully between. To let passionate moans escape her throat and waft upward through the palm fronds overhead. To give herself over to sensations she hadn't experienced since she was a much younger woman in a much different place and time.

She pushed his shirt up over his stomach, wanting to feel him, too, and he withdrew his touches just long enough to yank his shirt open and off. She didn't hesitate to let her fingers play over the muscles in his chest and below, getting to know his body as he returned to exploring hers.

As she touched him, taking in the hard arcs and planes of his stomach with her eyes as well, his gaze dropped to where she touched him, too. And she hurried to voice the thought that rushed to her mind. "I'm sorry my hands are so rough."

He blinked, peering down on her. "Huh?"

She drew in her breath. More honesty. Funny how quickly she'd gotten so comfortable with that. "It's from the work I do, the pottery and glass work. It's . . . rough on my hands and nails. They're not, you know, soft." *Now* she felt embarrassed because she'd started sounding a little self-deprecating again.

His eyes moved back to where her fingers had gone still on his skin, but just as quickly returned to her face. "I hadn't noticed," he said deeply. "I was mainly just thinking it feels good for you to touch me."

"Oh." She pulled in her breath, his words making her surge with moisture below.

And then Jeremy wrapped one hand around her fingers, warmly enclosing them in his fist, then drawing them up closer to his eyes. He studied her fingertips silently. And then he kissed them. One by one, he lowered kisses gentle as falling raindrops to the work-roughened tip of each finger on her hand.

He said nothing more in response to her self-conscious concerns, and he didn't have to. The kisses had said it all. They said her fingers were as lovely as the rest of her. They said to stop worrying and just let them enjoy each other, flaws and all.

More kisses fell on her breasts over the fabric of her dress as he drew her panties down and off, along with her shoes. She let out a hot breath of anticipation as the undies left her, feeling at once exposed and in truth still a little nervous, but she forced that away and remembered she wanted this and was oh-so-ready for it.

When his fingers dipped between her thighs, a harsh moan erupted from her throat. Oh Lord, she'd thought she'd never feel this again. And yet, here it was, like a sweet, hot dream. And she was so, so thankful she'd finally let down her walls and welcomed him in.

And . . . ohhh, did it somehow feel even better than it ever had in the past? As his fingers stroked through her most sensitive flesh, she bit her lip, wondering if it was possible to die from pleasure.

When he pushed first one finger, and then two, up inside her, a low groan left her. Oh God, that feeling—another one she'd thought she'd never experience again. She found herself clutching at him, digging her fingernails into the soft flesh of his shoulders and neck, pulling him down to her, kissing him with every shred of desperate need inside her that she'd been trying to ignore. None of it had gone away—it was all still there, and now, finally, it was being fed.

"You're so wet, honey," he murmured near her ear in between kisses.

"Yes," she breathed—it was all she could manage.

And then his thumb pressed onto the most sensitive part of her body of all—and began to rub sensual circles over it.

Sensation expanded inside her as she shut her eyes tight, her mouth falling open.

She bit her lip, wanting to move against his hot touch, wanting to let her whole body go.

But . . . she couldn't. She just couldn't. *Oh no, what the hell is wrong with me?*

Now she clenched her teeth in frustration, her body beginning to freeze up. She wished it were darker, wished the moon weren't so bright tonight—along with the nearby fire and the lights in the trees.

"What's wrong, Mary?" he whispered.

Honest. Just be honest. It seemed to fix everything between them, seemed to take all the confusion and hardness away from their interactions. *So just do it again now.*

And Tamra looked inside her beaten-up heart and said, "I feel you watching me. And that makes it harder for me to . . . really let myself go completely. I guess . . . I'm one of those people who finds it easier with the lights out."

She bit her lip, back to feeling self-conscious. Until he said, "Why? I mean, you've . . . seen me at my worst. Or damn close to it." He let his gaze wander the length of her body before bringing it back to her eyes. "Let me see you at your best."

She blinked, taken aback. "You think this is my best?"

Above her, Jeremy tilted his head slightly in the hammock. "I'm not sure—I haven't spent enough time with you to know your best. But I just meant . . . you're beautiful, and seeing you enjoy connecting with me . . . that's beautiful, too. Not a thing to be shy about or hide. Let me take you there, Tamra. Let me take you all the way."

And like before, his words, his truth, changed everything. Somehow, he made it okay. Okay for her to close her eyes and just feel. Okay to sink back into the moment, and into the pleasure, and into the feel of his thumb caressing that now-swollen spot between her thighs. Okay to softly, gently, begin to move against his touch. Just a little. And then . . . more.

It was okay to let out the sighs and moans that the sweet, hot, consuming sensations elicited. It was okay to let her pleasure show.

She wasn't sure how much time passed—she'd ceased thinking in terms of time; she'd ceased thinking at all. She wasn't sure anything had ever carried her away as completely as his touch did just now. And it was without much warning that she toppled into pure ecstasy.

The orgasm washed over her in waves as rough and consuming as any ever driven to shore by the ocean—it vibrated through her, rocking her senses, taking hold of her soul.

Tamra wasn't a woman given to frivolities. Maybe that was why she'd been so resistant to her own body's sexual needs—in comparison to lasting things like relationships and work and art, it was easy to see something like an orgasm as fleeting, trivial. But in the moment when she'd traveled all the way to heaven and back . . . well, it didn't seem trivial or frivolous at all. It seemed . . . like she'd reached a destination. One she hadn't quite known she wanted to arrive at so badly, but getting there had surpassed all her expectations.

She lay there for a few seconds after, recovering, absorbing all the emotions it brought, with her eyes shut. But then she opened them, surprisingly comfortable to find herself peering directly into Jeremy's. If any insecurities were going to rear their ugly heads, surely right now, after all, would be the time.

"Wow," she said, biting her lower lip as she gazed on him with pure affection. Because he was somehow making things that were hard for her . . . so much easier.

His mouth quirked into a sexy grin. "That's what I like to hear."

The trill of laughter that left her sounded utterly girlish, even to her own ears. "Isn't it amazing?" she mused aloud.

"Isn't what amazing?" he asked, flirtatious grin still in place.

"That the human body can do that? That we're wired that way."

Now he was the one to chuckle. "I never thought about it that way, but yeah, I guess it is."

She shook her head lightly, compelled to make him understand what she meant. "I'm just usually . . . a practical person. I view life through that kind of lens."

"I kinda already knew that about you, Mary," he said on a wink.

"And this is just reminding me that . . . sometimes throwing practicality out the window is a perfectly good idea."

His grin widened. "Sometimes it's the downright smart thing to do." Only . . . then his gaze darkened when she'd least expected it. "But not all the time."

"What's wrong?" she asked. *Please don't let him be changing his mind.* She was in this now, all the way. *God, please let him be, too.*

"I can't freaking believe this, honey, but . . . I don't have a condom. And I'm betting you don't either."

Her eyes went wide. She hadn't even thought about that. It had been a million years, after all, since she'd even had sex. And thank God he wasn't pulling back on this thing between them, but . . . this was bad in a whole different way. "No," she whispered. "I don't."

They lay in silence a moment, both absorbing this new reality.

Only then, she remembered. "But I'm taking birth control."

He blinked. "Why? I mean, it's none of my business, but you said it had been a long time . . ."

"For other female reasons," she explained, keeping it simple.

Jeremy met her gaze. "So then, how long is a long time? Since you last . . . ?"

Okay, she was still a little embarrassed by that. "Years," she said, keeping that simple, too. "Long enough that, well, I know I'm . . . safe."

"It's been a few years for me, too, and I got a clean bill of health before I was discharged from the Marines."

"So . . ." she said, considering the situation.

"So . . ." he repeated—but he finished the thought. "We might be the two luckiest people on earth right now—because we don't really *need* a condom."

The idea made Tamra laugh. Since that did make her feel extremely fortunate. And excited. Enough that she kissed him, hard. It was like . . . a whole new surrender. To everything. With Jeremy.

"I want you." The words spilled from her lips without thought. Or regret. Or any trepidation now.

In response, Jeremy pressed his hand over hers, where it rested flat against his chest—and he slid it downward, over his stomach, past his belt buckle, and onto the rock solid column behind his zipper.

Tamra gasped as her desire flared. The space between her thighs felt empty, aching to be filled. Her whole body pulsed with the beat of her heart as she let her fingers close gentle but firm over the stone-like bulge beneath her touch. And like before, she didn't even ponder her words, just spoke her heart. "Don't make me wait. Not another second. I've waited too long already."

A deep groan echoed from Jeremy's throat as their gazes locked.

But then he broke the stare to start undoing his pants.

Tamra kissed him some more as he worked the belt and button and zipper—and when he lifted slightly to push them over his hips, she instinctively parted her legs and shifted her body, pulling his weight onto her.

Oh God, his erection rested against that softest part of her, and one more unplanned word echoed from her lips. "Please."

She didn't have to ask again. Planting his hands on her bare hips under her dress, Jeremy thrust his way firmly inside her.

. . . she always said that what happened
almost at that moment was Magic.

Frances Hodgson Burnett, *The Secret Garden*

Chapter 16

AFTER SO very long, it was a jolt to her body to be
entered that way—and tears nearly sprang to her eyes.
But they weren't tears of pain—because a split-second
past that initial discomfort came the soul-searing satisfaction of being filled by him.

The tears she held back were because this was how
men and women were supposed to come together,
what their bodies were made to do, and she was—at
last—experiencing that. And to think she'd tried to
push away her need for it, her natural desire. Attempting to deny it seemed so pointless now.

Of course, until now no one had come along to help
her have this. And so she knew it was all unfolding
as it was supposed to. She didn't know what would
happen between her and Jeremy after this, but she
knew in her soul that he was the man meant to unlock
her desires, the man meant to make her open herself to
romance again.

Jeremy peered down into the eyes of the woman beneath him. They were glassy, wet, but her lips were parted in passion.

And shit—she was so, so tight inside that he was afraid he'd hurt her at first. But now, as he began to move in her in slow, firm, deep thrusts, small whimpers of pleasure left her, fueling his desire.

God. Yes. Damn, was it possible he'd actually forgotten how good this felt?

Tamra wasn't his usual kind of woman. The truth was, she was right—in the past, he'd gone for the more typically pretty girls, the ones who'd once been cheerleaders and homecoming queens. Those girls usually knew how to be outgoing, how to flirt, how to *be* with a guy—and that made it easy.

But the further truth was—none of that had ever crossed his mind until she'd started pointing it out to him, telling him everything she thought was wrong with her. And he'd instantly realized that maybe he wanted her *because* she was different. He was finding his way in life to a whole new normal, and maybe wanting a different kind of woman than he ever had before was just one more part of it.

And she was a funny little thing in ways—in, out; up, down; stop, go. But all that mattered right now, in this moment, was that she hadn't stopped *this time*.

Not having a condom was a blessing in disguise. She was so wet, clearly so ready, and now he moved in and out of her snug warmth with smooth precision, each stroke echoing outward from his cock through the rest of his body.

"You're a beautiful woman, Tamra," he breathed. He'd told her that before, but he needed her to know it now. Needed her to feel that. One hand still gripped her hip, the other he'd lifted to brush the hair from her cheek, helping the moonlight illuminate her face.

And he'd nearly called her Mary—a nickname that had somehow stuck in his head because it fit her so well, because she *was* so contrary. But in this moment, none of that mattered. In this moment, she was Tamra.

She expelled a rough breath, and brought her hands to his face as well. She ran them over his cheeks, jaw, beard, like a blind person seeing someone through the use of their touch. "And you're a beautiful man," she whispered. "I'm so glad you let me . . . see you."

And he was, too. It had gotten too easy to hide behind overgrown hair, too easy to just quit taking care of himself. Seeing how he looked after his haircut had reminded him . . . of who he could be. He wasn't the old Jeremy Sheridan—clean-cut war hero—but he was . . . a better guy than the one who'd been hiding up at Whisper Falls. And now Tamra could see that, as well. "Me too, honey," he told her. "Me too."

Soon, though, there was no more room for words between them—there was only thrusting, driving deep within her, making her cry out, knowing the distinct pleasure of making her feel exactly how connected their bodies were right now.

Soon, there was only the wetness and the heat. There were only his fingers digging into her ass as hers clutched at his shoulders. There was only the garden, surrounding them, cocooning them in the lushness of the trees and flowers and big, waxy leaves of tropical foliage.

Soon there wasn't even room for thought, only sensation. His body pulsed with every hard plunge into her.

Her hot whimpers echoed in his ears. Blood drained from his face, rushing south, gathering between his legs as the fever she inspired in him mounted, nearing that point of no return.

And then, he reached it. And a few ragged words spilled from his mouth. "Aw. God. Now, honey."

And his eyes fell shut, brilliant flashes of color exploding behind them as he came, like what you saw when you looked directly into the sun. He erupted inside her, driving hard, hard, hard, loving the way it made her cry out even as the climax threatened to consume him

FLETCHER drove toward his cottage on Sea Shell Lane, same as any other time. Same as any other time except that a glance toward the passenger seat revealed that Kim was sitting beside him. It was like riding with a ghost, a ghost of happiness past. He kept looking to make sure, to confirm he wasn't imagining the whole thing.

"You look so different to me," she said musingly, head tilted as she peered over at him. "When did you shave your beard off and cut your hair?"

"A few hours ago," he answered stiffly. He didn't *mean* to be stiff—it just came out that way. He *felt* stiff. She was the woman he'd loved his whole adult life, and yet at the same time she was a stranger to him.

Her eyes widened in surprise. "Really? Just a few hours? If I'd arrived yesterday, it still would have been there?"

His short nod came out equally as stiff.

"Timing is everything in life, isn't it?" she observed.

He swallowed back the urge to reply, but thought she'd just said a mouthful.

"You look really good, Fletch. Really good." Then her voice went lower, her tone changing. "How are you? Are you doing okay?"

Funny, he'd been waiting four years to pour his heart out to this woman, four years waiting for her to care, but now he found himself wanting to keep his thoughts private, even from her. "I'm fine," he said.

As he made the left turn onto Sea Shell Lane, he felt Kim looking at him, perhaps sensing the gravity in his words. But then she took in their surroundings. "Wow, you live here? It's like . . . a storybook. Or some old-fashioned postcard."

I was hoping you'd like it. It had been more than a place to wait for her, after all. He'd made a home here, all with the idea of it belonging to both of them one day. But that was one more thing he found himself not especially eager to reveal at the moment. So he said, "It's nice."

"Right by the ocean, too," she noticed aloud as they pulled in his driveway.

"Yeah." He turned off the engine.

"So . . . you've been performing on the beach all this time? In this one spot? Waiting for me?"

Somehow, now, he was embarrassed to confirm that. The waiting part. So, still sitting in the car, he turned and looked at her. "Where have you been, Kim?"

Her eyes grew wider again, but her voice stayed calm. "Can we go inside to talk? Or maybe sit on your porch?" She pointed.

Yet suddenly Fletcher didn't want to share *any* of that with her, *any* of his home. *His* home. That *he'd* made here. He'd always planned on sharing it with her—he'd *longed* to share it with her—but somehow, now, it wasn't that easy. *Nothing* was as easy as he'd expected it to be. "Here is fine for now," he said.

She looked appropriately cowed as she softly replied, "Okay." Then she paused, thought. "I've been . . . a lot of places. I spent some time on the California coast. And a few months on Cape Cod after that. I was in the Chesapeake area for a while. And for the last few months I've been at my mother's house in Iowa. Thinking about what I really want. And figuring out that it's still you."

This next question was harder to ask. "Wh-why did you go?"

She bit her lip, looked nervous. Yeah, this was definitely the hard part, for both of them. "I . . . I need to be honest here, Fletcher, so I'll just tell you. I met someone. Here, on the beach, a few days before I left. I know it'll hurt to hear this, but . . . he made me feel new things, exciting things, and he made me question everything about where I was, what my life was about, what I wanted. He was leaving for L.A. and asked me to come. There was no time to think carefully. I wasn't completely sure about any of it—but I made the decision to go. And I hated hurting you—I hated it. But I believed we would both ultimately be better for it in the end.

"After all, if I wanted to leave, that meant it was best for you, too, right? How could we be happy if I stayed where I wasn't fulfilled?" She stopped, shook her head. "I'm not explaining this very well, but my feelings then were complicated."

"And now?" he asked.

She met his gaze fully. "Now they're much simpler. I've gone on that journey. And the journey has ultimately led me . . . back to you. But now I want to be here. Now I want to be your wife. Now I want our life together, just as it was—I want to see the world with you and meet new people with you and make what we had together even better. I'd reached a place of taking you for granted, Fletcher. But I won't do that again."

Fletcher could barely wrap his mind around all she was saying. It answered some questions, but created so many more. Was he happier now, now that she'd come waltzing back into his world? He was happy to know she was alive and well—but beyond that, he wasn't sure.

"The L.A. guy." He swallowed back the lump in his throat. He'd known that she was probably with someone, but having it verified still stung. "What happened to him?"

"We split up after a few months. He . . . wasn't a very good guy, it turned out." She looked sad, like that wound hadn't yet healed. And that stung, too. Because he sensed all her wounds were about someone other than him.

"There were other guys?"

She gave a short nod. "But in the end, they meant nothing."

"You mean in the end, they let you down."

She confirmed it with another nod.

And he explained, "When someone lets you down, it means something—*they* meant something. Otherwise, you wouldn't have been let down."

"Oh . . ." she said, clearly seeing his logic. "But . . . well, they meant nothing compared to you, Fletch."

He pulled in his breath. Pretty words. He wanted to believe them. "This is a lot to take in," he told her.

"I know." She reached to cover his hand with hers where it rested near the gearshift between them.

Instinctively, he pulled it away. "Sorry," he said. "It's just . . . awfully soon for touching." Even though he couldn't have imagined, even a few days ago, ever pulling away from her.

After a long, awkward moment of silence, the only sound that of crashing waves in the distance, she asked softly, "Who was that girl?"

Fletcher sighed and answered honestly. "She was the first woman to start making me think about someone other than you. But like you said, timing is everything."

"Meaning . . . I came back in time?"

He didn't know how to answer.

And before he concocted a reply, she asked, "Do you still love me, Fletch? Do you still have a place in your heart for me? Can we start over? Let me make things right. Let me make it all better. I know I can, if you'll just let me."

Fletcher could have said many things. He could have weighed many things. His heart hurt right now—far more than he'd have thought possible. When he'd envisioned Kim coming home, he'd expected only elation, pure bliss—and this was a far cry from that.

And yet . . . didn't he owe it to himself to keep believing?

He'd believed in this for so long, so long that he'd finally gotten what he wanted—so what sense would it make to turn his back on it now?

So he gave his wife one more simple reply. "Yes, Kim. The answer to all your questions is yes."

"So what exactly is up with you, Mary?"

Tamra lay wrapped in Jeremy's arms in the hammock. They still wore most of their clothes, albeit in a disheveled fashion, but now curled up in a blanket she'd grabbed on her way back from a trip to the bathroom.

Her head rested on his chest, but the question made her lift it slightly and peer down at him. "Up with me?"

He was grinning. "What makes you so contrary?" he asked, adding a wink.

She relaxed against that muscular chest again, thinking through her reply. She could have denied it again, but she knew it was true—at least with him. And yesterday, she wouldn't have dreamed of getting into something so personal with him—but given how much she'd opened up to him already, somehow it felt safer now. And maybe she even wanted to. So he'd know she actually had a *reason* for being a little contrary.

"I told you once before that I was raised on a commune."

"Yeah," he said, clearly ready to listen.

"Until I was ten, I led a pretty normal life. I lived with my parents and big brother in a suburb of Peoria, Illinois in a three-bedroom ranch house in a typical subdivision where all the kids rode bikes up and down the street and the dads took pride in their lawns while the moms baked cookies and hosted Mary Kay makeup parties. And I had no idea how good I had it until that life was taken away from me."

"What happened?"

She felt him looking at her but kept her eyes down, taking in the hair that sprinkled his chest, and her fingers, resting there, touching him. And she swallowed back the small lump that had risen to her throat.

Funny she still couldn't talk about this with ease—it was so long ago—but her feelings about it never really got easier; they only got pushed aside and replaced by better things. To talk about it was to go back there in a way, to relive it.

"My parents started going to church—but kind of a left-of-center church. My dad was really into it, and then Mom got into it, too. And at first it seemed . . . nice. That first Christmas after they started going, they asked my brother and I to give up a few of the gifts we would have normally received to donate to a needy family. And that was good, you know? It taught me not to be selfish, and made me aware that there were people who weren't as comfortable as us.

"Only then it got more radical. They spent more and more time with their church friends. And the next thing I knew, they were selling our house, packing up our things, and driving us in a caravan with five other families to a commune in Arizona."

She paused for a second, remembering the hardest parts. "I had to say goodbye to everything I knew—and then, after that, we suddenly weren't a family anymore. My parents became Don and Debbie, just two more adults in a place where I was suddenly told they were *all* my parents. I no longer lived with them or my brother—I was put in a bunkhouse with seven other girls near my age and a woman who supervised us. The whole commune ate in a big dining hall. We cooked together, we ate together, we planted a garden together, we attended daily worship ceremonies together. All as one, everything shared, the equity from our house and other assets going into the communal bank account.

"And so . . . if I'm a little weird in ways, that's why.

I was *raised* weird." She tried to give a little laugh, but thought it came out sounding as cynical as it felt.

"I can't imagine what that was like," he said. "To suddenly have your family not be . . . your family anymore."

"Yeah," she said on a sigh. "It was pretty awful. To suddenly have the people you love and depend on, the people who are supposed to love you back, just seem to . . . stop. They talked a good game about there being even more love for all of us there, but I never felt that."

"Seems like . . . a decision you shouldn't inflict on your kids," he said.

And she felt grateful that he understood. As much as anyone could understand without having lived it. "Exactly. And I've always resented them for that. It was a very strange existence. People there talked about love and caring all the time—they talked about how we all loved one another equally. And yet, when your family gives up their ties to you, it doesn't feel much like love. And even relationships formed with other people came without . . ." She stopped, trying to find the right words.

"Without?" he prodded.

"Reverence. Or accountability." And that made her tell him the rest. A short version anyway. "When I got older—sixteen, seventeen—more than one man there acted . . . well, as if he loved me. But all the talk about how much we all loved each other just painted a pretty face on sex—you know, they claimed it was all just them wanting to express their love and wanting me to express it back, but . . ." She stopped because it was difficult to share this. Even though she'd been young at the time, it still embarrassed her how easily she'd been taken advantage of.

"But they were only using me. And I guess I was pretty hungry for love of any kind by then. Real love, I mean. What my parents had taken from me. I had no one in my life that I could claim a meaningful relationship with. And each time a guy came along telling me I was pretty, and special, I bought into it, thinking they were going to love me in a real way.

"They never did," she added, even though she knew that was pretty obvious by this point. "And I just kept getting hurt over and over. And the odd thing was . . . most of the other people there had been so brainwashed that they didn't feel the emptiness of it like I did. Don and Debbie never regretted the move. They were still there when I left, and I haven't talked to them since, other than an occasional postcard. My brother learned to be happy there, too—but he found someone there to love who loved him back, and I suppose that could make a big difference."

"What made you leave?" Jeremy asked.

"The last man who let me down. He told me how much he loved me—at the same time he was telling three other girls the same thing and hopping from bed to bed and, as far as I could tell, believing this was entirely okay and that I was crazy for misunderstanding. I was twenty-one—he was thirty." She shook her head. "I was so vulnerable. And that's why . . . why I don't like to be vulnerable now. I like to be in control of my life and my feelings."

"Where did you go when you left?" he asked.

"I was given a little money—to be exact I was given one one-hundred-and-forty-seventh of what was in the communal bank account because there were a hundred and forty-seven people there at the time. It was enough to buy a used a car and rent a crappy apartment outside Tempe for a few months. I worked as a waitress at a truck stop and didn't like the clientele much. And so I saved just enough to keep myself afloat as I moved from place to place, selling as much of my art as I could, but it's a hard thing to get started in—clay costs money, glaze costs money, firing costs money.

"The whole time, though, I just had this idea that if I could get to Florida, I'd be happy. Crazy, I know," she said, shaking her head lightly against his chest as a slightly self-deprecating smile took her, "but I always idealized Florida. We'd taken one family vacation there when I was eight. I met Mickey Mouse and walked through Cinderella's castle and got to feel sand on my toes—and it all felt magical. Like a dreamland.

"And the really amazing thing is . . . I eventually found *this* place. Coral Cove. Six years after I left Arizona. And it doesn't sparkle like Cinderella's castle, but in its own way, for me, it's just as magical. Because it feels like home. Because my friends feel like family. Because it's safe, and a little old-fashioned, and no one in this town would ever stop loving their kid for no good reason.

"I've spent the time since then sort of . . . rebuilding my understanding of life, and reinventing my own. And mostly, I've done pretty well, I think."

"I'd say you've done amazing," Jeremy told her, and he meant it. Because damn, he couldn't have imagined everything hiding inside her. But now that he knew . . . well, it took everything murky about her and made it crystal clear. She wasn't so contrary, after all—she was just . . . surviving, the only way she knew how. Kind of like he'd been doing—except he thought Tamra had done a much more respectable job of it.

He was surprised when she lifted her gaze briefly to his, but then pulled her eyes back down, looking uncharacteristically sheepish as she said, "I wouldn't go so far as amazing."

"I would. Most people don't have what it takes to go after the life they want when it's that far out of reach."

She shrugged. "I suppose, but . . . it's not as if I don't have my issues."

He raised his eyebrows and teased her, saying, "Issues? What issues?"

"Like I said, sex and relationships were cheap where I grew up. Turned me off of it for a while."

"But I turned you back on?" he asked, casting a flirtatious grin. Damn, she drew that out of him so easy.

"Don't be smug," she kidded.

He just laughed. Something about her made him want to flirt and play. And given how long it had been since he'd felt that way, he kept wanting to indulge it. "Just wondering why me," he told her.

"Good question," she said with a smile—and he laughed out loud.

Though then it hit him. She'd just told him she hadn't had sex since she was twenty-one. And damn, that was . . . big. But rather than point that out, he decided to just be thankful he was the man who'd broken her long drought.

"There aren't a lot of single guys in Coral Cove," she pointed out. "And so I guess I'm just lucky you didn't get put off by my . . . being contrary."

"Who said I didn't get put off by it?" He flashed another grin, an additional wink.

And she smiled back at him. "Well, you've been willing to put up with it. More or less."

At this, Jeremy shrugged. "Musta thought you were worth it."

"You can be pretty contrary yourself, you know."

The accusation drew another chuckle from him. "Fair enough. Maybe we're birds of a feather."

Another contented expression reshaped her face, and he could tell she liked that idea. "Maybe *that's* why you."

Still, it made him laugh a little more. "Because we're both so hard to put up with that nobody else will?"

She laughed, too, and he squeezed her to him a little tighter, using one hand to grab playfully onto the feminine fingers resting against his chest.

She was right—they were rougher than most women's. And yet he liked something about that—the realness, the lack of affectation. Because that was how *he* was. Not how he'd always been—but how he was now.

"So what makes *you* so contrary, Mr. Bird of a Feather?" she asked.

He answered bluntly. "War. Post-traumatic stress syndrome, to be more exact."

"What kind of stuff . . . happened to you over there?"

He just looked at her. He hadn't expected her to ask so directly. Most people didn't. Most people knew that a guy with PTSD didn't want to talk about his PTSD.

And he suspected she could read that in his expression right now, but instead of backing away from the topic, she said, "I told you mine. Tell me yours."

Shit. She was right.

He still wanted to cop out, though. Because her stuff was a long time ago. And yeah, it was worse than he'd expected. But his stuff . . . his stuff couldn't be said. He'd only ever said it once, to Lucky. A drunken confession. But he wasn't drunk now. And felt suddenly thankful that he'd only had one of those little green mojitos they'd been handing out at the party—since he wasn't ready to tell her or anyone else his darkest secret.

Fortunately, however, there was plenty else he could fill in the blank with. Stuff that had scarred him, just not as bad as the part he didn't talk about. So he constructed another honest answer—just made it one he could handle. "I lost friends. Saw a lot of other death, too. Not sure what was worse—civilian casualties or seeing my buddies die. Fucking hated how out of control it all felt." His chest contracted—everything inside him had tensed, in fact. He wondered if she could feel it, too.

"Did you have to kill people?"

His eyes flew to hers. Damn, talk about direct. And she had no idea what a big question she was asking. "Yes," he said. Just that, nothing more.

"I'm sorry," she whispered.

"Thank you," he answered tightly. "Can we change the subject?"

She bit her lip, looking thoughtful, pretty. He liked how messy her hair appeared in the moonlight. "Maybe I should just . . . give you something better to think about."

"Like what?" he asked, eyes narrowing on her.

"Like this," she said.

And then she eased her hand down between his legs, directly into his still-open shorts.

"Let her run wild in the garden."

Frances Hodgson Burnett, The Secret Garden

Chapter 17

JEREMY LAY beneath her, a willing captive, as she straddled him in the hammock, hovering above him like some sexy angel. And then she lowered herself onto him, sheathing his hardness in her moist warmth. They both issued low moans at the pleasure of reconnecting.

He explored her body as she moved on him in that timeless rhythm, letting his hands glide over her soft thighs and round hips, letting them push upward to mold and caress her ample breasts. He stroked his thumbs over the taut nipples that jutted through her dress and bra. Damn, he hadn't even seen them yet—but he supposed there was plenty of time.

When she leaned her head back in passion, he took in the long swath of her neck, the curtain of messy auburn tresses that fell down her back and over her shoulders. He liked when her fingernails dug lightly into his chest.

And then he got to see her come again. And it was

a beautiful thing. Beautiful in any woman—but more so in her. Because it was the other side of her, the side she'd clearly spent years running from and denying. The side he and only he had brought out of her.

Watching her face flush with the climax, listening to her cries of sweet release waft downward, excited the hell out of him. So much that—aw God, yes—he was gonna come, too. She'd just barely finished, relaxing her body, bending to rest against his chest—when he said, "Aw—me too, honey, me too," and thrust himself upward in three rough drives that sent him blasting almost violently into her cocooning warmth.

Like last time, they didn't talk at first afterward, content to lie in each other's arms just soaking up the night.

Though after a few minutes, it crossed his mind that maybe she was being *too* quiet, and wondered if it was a hint. "Um, do you want me to leave, Mary? Not stay the night?"

She raised her head from his chest, a hint of alarm coloring her eyes. "No. Why?" Then she blinked, looking a little nervous. "Unless you want to."

Okay, he'd read her wrong. Good. But with someone who could be as prickly as her, he'd figured he'd better ask. Even if she'd stopped being prickly. Never knew when she'd start up again, after all. "I don't, and just checking," he told her with a wink.

A minute later, as he gazed up at the expanse of stars stretching out overhead, he said, "I like your hammock. You use it much?"

"Mmm hmm," she replied. "But . . . I've never used it this *well* before."

Her playful, contented smile was the last sight he

remembered before falling into one of the most peaceful sleeps he'd experienced in the last two years.

WHEN Tamra woke the next day, Jeremy still slept soundly beneath her. She lay watching him in the early morning sun, filled with awe. *Did last night really happen? Did I finally let go of all those old hang-ups? Am I really lying here with him right now? And is he really that hot?* She was still adjusting to how he looked now, wondering why he'd hidden that handsome face.

She bit her lip, stunned to recall how naturally she'd initiated that second round of sex, how easy it had suddenly felt to touch him, and to *be* touched by him.

He'd somehow given her back the confidence she'd lost so long ago. She felt . . . free, alive, and like anything was possible. It was like breaking out of a jail she'd built around herself without ever realizing it.

She smiled down on his sleeping form for a moment—and then eased out of the hammock without waking him. Heading inside, she put on a pot of coffee, then traded her dress for a pair of cotton drawstring shorts and a T-shirt.

After pouring coffee into a couple of big mugs, she carried them out to find him sitting in one of her Adirondack chairs.

"I don't know how you take yours," she said, handing him one of the large cups.

He accepted it and said, "I'm easy," with one of his cute winks. Winks that, a few weeks ago, she'd have called lecherous. But she'd learned to appreciate Jeremy's flirtatious streak.

She took a seat in the chair next to his, again think-

ing about how he'd entered her garden, her private
sanctuary, but how it was a richer place now for his
presence. And how it would now hold new memories
of a very different kind, how the space would take on
a whole new positive sort of energy for her. It had already been a place she loved and cherished, but she
suddenly loved it more for having shared it.

After they finished their coffee, he set his empty
mug on the stone wall of the fire pit and said, "I should
probably get going, Mary."

"Your cat is probably wondering where you are,"
she suggested with a grin.

His reproachful look came with an indulgent grin.
"He's not my cat. I'm a—"

"A dog guy, I know." She placed her cup beside his.
"I heard you named him."

He shrugged it off. "He hangs around all the time—
had to call him *something*."

And she replied with a playful roll of her eyes.
"Whatever you say, dog guy."

As he stood up, she did, too, pleased when he pulled
her into an embrace and gave her a long kiss goodbye
that left her literally weak in the knees. Not to mention
tingling between her legs again.

And as they walked toward the gate, hand in hand,
she couldn't help thinking that for a night she'd very
nearly screwed up, it couldn't have turned out any
more perfect.

Stopping at the garden's entrance, she thoughtfully
bit her lower lip and peered up into those striking blue
eyes of his to say, "I don't know if there will be more
of this, but . . . it was the nicest thing to happen to me
in a long time."

In response, Jeremy's gaze widened. "Why wouldn't there be more?"

She liked that answer.

Then he tilted his head. "I mean, unless . . . do you *want* more?"

"Yes." It was so much easier to just be bold with him now, just say what she meant.

"Me, too," he said with a confirming nod.

"Okay, then." She smiled up at him. "There will be more."

"So much more you might not be able to walk straight," he informed her.

At which she sucked in her breath, both in shock and anticipation.

One more wink from him as he said, "Bye for now, Mary." And then he was gone.

ALMOST as soon as Jeremy was gone, she found her phone and texted Fletcher. ARE YOU AWAKE? WE NEED A CATCH-UP SESSION. Normally, she might not go shouting such private news from the rooftops, but given her deal with him, it made sense. And she felt too good to keep it bottled up.

His reply a moment later: YOU HAVE NO IDEA. COME ON OVER. I'M ON THE PORCH. WE'LL HAVE WAFFLES.

Tamra wasted no time crossing the street, eager to hear what had transpired for her friend last night with Bethany, and just as anxious to share her own happy news. When she bounded up onto the covered porch that faced the ocean, she found Fletcher sitting at the wicker table already eating a waffle—and a plate with a second waffle set for her.

"Yum," she said.

"I woke up early—needed to do something, so I made waffles."

Two things struck her as she pulled out a wicker chair and took a seat. First, she still wasn't used to Fletcher's new look. And second, his clean-shaven face didn't appear nearly as happy as she might've hoped. "Why do you look bummed?" she asked.

But he shook his head. "You go first. My news is bigger than yours, and more complicated, so we'll save it."

She flinched, sitting up a little straighter. "That's a bold statement considering that you don't even know my news. It might be astronomical. In fact, I'd say it *is* astronomical."

"It can't beat mine, promise. Now spill." She'd seldom seen her friend look so tense.

And that sort of took some of the wind out of her merry sails, but she still tried to sound as joyful as she felt inside when she said, "I had sex with Jeremy last night. Twice. And it was amazing! I feel like I'm on top of the world. He just left." She paused, then gave a confident nod. "Astronomical, right?"

Next to her, Fletcher smiled. "You're right—astronomical." He set his fork on his plate to reach out and squeeze her hand. And he seemed more like his usual, happy Fletcher self when he said, "You look really happy. I'm so glad for you, Tam. I knew good things would come to you if you'd just drop your guard enough to let them in."

She nodded, because he'd been right about that. "So, do you still think your news is bigger?" she challenged.

And he picked his fork back up, cut off a bite of

syrup-covered waffle, and said, "Kim came home." Then shoved the chunk of waffle into his mouth.

All the blood drained from Tamra's face. "Okay, you got me. Your news is bigger."

"Yep," he said, still seeming a little too preoccupied by his breakfast.

She couldn't believe it. All this time he'd been right—his blind faith had actually somehow brought his wife back to him. Wow.

Only . . . why wasn't he out of his mind with joy? And that was when it hit her to ask, "Um, how come you're eating waffles with me and not her?"

"She's still asleep. We were up late talking."

"And, and, and . . ." Her mind raced—there was so much to ask that she could barely summon questions. But then she did. "Did she come find you at the party? How did she know where you were exactly? Where has she been? And . . . why don't you look happy about all this?" She *hated* that he didn't look happy. Because if you get the one thing in the world you want most and it doesn't make you happy . . . could anything?

He nodded. "Yeah, she came to the party. Later she told me she'd planned to start at the Happy Crab because that's where we were staying when she left. She didn't know if I'd still be here, but she had nowhere else to start, as I always knew would be the case.

"As for where she's been, a lot of places." He stopped, sighed. "Long story short, she was . . . unfulfilled. So she connected with other guys. Which sucks. But then she decided she wants me more than any of them. And I'm sure I'll start feeling the good part of that . . . once I process the rest."

Tamra's heart sank for him. "Oh Fletcher," she said softly. "That's the one thing we never thought about, isn't it? That when she came back, the reasons she went away might hurt."

He shrugged. "Maybe I knew they would. But I thought I'd be so happy it wouldn't matter. I guess something about having Bethany in the equation changed that. Maybe because, for the first time, I had started looking in another direction for that kind of happiness. And in one way, it scared me to death—but in another, I kinda liked what I saw."

Tamra drew in her breath, thinking it through. "Were you with Bethany when Kim showed up?"

He nodded, wiped a napkin across his mouth. "It was awkward and I felt bad about it."

"The timing's not your fault."

He nodded once more.

"I'm just sad that . . . *you* seem so sad. This isn't how it was supposed to be."

"I know," he said quietly.

Tamra tilted her head. "I mean, I was never really sure I believed she'd come back. But when I envisioned it, I always imagined you being . . . overjoyed."

"I saw it that way, too." His eyebrows knit as he dropped his gaze to his half-eaten waffle, then raised it back to her. And his expression again shifted to that of the more content, peaceful Fletcher, the man who had it all completely under control. "And it'll be that way. Soon."

Just then, the screen door behind them opened and a thin woman with shoulder-length brown hair stepped through it, wearing a too-large bathrobe that probably belonged to Fletcher. She smiled at him. "Good morning, Fletch." Then she shook her head, as if stunned by the sight of him. "It's so good to wake up to that face. More of that face that I've never even seen before," she added on a light laugh, and Tamra assumed that meant his wife hadn't ever seen him without a beard either.

"Morning, Kim," he replied, meeting her gaze, and Tamra could see him taking her in, too, still adjusting to the newness of it all.

Then she turned to Tamra. "I'm Kim. You must be Tamra. Fletcher told me so much about you last night. It's a real pleasure to meet you." She held out her hand and Tamra took it, gently shook it. "I hope we can be friends."

And Tamra said, "I hope so, too." Though what she really meant was, *I hope you'll spend every second of every day of the rest of your life treating this man like the prince among men that he is—and maybe then I can like you enough and forgive you enough that we can get along.*

"Should . . . I join you for breakfast?" Kim asked. "Or are you catching up and would rather talk privately? I can go take a shower or something." She pointed over her shoulder to the door she'd just exited.

But Fletcher said, "No, of course not—grab a plate. And there are more waffles in the kitchen."

Tamra had to admit Kim seemed polite. But she still wished Fletcher looked happier.

And she also thought the two of them probably needed alone time more than company right now. So, though she'd only eaten a few bites, she said, "Actually, I should run. I promised to help clean up after the party this morning." She pushed back her chair. "You two enjoy breakfast together, and . . . welcome home, Kim."

"Thank you," Kim said with a warm smile.

Yet even as she'd spoken those last words, it had struck Tamra that this wasn't Kim's home. Not yet anyway. It was Fletcher's home. And it was her home. And it was Reece's and lots of other people's home. And it was a great place to *make* a home. But Kim hadn't done that yet.

TAMRA soon joined Cami and Christy behind the Happy Crab to begin dismantling the props and decorations for last night's soiree. She dove right in, untying thick ribbons and colored netting from the backs of chairs, and stripping cloths from the round, rented tables. As the three of them moved around the space, Christy said to Tamra, "Have you talked to Fletcher? Do you know?"

Tamra nodded as she untied a bow. "Yep, and I just met her over waffles at Fletcher's."

Christy and Cami both stopped what they were doing to look at her.

"Well?" Christy asked.

"What's she like?" Cami inquired. "Are we going to like her?"

Tamra sighed. "Jury's still out. She was friendly, but . . ." She shook her head, looking back down, removing the next ribbon. "Fletcher seemed . . . sad."

Christy tilted her head. "I've never seen Fletcher sad before."

"Exactly," Tamra said. "Me, neither. It just seemed like . . . having her come back wasn't what he'd expected."

"Well, that truly sucks," Cami replied on a sigh of

her own as she carried a handful of used napkins to a large garbage can. "To wait so long and then not have it turn out the way he wanted." She shook her head. "Doesn't seem right."

"I know," Christy said. "Especially for the nicest, most optimistic guy in the world."

And then it occurred to Tamra to ask, "How'd Bethany take it?" She looked to Christy, who was packing up centerpieces.

She joined in on the sigh fest they seemed to be sharing. "She tried to shrug it off, claimed it was no biggie. And on one hand, I know they'd just met, and she rolls with the punches more easily than I ever did. But on the other, she's had a lot of letdowns with men. I hate that this is just one more. I'm afraid she'll give up on love completely—if she hasn't already."

Tamra's heart went out to Bethany. She understood about giving up on love. She knew what it could cost you, the walls it could make you build. "That's a shame," she said, but then it hit her to ask Christy, "Hey, what are you even doing here? It was your party and we threw it. You're not supposed to be cleaning it up, Miss Bride."

Christy offered an easy smile. "I'm filling in for Bethany. She was feeling crappy enough—even though she tried to hide it for my sake—that I insisted she take the morning to work. She's been painting some seascapes since she got here—that's new for her—and I thought getting absorbed in her art might make her feel better."

Tamra nodded. "Yeah, that always works for me, too. You're a good friend. Though Cami and I could handle this on our own, you know."

Christy replied, "Well, after all the Fletcher excitement last night, and all the big changes in people's appearances, maybe I wanted to get together and just . . . debrief." She raised her eyebrows.

And Cami, now breaking down the tables that had held the buffet last night, added, "I love your hair so much, Tamra—seriously! And your dress . . . well, let's just say you should show off your shape more often."

Just then, a big gray one-eyed cat came trotting up the same dock where Tamra had walked with Jeremy last night, and a few seconds later Jeremy followed, now wearing a T-shirt and blue jeans—which Tamra couldn't help noticing fit him just right.

"I second what she just said," he directed toward Tamra with a small, flirty smile.

She returned it. But then dropped her gaze to the other newcomer on the scene. "Out walking your cat?"

He laughed. "Um, no. Again, not my cat."

And when Tamra looked skeptical, he added, "We just . . . happen to be in the same place at the same time."

"You know," Cami said to Jeremy teasingly, "I own a cat leash. Though . . . it's purple. But you could borrow it if it wouldn't put a big chink in your masculinity. Or the cat's."

They all laughed, and Jeremy said, "Um, I'll pass. I don't think either one of us could handle that."

The cat had woven a path between the tables and made its way to the breezeway next to the office, and Jeremy had followed as they'd chatted with him. Though before passing through it, he looked back to ask, "You ladies need help with anything?"

"No, we're good," Cami said, "but thanks."

"All right then. Have a good one."

And Tamra said, "Have fun walking your cat."

And he tossed one more playfully sexy glance her way—just before he disappeared.

Turning back around, she let out a happy sigh and smiled to herself as she resumed her work on the bows.

And Cami softly said, "Oh my God."

Tamra looked over to find Cami eyeing her suspiciously and asked, "Oh my God what?"

"You had sex with him," Cami accused in a low but celebratory tone.

"What?" Christy chirped, her eyes nearly leaping from her head.

"Sex!" Cami said again. "You had sex." She looked to Christy. "They had sex."

"You want to keep it down," Tamra warned, teeth clenching slightly. "And quit saying *sex* over and over again."

Cami smiled. "But you did, didn't you? I could tell from the way you were looking at each other. And you haven't denied it."

Tamra took a deep breath. Then paused, hoping Jeremy was far enough away that he hadn't heard Cami—and that he wouldn't hear this, either. "Yes," she said in a hushed tone, stepping nearer to them. "We totally had rockin' hot sex in my garden." She couldn't hide another small smile.

"In your garden?" Christy asked, eyes still huge.

"In my hammock," Tamra specified.

And Cami began gently clapping her hands. "Oh my God, I'm so happy for you."

"Me too!" Christy said. "Especially now that he's so

darn cute! I mean, wow—I remembered he was always cute before, but I think he's even more handsome now."

"Do you think you'll do it again?" Cami asked.

"Yes," Tamra replied boldly, still smiling.

"Are you, like, a couple now?" Christy asked.

And Tamra tilted her head. "I don't know. I think we're just taking it one day at a time. But either way, I'm happy."

And the secret garden bloomed and bloomed and
every morning revealed new miracles.

Frances Hodgson Burnett, *The Secret Garden*

Chapter 18

IN THE days that followed, Tamra and Jeremy resumed work on the golf course. Since the artificial grass
had been installed on all the holes the previous week,
Jeremy began cutting and attaching the wooden borders around each green. While most modern courses
were using more natural boundaries like stone and
other landscaping materials, the Coral Cove Mini-Golf
Paradise had been designed to resemble those from an
earlier era, with a retro feel, right down to the coral-
colored details accenting it all.

And that was mostly what Tamra worked on—
painting the borders before Jeremy put them in place,
and finishing painting the hut. She was also busy placing orders for a cash register, snack foods, a soft drink
dispenser, golf clubs, and an array of colorful balls.

Of course, working together was entirely different
now. Now Tamra welcomed Jeremy's flirtation—even
if she sometimes had to bat his grabby hands away,

only because the course was situated right in the center of town where anyone could see them.

After the first day they worked together, Tamra wondered if Jeremy might come over that night. She sat outside in one of the Adirondack chairs with a glass of wine, almost waiting on him, almost willing him to come—but time passed and it got late and she realized it wasn't going to happen.

She looked at her cell phone and considered texting him, inviting him. Yet she decided against it. She didn't want to seem like she wanted him if he wasn't . . . in the mood. Or maybe he didn't want it to become a big, every night thing. Whatever the reason, despite her new confidence, she still decided to leave the next move to him.

The following night, as they were finishing up the day's work, Jeremy said, "So what's up tonight? Any chance I can interest you in grabbing a pizza with me at Gino's?"

And crap—she had plans. "I'm sorry—Fletcher and Kim invited me over to dinner after the Sunset Celebration. I think they want to try playing ordinary husband and wife. Or maybe she wants to get to know me. I'm not sure, but can't say I'm looking forward to it."

Jeremy had tilted his head and flashed a cute look. "Could always blow it off. And we eat the pizza in private somewhere so they never know."

Wow, she *so* wanted to eat pizza someplace private with Jeremy. And then do other things with him in private, too. But she let out a sigh and said, "I can't. He's too good a friend and this situation is too weird. I don't want to let him down. Another time, though?"

"Sure," he said. Perhaps a bit too easily, as if he'd felt *he'd* been blown off.

And she'd felt awkward.

Her dinner with Fletcher and Kim held some awkwardness of its own. They were both trying too hard to be normal, but it was apparent to Tamra that *nothing* was normal, at least not yet. Afterward, Fletcher walked Tamra back across the street to her house. "It's getting better," he told her. "We're talking a lot, working through issues. And she loved all the little gifts I got for her while she was gone. I've even convinced her we can be happy if we stay here and don't go back out on the road."

Tamra's eyes had gone wide. "She's trying to make you leave? Sell your house?"

"Don't worry—I've made her understand this is my home now. She's just afraid people here won't really accept her. But I've assured her they will. That's why I wanted you to come over tonight. And thanks for being pleasant to her. I know that might not be easy for you."

"I'm trying. For you," she said. Then admitted, "She's actually pretty nice."

"And what's up with your new *lover*?" he asked teasingly.

Her face warmed at the word, as he'd clearly intended. "Well, nothing new, but . . . let's just say we get along at work a whole lot better now." And she'd ended with a smile, but she also hoped there'd be something new to share soon.

It was two days of frustration and flirtation later that she was bent over Hole 14, inserting the little metal cup that would catch the ball, when she turned around and caught Jeremy checking her out.

She cast a playful smile. "See something you like, Mr. Dog Guy?"

"Sure do, Mary. Your ass."

She blushed hotly at his bluntness.

"Can I just be honest with you about something here?" he asked.

Hmm. She got to her feet and turned to face him. "Yeah, okay."

And her cheeks got even hotter when he said, "I'm so hard for you right now I'm about to bust my damn zipper. And I've been hard for you since about Sunday morning, since about an hour after I left your garden."

After a small gasp left her, a lump of something like anticipation rose to Tamra's throat. "Really?" Part of her couldn't believe he'd just said that, but then she remembered that Jeremy seldom minced words.

"Yep, really."

She tried to swallow back that anxious lump as a tingly sensation cocooned her whole body. "Then, um, what should we do about it?"

His eyes narrowed on her. "You could invite me over later. We could build a fire, eat that pizza next to it. And then we could have fun in your hammock again."

He was possibly the boldest man she'd ever known. The ones in her youth—they'd been bold, too, but in a different way. They'd been all about taking advantage of her innocence, deceiving her. But Jeremy was without guile. He was just himself, no pretending or strategizing or tiptoeing around anything. And even when it caught her off guard, she kinda liked it.

After all, *she'd* been tiptoeing around this for the past few days and it had gotten her nowhere. Clearly Jeremy had tired of that and had now taken them somewhere with a few simple sentences.

She let out a breath. "Okay, consider yourself invited."

WHEN Jeremy arrived with pizza following the Sunset Celebration that night, he found her in the garden, waiting with two glasses of wine beside a small café-style table he hadn't noticed on his previous visits. It was tucked away at the end of the stone path, painted in an array of colors and swirly designs, and he suspected she'd done the artwork herself. And for some reason, he had the feeling she'd never sat at the table with anyone else before. It felt like . . . a private place within her private place.

Music played softly over speakers he couldn't see—Marie Lambert singing about her secrets—and the lights in Tamra's trees gave the whole garden a magical essence.

She must have sensed him taking it all in because as she handed him a wineglass, she bit her lip and asked, "Too much?"

He shook his head. "No. Perfect. In fact . . . I can't think of anyplace I'd rather be with you."

Her expression softened, those pretty red spirals falling around her face, and he could see the sentiment touched her. "I'm glad you like what I've created here. It's . . . special to me."

"I guess I kinda feel that." He gave her a quick wink. "And even though I'm doing a hell of a lot better about being with people, there's still something pretty damn comfortable about . . . not. Being with them." Then he winced. "Not you, I mean. You I like." He leaned his head back, sighed. "I like lots of people. I just . . ."

"It's okay, I get it," she said on a soft trill of laughter. "I'm not always crazy about hanging out with other people, either. Why do you think I made this place?"

After they sat down and started eating slices of greasy pepperoni pizza on brightly colored plates she'd brought from inside, he asked about the table and chairs and learned that she had indeed painted them.

"I'd like to see more of your art," he told her. "Maybe after we eat you can show me."

Her eyes lit up. "Sure. My art is . . . what sustains me. Not only financially, but in my heart, I mean." Then she lowered her chin and looked more vulnerable than usual. "But . . . I kinda thought you weren't interested in that."

He blinked. "Why?"

She dropped her gaze to her pizza, yet then peeked back up at him. "Well . . . I invited you to come see it at the Sunset Celebration. But you weren't into it."

Aw damn—she'd misunderstood. But then again, he hadn't bothered to explain. Back then, it would have been too personal. Now, though . . . he could tell her. "It wasn't that I didn't want to see you, or your art. It's . . . crowds. Crowds aren't my thing, Mary."

She looked earnestly curious as she asked, "Why not?"

And Jeremy drew in a breath, let it back out. He was okay with telling her this, but it still made his chest tighten. "It's a war thing. When you're over there, crowds just mean trouble. They're unpredictable. You can't keep an eye on everybody—you can't control what happens."

"Oh." She looked both understanding and sad. "I never thought of it having to do with that."

He nodded. Most people didn't get it, he knew. "When I'm on the jobsite with you, or in the Hungry Fisherman, or hanging out behind the Crab, there are few enough people around that I can monitor the situation, keep a lookout for anything suspicious or weird."

"And you do that? In all those places?"

"Everywhere," he admitted. His thoughts went back to the Home Depot where he'd picked up work supplies several times now. "Not crazy about big stores, either, but doing better with that. And I'm cool with jogging on the beach at night when it's mostly quiet, or walking up the street to Gino's for a couple slices when there aren't too many cars driving down Coral Street. But the Sunset Celebration—or hell, even the beach in the middle of the day . . ." He stopped, shook his head. "I know, logically, it's fine. I know there aren't suicide bombers hanging out on the pier. But . . . just not my scene, like I said."

"I understand now," she told him. "Though . . . I'm sorry you miss out on it. It's nice. I think you'd have a good time. Without the crowd issue, I mean."

He just nodded. It embarrassed him a little, made him feel like a tough kid in the schoolyard letting his insecurities show. But at the same time he was glad to clear the air on it.

"Can I ask you about something else? Something that's none of my business?"

Hmm. *This is what you get when you start opening up to someone.* The question reminded him that everything came with a price, even something as simple as letting someone get to know you. "Sure, you can ask me anything." Then he grinned. "Can't promise I'll answer, but you can ask."

She returned the smile. "Fair enough. I'm just wondering how you ended up . . . well, without a home or income. Because, I mean, they pay you in the service, right? Even if you didn't get a job right away after coming back, I would have just thought—"

"I gave it away," he replied.

"What?" She looked surprised.

"I'd saved most of my pay the whole time I served. But I gave it all to someone after I was discharged. Someone who I thought needed it more than me."

She regarded him from beneath shaded eyelids. And he realized he'd have to tell her more. He'd answered without forethought, wanting her to understand his circumstances came with reasons—but if he didn't tell her who he'd given his money to, he'd seem like a guy who kept secrets. And in truth, he *was* keeping a secret—a damn colossal one. But he didn't want to seem shady or suspect. With Tamra, he didn't want to be that guy anymore.

"I had a buddy in Afghanistan named Chuck." He stopped, pressed his lips together, felt the weight of what he'd just said. "No, he was more than a buddy—he was my best friend. We went through a lotta kinds of hell together."

He stopped, remembering Chuck's face, his big goofy grin. He'd been the guy who could laugh through the rough times, lighten things up. The muscles in Jeremy's chest tightened, but he shut his eyes a second, pushed that away, and went on. "Chuck was killed."

"I'm sorry," she whispered.

He just shook his head. It was nice of her, but she shouldn't be sorry for *him*. "Thing is, Chuck had four little kids. The oldest is only ten now. And I knew even with death benefits, it just wouldn't be enough. And Chuck had big dreams for them. He wanted them to have opportunities, wanted them to go to college—the two oldest ones are bright as hell. So . . . not long after I got home, I drove from Ohio to Texas and wrote his wife a check."

"For all of it?" She looked a little amazed.

"Yep," he said. Then he let out a self-deprecating laugh. "Now thing is, when I did that, I thought I was in better shape. I thought I'd get a good job and be the hero everybody in my hometown thought I was. Only . . . it didn't work out that way. And hell . . ." He laughed again. "If I'd known then what I know now, I'd have kept a little of that money to help me get by. But guess I didn't think through that grand plan quite well enough, huh?"

"What happened, Jeremy?" she asked gently. "Why didn't you get that job? Why *weren't* you the hero your friends and family . . . thought?" She'd paused toward the end, her voice gone softer. And he heard it, that second when she realized what he'd said—*the war hero they thought I was.* And she knew now that there was something people didn't know.

Jeremy parked his chin in his palm, his elbow on the table. His fingers, curled into a loose fist, pressed against his mouth as he let his gaze drop to the open pizza box between them. And it struck him then—the military shrink had pointed out this gesture to him. "You do that when there's something you want to hide, something you don't want to say—you cover your mouth, cover part of your face." Even so, in the end, Jeremy had convinced him he was okay.

Tamra tuned in to his unease. "You don't have to tell me if you don't want to. And the fact that you gave your income to that family—Jeremy, that's tremendously selfless. You should be proud of that."

Still letting his fist cover his mouth, he raised his eyes to her. "Proud? No," he said. "It's not a pride thing. It was just . . . the thing I had to do. The only *decent* thing." He stopped, drew in a breath. "If anything about any of it could be called decent," he heard himself mutter.

Across the table, she bit her lower lip, and he could see her trying to read what was going on behind his eyes, wanting to know more. Shit, how had things gotten so freaking serious here? This wasn't what he'd had in mind when he'd suggested this.

And . . . hell, she was so pretty. He'd always thought that, but he could swear that just since the party she'd somehow gotten even more so. It was as if her skin was softer, glowing, her eyes a deeper shade of green with a brighter sparkle. Her hair now fell about her face in a way that softened everything in her demeanor. Or . . . maybe *he'd* done that. In the hammock with her.

"Would you mind," he asked, "if we didn't talk anymore?"

Full darkness framed her face now, her eyes as illuminated as the tiny bulbs strung in the trees. "Sure," she said. Though she looked as if she felt bad now, and he didn't want that.

"I came here," he told her, "because you make me feel . . . better. Better than I do most of the time. And I think I make you feel good, too. And I'm looking at your beautiful face and thinking: Why the hell am I telling her all this heavy shit when all I really want to do is have my way with her?"

Across from him she sat up a little straighter in her chair, tensing slightly. Her lips pressed into a thin, straight line. And he thought maybe he'd said the wrong thing—until she replied, "Then I think you should have your way with me."

> "The magic in this garden has made me
> stand up and know I am going to live . . ."
>
> Frances Hodgson Burnett, *The Secret Garden*

Chapter 19

*H*E SAT up straighter, too. He hadn't seen that coming. But damn, he liked it.

And after that, things went fast. He stood up, reached down for her hand, pulled her to her feet as well. He drew her to him by planting both his splayed hands on her ass, his fingers curving tight into her flesh. And despite how somber things had gotten there for a few minutes, almost as soon as his pelvis connected with hers, he went hard as granite.

She sucked in her breath, and he locked his gaze on hers. "See what you do to me, Mary?"

"I'm not feeling very contrary right now, just so you know. I'm feeling downright agreeable, in fact. To about anything you want."

A low groan left Jeremy's throat. He gazed down on her darkly. "Who knew you'd become my dream woman?"

She bit her lip, looked sweet and sexy as hell at the

same time. "Didn't exactly think you'd become my dream guy, either—but here we are."

He kissed her, hard. Because yeah, being anyone's dream of anything had seemed pretty damn far out of reach even a couple of weeks ago. So her words were like a gift to him, and he wanted to give her something back, even as he took from her.

He stopped the kisses long enough to look down, take in all that she was. She wore a long, pretty skirt like he'd seen her in before, but her top was more delicate, feminine, and low cut, a swath of lace making a "U" across her breasts. He let his hands glide upward over her curves and onto that lace. Like the last time he'd touched her there, his thumbs instantly found nipples hard enough to jut through her bra and top.

"My one regret last time was not getting to see these, kiss these," he told her.

A soft whimper left her. A perfect invitation.

And so he reached for the hem of the fitted lacy tank and said, "Lift your arms, honey."

She obeyed—and he took the top off over her head.

Her bra was cotton candy pink and couldn't have hugged her bountiful curves more beautifully. And the color of the bra—it felt the way discovering this garden had, like one more soft piece of her most people didn't get to see, one more soft piece of her he'd sensed all along and was happy to uncover.

He didn't want to leave it on, though—so he reached for the straps on her shoulders and drew them gently down. She gasped slightly and he grew even harder behind his zipper. "I want to see you," he rasped.

And in response, she reached up behind her back and smoothly unhooked the bra. A second later, it fell between their feet. And Jeremy wasn't sure he'd ever seen a prettier sight than Tamra standing topless in her garden, seeming all the more pure and natural for it.

He followed the urge to take her lovely breasts back into his hands, to mold and knead, to bend and take one taut pink peak into his mouth. The whimpery moans that followed fueled him; her fingers threaded through his hair. And part of him wanted to kiss and lick and suck her breasts forever—but that quickly he needed more, needed to kiss her someplace else entirely.

Rising up, returning his kisses to her lush lips, he reached down to begin gathering her skirt into his fists. And then he eased her back, back, off the stone path and up against the thick trunk of a palm tree.

When she spoke, it came out broken, thready, breathless. "Should—should we go somewhere? Else?"

He was already dropping to his knees before her in soft grass, the light fabric of her skirt still between his fingers and pushed to her hips. "No," he said firmly. "Here." Then he lowered the pink-flowered panties he discovered underneath. She gasped. And he liked exciting her.

"Hold up your skirt." He spoke more softly now, pleased when she did as he asked, using both her hands to raise it to her waist. Taking in every feminine curve and plane of her body, he pushed her panties the rest of the way down until they dropped to her ankles—and then she lifted her sandaled feet one at a time to shed them completely.

After which he used both hands to part her thighs.

Above him, her quick intake of breath drew his

gaze to her face. He found her head tipped back, eyes shut. Her easy surrender to a pleasure he hadn't even yet delivered tightened his chest—and his cock. Somewhere in the recesses of his brain he became aware of Hoobastank singing "Disappear," and realized he felt like that, about her, right now. She made the whole *world* disappear when he was with her.

When Jeremy's tongue pressed into her most intimate flesh, Tamra whimpered—then curled her fingers more snugly into her skirt as the sensations flowed through her as thick as hot lava, as fast as lightning. Part of her couldn't believe this was really happening, and yet in another way, it felt entirely natural, like exactly how things were supposed to go. For the woman inside her who'd run from men and sex for so long, it felt foreign, daring, and yet for the part of her that had burned with desire lately, it only felt . . . perfect.

She bit her lip as jagged pleasure zigzagged through her body—each movement of his tongue, mouth, rocketing her higher and higher. Orgasm didn't take long arriving, and as it rushed through Tamra with the power of a mighty storm, she'd never felt freer. She didn't try to squelch her cries of bliss, she didn't resist the need to drive the crux of her thighs against his mouth—she drained every last drop of pleasure from it before she went quiet and still.

She opened her eyes long enough to lock gazes with the man on his knees before her, but then her own knees gave out and she let her eyes drop shut again as she began to slide down the palm tree, needing to recover.

Only Jeremy bolted to his feet just then—and caught her in his arms, and after a quick kiss to one of her breasts, he rasped near her ear, "Turn around, honey."

"Huh?" she murmured, tired.

But he was already shifting her to face away from him, toward the tree. After which he took her hands in his from behind and pressed them to the palm's wide, smooth trunk, covering them with his own. Her skirt had fallen back into place, but that didn't stop her from feeling his sturdy erection against the center of her ass. "Oh . . ." she moaned. For a few seconds she'd thought she needed that recovery period pretty badly. But maybe not.

His palms slid up her arms, over her shoulders, down her back, onto her hips, his thumbs digging into the soft flesh of her bottom. Instinctively, she arched for him, thrusting her rear against that perfect hardness between his legs.

And then he was wadding her skirt back in his fists, using one hand to free himself from his blue jeans, and then—oh God, he was pushing his way into her waiting body. She bit her lip, shut her eyes, drank in the evening air cooling around them, and arched a little further.

"Mmm, yes," she whispered as he sank deeper, filling her to the brim.

As he began to plunge into her, again, again, each stroke vibrated outward, all the way to her fingers and toes, until she went light-headed with the resounding pleasure. It was like the hard beat of a drum that sounded over and over and over, each beat taking her farther into a heady oblivion she'd never experienced.

When she'd been young, her sex had been focused around climaxing—that had been the one and only part she enjoyed. But this, now, was more. Maybe it came with maturity. Or maybe her body and needs had changed. Or maybe Jeremy was just a magnificent lover. But the pleasure that pummeled her over the next few minutes had nothing to do with orgasm and everything to do with having her body rocked and filled and consumed with near-blinding sensation.

She cried out—again, again. And at one point, it occurred to her that the neighbors might hear—but then she let go of the thought. Which was careless for her—but it was also care*free*, and that seemed like a quality worth embracing.

"Aw, aw God, baby," he murmured behind her, his voice thick and deep with passion. "God, I'm gonna come now—hard."

And he did. So hard that Tamra had to clench her teeth, her high-pitched cries fighting their way through as he pounded into her in four last mighty plunges. It nearly brought tears to her eyes. But when he went still, when it was over, she realized they were tears of pure, undiluted joy.

HALF an hour later, she sat curled up in Jeremy's lap in one of the Adirondack chairs next to the fire he'd built. They were wrapped in a blanket, drinking wine from the bottle she'd opened earlier. She'd turned the music off—the only music now was the crashing waves in the distance.

Beneath that palm tree with him, she had experienced a passion so profound she'd not have believed she could share it with someone she'd known such a short time. But then, she supposed it had come with being so open.

The truth was, there were moments when she felt hints of awkwardness—when she was still learning how to touch him, still learning what it was like to *be* touched. But she supposed awkwardness was only truly awkward when you let it be. When you were with someone who made you comfortable, it wasn't really awkwardness at all—it was just . . . trial and error, learning how to connect together. It was . . . a form of trust. Wasn't *all* sex a form of trust in a way? Trust the other person to like what you do, to make you feel good about it as you let them see those private, personal parts of you that come out only at the most intimate moments in life.

The thoughts brought to mind something Jeremy had said to her the first night they were together, back before she had achieved that trust. "Were you right—is it my best? When we're having sex?"

Tipping the bottle to his mouth, he appeared to be thinking it over. "I'm not sure it's the *best*," he said a moment later, "because there's a lot *to* you, and a lot of best in you. But either way, it's a damn good part of you, I promise. And I love getting to see it."

Her heart warmed. And given her past, the sweet talkers of her youth, it would be easy to doubt, grow wary—but she'd didn't. Because she could feel his honesty—always had. Whether he was threatening to drop a bush on her feet or telling her she was beautiful, there was no pretense inside him.

"It's nice to be able to . . . be open. It's not my usual way."

He shifted his gaze in her direction, gave her one of his sexy winks. "I gathered that, Mary."

It eased a smile from her. "Thank you. For helping me . . . be that way. Giving me someone I can be that way *with*."

"Just so you know, you kinda do that for me, too." He took another drink, then passed her the bottle.

"You don't seem like you could be any other way," she told him. "You're always just so . . . you."

And he gave his head a speculative tilt in reply. "That's . . . good, I guess," he said. "Truth is that I used to be pretty good at . . . hiding my feelings. Being who people wanted me to be. A couple years of being anti-social took that outta me, I guess. And I didn't think it was a good thing. But maybe it's okay."

She wanted to reassure him. "With you, I always know I get the real thing, the real you. And mostly, that *is* a good thing. Except for maybe when you're shoving people out of your way with large pieces of landscaping."

He let out a laugh and she noticed how his shortly trimmed beard allowed her to see dimples she hadn't before. "I've told you a thousand times, it was heavy!"

She laughed, too. Took a drink of wine. But then got a little more serious. "About before . . . I'm sorry if I pried." It was the only time in their acquaintance that he'd refused to tell her something, the only time he'd held back.

But Jeremy shook his head. "No—I'm glad I got to explain. I don't like you thinking I'm really some homeless-type dude. Thing is, I'd accidentally sponged off my sister and her husband too long before coming here. And that's why I didn't tell John and Nancy Romo

I was in town—I didn't want to end up taking advantage of their kindness, too. They're good people and would have insisted on helping me out, but I needed to make my own way—even if it came with a rough start."

"If you . . . wanted to tell me about what you didn't before, about your friend, you could. You don't have to, but you could."

Jeremy took back the bottle Tamra offered, thinking about what else she'd just offered, as well. He swallowed another drink, feeling the wine—they'd nearly killed the bottle and it had seemed like unusually potent stuff.

He knew he should just shut up and kiss her.

And yet instead . . . he heard himself beginning to tell her. Just a little. "I was a squadron leader. Helmand Province. That's where a lot of action took place."

He wouldn't tell her everything. But just a little would be okay.

"It was cold in winter, just like it is here, up north. A lot of people think it's always hot over there, but they have winter just like us."

Because it touched him that she wanted to know, and that she cared.

"We'd been stationed near Kandahar a couple months."

"When Chuck died, you mean?"

He nodded. For him, everything about Kandahar revolved around when Chuck had died. "The weather had just turned, the temps dropping quick at night to below freezing." He took the last drink, draining the bottle, then gently lowered it beside them onto the stone pavement beneath the chair. "We were all surprised how cold it was—even with our gear on." He glanced over at her. "We were out on a night raid in a nearby village. Mostly deserted except for Taliban."

"Were you there when it happened?" she asked softly. "Did you . . . see it?"

When Chuck died. That's what she meant. He didn't have to ask. "Yeah," he said, staring into the fire—but seeing other things.

"I'm sorry," she whispered.

It made Jeremy give his head a brisk, short shake to correct her. "Like I said before, don't feel bad for me. I don't deserve any sympathy. It was my fucking fault."

Shit, he'd really just said that.

The air around them felt thicker than it had a moment before, seeming to stand still. No breeze, no palm fronds swaying overhead, no nothing.

His heart suddenly beat too hard, and his stomach sank like a stone.

And a veil of silence dropped over the garden—until she said ever-so-gently, "How? How could it have been your fault?"

When he didn't answer, his throat threatening to close up, she said, "I'm sure that's survivor's guilt speaking, Jeremy."

The words made him dart his gaze from the fire to Tamra's face. "No, it's way worse than survivor's guilt. Don't worry, I have that, too—I lost more friends than just Chuck and there's no understanding why them and not me. But . . ." It was hard to keep talking around the thickness in his throat now, almost even hard to breathe. "What happened with Chuck was different."

"Different how?" asked the woman in his lap.

Different how? Simple question. Fucking complicated answer.

Or . . . then . . . maybe it wasn't complicated at all. Maybe it was only complicated and muddled in his head. Maybe the real answer was way simpler than he wanted it to be.

And he knew he didn't have to reply. He knew she probably wouldn't push him if he shut her down, like before. But for some reason, more words— the honest, simple truth of the matter—went spilling from his lips. "I'm pretty sure I did it. I shot him."

"When I lie by myself and remember, I begin to have pains everywhere and I think of things that make me begin to scream because I hate them so."

Frances Hodgson Burnett, *The Secret Garden*

Chapter 20

*H*ER GASP was quick but audible. Followed by one word. "No."

He'd looked away from her again, letting his eyes get lost in blue flames a few feet away. But now he peered back at her. Met her gaze head on. Even if it was harder this time. "Yeah," he corrected her. Only then he began to tremble, just slightly. "I didn't mean to."

"Of course not." Horror filled her eyes now and he was sorry as hell he'd told her.

How the fuck had that even happened? Since when did he go spilling his guts to *anyone*, and spilling his worst, deepest, ugliest secret at that?

He felt like . . . a monster. Someone who hurts people.

Was that how she'd see him now?

"I'm not—it was just—" Shit. He stopped talking, tried to catch his breath.

Beneath the cover, she was touching his chest now, then running one hand up over his shoulder, neck, trying to soothe him. "It's okay, Jeremy—it's okay."

But no amount of comfort could make this better. "It's not okay. It'll never be okay."

"You—you didn't do it on purpose. And . . . you said 'pretty sure.' What does that even mean? Why do you even think . . . ?" She trailed off and he knew she didn't want to push him any deeper into the memory, but at the same time she wanted to understand.

And hell—now that he'd dropped this shit on her, *he wanted her to understand, too. As much as possible* anyway. Although, even now, there really wasn't any understanding it. He gave his head a quick shake, trying to clear it, trying not to get too mired in the ugliness.

"There . . . there was gunfire all around us," he told her. "My buddy Marco was with me, but we were separated from the rest of my guys." His heart boomed so hard against his chest it hurt, but he tried to keep talking, tried to stay as calm as he could. "We took cover." *Breathe in to four, breathe out.* "In an abandoned stone hut." *Breathe in to four, breathe out.* "But we knew the bad guys were coming. Saw them headed our way before we ducked inside."

Shadows. Images of them filled his head. Dark shadows moving through the dark night. Shadows with guns. Same as he'd been a shadow with a gun.

"Three, four, five Taliban came in bullets flying," he said, "and we returned fire."

War games. He'd always been so good at them. Praised. Promoted. Trusted.

He'd trusted *himself*, too.

He never fucked up. Never.

Until . . .

"And then a sixth man came in . . ." His chest went hollow. "And I thought he was one of them." Stomach, too. "But when it was all over . . ." More thickness filled his throat. "Chuck lay there dead."

He let out a sigh. "He'd been coming for us, coming for me and Marco. I don't even know where from—like I said, I'd lost the rest of my squadron. Somehow Chuck had been more plugged in on my locale than I was myself." *Breathe in to four, breathe out.* Hell, was there irony in using breathing techniques learned in the military for combat situations to get him through talking about killing his best friend in one?

It had been a long time since Tamra had spoken—and when she did, damn, the sound of her sweet voice reminded him he was in a safer place now. No more Helmand. No more shadows. At least not the kind with guns.

"But you're not sure," she said. "Not sure you did it."

He swallowed past that damn lump in his throat—it was getting on his fucking nerves. Made him realize he hadn't felt that so much in a while. He used to feel it all the time. "Not a hundred percent, no," he told her. "Too many bullets flying. But the way we were positioned . . ." *Breathe in, breathe out.* "It's unlikely the fire came from an enemy gun."

"Don't they investigate stuff like that?"

Breathe in, breathe out. "When they have reason to suspect friendly fire, sure—they investigate the hell out of it." *Breathe.* "But not all friendly fire ever gets reported." *Breathe.* "And it's not something the military likes hearing about—hell, nobody likes it. For obvious reasons. But it happens." *Breathe.* "Probably more than people want to believe." *Breathe.* "In close combat, it's fucking hard to keep track of what's going on—I don't care what anybody says."

"I can understand that," she said. Her voice stayed sweet, calm. He'd never noticed that before, that sweet quality. He let himself focus on it—let it calm him, too.

Even as he let the rest out.

"And so, I'm pretty sure I killed my best friend. And I guess when you break it all down . . . that's why I have nightmares, that's why I hid at my brother-in-law's for so long, that's why I didn't give a shit about anything. Because . . . it was just hard to want to live after that. Hard to look in the goddamn mirror." And it hit him for the first time. *Maybe that's why I quit taking care of myself. Easier to look in the mirror if I don't really see myself there.*

He was done now, spent, ready to shut the hell up.

Maybe she sensed that because she lifted her hand to his face, cupped his jaw, gently kissed his lips. And it was perhaps the nicest kiss he'd ever received.

"I think," she began gently, "that you should try to let this go."

He flashed her a stunned look, but before he could say a word in protest, she pressed one art-roughened fingertip over his lips and went on. "Your heart is broken, I know. But you've done all you can."

"I . . . I never . . . told anybody." It came out sounding hoarse. "His wife. My commanding officers. The shrink I saw before discharge."

"What good would that do? What good would it do *anyone*? It wouldn't, and you knew that. And you've tortured yourself enough. I'm sure your friend wouldn't want that. And I'm not suggesting that letting go of it is easy. And I'm not suggesting forgetting about it. I'm just saying you should . . . consider forgiving yourself. That's all."

"But—"

She literally reached out and clamped his lips together between her fingers. "No *but*," she said in that same gentle tone. "All I'm looking for here, all I'm wanting you to say is: 'I'll try.' "

She pulled her hand away, and he instinctively began to say, "But I—"

This time her fingertips only pressed down on his mouth, effectively shutting him up again. "*I'll try*," she said, enunciating very clearly, eyes wide on his. "That's all I want to hear, nothing else."

"Or?" he challenged her.

She pressed her fingers back down over his mouth. "Or this. I can do this all night, you know. So you might as well just see things my way. Now—what do you have to say for yourself, Sheridan?"

She drew her fingertips away. Waited. Oddly, part of him wanted to laugh—it was funny, her physically shutting him up. And that made it easier. To think it over for a minute and to just give her what she wanted. "I'll try," he said.

And he didn't think he meant it. Except when the words left him . . . well, sometimes it was hard to say something without feeling it. Especially given that he quit putting on acts a long time ago. So he was saying it only to appease her, but . . . at the same time, deep down inside, there was a tiny part of him that meant it.

And as they went quiet again, letting the crackle

and pops of the fire compete with the distant roar of the surf, Tamra snuggled more closely against him, resting her head on his shoulder. And it was nice. Nice to have . . . her forgiveness, even if he didn't have his own. Nice to let the crash of waves—rolling in, rolling out—soothe his soul.

Nice sound. *Worth coming to the beach alone just for that.* The slow rhythm of it was like . . . breathing. And that was when he realized his own had relaxed. *Everything* in him had relaxed.

He'd been wrong. About her comfort.

It worked.

ALTHOUGH he sometimes drove out to Route 19 to grab some fast food when the urge for something different struck, most nights Jeremy still got his dinner at the Hungry Fisherman or Gino's, and he'd also gotten in the habit of doing it while the Sunset Celebration took place. Because when people were at the beach, they weren't at the Hungry Fisherman or Gino's.

And since his talk with Tamra the other night, he'd connected with her most evenings *after* the Sunset Celebration, and he had plans with her tonight too, but was stopping into the Fisherman in the meantime.

After baring his soul to her, two things had happened.

He'd realized that maybe telling someone had actually been an okay thing to do. Giving it voice was hard—almost like . . . reliving it. But it had also shown him that maybe he *wasn't* a monster. He didn't want to be absolved—he still didn't think he *deserved* to be absolved—but it had shored up something inside him to find out he could tell her something like that and not have it change how she saw him.

The other thing was that . . . well, he was a long way from forgiving himself, but . . . getting *her* forgiveness made him feel something new. That life was going to go on. *His* life. He'd put that on hold for a long time now. And even coming to Coral Cove had only been one tiny change, mainly driven by the desire not to burden his relatives. But something in that unexpected conversation had made him realize that if he was alive, existing, breathing, he needed to keep moving forward.

As he walked across the parking lot that led from the Happy Crab to the Hungry Fisherman, he found a certain cat underfoot. It was freaking uncanny sometimes how quick the cat appeared from nowhere the second Jeremy stepped outside. "Do you lie in wait for me or something?" he asked Captain as they crossed the asphalt.

"Meow," Captain said.

Jeremy rolled his eyes. "I'll take that as a yes." Then, nearly tripping over the damn cat as usual, he said, "Bud, couldn't you just hang back at the motel? The fish is coming. You know that. So be cool, huh?"

Of course, Captain didn't seem to take that to heart. A dog would. Even if a dog didn't exactly speak English, they still had a way of grasping what you wanted them to do and doing it—at least some of the time. *Which is why I'm a dog guy.*

Fortunately, Jeremy got in the door of the restaurant without the cat getting in, too. He sat down in his usual booth and, fifteen minutes later, Polly had taken his order and brought him a fish sandwich, coleslaw, and fries.

He was halfway through the sandwich when Abner, wearing a Tampa Bay Buccaneers winter hat complete with a fuzzy ball on top, slid into the padded seat across from him. "How's your fish?" the older man asked.

"Good," Jeremy said, a little taken aback as usual when Abner engaged with him.

Then Abner abruptly changed the subject. "You look serious tonight. Somethin' on your mind?"

Jeremy thought he probably looked serious *most* nights—but maybe the recent haircut revealed his expression more. And having the man offer to lend an ear caught him off guard just as much as everything else with Abner. So Jeremy said, "Guess I'm thinking about my future."

"That's a mighty big subject, son."

"Yep," Jeremy agreed. "But the golf course will be done soon. I'm gonna need another job, and hopefully something not as temporary."

Across from him, Abner nodded repeatedly, appearing to think this over. And finally he said, "Jobs are a dime a dozen. I could put you to work in the kitchen or you could get any of twenty different jobs if you headed out to all the retail on the highway. But seems to me it'd be a good time to start doin' somethin' you feel passionate about."

"I've been thinking the same thing," Jeremy confided.

"Then what do you feel passionate about?"

He'd been thinking that over, too, and kept coming back to one thing. "I like building." He'd liked it more lately than he had anticipated. Maybe it was like . . . his own personal kind of art. Not the same thing as what

Tamra did, of course, but he'd discovered it felt good to create something that hadn't been there before.

"Well, that's handy, 'cause there's always construction goin' on up and down the coast."

"Problem is," Jeremy said, "I'm not skilled enough, haven't had much training. I know enough to put up a golf hut. And I can follow instructions and learn. But I probably couldn't handle a project much bigger than that on my own."

Abner turned that over in his head for a minute before he said, "Seems to me like you need some sorta mentor, somebody to teach you those skills."

Jeremy hadn't thought he'd want to be anybody's student at thirty-four, but damn, that suggestion sounded good. The idea lifted his heart unexpectedly.

Though he had no idea where a guy got such a mentor. And he was just about to say that when Abner read his mind. "Let me call up a friend of mine, a fella who owns a big construction outfit, see if he'd he willin' to hire you on, teach you some of what he knows."

"You have a friend?" Jeremy asked without missing a beat.

And Abner laughed. "See why I like you? You aren't afraid to give me a hard time. Most people don't pay me much attention and I'm good with that. But . . . gotta admit I like you."

"It may surprise you to hear this, Abner, but I've grown fond of you, too."

When Abner stood to go a few minutes later, he said, "Have a nice evenin' and enjoy feedin' your cat the fish Polly slips you across the counter."

"You know about that, huh?"

" 'Fraid so. I notice more than folks realize, includin'

that one." Abner motioned over his shoulder to his wife as she headed toward the kitchen.

"I can pay for the cat's food." Maybe that made sense, actually, now that he was getting more financially stable.

But Abner swiped a hand down through the air and said, "Naw, no need. As long as I don't have to live with a cat or have a cat runnin' around in here, you two can feed the thing all ya want."

He started to walk away then, but Jeremy felt the need to correct him on something. "It's not my cat, just so you know."

And Abner simply chuckled. "Whatever you say." Then went on his way.

Jeremy just rolled his eyes, even though there was no one there to see it.

These cat accusations were getting ridiculous.

A week after Jeremy had told Tamra his big secret, she sat at a table on Christy's side porch with her and Bethany, helping to decorate tiny bottles of bubbles to be blown at the wedding in lieu of throwing rice or birdseed. The calendar page had turned to October and the wedding was only a couple of weeks away now.

"Did you decide which one you want?" Bethany asked Christy. Now that Tamra's fellow artist had painted a number of beachscapes, Christy planned to select one as a wedding gift. Tamra had seen the paintings and was duly impressed. She'd never seen Bethany's cityscapes, which she understood had been her primary focus up to now—but she thought the girl had been born to paint the beach.

"I'm leaning toward the sunset with the most pink

in it," Christy said. "That one just glows—it's like you captured light on canvas."

"Excellent choice," Tamra said, then shifted her gaze to Bethany. "And now that Christy has made her pick, I'm going to look at the rest and buy one from you, so think about what you want for the various pieces."

"That's generous, Tamra," Bethany said with a smile, "but I'd be happy to just give you whichever one you like."

"No, *that's* generous," Tamra replied. "But I'm big on supporting other artists and I know you are, too—we all need that to get by in this business. I'll be getting a beautiful piece of art for my home and I want to give you what it's worth." Then she tilted her head, adding, "And that reminds me—I've been thinking you should set up a table at the Sunset Celebration. It's a great venue."

Bethany had attended the nightly event with Christy several times since her arrival. "Oh, I agree it's great. But . . . don't you think my pieces are too big, and maybe a little too pricy, for the vacation crowd?"

Tamra turned that over in her head. "Maybe, maybe not. People will spend a lot on something they love. And . . . you could also start doing smaller canvases that could be priced lower. Everyone wants something to take home from their beach vacation."

Bethany narrowed her gaze and scrunched her lips a little, thinking it over. "Hmm," she said. "Okay, sure, why not. What do I have to lose?"

Tamra had really come to admire the younger woman's bold, go-for-it attitude. Especially now that she was reaping some benefits of going for something *she'd* wanted.

Jeremy and she had connected more nights than not

in the past week, and it had remained mind-blowingly hot even as it grew still more comfortable. Now they discussed their plans with ease rather than tiptoeing around the issue. If one of them was tired and wanted to just lie low, the other didn't take that personally. And on the rest of the nights, well . . . heaven had come to Tamra's own backyard.

Her garden had quickly come to feel more like *their* place than hers alone now. Sometimes it was all sex, sex, sex—sex in the hammock, sex by the fire, occasionally even sex in her bed of all normal places. Other times, though, it was talking. About her past and his. They never pushed each other, but it had just become easy to share now, in a way she knew neither of them shared with anyone else.

And Jeremy had finally seen her art and seemed impressed—he'd even commissioned special pieces for his sister and mother for Christmas, along with one for Polly, as well.

That had surprised her. "Polly?" she'd asked.

"She's been good to me," he'd said easily. "And she doesn't have a lot of pretty things in her life—so she might like something pretty, something that catches the light." For her he'd requested a stained glass suncatcher shaped like a cat.

"But you're not a cat guy," Tamra had reminded him, her voice dripping with sarcasm.

"Nope," he'd insisted. "This is for Polly, not me—remember?"

The sounds of muffled voices from behind Christy and Jack's cottage brought Tamra's thoughts back to the present, reminding her that Fletcher and Jack were currently finishing up the arbor in the backyard.

And Tamra hoped this wouldn't be a bad subject to broach, but decided to anyway. "About Fletcher," she said to Bethany, "I'm really sorry about how things turned out. I know he really liked you and wanted to get to know you better."

Bethany let out a wistful sigh. "The hell of it is that he turned out to be so cute. Still not my usual type, but . . . there was something about him I really connected to." Then she shook her head. "Crazy of me, right? To think things would ever work out with a guy I really like?"

"Stop that," Christy admonished her. "The right guy will come along."

"I'm not necessarily looking for my Prince Charming," Bethany argued. "Just someone to . . . connect with, like I said. Someone steady and nice."

"Well, then I'm sure *that* guy will come along, too," Christy-the-eternal-optimist said.

Bethany only shrugged. "Maybe. But where is he?" And before either of them could reply, she looked to Tamra and said, "I guess things are working out for him and his wife then." It was a statement, but also, Tamra knew, a question.

"As far as I know." Between work and Jeremy, Tamra hadn't seen much of Fletcher lately, but in the brief conversations they'd shared, things had sounded the same—like he and Kim were busy rebuilding their relationship.

"Well, I'm happy for him," Bethany announced. "It might not seem that way, but I am. I mean, to think he believed all that time that she would come back and then she did. There's something special in that, right?"

And it was hard for anyone to argue that. Even Christy stayed quiet. The silence among them was its own answer. It was difficult to question an honest-to-goodness miracle.

"Well," Christy finally said, ending the quiet contemplation, "Tamra is living proof that the perfect guy can come along when you least expect it."

Tamra's face warmed slightly as a blush stole over her. Sometimes it was still hard to believe the way things had unfolded for her and Jeremy. And maybe that wasn't a miracle as big as Fletcher's, but given the romantic drought that had stretched through most of her life, it still felt pretty darn miraculous in its own way. She'd written Fletcher that note at the party about it being a night for miracles, but maybe it was just a *time* for miracles, a time for change, for all of them. Maybe Bethany, too—even though Tamra had no idea where Bethany's own personal miracle might come from.

"It's true," Tamra replied. "Things can change in a heartbeat."

Christy gave her head a thoughtful tilt. "And if you don't mind my saying, you've been a ray of sunshine lately. You seem happier than I've ever seen you."

"And now we hear all sorts of interesting noises from your backyard at night," Bethany added, punctuating the statement with a sly grin.

The heat of another blush crept up Tamra's neck and onto her cheeks.

But Bethany quickly added, "Oh, hey, don't worry—I'm not modest. I've had sex in lots of weird places. And he really turned out to be a hottie—so have fun with it."

Though what Tamra shared with Jeremy had gotten to be more than just fun. She cared about him. A lot.

How could she not? He'd brought her back from such a barren romantic existence. He'd taken her from having nothing to feeling like she had it all—laughter, passion, companionship, and . . . trust. The trust he'd shown in her had blown her away. So she liked to think she'd helped bring him back from a pretty bad place, too.

A few hours later, she found herself in the spot on the pier where she sold her wares most evenings, sorry to notice a slight chill in the air setting in earlier now that summer had passed officially into autumn, but happy enough about other things.

Bethany had brought her paintings tonight—Christy and Jack had provided a folding table for her to sit at with her work propped up in front of it and also behind her, against the pier railing. And she'd seemed utterly surprised when an older woman walking a Chihuahua had purchased one of her paintings for $75 in the first half hour. It had reminded Tamra to go ahead and select the one *she* wanted, too, after which she pointed out with a wink, "Two official sales already—not bad."

Plus she had plans to meet Jeremy later—he'd suggested getting slices of pumpkin pie at the Hungry Fisherman, which Polly started offering this time of year, and then seeing where the night led them. And she hoped the night would lead straight to sex. Wild, crazy, hot, naughty sex. Because she was finally comfortable wanting that and not being shy about it.

Just then Reece came strolling up, walking Fifi on the pink leash Tamra had given him a few Christmases ago, and he paused to say, "You've got a suspicious grin on your face."

She let her eyebrows rise. "I do?"

"Yep. And that's new on you. And I like it."

"Is that so?" She gave her head an inquisitive tilt.

"Yep. Because I'm pretty sure I know what it's about."

She blinked. "You are?"

"Yep. The guy staying in Room Eleven," he said—and then he tossed her a wink before Fifi led him sauntering away.

Soon after, Fletcher walked by hand in hand with Kim, raising a casual wave to Bethany as Kim stopped to say to Tamra, "I'm going to pick out the perfect sun catcher for our kitchen window." And Tamra realized that maybe some of her happiness with Jeremy had come along . . . because Fletcher had made her believe in miracles. And ever since then, she'd felt like more and more of them were possible.

She watched as they proceeded up the pier, a little sad for Bethany, but feeling like things must be working out the way they were supposed to. After all, that was what Fletcher always said. And she pretty much considered him the authority on that now.

"Hi, Mary."

She jumped at the sound of the familiar voice, deep and sexy, and looked up to find none other than Jeremy himself standing in front of her. She blinked, stunned. "What are you doing here? Is something wrong?"

He laughed, even if it appeared a bit forced, and said, "No, something's right. It's just . . . time I came here. Time I started getting past some things. I should have come the first time you invited me, but better late than never, right?"

She smiled up at the man who had brought her so much joy, so much passion. "So why tonight? What brought this on?"

"Guess I just wanted to surprise you."

One more little miracle.

And each day his belief in the Magic
grew stronger . . .

Frances Hodgson Burnett, *The Secret Garden*

Chapter 21

"So," SHE said, keeping her voice low so no one around them would hear, "are you okay? Being here?"

Another forced chuckle. "Can't say I'm completely at ease." His glance darted to a couple walking past, and Tamra realized he was instinctively keeping an eye on as many people as possible. "But . . . it's fine."

"I'm glad you came," she told him, beyond touched that he would do this for her—even while she knew he'd done it for himself, too. "But you don't have to stay if you'd rather not."

Yet Jeremy shook his head. "Nah, I'll hang out a while. Try to act like a normal human being." He managed a wink. "Maybe I'll finally catch Fletcher's show."

She'd nearly forgotten he'd never seen it. "You should. It's amazing."

"Might just watch it from up here on the pier with you, though." He flashed a playful grin. "Keep a better eye on the perimeter that way. Watch for any Sunset Celebration snipers."

A quick laugh escaped her, and he chuckled, too. She liked that he could laugh at himself a little.

And so Jeremy hung out with her, clearly inspecting his surroundings while trying not to look like a guy who kept inspecting his surroundings. But occasionally, when a shopper or passerby stopped to converse with her, he meandered to some of the nearby vendors, looking over their art, and chatting with Bethany about her paintings.

Given the lighter crowds due to the change in season, the pier emptied during Fletcher's tightrope act and all the vendors stood at the railing to watch as well. Tamra liked watching the show with Jeremy, liked seeing him take it in for the first time. But it was a little melancholy to watch it with Bethany—because Kim stood prominently in the front row of the crowd gathered for the performance, and given that Tamra could feel her presence even more than she saw it, she was pretty sure Bethany could, too.

Once upon a time, Kim had served as Fletcher's assistant, and while he hadn't yet brought her back in on that same level, she was quick to pass him the props he needed throughout the performance, and it was obvious she was eager to resume her old role. Well, both of them—assistant and wife. And Tamra knew she really would have to forgive Kim—she'd come back, and she was going to be part of their lives now, part of their circle.

As Fletcher balanced on the rope, juggling flaming torches in the air as he merrily flung banter into the crowd, Tamra leaned over and whispered to Jeremy, "Amazing, right?"

He met her eyes briefly, nodding, before refocusing on the show. Then, gaze still on the tightrope and the man atop it, he murmured, "And to think I've been missing this out of fear." He shook his head. "No more. That stops now." He glanced back over at Tamra. "Because what else am I missing? I don't want to miss anything."

The sun was beginning to set earlier these days, ending the celebration a tiny bit sooner with each passing night. By the time Fletcher's act had ended, most of the shoppers were heading to their cars and back to their homes or to the resorts up the road.

Bethany was excited to have sold three paintings, counting the one to Tamra, and thanked her for suggesting she come.

Jeremy had walked from the Happy Crab, so he helped Tamra load her things into her SUV, and together they drove to the Hungry Fisherman.

As they dug into their pie, Jeremy said, "I have some good news. Wanted to wait until we were alone."

She looked at him across the table, curious. "What is it?"

"When the golf course is done in a couple of weeks, I'll be starting a new job. On November first. I got on with Sun Coast Builders. Interviewed for it a few days ago, but I didn't mention it in case it didn't work out. It did, though, and the owner, Bob Metzger, is going to mentor me this winter. And whenever he thinks I'm ready, he'll make me a foreman."

Tamra sat before him stunned.

And when she didn't reply right away, he went on. "I've been giving it some thought, and turns out I like building. A lot. Don't know why. Maybe building

something feels . . . I don't know, just a lot more productive than war." A sheepish chuckle echoed from
his throat as he shook his head. "I don't mean to make
it more than it is, but I just want to learn something I
like doing and get good at it. So I can rest easy knowing I'll be able to keep a roof over my head. So that's
my news, Mary."

She'd been smiling at him the last few moments—
ever since she'd gotten over her initial shock. And
now she said, "It's *great* news! *Phenomenal* news! I'm so
happy for you."

He gave Abner credit for his help getting the job,
after which he informed her that he'd been thinking
about other aspects of his future, too. "I'm going to
keep living at the Crab 'til spring since I know Reece
could use the business through the winter. But come
February or March, I'll find myself an apartment and
get settled here for good."

And though she'd been happy enough already,
now it felt as if something in Tamra's heart broke into
full bloom—just like one of the flowers in her garden.
Because she hadn't allowed herself to think very far
ahead with Jeremy; she'd been taking one day—and
night—at a time, living in the moment and enjoying
each for all it was worth. But at the same time, she'd
been aware that he had no real roots here. And she
couldn't be sure he'd stay—until now.

"I think this calls for a celebration, Mr. Sheridan,"
she told him coyly as he ate his last bite of pie.

He narrowed his gaze on her, his expression flirtatious. "Exactly what do you have in mind, Mary?"

She bit her lip, then spoke lowly. "I was thinking we
could get naked in my backyard."

He didn't bother replying—just called across the restaurant, "Polly, could we get the check?"

THE following evening just before the sun dropped below the horizon, Fletcher balanced atop his tightrope on the beach, as he did every night. Something about the experience felt otherworldly to him—it had always been that way, since he'd first started performing.

Maybe it was the unique vantage point it gave him. It wasn't the kind of freedom that came with, say, being a bird, but it still allowed him to see farther, more clearly, than you could on the ground, and peering down on awe-filled faces had always struck him as a view one might have from heaven.

Or maybe it was because man wasn't meant to balance on a tiny rope strung high above the sand. And perhaps even now, each step he took upon it reminded him that we each set our own limitations in life—and that we could all do amazing things if we only believed we could.

Regardless of the reason why, though, he always felt a little magical up there. Always—every single time.

Just then, with those thoughts rolling through his mind even as he addressed the crowd—he could do that part without thinking now—he caught sight of one particular face there. Kim. Just like he'd visualized.

And she loved him again. Just like he'd visualized.

That felt like magic. To have held that faith, to have seen that vision in his head and experience the reality of it now. So he let himself grab onto that feeling for a moment—because it reminded him how powerful he was, how powerful we all were.

There was only one thing wrong with the whole situation. He still hurt inside.

That hadn't been part of his vision. Nope, not at all.

She'd come home—but everything was different now. No matter how hard they tried to make it the same, everything was different. Their *history* was different. It had this big, ugly blight on it now—a big, open, festering wound.

It almost made him want to laugh at odd moments. He'd believed in this so hard that it had actually happened, yet he hadn't factored in that one enormous component of it all—that when someone leaves for four years, even if they come back, it isn't the same. What a colossal oversight.

He'd built a whole life without her. Her departure had, in so many ways, made him into someone new, someone much different than she'd left behind. He had a new home, new friends. He'd become part of a community in a way he valued far more than he ever could have anticipated. He'd accumulated possessions that were his and not theirs; he'd fallen into routines that were, again, his and not theirs.

And she, too, had seen places and known people and done things that were wholly separate from him. There were parts of her life he would never know, never be a part of, even peripherally.

Though . . . if there was one thing that bothered him most about all this, it was that she seemed relatively unchanged or unscathed by any of it. In fact, a certain naiveté hung about her. She seemed unaware of the gulf four years had placed between them. Unaware of the level of pain she'd caused him. Unaware that his staying exactly where she'd left him all this time, waiting for her, was a miracle.

She can't win with you. You're mad because of ways she's changed and mad because of ways she's stayed the same.

But it'll heal. It'll heal. You just have to let it heal.

This was meant to be; you just have to let it be.

The song entered his head then, Paul McCartney singing those soothing words, and he let the lyrics run through his mind, let them bring him a little peace.

In the end, it's all we have. The peace we let ourselves experience. And love.

If you're lucky enough to be loved by someone who loves you back, you have something truly rare. Which was one more reason among many to forgive. And he would.

When we're old, none of this will matter. The last four years will seem like nothing but a dream.

And . . . if it hadn't happened that way, he wouldn't be here right now. He would have long since left Coral Cove and its quirky charm and accepting people behind. He wouldn't know as much as he now knew about friendship. Or loyalty. Or simple caring. He would have missed so much that comprised his world now.

Kim had to leave you for you to discover all that.

And now she's back, like you wanted, so you can have it all.

Everything happens for a reason. Now heal. Now forgive.

Even as those thoughts tumbled through his head, he'd been doing his act, focusing on his balance, and now he began to juggle the torches he'd just lit. The crowd roared for him, but it was Kim who his eyes caught on, down below, and she was smiling up at him.

Let it be.

SOME nights Jeremy spent the night with Tamra; others he came back to the Happy Crab and slept in the bed he'd begun to think of as his own. It was easy to be with Tamra, easy to be at the little cottage she'd filled with color and art and made uniquely her own. But something made Jeremy not to want to get too comfortable there. He still needed his own space. It was early days of being back in the land of the living, after all.

Though he felt more alive all the time. Having a job, with a future, a job where he'd learn something he could use the rest of his life, felt incredible. He'd acted cool when Abner's friend, Bob Metzer, had offered the position to him, and he'd acted fairly cool telling Tamra about it, too, but inside he'd felt wired—downright electrical. Like a part of him that had been unplugged for a very long time had suddenly gotten juice again.

As he awoke at the Crab, got a shower, and got dressed for another day of golf course construction, he realized he hadn't felt this hopeful and eager since his early days as a Marine, back when he'd thought he could save the world. Now he knew he couldn't, but he was perfectly happy not to be in the world-saving business anymore—it was enough to think he could simply be useful, be part of creating new things.

He'd called both his mom and his sister the previous night to fill them in. And it had felt so damn good—he knew they could each hear in his voice the shift in his outlook.

"What else is new?" his mother had asked once he'd given her the details about his job with Sun Coast Construction. "Nancy Romo said you're seeing someone she knows. An artist. Tell me about her. Nancy says she's nice."

He'd almost laughed realizing Coral Cove wasn't much different than Destiny in ways—in a small town, everyone knew your business. It had never occurred to him that information would make it all the way to Ohio without his knowledge. But he didn't mind much.

"Her name is Tamra. We're working together on the mini-golf course. And yeah, she's an artist—makes pottery and stained glass. She's friends with Christy Knight—lives next door to her."

"So is it serious?" His mom sounded hopeful. Why did the whole world want everyone to be "serious" when they were dating someone?

He just shook his head slightly, even though no one could see it. "We've only been going out a couple weeks," he told her, "so don't get all excited and blow it out of proportion. It's a new thing. And it's nice the way it is."

"Maybe you can bring her up for Thanksgiving or Christmas. You *are* coming home for the holidays, right?"

Jeremy let out a breath. He loved his mother dearly. And he should probably go home for the holidays, now that she mentioned it. But he hadn't given it a thought—he'd been way too into living life one day at a time to be thinking that far ahead, even though

Thanksgiving was next month. So he said, "I'll have to see what my work schedule allows for—I'll be the new guy on the job, after all. But if I make it home, I'll be on my own."

"Well, your father and I will probably take a week away from the winter weather in Coral Cove after the new year, so we'll meet her then."

"Fine," Jeremy said.

Another big improvement in his life? Very few nightmares lately. He had better things filling his head these days, he supposed. And okay, yeah, he'd woken up in a cold sweat one night last week after visions of being trapped in a bunker with gunfire and dark shadows—but at least that happened way less now.

He almost felt guilty when he didn't have Chuck in the back of his mind, but . . . he supposed it was healthier. He supposed things Tamra had told him were true. That Chuck wouldn't want him to keep suffering. That he couldn't fix what had happened.

And sure, there were moments when a little voice inside him argued, told him that was taking the easy way out, letting himself off the hook, that he should keep punishing himself since no one else was going it do it for him. But then he remembered that torturing himself just made him a useless human being who became a burden to people. Healing, trying to inject a little good into the world however he could, was starting to make a lot more sense to him.

He walked out the door to another beautiful day in paradise. Damn, he liked it here. It felt . . . downright strange in a way to realize he looked forward to each day. He looked forward to working alongside Tamra at the course, he looked forward to whatever the evening would hold, too. He looked forward to seeing the people who'd become pleasant parts of his life now—Polly and Abner, Riley, Reece and Cami, and all the other people who'd made him feel at home here in one way or another.

Life was good.

And a month ago, he wouldn't have dreamed he could feel that way in such a short time.

As he pulled the door to Room 11 shut behind him and walked toward his truck, he took a long glance up Coral Street, quiet at this hour, and another across the way to the beach, flanked by the row of tall palm trees that swayed in the breeze. This place had saved him. The thought seemed cheesy, but he knew it was true. Coral Cove had turned his life around.

When he got in his truck and slammed the rickety old door, his eyes were drawn to the passenger seat—or more precisely, to what was in it. A big brown shopping bag. What the hell?

Perplexed and a little cautious—because he disliked mysterious things appearing out of nowhere in the same way he disliked crowds—he leaned over to peek warily inside.

And he found . . . cat stuff. A litter box and bag of kitty litter, some dry cat food, a couple of bowls with cartoony cat faces on them, and—holy shit—even a collar. Powder blue.

Then he noticed a little white envelope on the seat next to the bag. He didn't have to open it to know who it was from. He tossed a suspicious glance toward the restaurant next door as he ripped into the envelope and pulled out a folded sheet of Hungry Fisherman stationery that looked like it had been around as long as the restaurant—the edges were even yellow. *Polly's probably been trying to use up this paper since the seventies.* He read the handwritten note.

> *That cat needs a real home. Consider this a housewarming gift for him. But if Reece ever finds out you got an illegal boarder in your room, you never got this stuff from me.*
>
> *Polly*

Well, shit.

He loved Polly—he really did. But this was going too far.

He'd looked out for the cat some, but God knew it was early enough in his recovery that he had no interest in being permanently responsible for anyone else's care—even a tomcat.

Just then, out of nowhere as usual, the big gray cat bounded up onto the hood of Jeremy's truck.

"Shit!" he bit off through the windshield, immediately relieved it was only the cat but still feeling a little bit stalked.

"Meow," the cat said, though it was muffled with the windows up.

"I'm pretty sure you only like me for my fish," Jeremy muttered toward him.

"Meow."

He shook his head. "You're not even skinny anymore. Kind of a hog, really."

"Meow."

And then Jeremy made a decision. He wasn't going to be shanghaied into this. He might be fond of Polly, but he didn't like these tactics. And he'd felt charitable toward the damn cat, but having it around constantly was getting annoying.

"Look," he said through the window, "we're not gonna do this anymore, okay? I got too much else going on."

"Meow."

And something in the cat's plaintive tone made Jeremy realize he had to quit playing softball here—he was being too nice. So he yelled through the windshield, "Get outta here!" He waved his arm, shooing the cat away.

When the cat didn't go, Jeremy opened the door, got out, and reached up onto the hood. And, grabbing the cat by the scruff of his neck, he flung it off the truck. The cat let out a yowl in midair, landing on his feet on the asphalt, then darted around the building and out of sight.

"I'll take care of you."

Frances Hodgson Burnett, *The Secret Garden*

Chapter 22

Aw crap—what did I just do? Jeremy's heart felt like a lead weight in his chest.

What's next—I punt him off the deck of a boat?

He let out a breath. "Shit, I'm a jerk."

It wasn't the cat's fault he'd suddenly felt too pressured by Polly. It was his own problem—still not wanting to be responsible for keeping anyone safe.

"Here kitty," he said, circling around to the pool area and picnic table. "Here kitty kitty."

After a minute, he caught sight of Captain crouched at the edge of a little storage shed behind the pool, looking tense.

Keeping a good distance away, Jeremy stooped down, making eye contact with him—and still feeling shitty. "Here kitty." And maybe he was making too much of it—but something inside him insisted he set things right. "Come on, buddy. I'm sorry. I won't hurt you, promise." Somehow scaring this innocent animal who couldn't understand felt almost as bad as things he'd had to do in the name of war.

"Forgive me, Captain?" he asked as the cat took one gentle, tentative step forward. "Yeah, that's right—come on out. Come on over." Jeremy wished he'd grabbed the box of dry cat food from Polly's bag so he'd have something to lure the cat with, but as it was, he had only his good intentions. "Here kitty. It's all right."

Slowly but surely Captain came out of hiding and made his way to Jeremy. Though when he got close and Jeremy reached out, the cat flinched and drew back. And Jeremy felt all the worse—he'd made the cat fear him.

But after a moment, Captain let Jeremy pet him And finally Jeremy drew the big, hulking cat into his arms, against his chest. He scratched behind his ear and Captain began to purr. And when Jeremy next spoke, it was in a whisper. "I'm really sorry, buddy."

He hoped when he put the cat back down that the incident was truly mended.

And when the cat followed him, nearly tripping him, he was pretty sure they were friends again. "Lucky me," he murmured on a laugh, rolling his eyes as he got in his truck.

Then he started the engine and drove away.

But he was pretty sure he was going to end up adopting that damn cat, like it or not.

THE following Saturday night after the Sunset Celebration, Tamra sat in her garden wearing jeans and a cozy sweater to ward off the night chill, drinking a cup of hot tea, and smiling at nothing.

But, of course, she was really smiling because of . . . everything.

She and Jeremy had spent the last week installing the wooden obstacles that she'd designed and he'd built—the miniature versions of Coral Cove landmarks—onto each hole. The retro mini-golf course was almost done. In the beginning, this had been a job to her, and a way to improve the town she loved. But now, it had become a project near and dear to her heart, for many reasons, and she took true pride in it.

All that remained were finishing touches. A custom-made sign, designed to echo a 1950s seaside tourist sign, was due to arrive in a few days, and the clubs, balls, and scorecards had already come. Yesterday she and Jeremy had hung the Grand Opening banner with the date, a week away, when the town would finally get to play miniature golf. Cami had hired the Happy Crab's part-time maid, Juanita, and two of her sisters, to work at the course—though Cami and Tamra would both train them and take some shifts at first, too.

Part of her would be sad not to labor side by side with Jeremy anymore. But she couldn't have been happier that he'd soon be moving on to a wonderful new opportunity—and she was so proud of him for finding a new direction. He'd transformed in so many ways since they'd met.

In fact, he'd even let the big gray cat who'd originally gotten him in so much trouble start living with him. He claimed it was temporary, until he could find him a better home—but apparently Polly had given him some cat supplies, and when it had rained that very night, Jeremy had brought the cat inside and not put him back out the next morning. It was a secret from Reece, who didn't like pets at the motel, but he seemed to be the only one who didn't know about it.

Though Fletcher and Kim still kept to themselves a lot, they appeared happy when Tamra saw them during his act in the evenings. And she thought Fletcher now looked more at ease.

And though she still wished he'd gotten to know Bethany better, she seemed fully recovered now—and had just last night announced to all the girls over drinks on the Hungry Fisherman's patio that she'd made a monumental decision: She was going to stay in Coral Cove, even after Christy's wedding.

Although she'd had one gallery showing at home in Cincinnati, sales at the Sunset Celebration had made her realize there was more than one way to be an artist and that selling her paintings to tourists on a pier made it so that "I actually have an audience!" she told them. "And who doesn't love the beach? And warm winters?"

She'd then said that although she'd been staying with Christy and Jack, now she needed to find an affordable place of her own. And Cami had told her, "Well, don't worry, if you don't locate anything right away, there's always the Happy Crab. Even if you can't afford the room rates." She winked. "Reece has been known to be generous that way."

And Christy's wedding was coming up fast, the week after the golf course grand opening. Since Fletcher was the best man and Bethany the maid of honor, everyone wondered if that would be awkward now, but Bethany had been quick to assure Christy, "I wouldn't ever let anything overshadow your day."

So all seemed right with the world on this quiet night.

And though Tamra and Jeremy hadn't made plans to see each other tonight, inspiration struck her. And she thought of calling or texting him, but they were comfortable enough now that she didn't even bother. She simply slipped on a pair of comfy flip-flops, got in her SUV, and drove to the Happy Crab.

As she approached his door, her heart rippled. *I should be used to it by now, the way he makes me feel. But I'm not. And maybe I never will be.* Maybe it was premature, but the very notion of such an enduring desire made her smile as she knocked on the door of Room 11.

He pulled it open, looked surprised to see her, then laughed.

"What's funny?" she asked with a smile.

He gave his head a small shake. "Normally I don't like surprises. But this one I do. What's up, Mary?" He tilted his head and flashed her favorite sexy grin.

She bit her lip and said, "I had a wacky idea."

His eyebrows shot up. "Booty call? Because if so, I'm okay with that."

She let out a laugh. "You wish."

"I do."

She glanced at her watch, and then back up at him. "Here's the deal. It's after eleven—the streets are all rolled up for the night, not a soul out and about."

"This is still sounding booty-call-like, just so you know. And I'm still okay with it."

She ignored his silliness and went on. "I was thinking . . . that you and I should . . ."

"Yeah?" he asked eagerly when she trailed off.

"Inaugurate the golf course. That we should play the course, just you and me, one time, before anyone else gets to. It's really ours, after all. We made it. We should play it. As a little way of celebrating it."

A slow smile formed on his face, but he didn't answer.

So she said, "Is that stupid?"

"No," he said. "It's genius. Let's go."

JEREMY found it both peaceful and downright fun to secretly play mini-golf with Tamra on the course they'd built together. Instead of turning on the course lights, they lit their way using a portable floodlight already on the jobsite. That made playing a little more challenging, but it reminded Jeremy that some challenges in life he actually liked. And, of course, the woman he was playing golf with was the biggest part of the appeal. Her smile shone nearly as bright as the flood lamp when he glanced at her. She smiled so much more than she used to.

"Damn," he said as his ball completely missed the opening in the tiny Happy Crab sign on Hole 7, colliding with one of the little red wooden pincers with a thud. "Maybe I should have made that slot bigger."

"Or maybe you're just bad at mini-golf," she quipped.

He cast her a sideways glance. "Gettin' saucy on me, woman?"

She laughed. "Just telling it like it is, Sheridan. We want the course to be challenging." Then she shifted her weight from one flip-flop to the other. "However, given the poor lighting, I'm willing to give you a do-over."

The competitive part of Jeremy didn't want to take it. But . . . "It's damn hard to see this hole right now, so I'll take your do-over. And you get one, too. But that's it. One apiece. After that, we let the balls fall where they may."

She nodded succinctly. "Fair enough."

"And after the place is open, we play again, in normal lighting."

"You sound like a guy who's afraid he's going to lose," she said playfully.

"No way," he claimed. "I was a star athlete in high school."

She shrugged. "Ancient history."

And he laughed. And took his do-over. This time, the ball went through, dropped onto the Astroturf on the other side, then rolled neatly into the hole. "Sweet success."

Another shrug from his opponent. "If you don't count the do-over."

He lowered his chin, gave her a look. "That's kind of the point of a do-over—not to count what happened before. You'll need yours soon enough, Mary Mary Quite Contrary."

And she did, on the twelfth hole. She'd continued being pretty smug until then, but that turned the tables, and by the time they started the last hole on the course, they were tied.

Concentrating, and maybe wanting bragging rights for winning the first game ever played here—secret or not—Jeremy strategically putted his ball, trying to put just the right amount of power behind it, along with careful aim. They both watched as it traveled briskly up a ramp to a higher level, where it veered to the right and neatly ricocheted into the hole. "Ha!" he said. "Hole in one." Then he glanced over to the woman beside him. "Didn't know you were dating a miniature golf pro, did you?"

"No," she said coolly. "But since we're dead even before this hole, I'm not sure I'm very impressed."

He stepped aside as she moved up to the putting pad and said, "Let's see what ya got, Mary. Pressure's on."

"Quiet," she instructed.

Then she sized up her shot, gave the ball too hard of a whack, and sent it catapulting up the ramp, where it hit a small wooden palm tree, then flew to smack against one of the coral borders, then ricocheted wildly against still two more borders, before rolling, rolling, rolling . . . into the hole.

Jeremy's jaw dropped. "What in the wide, wide world of sports was that?"

The woman next to him gave him one more smile. "I believe it's called a hole in one."

"I'll be damned," he muttered, then laughed. "Guess it's kinda fitting, though."

She raised her eyebrows. "Oh?"

"I feel like everything we did together to build this place was pretty even, fifty-fifty. Makes sense this would end in a tie." Then he held up one finger. "But I still want a rematch."

"Don't worry—you'll get your rematch," she promised. And he thought her voice held a little flirtation. And even in jeans and a big sweater, she was sexy as hell. Funny, once upon a time he might not have thought that, but . . . she was different now. More confident. It flowed out of her like something liquid and hot.

He didn't hesitate to follow the urge to ditch his club on the green in order to step up and ease his arms around her, letting them settle on her ass. "Now *I* have a wacky idea," he told her.

She'd abandoned her putter, too, and pressed her palms against his chest. "What's that?"

"We could christen the golf course in a whole other way." He winked and whispered seductively, "Wanna do it on the eighteenth hole?"

Her eyes flew wide.

So he quickly added, "We can turn the lights out. And like you said yourself, no one's around, the town is rolled up, and—most importantly—I want you, honey."

A hint of temptation flickered in her green eyes for a second—before she said, "The answer is still no. Sorry. But it's too big a risk. We live here, you know?"

Jeremy saw her point but was loath to admit it, lest it make him feel old and sensible at a time when he was just starting to see the fun in life again. So instead he said, "You're no fun."

"I'm plenty of fun," she countered.

"Show me then," he challenged.

She peered coyly up into his eyes. "You know what's fun?"

"Mini-golf course sex?" he asked.

And she said, "No. Getting naked with you in my garden."

She didn't have to say another word. "I'm a sucker for naked in your garden," he replied. "Race you to the car."

* * *

THEY'D had sex in the garden twice. But then they'd moved in to Tamra's bedroom because it had gotten chillier outside. Already she looked forward to warmer evenings—but she also had no complaints about having Jeremy in her bed. Nights they ended up there tended to be nights he stayed over, and she liked that. It was nice to snuggle with him while they slept, nice to wake up with him.

It was late, past two, but they were still awake talking. About everything and nothing. The grand opening next week. The upcoming wedding. Jeremy's new job. Places where he might find an apartment. "Which I guess," he added, rolling his eyes dramatically, "has to allow pets, since I seem to have one. For now anyway."

But soon she was ready to stop talking. She wanted more sex. And it was more than just a physical thing—it was about . . . closeness. All the different kinds of closeness. As their warm, naked bodies mingled together under the sheets, she eased her hand down between his thighs and whispered, "I want you again."

"God, woman, you're an animal tonight," he told her with a playful smile.

"I kinda am," she agreed—then leaned in to begin kissing his bare chest.

"Mmm, I like it," he growled.

And she liked pleasing him. Almost as much as she liked *being* pleased. When she'd been young, her older lovers had often been pushy, at times demanding. But Jeremy never pushed her. He playfully suggested sex on the golf course, sure; and he could be . . . commanding during sex, yes. But commanding and *de*manding were two different things. Commanding was knowing what would please them both. *De*manding was selfish. And Jeremy was never a selfish lover.

And that was probably what compelled Tamra to follow the instinct to kiss her way down onto his well-muscled stomach—and then lower. She'd never done this with him before. He'd never asked. But she wanted to give him something new, something wholly selfless. He'd taken her to places she'd never thought she'd go—she wanted to take him someplace amazing, too. And the low groans that began to echo from his throat told her she was on the right track.

She held his solid erection in her hand, stroking firmly, as she studied it in the moonlight seeping in her window. Another way of getting to know him, of growing closer to him. And he'd pleasured her this way so many times without ever asking her to do it in return. She gingerly kissed the tip and he let out a deep sigh that fueled her. Then she began to run her tongue down his hard length and back up again, experimenting, getting used to the feeling.

"Aw." Another hot groan from him. "Aw baby. That feels so good."

Now she licked, holding onto him as if he were an ice cream cone, still tentatively finding her way. "You . . . you've never asked me to," she observed. Although her experience was limited, every guy she'd been with in her youth had asked her to, indeed pushed her.

"I wouldn't want you to do it because I asked you," he told her deeply. "I only want you to do it if you really want to."

"Well, I really want to, Jeremy," she said. And then she parted her lips and sank her mouth over the shaft in her hand.

"Aw—aw God, that's good."

Her chest expanded with an unexpected pleasure of her own as she began to move her lips up and down on him. God, she hadn't anticipated the satisfaction it would bring her—that it would feel like more than just giving—but it truly pleasured her as well. And being this intimate with him, this real and raw, made her feel more connected to him than ever before.

Though eventually she needed him inside her. And told him so. He rasped, "Anything you want, honey—I want to make you feel so damn good." And he did. She straddled his body, he pulled her down onto him, filling her, and soon she was screaming her orgasm, thankful it was cold enough to have the windows closed.

"Aw, Tamra honey—I'm gonna come, too," he murmured deeply, and exploded inside her in three hard thrusts that nearly lifted her from the bed.

When it was done, she let her body fold over onto him, exhausted, ready to settle warmly against him and fall asleep.

Though she'd been thinking a lot about her feelings for him—and she knew she'd fallen in love with him. She'd avoided saying it, even to herself, because it was a big place to go emotionally. But now it seemed silly to deny it. And like if that was the feeling flowing through her veins as thick as blood, she should just say it. Things were that easy between them now—it wasn't even scary. It was just being real with him, same as always.

"I love you, Jeremy," she breathed in his ear. Then snuggled tighter against him.

And his body stiffened beneath her. So much that

the tension shot through her like the shock from an electric prod.

Then she went tense, too. Because she knew already, before either of them even said another word, that she'd just ruined everything.

... the immense, tender, terrible,
heartbreaking beauty ...

Frances Hodgson Burnett, *The Secret Garden*

Chapter 23

HER FIRST impulse: damage control. "You—you don't have to say it back. I . . . wasn't trying to make some huge statement or anything." She rose up, peered down on him, wanting to make eye contact, put him at ease.

But he didn't *look* at ease—even in the dark she could see that. "Well, it feels kind of huge."

And obviously not in a good way. Her heart was breaking inside her chest, but she girded herself, still following the instinct to try and save it, try to fix what she'd obviously messed up. "I didn't mean it to be. I just . . . said what I felt in the moment."

She still looked down at him, but he'd broken eye contact. "Tamra, I like things the way they are, the way they've been."

"Well, that's good, because nothing has changed. I mean . . . it's not like I suddenly woke up feeling this way. It's grown. Developed. Over time." But oh God, she was saying too much. Even though she meant her words to relax him, she could see the fear in his eyes actually increasing. *Shut up already.*

A heavy sigh left him, and her heart dropped a little more even before he said, "I just . . . thought we were on the same page."

Tamra began to feel smaller inside somehow than she had a mere moment before. She instinctively drew her body slightly away from his, disentangling their limbs, as she lay down next to him. *She* didn't want to be looking into *his* eyes anymore either now. "What page is that?" she asked.

"That we're just . . . having fun. That it's the same as it's been up to now—casual."

Huh. Wow. "What we've been isn't casual, Jeremy," she informed him.

And sensed him going a little more rigid beside her. "We never made any promises," he nearly snapped. "And I don't want anything serious. I thought you *got* that. I mean, I'm just now getting my life together. I'm not into being all bogged down by a relationship. I've got too much other stuff to worry about first."

Tamra took all that in, let it settle inside her.

Everything had just changed. And it was her fault, for trusting in what they had so much, for feeling so unguarded with him that she'd expressed her love assuming it would be gratefully received. She'd wanted nothing back—she'd simply followed the urge to let this man know he was loved. And she'd thought—mistakenly—that maybe mature adults could do that, that they could acknowledge their feelings, give and take true affection from each other, without it redefining the relationship.

But she'd been naïve. As naïve as she'd been as a teenager. Nothing much had advanced, she now realized, between the way relationships had worked then and the way they worked with adults. When you put your emotions out there, it changed things. For better or worse.

And it hurt to find out Jeremy didn't feel the same way about her as she did for him. Or that even if he did, the idea of "being casual" was more important to him. Whichever answer was the truest didn't much matter—either way, it hurt like hell.

Because she'd given so much of herself to him. And she'd trusted that he'd valued all those personal pieces of herself she'd shared—the physical intimacy, the secrets told and confessions given, every moment she'd spent with him that was out of choice and not obligation. She'd thought they'd truly connected.

But now that he was claiming they hadn't . . . well, that changed things for her, too.

And it changed them even more when he added, "Love's the last thing on my mind here. I'm not interested in love, Tamra, and I doubt I ever will be."

In fact, that . . . *killed* things.

"Oh," she said, stunned, even insulted.

And it left only one horrible option for her, the only saving grace being that she felt absolutely certain about it. She forced back her emotions and attempted to be stoic as she delivered it. "Okay then, I understand. But . . . I don't think I can see you anymore, Jeremy."

Next to her in the bed, he flinched, bolted a sharp look her way. "What do you mean?"

"What I just said."

He blinked. "Why can't things stay like they've been?"

"Because you're right—what I said was huge. I didn't realize it when I said it, and it wouldn't have been a big deal if you'd been okay with me feeling that way. But you're not. You're still in casual mode." She stopped, rolled her eyes, and muttered, "Don't ask me how, mind you, given some of the stuff we've talked about." Then she spoke louder again. "But that doesn't matter. What matters is . . . *I* don't feel casual anymore. And if you already know you can never return my feelings, there's really no point in going on. I'd always just feel . . . embarrassed with you now. Weak or something." She shook her head.

Jeremy just looked at her. And she looked back. Into eyes of blue fraught with pain and beauty. She'd seen less pain there recently—and a lot more joy and laughter—but right now, all she saw was sadness trapping a beautiful man inside.

"Are you sure?" he asked. He sounded taken aback, as shocked as *she* had a few minutes ago when he'd called them casual. "Sure you don't want to try to work this out, see if we can meet in the middle?"

Something in his voice nearly made her feel compassion for him—but maybe she'd shown him enough compassion. Maybe it was time to get back to taking care of herself. "Be careful," she cautioned. "You almost sound like you care."

"Well, of course I care." His tone implied that she was acting ridiculous. "Just because I don't want something big and serious here doesn't mean I don't care."

"Not enough," she said quietly, firmly.

And sure, it would be easy to sell herself short here,

take what she could get from him. Many women in her position would. They'd keep hanging on and trying to figure out how to make him love them back. They'd clamber and cling and hope and pray—they'd dig themselves deeper and deeper into love with him, become more and more invested in trying to make him feel the same way. They'd lose themselves there. All for nothing. Because if love wasn't freely given, what was it worth? If love wasn't freely given, it wasn't real.

He still looked confused, a little broken, in a way that tugged at her heart even now as it crumbled inside her. But at the same time, she felt so shockingly sure she was doing the right thing that it kept her strong. Her resolution never wavered, even as she explained, "I don't want anything from you that you don't want to give me, Jeremy. But I know what I'm worth, and I don't want to settle for less than that. *Now*, if we went on seeing each other, I'd *feel* that every single time I saw you, that I was getting less than I'm worth."

"Why do women always have to make such a big deal out of everything?" he muttered on a heavy sigh.

But she gently said, "Well, it's a big deal to *me*. My mistake."

"Look, I don't mean to hurt your feelings. I'm just being honest." He gave a shake of his head. "I feel like I can't win here, like nothing I say will be the right thing to fix it."

"That's probably true. Some things can't be fixed."

And as they stared at each other in stark silence, she knew they were both feeling the enormity of her words. She and Jeremy had both fixed a lot in each other in recent weeks—proving that some things *could* be repaired. But some things couldn't. There were some things you could only try to heal from. What had happened to his friend, Chuck. The loss of her deluded parents' love. And . . . this. This would take some healing, at least for her.

"I'll be fine," she promised him. In case he was worried about her feelings at all. The truth was, she didn't know. She suddenly didn't know how much he cared or *didn't* care; maybe all he was experiencing the loss of right now was something he'd grown accustomed to because it took his mind off the cost of war.

After a long moment, Jeremy sat up in bed and reached for the clothes he'd brought inside after their garden romp. Only after he was almost completely dressed did he quietly say, "This doesn't make sense to me, Mary. One minute we're fine and the next . . ."

"And the next, I tell you I love you and you freak out and—"

"I didn't freak out," he argued.

"You did, a little. Quietly," she insisted, still calm, stalwart. "And it told me all I need to know. I think we started out on the same page, but we're not there anymore. My page turned and yours didn't—that's all. No harm, no foul."

He still wore that same shell-shocked look, but she forced herself to become more inured against it. She was the wounded party here, not him. And it wasn't as if he'd suddenly started saying all the right things.

As Jeremy stood up, peering down at her as if still waiting for her to change her mind, she felt sad— brokenhearted if she was honest—to discover he didn't love her back. She wasn't sure when it had turned into love, but she could have sworn they felt the same way. And yet . . . another part of her felt even sadder *for him*.

For not loving her. Or for not letting himself. Either way, he was missing out on the amazing person she was. And he was closing the door on all the good things they'd given to each other.

"Do you want me to drive you home?" she asked, remembering she'd brought him here.

He shook his head. "I'll walk the beach back."

She nodded.

And he let out one last sigh, then turned to go.

"Jeremy," she called, realizing there was one more thing to say.

He looked back. And she tried not to see hope in his eyes, because what she had to say wasn't about that.

"Thank you," she told him. "For bringing me back to life inside. I'll always appreciate the time we've had together. It'll always mean something to me."

Jeremy knew he should be saying something in reply, saying the same kinds of things—but he didn't. He was still too stunned. And he kind of just wanted to shut down.

So he simply nodded, then ducked out of the bedroom. He was ready to be gone, out of this situation.

He exited through the back, just because it was how he'd come in. But he walked briskly—through the garden, out the gate—purposely not taking any of it in. He wouldn't be back here, after all. He was leaving for the last time.

He gave his head another quick shake as he hit the path that led to the driveway. This felt unreal. He hadn't felt anything unreal since . . . Afghanistan. There, unreal shit had happened all the time—unreal shit had become a way of life. But back here, even mired in depression, not a lot had thrown him. Even since coming to Coral Cove, life had been mostly . . . predictable, steady. And the only surprises had been mostly good ones. Mostly related to Tamra. So walking out of her house in the middle of the night, suddenly knowing it would be the last time, was a little jarring.

As he'd told her, he headed for the beach. He'd grabbed his shoes on the way out, but hadn't bothered putting them on, and it felt good, after descending the worn steps at the end of Sea Shell Lane, to sink his toes into cool sand and to let the sound of the ocean wash over him.

He headed toward the water, walked along the edge of where it met the shore, purposely keeping his feet in that soft, dry sand. Maybe there was something . . . grounding in that. He just wanted to keep feeling it as he put one foot in front of the other.

Parts of their conversation blipped in his brain. She loved him. But if he didn't love her back, she didn't want to see him anymore. She didn't want anything from him he didn't want to give. But apparently she didn't want the things he *did* want to give, either.

Though maybe this was best. Because he just wasn't into tossing the L-word around—it made things serious, no two ways about it. He just didn't know how somebody said it without realizing that.

Everything in his life right now was new, and he was doing the best he could. He'd already committed to a job, and to moving here permanently. And he seemed to have committed to that damn cat, who would probably be weaving figure-eights around his ankles the second he walked in the door. And hell— that was enough. *More* than enough.

So he had a perfectly full life without Tamra in it, and he just didn't need the kind of drama that L-word brought.

And the truth was, being alone wasn't always so bad. There was no guesswork in being alone, no curveballs. There were no bombs being dropped—figurative or literal.

And with that thought, he closed the door on the topic. He turned his brain back to the rush of the surf and the sand beneath his feet. And sleep. Because it was late and he was tired. He banished all other thoughts from his mind.

How real that dream had been—
how wonderful and clear . . .

Frances Hodgson Burnett, *The Secret Garden*

Chapter 24

*T*AMRA SAT in her garden drinking wine and feeling a little weepy. She'd cry a little and then stop, cry a little and then stop. It had been that way for the last two days.

She'd told Jeremy she'd be fine, and she would—eventually. But for now, things were hard. For now, she missed him.

She missed his sexy grin, she missed his smart mouth, she missed his touch, she missed his kiss.

She missed knowing she'd helped him . . . be better, get better. He'd never told her that, but she knew.

She missed having someone who wanted to be with her, who *chose* to be with her. She missed the simple companionship.

She missed having someone to be with who made it so . . . she didn't have to try. At all. She could just be. She missed that comfort, that ease. She loved him, but she also sincerely *liked* him—she liked who he'd become with her.

And she missed the sex. She wasn't sure when she'd have that with someone again—how she'd ever find someone she *wanted* to have it with again. Maybe for other women it was easier, but for Tamra . . . well, it had taken half her life for someone to come along who made her want him enough to trust him enough.

Funny that for a woman who used to downplay the importance of sex, she thought the sex she'd shared with Jeremy was about as close as you could come to heaven on earth. It had been hot and fun, but . . . more. Deeper.

Well, for her anyway.

She still didn't know if she believed that he really didn't love her. But it still didn't matter much. Either way, she was content in her decision. It had, in fact, felt like a secret she'd stumbled upon and would carry with her always—to only want love, of any kind, that was freely given.

The garden felt . . . lonely now. But it was still a good place to hide, lick her wounds. In fact, she'd spent the better part of the last two days digging, weeding, loving her garden, sinking her hands into the dirt—and trying to remember the other things in her life that had moved her before Jeremy entered it.

She hadn't spoken to Fletcher, because now that he shared his house with Kim, things were different. His attention was focused elsewhere—she understood that. But she missed her best friend right now.

Just then, her phone chimed, indicating a text message. She rushed to pick it up from the arm of the Adirondack chair, realizing as she looked that she hoped it might be from Jeremy.

Her heart sank seeing it was from Christy instead—*how silly*. She clicked to open it.

HEY, JUST WONDERING IF YOU'RE OKAY. WHY HAVEN'T YOU BEEN AT THE PIER?

Indeed, Tamra had skipped the Sunset Celebration the past two nights. And her friend's concern touched her.

Her first impulse was to tell Christy she was fine, just busy, or tired or something. Her impulse was to go back behind the wall she'd had up before Jeremy had come into her garden. It was the easy way, the easy answer.

Or . . . was it?

She'd started to reply, but stopped typing. *Was* it easier to keep everything bottled up just because it wasn't fun to talk about bad stuff? Was it really easier to deal with trouble—heartbreak—alone? Was it easier to sit here behind a closed gate crying into a glass of wine . . . than it was to keep on living?

After all, did she really want to go back there, behind the wall? Had it been so great? Safe maybe, but . . . the truth was, it had been kind of lonely. She just hadn't understood that until she'd come out from behind it.

So she followed a new impulse without even weighing it.

JEREMY AND I BROKE UP. I'M IN MY GARDEN AND I WOULDN'T MIND SOME COMPANY IF YOU HAVE THE TIME. BUT IF YOU'RE BUSY, IT'S OKAY.

A moment later, another text arrived. OMG. BETHANY AND I WILL BE OVER IN FIVE, AND I JUST TEXTED CAMI, TOO.

It was the first time she'd ever invited her friends

into her garden. Because she didn't want to be alone there anymore. And because it was a place to be shared. All those Adirondack chairs proved it. This would be the first time they were filled.

"OH my God, what happened?" Christy asked, her eyes fraught with distress as she came rushing in through the gate, Bethany on her heels.

"And why haven't I been invited over to see this beautiful garden before?" Bethany asked, clearly awed by her surroundings. "This is breathtaking. I may need to paint it."

And as Tamra tried to think where to start, she broke into tears again.

And she pretty quickly remembered why she'd valued her solitude for so long—it was hard to cry in front of someone, even a friend; hard to let someone see you so vulnerable and raw. But Christy came over and bent down to hug her, telling her it was okay. And by the time Cami showed up, Christy was crying, too.

"Oh my God, what did he do?" Cami asked, bursting through the gate like a woman on fire. "Do I need to kill him?"

"No," Tamra said through her tears. "He didn't really do anything wrong. He just doesn't love me."

Cami's spine went ramrod straight. "That's wrong enough. I'm going to kill him. It's my fault you even met him, after all."

But Tamra was shaking her head. "No, I'm glad I met him. It was wonderful. And . . . and . . . I'm glad I love him even if he doesn't love me. I mean, it's kind of amazing to feel that way about someone, don't you think? Even if they don't appreciate it."

"Tamra, what did he say exactly?" Christy asked softly.

"That we were just casual. That he wasn't interested in love."

All three women gasped their collective horror.

"Asshole," Bethany bit off, taking a seat in one of the chairs next to the fire. Then she held up a bottle. "I brought wine."

"I already have a bottle open," Tamra said on a sniff.

Bethany just shrugged. "That's okay—we're gonna need more."

Over the course of the next half hour, Cami filled her girlfriends in on what had happened. How she'd so haphazardly professed her feelings, only to have Jeremy not return them, and why she'd had to end things with him.

"He's a fool," Christy proclaimed. Then sighed. "I'm only sorry he got so good-looking, since this might have been easier if he'd still been rocking the homeless vibe."

"But you're so wise," Bethany told her reverently. "As in, you're my new hero."

Tamra blinked, caught off guard. "Really?" The truth was, she hadn't expected them to understand how she'd felt, why she'd sent him away.

"If it had been me, I'd have probably hung on for dear life," Bethany confessed. "Because love is just so . . ."

"Intoxicating," Cami replied.

And they all nodded, and Bethany went on. "It's so potent that you just want more and more of that feeling, even when it's not good for you or not going the way you want. It's . . . blinding," she said. "But you're not blind. You're smart. Smart enough to walk away and keep your dignity. I dig that, man."

They were deep into the second bottle of wine—and Christy had just suggested they were going to need a third—when Tamra caught Cami giving her the strangest look, so much so that she asked, "*What*?"

And Cami said, "Thank you."

"For what?"

"For being so real with us about this. For just . . . letting it all out. You wouldn't have done that a few months ago. And I know this is awful, and my heart is breaking for you, but in another way, it's . . . nice. To be your friend this way."

And that nearly started Tamra crying again, but she girded herself this time, and got all the more honest. "A few months ago, I wouldn't even let anyone into this garden with me."

"It's beautiful," Cami said, looking around, clearly taking in the lights and windchimes in the trees. "I'm glad you did. And I hope we'll be here a lot now."

"You will be, I promise," Tamra told her. "Because the thing I'm learning is . . . it feels better to cry with friends than to be strong alone."

"Oh wow," Bethany said, hand to her heart. "Hero. Role model. You need to teach a class or something, girlfriend. You've so got it goin' on."

"Only I didn't before," Tamra said, shaking her head. "Not until now. And the really awful, tragic thing is—it was Jeremy who helped me open up and quit being afraid of letting people in. But he doesn't love me!" More tears sprang from her eyes.

And as Cami and Christy offered soothing sounds

of comfort, Christy reaching out from the chair beside her to squeeze her hand, Bethany said through clenched teeth, "Oh, the hideous irony."

"But . . . it's kind of poetic," Christy suggested sadly.

"In a tragic way," Cami agreed.

And that was what Tamra felt. A tragic loss. And she knew it wasn't *tragic* really. It wasn't death and destruction. It wasn't the horrible things Jeremy had endured in war. It was only love. But it still hurt like hell to love someone who didn't want you to, and who didn't love you back. "I put my heart on the table and he smashed it with his fist," Tamra whimpered. Then added, "Though I think this is partially the wine talking. Making it extra dramatic."

"Know what you need?" Bethany said.

Tamra looked up, across the fire at her. "What?"

"A new guy."

"I don't want a new guy," she whined. "I want the one I had."

"Doesn't matter," Bethany said, rejecting the thought with a swipe of her elaborately manicured hand down through the air. "A new guy makes you feel good. A new guy gives you something else to think about. A new guy is always a good idea."

"This soon?" Tamra asked, aghast at the thought. Then she let out a sigh. "But why am I even worried? There aren't exactly new men coming out of the woodwork around Coral Cove."

"True," Cami agreed, "but I believe you said something very similar right before Jeremy showed up."

She gasped. "Crap, you're right." Then blew out a tired breath.

"Just . . . be open to the new," Bethany suggested. "Because you never know when something new is going to arrive."

The truth was, Tamra didn't think a new man was going to magically appear on the horizon. And the further truth was, even if he did, she didn't think she'd be ready to dive right back into the dating pool while she was still in love with the ex-Marine up the road.

But there was a whole new truth inside her now, too: While she knew in her heart that no one would be a substitute for Jeremy, she also knew she no longer wanted to be a woman who sat around waiting for life to happen to her.

So she meant it with her whole heart when she said, "Okay. I'll be open to the new."

And then her heart broke a little more, remembering that she'd just lost a guy who she truly thought she could be happy with, and what a rare commodity that kind of love really was.

But he doesn't want my love. And I refuse to let heartbreak paralyze me again. No matter how bad it hurts.

THE following Saturday morning marked the Coral Cove Mini-Golf Paradise's festive grand opening. A sizable crowd of Coral Cove residents were in attendance, the large Grand Opening banner waved in the breeze, and colorful balloons dotted the course.

Before golfing officially began, though, Cami took the microphone she'd hooked up and thanked everyone for coming. "Welcome everyone!" she said to the crowd at large. "Look at this place! Isn't it amazing?"

And Tamra had to agree. She'd always been confident it would turn out well, but now that all the finishing touches were in place, she couldn't have been more pleased. The retro miniature golf course was the perfect addition to their beach community.

Of course, the only downer was that she was standing next to Jeremy. Because they had spearheaded the project together, Cami insisted on thanking them. "I know it will be a little awkward," she'd told Tamra, "but it only makes sense. You both worked hard on it and you should both be there to celebrate it, regardless of your relationship outside the job."

And since this had been planned for weeks, it would have been hard to disagree—and even harder to not show up and let Jeremy think he'd destroyed her that much.

So far, the two of them had exchanged only murmured hellos. So, yeah, it was awkward. And seeing him brought on a sense of loss she felt in her bones. But she'd survive. Cami had promised this part would only take a few minutes. And besides, they lived in the same tiny town; she would run into him sometimes, so she might as well get used to it.

Now Cami announced that there were free hot dogs and face painting, and that later there would be a hole-in-one contest and door prizes.

"What are they gonna paint on kids' faces?" Jeremy muttered, sounded truly perplexed. "Golf balls?"

And when she least expected it, Tamra smiled. Though she tossed him only a short look. "Probably animals or something."

"Mmm," Jeremy replied, tipping his head back slightly. Then added dryly, "Probably cats."

Tamra listened to Cami for a few more seconds

before saying to Jeremy, "You could probably request a dog. Since you're such a dog guy and all."

She caught the quick, quietly amused glance he tossed her way. He didn't crack a smile as he said, "Maybe I will. I think it would look good on me."

"Captain wouldn't let you back in the door, though."

"Captain's not the boss of me," he assured her. But she had a feeling Captain was the boss of Jeremy a little more than Jeremy even knew. She kept that to herself, though.

"Before we start playing golf," Cami was saying, "I have an exciting announcement! Another new business will soon be erected in our humble town, at the south end of the beach"—she pointed—"and right on the water. Jack DuVall, proprietor of our wonderful new miniature golf course, has just agreed to finance an establishment called the Barefoot Bar! The Barefoot Bar will offer a full bar with beer, wine, and specialty drinks along with a small menu of burgers and other light fare. The laid-back open-air restaurant will be the perfect place for drinks after the Sunset Celebration or to have a light lunch or dinner while enjoying Coral Cove Beach. In the words of Kenny Chesney, no shirt, no shoes, no problem. Sun Coast Construction has been hired as builder, and groundbreaking is scheduled for late next summer."

The crowd applauded before Cami continued with, "Jack and his fiancée, Christy, will christen our quaint little course here by playing the first game on it"— though this made Tamra and Jeremy exchange quick glances before turning their eyes back on Cami.

"First, though, we would be remiss if we didn't thank the two people who made this course a reality.

Tamra Day designed the entire course from the layout to the landscaping and color scheme. She even designed the gorgeous retro sign at the entrance. We're so lucky to have such a versatile and creative artist in our midst." Cami extended her hand Vanna White style. "And beside Tamra is Jeremy Sheridan, who provided the craftsmanship and hard labor. Jeremy built everything you see here, including the miniature buildings and other props on the holes, and he also served as a Jack-of-all-trades, pitching in on landscaping and anything else Tamra needed from him."

At that last part, Cami flicked a glance at Tamra, cringing slightly, apparently hearing her own double entendre—though it would have passed unnoticed had she not sent the glance and the cringe.

"So let's give these two a big round of applause for creating this wonderful golf course!" she finished. Finally.

"Smile and wave a little," Jeremy said under his breath and Tamra realized he was already doing those things, so she did, too. As opposed to standing there looking mildly horrified, stuck back on the idea of Jeremy giving her what she needed.

"How do you know to do that?" she asked quietly around her smile as the crowd clapped.

"War Hero 101," he said.

And she realized how often she forgot that Jeremy had once been a leader both in the military and his hometown. She didn't see him that way, and was so glad he'd let that image go. She liked the guy underneath much better—even if he could be a smart-ass.

As the applause died down, Cami announced it was time to play golf and that the line for clubs and balls formed at the hut. And Tamra turned to Jeremy to say, "We really did do a great job on this place. Thank you for that. For helping me create something really nice."

He met her gaze and she realized how much she missed looking into those eyes. "You're welcome," he said, "and thank you, too. For giving me the opportunity. It changed things for me, for the better, in a lot of ways."

Tamra heard them both saying things that skirted the bigger picture—attributing things to the golf course that were really much more about them, their relationship.

"Will you be working on the Barefoot Bar?" she asked.

He nodded. "That's the plan."

"I guess you start with Sun Coast soon."

"A week from Monday."

She nodded.

And he said, "How are you, Mary? Are you okay?"

She drew in her breath. Because he was ditching the small talk so suddenly.

And then she lied. "I'm fine." She wasn't fine at all. She still felt empty inside, and like Jeremy had left a space in her heart no one else would ever fill. But she'd be damned if she'd let him know that. And that brand of not being open wasn't about putting walls back up—it was just a little self-preservation. Two different things.

"And I'm sure you're fine, too," she added. Hoping it didn't sound sarcastic because it wasn't intended to be. Because if he didn't love her, being without her shouldn't be a loss.

"I'm okay," he said with a quick nod. Just as she would have expected.

And then there seemed to be nothing more to say. People milled about now—heading for the hot dogs or the golf clubs—and standing there staring at each other got officially awkward.

So Jeremy hiked a thumb over his shoulder to say, "Well, I'd better go get in line for that face paint dog," adding a small wink.

And she nodded. "I hope Captain forgives you."

"He will. I bring him fish."

And then he was walking away into the crowd.

Tamra watched him go, then stood there a moment catching her breath. She was in the process of deciding what to do next—go home and lick her wounds a little more or force herself to stay and try to have fun—when a shockingly handsome, shockingly muscular dark-haired man said, "Hi, my name is Alejandro." It came with a thick accent, a rolled "r," and a dash of dramatic flair. When she gave him a look that probably bordered on astonishment, he laughed and said, "But most people call me Alex."

"I'm Tamra." She was still confused, no matter what his name was, but tried to roll with it.

"I am new to Coral Cove," he informed her.

She nodded.

"I am from Brazil," he added.

"Ah," she said.

"And I am pleased to find a lady who is both so lovely and so talented this soon after my arrival."

Just then, Bethany came whisking up on high platform heels more appropriate for clubbing than miniature golfing. She wore a big smile and said, "I see you've met Alejandro. I told him you might be interested in showing him around Coral Cove. Isn't it wonderful to have a handsome new man in town?" She ended with a sly wink.

And Tamra felt like she probably wasn't ready for this. And she wasn't sure Alex here was her type.

But she'd promised herself to be open. Better that than spend the next fifteen years pining over a man who didn't really want her. So she said, "Welcome to Coral Cove," then held out her hand.

Which he promptly took into his and kissed.

"He's not going to trouble himself about you, that's sure and certain."

Frances Hodgson Burnett, *The Secret Garden*

Chapter 25

JEREMY STOOD eating a hot dog, trying to look like he wanted to be here. The truth was, he felt a little more like he *used* to feel—like he'd prefer heading back to his room. This was too big a crowd, too many people. He was getting better about that, but he still didn't like it.

Suddenly, a shot sounded. Jeremy's heart nearly exploded in his chest as he scanned the area—only to realize a balloon had popped. Shit. He hated balloons. For this very reason.

When his heart slowed back to normal, he resumed eating his dog—as opposed to really getting one painted on his face.

Just then, though, as a family near him got their hot dogs and moved on, it cleared a visual path between him and Tamra—and the dude kissing her hand. What the fuck?

But he lowered his eyes so he wouldn't be caught staring.

And what did he care anyway? If she wanted to let some he-man type kiss her hand, it was none of his business.

Even if the guy looked like kind of a clod.

And damn, she'd moved on pretty fast for somebody claiming to love him so much.

But whatever—he didn't care.

Just then, Reece stepped up beside him. "Really nice job on the course, man."

"Thanks," Jeremy replied absently. Then, realizing he was still watching Tamra talk to the big musclebound dude even though he'd intended to look away, he said to Reece, "Who's that?"

Reece followed his gaze and said, "New lifeguard."

Maybe Jeremy looked puzzled because Reece added, "You didn't want the job, remember? Town found a guy who did."

"Huh," he said.

"Name's Alejandro. He's from Brazil."

Jeremy felt his brow knit. "Ali what? Handro? Like with an h? What the hell kind of name is that?"

Reece laughed. "I don't think that's how it's spelled, but that's how you say it. And guess it's a Brazilian one, dude."

So a Brazilian lifeguard was kissing Tamra's hand? A big, burly one at that. A guy who'd taken a job he didn't want. *Ignore the irony in that, seriously.*

It was her business who she hung out with, even if something about the guy rubbed him the wrong way—even at this distance. But he decided he'd had enough grand opening for today.

"I'm takin' off," he said to Reece.

"Not gonna play a round?" Reece asked, eyebrows raised. "I mean, you built the place."

He could have—probably should have—given Reece any number of explanations for why he was leaving, but instead he just said, "No, man—gotta go."

And as he started to walk away, Reece said, "It's none of my business, but for what it's worth, you're starting to seem a lot more like . . . you used to."

Jeremy stopped, looked back. "What do you mean?"

"Some people might call it moody," Reece said. "A few might lean more toward . . . asshole-ish."

Jeremy tipped back his head in understanding. He wished he cared more, but right now he didn't. Right now he just needed to get away from this whole scene. So he walked off without another word.

He intended to head back to his room, but as he trudged down Coral Street, he found himself stepping inside the Hungry Fisherman instead. He wasn't sure why, but that was where his feet led him.

The place was dead quiet inside, with no lights on, making it even darker than usual. Abner called over, "We're not open yet, son," and Jeremy spotted him in his usual booth. "Polly's over at the big golf to-do, so we're openin' late today."

"Mind if I just sit?" he asked.

Abner shook his head. He wore a multi-colored beanie, complete with propeller on top. "Nope—help yourself."

Jeremy took his usual booth on the opposite side of the restaurant. He actually didn't mind them

being closed as he was in the market for some solitude. Maybe that was why he'd come here—the dark,
woody interior didn't let in much of the bright Florida
sunlight—and right now that suited him just fine. It
made it easier to forget where he was. Normally he
liked being at the beach, in a land of sun and sand, far
from war and far from the hometown where he'd let
people down. But right now he didn't want to be here
either for some reason.

Tamra's here. Tamra's here letting some guy kiss her
hand.

But he pushed that thought away. It didn't matter
He leaned his head back on the booth, shut his eyes,
tried to be nowhere and feel nothing.

"You all right, Jeremy?"

He opened his eyes, surprised to find Abner had
gotten up and walked over. Always surprising him,
this guy.

"Fine," Jeremy bit off.

"Don't *sound* fine."

"Just . . . tired," he claimed.

"I'll leave ya be," Abner said—and Jeremy liked
that about the man, that he knew when to leave well
enough alone.

When he turned to go, though, his beanie fell off
and hit the floor behind him. "Well, I'll be dogged," he
said, then bent to pick it up.

And Jeremy still wasn't much in the mood for talking, but he knew Abner a little now, and he'd always
wondered the thing no one ever seemed to ask him,
so he decided to ask. "Got a question for you, Abner,"
he said. "Why do you wear all those hats? What's that
about?"

Abner tipped his head back, taking in the question, turning it over in his head for a minute before he replied. "Started when I was a boy. My father once told me a man who wears many hats can always make his way in the world. Bein' just a little fella at the time, I misunderstood his meanin' and took to wearin' different hats around. Thought the very act of wearin' 'em would made me smart or somethin'.'"

Jeremy cocked his head slightly. "But you kept on wearing them even when you figured out there was more to it than that?"

The older man nodded. "Reckon what I found out pretty early on was . . . folks kinda steered clear of me when I was wearin' a funny hat of some kind. Just thought I was odd, I guess. And thing was, I kinda didn't mind that. I was always a keep-to-myself sort, ya see."

Jeremy absorbed that and asked, "What about Polly?"

"Polly didn't care nothin' about me wearin' hats. She just shoved her way right into my life whether I liked it or not. You mighta noticed she can be kinda pushy," he said with a wink.

"Yep," Jeremy said, letting only the hint of a grin sneak out.

"And truth was, I liked that about her," Abner said. "Knew it made her the real thing, the one worth hangin' on to. But the rest of the world . . . I didn't care much about gettin' to know 'em. What it boils down to is . . . you make yourself off-puttin', it works—people leave ya alone. And that's mostly what I still want— 'cause it got to be a habit early for me, and habits can be hard to break."

Thinking over the life Abner had created for himself, Jeremy asked, "Any regrets?"

"Mostly no," Abner replied thoughtfully. "If I have any it's that . . . I reckon it makes things a little hard on Polly. But she's learned to get by well enough and don't seem to mind. And . . . guess it can make life a little lonely at times when ya keep people out. Who knows, if I had it to do over, maybe I'd listen to my mother when she told me to take off those silly hats so other kids would play with me—maybe learn to not want to be left alone." He stopped, shrugged. "I'm not an unhappy man—but sometimes I wonder if . . . well, if maybe life coulda been a little richer in ways . . . if I'd let it be."

THE next morning Jeremy awoke to find he had a text message awaiting him, from his buddy, Marco. SORRY FOR THE SHORT NOTICE, BUT GONNA BE PASSING THROUGH YOUR AREA AROUND LUNCH TODAY. ANY CHANCE WE CAN MEET UP?

ABSOLUTELY. Jeremy might have been in the mood to hibernate a little, but for his military brothers, it was different—being with them didn't require effort. They'd traveled the same road together, after all.

He met Marco at noon at the pier. When they spotted each other, they both broke into smiles and then did that guy hug thing that was mostly about slapping each other on the back.

"You look good, man," Jeremy told his old friend. Marco had aged a little since Afghanistan—and it reminded Jeremy that years had begun to pass since then, putting that part of his life further and further in his past now—but his friend looked strong, healthy, fit.

"You, too, bud," Marco said. "Hell of a lot better than the last time I saw you." He laughed and Jeremy recalled that he'd texted Marco a selfie on request several months earlier when Jeremy had admitted he hadn't shaved in a while. Jeremy laughed about it now, too.

"So on vacation with the family, huh?" Jeremy asked.

Marco nodded. "We're hitting the beach at St. Pete for a couple days, then headed over to Disney. The girls have appointments to meet Mickey Mouse and princesses and all kinds of fun shit like that." After more good-natured laughter, he added, "They're killing time playing that little putt-putt course up in town right now."

"I'll have you know I built that little course," Jeremy announced, realizing he truly took pride in it.

Even more so when Marco said, "No shit? Looked nice, man. Good for you. Good to see how much things have turned around for you."

As they meandered out onto the pier past the few fishermen and sightseers there, it gave him a chance to tell his friend about his new job and how he felt like he'd gotten back on his feet here. And he took pride in that, too. He really cared about something again. And it was a damn good, solid feeling.

When they reached the end of the pier where it was quiet, empty, they both sat down on a bench looking out on the horizon. Sun sparkled on the water. And a part of Jeremy wanted to just keep on like they were, talking about how good life was for both of them these days.

But the thing was—Marco was the one other guy

on the planet who'd been with him that horrible night Chuck had died. And even though he was doing a lot better about that, they'd never discussed it—ever— and now Jeremy wondered why. Maybe Marco had just wanted to let him off the hook by never mentioning it. But somehow it seemed important to . . . face the truth, accept it all the way, quit running. He might have run away from the golf course yesterday, but he suddenly didn't want to run from *this* anymore. And if Marco was here, well . . . maybe God had dropped in his lap the way to quit running from it.

"I don't want to take us both back to Helmand," Jeremy said to his friend, "but . . . there's something that's always bothered me, something I maybe need to get square on."

Next to him, Marco appeared tense, possibly troubled. "About Chuck."

Jeremy let out a heavy breath. Clearly they were on the same wavelength if Marco went there that quick. "Yeah, man," he murmured, not looking at his friend. In fact, he realized they were both staring out to sea.

And they stayed quiet for a long moment after that, until finally Jeremy said what he had to say. Maybe it was about true acceptance, or maybe he was seeking some kind of absolution from the man who'd seen it all go down—but whatever the reason, he had to. "I know it's my fault he's dead. I know I killed him."

He crushed his eyes shut against the ugly words— even now, to say it out loud was so much harder than just knowing the truth in his head.

Only that was when Marco said, "What? *You*?"

Shit. Did this mean they *weren't* on the same wavelength? Hell—that was going to make this harder. A lot harder. Now he turned to look at Marco, who met his gaze, and he swallowed past the lump in his throat as he said, "Yeah." Then more quietly, "Me."

Confusion reshaped Marco's face, and Jeremy was starting to feel a little confused as well, when Marco told him, "I thought it was me."

Jeremy's jaw dropped. "Huh?"

"I thought it was me," Marco repeated. "When he walked through the door, I thought he was more Taliban and fired."

Jeremy drew in his breath. "Me, too." Then he blinked, trying to clear his head, make sense of this. Because . . . whoa. "Man," he said softly, "are you telling me all this time I've been sure I was the one who did it when . . ."

"When all this time I've been sure it was me," Marco said.

They both went silent then, withdrew their gazes from each other, and Jeremy bent over slightly, ran his hands through his hair.

He wasn't sure what else to say. This reshaped his whole view of that night. He'd been so wrapped up in knowing he'd fired his gun in that direction that it had never crossed his mind that Marco had been firing, too, maybe also in the same direction.

Finally, Marco said, "To know you've been going through the same thing I have . . . it tears me up, dude."

Jeremy just nodded. Because yeah, to learn his friend had endured this same exact suffering, even if he appeared to have handled it better outwardly, ripped at his soul. "I hate this, man—hate knowing you've felt that way, too. Because it's . . . fucking torture. And . . ." He shook his head. "You probably didn't even do it. You've probably been punishing yourself for nothing."

"I could say the same about you," Marco pointed out. And it made Jeremy flinch. He was just so used to thinking—knowing—he'd been the one to fire the fatal shot, that it was hard to change that in his head, even now, even if this made things different in some way.

"I've just had this ingrained in me so long," he explained. "It's like . . . a part of me now."

"I know what you mean," Marco agreed. "Only . . . now it's a part of me, and you, that that we don't even know for sure is real. I mean, we couldn't have both done it."

"Actually, we could," Jeremy pointed out. Then reminded Marco, "It all happened fast."

Next to him, Marco nodded, pressed his lips together flat, looked off into the distance, clearly still weighing all this.

"I . . . confided in somebody about it recently," Jeremy confessed. "And she made the argument that it could have been the bad guys just as easily as me."

Marco nodded. "Yeah, I've always known that. I just thought . . . the angles made it likelier to be me."

"Or me."

"Shit—I don't know what to think anymore." Marco shook his head.

"Me neither," Jeremy agreed. His mind felt blown sky high, in fact.

Marco let out a tired sigh. "The upshot is, we'll never know for sure."

Jeremy nodded. "For better or worse." Then he looked at his friend. "This . . . gives it a new perspective, though. Because, I mean, I've been so sure. It never even occurred to me . . ."

"I know, man, I know." Marco stared back out to sea. "I guess it makes me wonder . . . what other perspectives we could be missing. Not that I want to let myself off the hook—I don't." He shook his head. "I mean, I take responsibility. Inside myself."

Jeremy nodded. "Me, too. But yeah . . . I guess if nothing else, now we share the burden."

Marco shrugged. "Better than carrying it alone, I guess." One more head shake. "Maybe. I don't know anymore."

"The person I told, she also said Chuck wouldn't want me to keep suffering. And I guess I've . . . started making peace with it."

Marco nodded. "She somebody special to you?"

Jeremy let out a breath. "No, not really," he said. But in that heavy moment, it felt like the biggest lie he'd ever told.

JEREMY had spent the last few days not doing much. He'd lain on the beach, trying to clear his head—on a lot of different subjects. He'd thought a week off between jobs might be nice, but he realized now that he'd had the last two years off and that working was good for him; not working gave him too much time to think.

Of course, maybe some of the thinking was good.

Though what he'd learned from Marco didn't absolve him from firing his weapon that night, at the same time it did force him to re-examine the whole event. It reminded him that just because he'd been there, that didn't make him a reliable witness—it was hard to process things in extreme stress and that had been about the most extreme stress of his life. So he didn't absolve himself, but maybe he was beginning to forgive himself a little more.

And he hoped Marco would, too. He planned to keep in closer touch with his buddy.

But some of the thinking was bad. Because it was about Tamra.

His conversation with Marco had also forced him to see he'd minimized what he'd shared with her. He'd tried to make it nothing when it was . . . something. More than something. She'd helped him turn his life around and that counted for more than he could measure.

He felt like an ass now for making so light of their relationship. But he'd been thrown into panic mode, shutdown mode. He'd been mentally running away.

That was what the whole last two years of his life had been about—running away. And he'd thought he'd stopped that, but the second she'd told him she loved him, he'd gone right back to running.

Now he sat outside behind the Happy Crab with his usual companion these days—one who happened to come with fur. At least he didn't talk much.

He peered down at him and said, "Know why you and me get along? Because you don't want anything from me besides fish. And I'm okay with that kind of superficial relationship."

If he was honest with himself, he'd felt a little lonely since parting with Tamra. But the hell of it was that . . . it just felt safer that way. And he could have hung out some with Reece if he'd wanted, or hell—probably Abner for that matter. And one night Riley, the nice old man who managed the motel, had invited him to watch a football game on TV. But Jeremy had passed. And he wasn't sure why. He only knew that it had something to do with Chuck, and also something to do with Tamra.

"I heard from Polly you adopted a cat."

He looked up to see Fletcher McCloud round the building.

Fletcher smiled. "Don't worry—I know it's a secret from Reece."

"I'm not really a cat guy," he told Fletcher. "More of a dog person."

Fletcher's gaze dropped to where Jeremy absently held down one hand to stroke behind the cat's ear. "You kind of seem like a cat guy."

"I was mostly guilted into it," he explained.

Yet it was clear the other man wasn't buying it. "None of my business, but sometimes it's wise to just accept certain things, learn to roll with what *is* instead of what was."

Jeremy took that in, turned it over in his brain. And then let out a giant sigh. Aw hell. He was a cat guy.

"I've been wanting to get to know you better," Fletcher said, "but our paths never seem to cross."

Jeremy forced a laugh. "My path doesn't cross many others. Tend to keep to myself."

"I'd heard that was changing."

"Well, changed back." Jeremy crossed his arms.

"That's unfortunate," Fletcher said. "Good people here. Knowing them has enriched my life."

It put Jeremy on the defensive. "They *are* good people. Guess I'm just not into . . ."

"Having friends?" Fletcher asked.

At this, Jeremy shrugged. "Makes life simpler, you ask me."

"Does it?" Fletcher countered. "I would get lonely without people. Relationships are the spice of life."

Jeremy just gave his head a short shake. "For some guys, I guess."

"What's the spice of *your* life then? If not people?" And when Jeremy didn't give him an answer, because he couldn't think of one, Fletcher added, "What else is there really?"

And Jeremy wanted to just shut up and let this conversation end, but he heard himself reply any way, with what he was really thinking. "People . . . make life complicated. They come with obligations. Or they need to be taken care of. Or they want to take care of *you*. Or they go away. Or they die."

"But it's a trade-off," Fletcher said without missing a beat, "and what you get in return is worth it."

"Is it?"

"Always," Fletcher replied. "Because it's the whole point of living. It's why we're here. Some people would say that to avoid relationships is to live your life in fear."

"Fear of what?"

"Fear of love. Fear of loss. Loving can mean losing, my friend. Some people mistakenly think it's easier to avoid the whole thing."

Jeremy let out a heavy breath. "Don't take this the wrong way, but . . . you're a very intense, philosophical dude. I mean, I was just sitting here enjoying the weather and . . ."

Fletcher let out a laugh. "I hear ya—and I apologize for turning a hello into an analysis. I was just looking for Reece." And as he started to walk past, toward the motel office, Jeremy thought he seemed like some wannabe therapist. But another part of him was forced to recall he'd once said something similar to Tamra— he'd told her sometimes you had to be bigger than your fears. Maybe it had been easier when they'd been talking about her, not him. Or . . . maybe he'd just been smarter *with* her than *without* her.

Regardless, he was glad the conversation was over. But something still made him call to Fletcher, "I'm glad your wife came back, man."

The tightrope walker had just opened the back office door, but looked over to say, "Thanks. Me, too." Then he disappeared inside.

Although it was a beautiful October day in Florida, Jeremy followed the urge to retreat even a little more and headed back to his room. Of course, Captain followed, ever Jeremy's furry shadow. It was the middle of the day, but a nap sounded good.

No, a nap is bad. Back at Whisper Falls, he'd napped too much. Especially during periods without many nightmares. During those times, sleep was sweet escape from life.

But he still lay down because sleep sounded good. He grabbed his phone, turned on some music, low. Bush singing "Glycerine." He got lost in the song's low, soothing tones.

Don't shut down. Don't start closing yourself off.

But he still wanted the nap.

The problem with that was the damn cat. He kept walking around on Jeremy. "Geez," he finally said, opening his eyes to look up at the cat whose big front paws were planted firmly on his chest. Captain peered back down at him through his one good eye.

Jeremy sighed. "You're pretty damn clingy for such a big tough guy," he said. The cat let out a small mew and their gazes stayed connected, and something in the connection softened Jeremy a little. "But . . . I guess you just want what everybody wants—to be loved, right?" And only because no one was around to see it, he hugged the large cat to his chest.

And then his own words echoed in his ears. About everyone wanting to be loved.

It's normal, what Tamra wants.

It would be normal for you to want it, too. Normal to be brave enough to want it.

His chest tightened. Because he knew he loved her, too. But he stuffed the thought down as soon as it struck him.

Shit, Fletcher was right. Except . . . it wasn't fear for Jeremy. It was a conscious choice. He'd already endured so much loss in war; he needed time to get over that. And the whole love thing with her—it was just too much too soon. It only made sense—for both their sakes—for him to let her go. He didn't know how to take care of someone and maybe he never would. He could just barely let himself feel responsible for a cat.

And this protected her as much as him. He'd put on a pretty good show with her—and with himself—for a while. But the truth was, he was still a man running away from life. And she deserved better than that.

"It was th' joy that mattered."

Frances Hodgson Burnett, *The Secret Garden*

Chapter 26

IT WAS a beautiful evening for a wedding in Coral Cove. Tamra stood at the top of the wooden stairs that descended onto the beach from Sea Shell Lane, looking out over the picturesque scene. The white arbor Jack and Fletcher had built for the occasion rested on a blanket of soft pale sand, rows of white chairs arranged neatly facing it. A spray of wildflowers, with pale yellow roses sprinkled in, was a finishing touch on the arch. A guitar player situated to one side strummed light pre-wedding music that wafted through the air.

Guests were beginning to arrive and take their seats for the sunset nuptials and Tamra had already met a number of Christy's friends from Jeremy's hometown of Destiny, Ohio. But she tried not to think of Jeremy as she spoke with them. She tried to focus on the night and the occasion and her friend who would soon walk down the aisle and marry the love of her life.

She'd been encouraging people to sign the guestbook, then directing them to the ushers—Reece and one of Jack's friends from up north. Christy and Bethany were in Christy and Jack's cottage getting ready. And Jack, who'd gotten dressed at best man Fletcher's house across the street, had just come out to start greeting guests as well.

And during that quiet moment as she stood back and took in the scene, a shocking thought hit her. *I want this.*

And the shocking part was . . . she'd never really let herself truly want that before. A wedding. Lifelong romance and love and passion. Happily ever after—the real deal.

And she wasn't sure she believed she'd ever have it, but . . . something in her had changed. Before Jeremy, the very idea of love had seemed distant and almost impossible, like something that just wasn't in the cards for her. And she'd blindly accepted that. Jeremy might not love her, or maybe he was just running from his feelings—she still didn't know—but either way, he'd opened up something inside her, shown her she could have what other women had, and that it didn't take perfection or being a certain size or a classic beauty. It only took letting her inner light shine, and letting someone see it. It only took letting someone in.

And Jeremy hadn't wanted to *stay* in.

And she was far from over him. The truth was—she didn't feel like the pain was ebbing at all. At the moment, she didn't feel like she'd *ever* be able to let go of her yearning for him, and for more of what they'd shared. She wanted to hold him when he was hurting. She wanted to make sure he healed inside. She wanted to let him help *her* heal some more, too.

But she'd always been a logical woman and that

hadn't gone *entirely* out the window with love. And she knew, logically, because people said so, that maybe someday she'd get over him. And that maybe, just maybe, it was okay to let herself begin to want and wish for what Christy had with Jack.

Of course, she worried for Jeremy. She knew from her friends that he'd been withdrawn lately and she didn't want him to relapse. She'd seen such light in him and she wanted it to shine just as badly as she wanted her own to.

She didn't know if he'd come to the wedding. He'd been invited, and there were lots of people from his hometown here who would surely love to see him, yet knowing him as she did, she realized he might just decide it was simpler to stay in tonight.

But don't let yourself get mired in thoughts of a man who doesn't want you. Be in the moment—be here for your friend's special day. So she did her best to shove thoughts of Jeremy aside and put back on a smile for Christy and Jack and the lovely wedding that was about to commence.

"Hello there, Tamra."

She turned to see Alejandro just as he grabbed on to her hand, closing it between both of his. He wore an eager smile.

"Hi Alejandro." She tried to smile back.

Jeremy had changed her life for the better and she was determined not to go back into her sullen shell. Even if that meant trying to talk to Alejandro. Even if he didn't seem to have much personality.

A few minutes later, during which he never relinquished possession of her hand, they parted ways. His thick accent kept her from always understanding him, but she thought she'd agreed to connect with him after the ceremony. For better or worse.

Just then, Bethany arrived at the top of the steps. "So, you and Alejandro."

Tamra sighed. "I don't know. His name is a mouthful. And he's very touchy-feely."

"Men of his culture are very openly affectionate," Bethany explained. "And at least he's hot. I know there might not be much else there, but don't knock hot."

Tamra nodded. "I know. Hot is nice. I'm trying." Then she checked her watch. It was almost time for the wedding to start. *Jeremy must not be coming.* But she pushed the thought aside as soon as it entered her head. It didn't matter.

"Do you have any idea what Jack's big surprise is for Christy?" Tamra asked. The last few days there had been whispers about a surprise, but no one knew what it was.

"Nope," Bethany said. "But I guess we'll find out soon." Then she got a faraway look in her eyes as a small smile stole over her. "You know, I have a feeling this wedding is going to be epic."

"I agree. Jack and Christy are perfect together and it's going to be a beautiful ceremony."

"Yeah. But . . ." Bethany gave her head a speculative tilt. "I actually mean more than that. I just think it's going to be a special night."

FLETCHER exited his house in the first tux he'd ever worn. For his own wedding, he'd been in a cheap suit, Kim in a flowy sundress—and it had been perfect for them at that beautiful moment of their lives. But time marched on, and just like when he'd fancied up for the engagement party, right now he felt pretty damn good in his monkey suit. He was honored to have been chosen as Jack's best man. And though he'd never been a guy who cared much about how he looked, maybe the recent responses to his change in appearance had given him a new confidence.

That confidence was confirmed when Tamra, standing with Bethany at the top of the stairs, said, "Whoa—look at you! You clean up nice, Fletch!"

He let his smile connect not only with Tamra's gaze, but Bethany's, too. "It's for a good cause," he said with a wink. "Jack just texted me. His surprise has arrived, so it's all systems go whenever Christy is ready to walk down the aisle."

Bethany drew in a breath. "Wow, this is really it."

And Fletcher felt that, too—the gravity of the moment. Though for him, there was more to it than just Jack and Christy saying their I do's.

"I'll go get her," Bethany said.

Fletcher and Tamra both nodded, and as Bethany started toward the cottage, Tamra asked, "Where's Kim? I haven't seen her today."

"She's, uh, not coming," he said. "In fact, she's gone."

At this, Bethany stopped, looked back, wide-eyed, mouth in the shape of an "O." "Gone?"

Wow, he liked her. He liked how direct she was right now, not hiding her interest in the situation. And so he decided to be just as direct. Because life was short. People had been telling him that ever since Kim's original departure, but only now was he really getting that. He knew things had unfolded exactly as they were supposed to, yet he also realized he didn't want to waste any more time.

"Yeah," he said. "She left last night—for good."

"Um . . ." Tamra said, clearly stumped for words.

As Bethany remarked, "Huh."

He met Bethany's lovely gaze full on as he told her, "I'm hoping you and I might be able to . . . start over."

And she beamed at him, her smile as brilliant as the sun dropping toward the horizon in the distance. Only then she took on a coy, playful look that he'd seen in her before. "It's a wedding, a time of new beginnings, right?"

And then she turned and headed toward the cottage to bring out the bride.

Only when she was gone did Tamra grab his wrist and speak in a hushed-but-freaked-out tone. "What the hell did I miss?"

Fletcher sighed. It had been a long couple of days, complete with a lot of soul searching, but he was truly at peace with how things had turned out. "I just had to accept the truth—we couldn't go back in time to who we once were and what we once had. I'm a different person now. And besides, my trust in her was shattered—I just never thought about that when I was waiting for her to come back. Neither one of us wanted to accept it, but we both felt it." He looked into his best friend's eyes. "I thought it would be easy, Tamra. I thought it would be just picking up right where we left off. But it wasn't."

She still looked just as taken aback as before he'd spoken. "But you waited so long and wanted it so much," she said. "And it seemed like such a miracle. How can you let that go?"

"It *was* a miracle. But I'm realizing now that some miracles aren't meant to be held on to—some miracles are just moments in time, amazing moments, and *that's* what you hold on to, the memory and wonder of the moment." He looked out over the sunset, then told Tamra the truth he understood now. "I had to get her back before I could let her go. I needed to . . . have that choice. I needed to see how things were between us. I've done that now. And it'll be all right. Just like she told me in that note four years ago. Everything will be okay. Everything *is* okay. I feel that in my soul."

Tamra reached out, squeezed his hand. And he squeezed it back, grateful for her friendship.

Then she tilted her head and said, "Did you know Bethany's staying? In Coral Cove? For good?"

Fletcher blinked, and suspected that now *he* looked freaked out. "Um, no. What the hell did *I* miss?"

"A lot, apparently. But I think you're about to get back on track."

He let himself smile. "I was on track all along, my friend. It was just a long and winding one. But I think it's about to get straighter, a little easier to navigate."

As Tamra took her seat, she spotted Jack's surprise. Christy's Grandpa Charlie stood at the end of the aisle, waiting to escort Christy down it—the key word being *stood*. The old man had been in a wheelchair the entire time Tamra had known him, with occasional outings on a walker. But now he stood in a tuxedo, looking proud as a peacock, with only a cane for support.

When Bethany appeared at the top of the wooden

steps that led down to the beach, the guitarist began to play a lovely version of "Here Comes the Sun," and the crowd turned to watch as she descended the stairs, passed Grandpa Charlie—giving him a smile—and then made her way up the aisle in a flowy, gauzy lavender dress.

And then Christy appeared, a wreath of flowers in her hair that matched the small bouquet in her hand, in an equally flowy, lovely white dress that struck Tamra as the perfect choice for a beach wedding. As all eyes went to the bride, Tamra watched Christy pause to take in the scene, and the moment—and then Jack, who stood with Fletcher and the minister in front of the arbor.

It was only as she descended the sun-bleached stairs, however, that her gaze fell on Grandpa Charlie, waiting there for her. She gasped, and her eyes fell shut for a moment, clearly holding back tears of joy.

"How did you do this?" Tamra heard Christy ask him quietly, glad she'd sat in the last row and could catch this exchange.

"Been workin' on it with Jack for weeks now. He's a good coach."

Christy switched her gaze lovingly to her husband-to-be for just a moment before she hooked her arm through that of her grandfather.

"Now I just hope we make it down the aisle," he told her with a wink.

And she said, "Don't worry—we will. We're in this together. I won't let you fall."

And then it was Tamra fighting back tears as she watched Christy and Charlie proceed slowly down the aisle, where he gave her away, and where she watched

Jack and Christy pledge themselves to one another, becoming husband and wife.

JEREMY had watched the wedding from up above. He'd shown up late and hadn't wanted to interrupt. Coming had been a last minute decision—but he'd made himself do it, because he knew he should, and he knew he'd probably be better off for it. Hiding in his room would have been easier, but maybe he'd decided he was tired of taking the easy road. The truth was, when he took the road that seemed a little rockier and required a little more effort, it always turned out to be a road that actually led somewhere. Usually somewhere good.

Another big impetus was his sister, Tessa. She and Lucky had been due to arrive only a few hours prior to the wedding, so they'd made plans to connect here. He didn't want to get back into the business of letting people down. Well, not his family anyway. He knew he'd already let Tamra down—but maybe he could keep his disappointing to a minimum and not spread it around the way he used to.

Now he stood off to the side watching the reception—also taking place on the beach. It was getting dark, so that made it easier to lurk in the shadows.

Polly and Abner were in charge of the food, using Christy and Jack's place as a home base, and the DJ had set up in their backyard, placing speakers in the sand below. And to Jeremy's surprise, there was no fish on the menu—Abner was grilling hamburgers and kebobs while Polly put hot dogs on spears for people who wanted to roast their own over a fire pit on the beach. Near the fire was also a s'mores bar, and a tower of pastel cupcakes decorated with candy shells, starfish, and seahorses, courtesy of the Beachside Bakery, next door to Gino's.

Old friends from Destiny milled about. Anna Romo, who he'd once had that crush on, and her now longtime boyfriend, Duke Dawson, looked happy roasting hot dogs together. Amy and Logan Whitaker stood talking with Christy, who made a lovely bride. And he spotted Anna's brother Mike Romo and his wife and young daughter near the s'mores stuff, preparing to roast marshmallows.

"Where the hell is Jeremy? Anybody seen him?"

He swung his focus to the sound of Lucky's voice to find his brother-in-law joining the crowd by the fire pit.

"Good question," Anna said. "I'd heard he moved down here, and I was hoping to say hello. How's he doing?"

"Really well, from what we've been told," said his sister, Tessa, now at Lucky's side. "He was supposed to meet us here."

Cami, who'd been helping at the cupcake table, called over, "I thought I saw him right after the ceremony, but I'm not sure where he went."

And then his eyes fell on Tamra as she came down the stairs from Sea Shell Lane, probably running back and forth, helping out. And damn, she looked beautiful. She wore another knockout dress that showed off her shape and made him wonder why she'd ever hidden it. And he was glad she was comfortable enough to let the world see that beauty. The difference between the way she looked tonight and the way she'd looked at the wedding shower was . . . she *was* comfortable now. She wasn't nervous; she wasn't wondering what anyone would think. She was just being her beautiful self.

His eyes were drawn from Tamra only when a more surprising sight came into view—Fletcher and Bethany looking as chummy as they had at the party. Something had changed here—something big. Clearly the wife was out of the picture. And Fletcher looked pretty damn happy, so Jeremy guessed that meant everything was okay.

They walked past close enough for him to hear Fletcher saying he had a lot to explain to her. But her eyes shone bright as the strings of lights now stretching across the beach around the reception as she took his hands in hers and said, "Later. Tonight is just about new beginnings and being happy. The dancing is going to start soon—I want to dance the night away and celebrate my best friend's happiness. With you."

Looking around the beach, it struck him that he was probably the least happy guy here. Hell, even Abner looked happy tonight, having donned his top hat again for the wedding, though now he'd changed to a fluffy white chef's hat as he manned the grill.

A sweet song about love and swaying palm trees called "Always" filled the air as Christy and Jack shared their first dance on the sand. And Jeremy looked at all the people at the wedding, all those damn happy people. And it hit him that . . . love didn't always come easy. He knew a lot of those people and he knew they'd had to fight to get where they were— they'd had to overcome troubles and hurt and demons, same as he'd been trying to. And the only difference between them was . . . they'd done it. And they'd let themselves be happy. They'd let themselves get over whatever fears held them down and let themselves love somebody.

Just then, the same big, muscle-bound lifeguard from the golf course opening came rushing up to Tamra, boldly took her face between his hands, and planted a kiss on her lips!

What the hell?

He didn't know what he'd missed between these two—he only knew he didn't like it! And he didn't really have a clear plan as he started toward her across the sand—but seeing another guy kiss her that way had just pushed him over the edge.

The guy was up in her face, whispering sweet nothings or some such shit when Jeremy reached her. He closed his hand over her arm and turned her toward him to say, "What the hell is happening here?"

She blinked, then looked a little outraged, which was maybe understandable, but he didn't care. "A wedding," she bit off.

"No, I mean *here*." He wagged his finger back and forth between her and the he-man. Who might pound him into the ground any minute, so it was probably a good time to be a Marine, which came with certain skills. But he wasn't very concerned about that right now, either.

"What do *you* care?" she snapped at him.

And he snapped right back at her, "I care because I love you, damn it."

"What?" she spewed, looking just as shocked as he supposed made sense.

He was kind of shocked, too, but he was in this now,

and ready to plow full steam ahead. "I love you," he repeated. And though some people were dancing now, he also sensed other people turning their attention in this direction.

"I thought you said you didn't," she replied.

And he decided this was a good time for them to step away from the crowd—he didn't want to make a spectacle of them at Christy and Jack's wedding. But he had stuff to say. Big stuff.

So he more gently took Tamra's hand and pulled her a few feet away from everyone else. And he spoke more softly but with just as much conviction as he said, "I'm a man with PTSD, Mary! Why would you take my word for something so important when you know I've got serious issues?"

She was blinking again, repeatedly now, just before she said, "Well, what am I supposed to think here? Yesterday you didn't love me, today you do—how do I know you won't say you don't love me again tomorrow?"

Jeremy took a deep breath. And suddenly nothing in the world seemed as important as making her understand, making her trust, making her believe in him. So he got as honest as he possibly could, and he let down every wall he'd ever put up. "First of all, I did love you yesterday," he explained. "And the day before that. And the day before that, too. I've just been running from it.

"But I don't want to run anymore, Tamra. And I know you don't have any reason to believe me, except . . . I don't put myself on the line lightly. That much you know about me. I don't say I love you to anyone I don't love. I barely say it to people I *do* love. So if I'm saying it to you . . . you know it's real.

"And I'm sorry I hurt you. I'm sorry I tried to make us . . . less than we were. Because you . . . saved me. You saved me the way Chuck tried to save me. And I . . . fucked up both attempts. But I'm done fucking things up, honey. I'm done throwing away the good in life. And *you're* the good in life. You're better than I deserve—I know that.

"I told you once not to make decisions out of fear, but that's exactly what I've been doing. Only I don't want to do it anymore. I just want to love you. I want to love you the way you *should* be loved. You're an amazing woman. And you and I . . . we fit together. And I want that. I just want that."

Jeremy was out of things to say. He'd said all that he could, all that was in his heart. So he stopped, waiting to see if he stood a chance with her—or if she'd do what she probably should and tell him to go to hell.

And when she said nothing, just stood there gaping at him, he concluded, "I've . . . I've been contrary."

"That's a nice way of putting it," she said.

"I know," he admitted. "Here's another way. I was a selfish ass. Caught up in fear. Old fears. That I want to let go of now."

"What fears are we talking about?" she asked.

"Fear of losing people," he told her. "Fear of not being able to keep anyone safe."

"I can take care of myself," she assured him.

"I know," he told her. And he truly did. "But when I love someone, I feel a responsibility to keep them safe. Body and soul. And Afghanistan made me think I couldn't do that anymore, keep anyone safe. Even a damn cat."

Her voice finally went a little softer. "You seem to be doing okay with the cat."

"Yeah," he said. "And now I'm thinking I'd like to try my hand with someone who doesn't just love me for bringing food."

"The cat loves you for more than that," she insisted.

He just shrugged. "He's an easy audience. He doesn't realize how contrary I can be. And he's pretty forgiving. Are . . . are you? Can you forgive me, Tamra? Give me another chance?"

Tamra couldn't believe this was happening. Because even if she hadn't known Jeremy long, she felt she knew him well—she understood him. And she understood about walls—she'd kept them up for so long herself.

And now he wanted her to forgive him. The request forced her to think of her past. The way her parents had emotionally abandoned her. The men who'd done the same. She'd spent a long time coming back from those betrayals. "Forgiving and forgetting are two different things," she pointed out to Jeremy now. "Forgiveness I believe in. Forgetting can be harder, though."

He took her hands in his. And oh—it felt so much better, so much more . . . right, than when silly Alejandro did. "I'm a troubled guy, Mary," Jeremy told her. "I know it, you know it. I can be moody as hell. I can get trapped in my own head. I've got ghosts all around me. And I feel I owe a hell of a lot to more people than I can count right now and sometimes that overwhelms my brain."

She saw him swallow. And understood that he was baring his soul to her. In a deeper way than he ever had before. "But I can be better. I'm so much better than I used to be. Except . . . on the day I hurt you. That day I messed up bad. I made an awful mistake. And I wish I could take it back, do it over again. But . . . I understand if that's too much to ask."

Tamra searched her heart. She'd told herself today that she was open to love. She'd promised herself she wouldn't close off that kind of hope. And so even if it was scary as hell in a way to trust Jeremy again, she knew she had to. She had to.

"Everyone gets a do-over," she said softly.

"Even in love?" he asked.

She nodded, slowly, surely. "Even in love."

"That's amazingly generous." He squeezed her hands in his.

And she gave him a gentle smile as she told him, "See? I'm not so contrary after all."

"Now," he said at the end of the story,
"it need not be a secret anymore."

Frances Hodgson Burnett, *The Secret Garden*

Epilogue

D<small>EAR</small> F<small>RIENDS</small>,

Season's Greetings from sunny Coral Cove, Florida!

The most exciting news in my life? A year to the day since we met, Jeremy asked me to marry him! There are no words for how happy this man has made me. Let's be honest—before him, I was a little bit of a stick-in-the-mud. But Jeremy has found in me lighter parts of myself I'd truly forgotten existed—and I'm pretty sure I've improved his life in many ways, as well. We're excited to be planning a small, intimate ceremony in my garden next spring, with a reception for the entire community afterward at the Hungry Fisherman. Hope you like seafood!

I continue to find success selling my art and to be inspired by the other artists I'm lucky enough to share this community with. Among them my next door neighbor and fabulous jewelry designer Christy, my incredible seascape painting friend Bethany, and her boyfriend and my best friend, Fletcher, who puts the fun in funambulist every night as he walks his tightrope next to the Coral Cove Pier.

Jeremy is rising rapidly through the ranks at Sun Coast Construction, and takes true satisfaction in his work. He was named foreman for the building of the Barefoot Bar currently being constructed on the beach right now. It's a wonderful coincidence that our dear friend and my next door neighbor, Jack, (Christy's husband, as luck would have it! Small world, right?) is the owner and financier of the project—especially since Jeremy and I met primarily through working on one of Jack's other business ventures, the Coral Cove Mini-Golf Paradise.

Speaking of Coral Cove businesses, the whole town is looking great! Another close friend, Cami, continues to serve as head of the town planning commission, and my oldest friend in Coral Cove, Reece, just put a new coat of paint on the Happy Crab to celebrate the fact that business there is booming again. Polly and Abner continue to make improvements to the Hungry Fisherman with Cami's guidance—soon the restaurant will sport a lighter, airier interior with a dockside theme. Polly has hired two new waitresses, and the biggest shocker of them all: she's retired her old uniforms, trading up to khaki capris! More and more new businesses are looking to make their home here, but Cami vows that our idyllic seaside town will always retain its quaint charm.

Jeremy and I are looking forward to spending Christmas in his hometown of Destiny, as we did last year, and it already feels like my home away from home. "Home" has been an iffy concept in my life, so I like the idea of having two! I met Jeremy's wonderful family over the holidays last year and I already love them! Family is another thing I've been short on, so I'm grateful to become a part of his.

Jeremy's cat, Captain, will be moving to my cottage along with him when we get married. Jeremy sometimes talks about getting a dog as well, but I don't think Captain would stand for it—he loves Jeremy to death. And the feeling is mutual, too, but you didn't hear that from me about my tough ex-Marine fiancé.

Who, by the way, I tried to make pose for a picture in a Santa hat, but he wouldn't do it. Captain didn't go for the reindeer antlers, either. They can both be pretty contrary, but I love them anyway.

From my humble beach cottage here on Sea Shell Lane to your home, wherever that may be, Jeremy and I wish you the happiest of holidays and a warm and prosperous New Year. May joy and love be yours!

Tamra

*Next month, don't miss these exciting
new love stories only from
Avon Books*

One-Eyed Dukes Are Wild by Megan Frampton
The scandalously unmarried Lady Margaret Sawford is
looking for adventure—and is always up for a challenge.
Her curiosity is aroused by a dangerous-looking stranger
with an eye patch, an ideal companion for the life she
longs for, no matter what Society might say. So when the
piratical gentleman turns out to be a duke, she can't help
but incite him to walk on the wild side.

The Earl's Complete Surrender by Sophie Barnes
Despite the diversions offered at Thorncliff Manor, former
spy James, the Earl of Woodford, has one purpose in staying
there. He must find an encoded book that exposes a
conspiracy within the British aristocracy. And he must do
so without revealing his purpose to the clever, tempting
Chloe Heartly, who has a knack for appearing wherever it is
least convenient: In the library, in the salon, and especially,
in his arms . . .

Caught by You by Jennifer Bernard
Months of alternately flirting and bickering with Kilby
Catfish catcher Mike Solo just turned into the hottest kiss
of Donna MacIntyre's life—and that's a major league
complication. Any hint of scandal could keep her from
getting her son back from her well-connected ex. Then
Mike comes up with a game-changing idea: a marriage
proposal that could help win her case—even as it
jeopardizes her heart . . .

REL 1215

*G*ive in to your Impulses!

These unforgettable stories only take a second to buy and give you hours of reading pleasure!

Go to *www.AvonImpulse.com* and see what we have to offer.
Available wherever e-books are sold.

AVONIMPULSE